JUSTIFIED VENGEANCE

Young Pistolero Series Book 7
by
Robert J. Alvarado

I0554002

OTHER WORKS

Robert J. Alvarado
www.youngpistolero.com

Non Fiction

Elfego Baca Destined to Survive
2013 Sunstone Press, Santa Fe, NM, First Printing
2016 Sierra Press, Albuquerque, NM, Second Printing

Fiction
Award Winning Young Pistolero Series
The saga follows Rafael Ortega de Estrada, a seventeen-year-old Mexican peón on the run, riding a stolen Appaloosa stallion. After shooting the haciendero who raped his younger sister, Rafael heads north and enters the United States in 1866 and finds life on the other side of the border holds new dangers along with the promise of a new life.

This gritty tale is set in the American Southwest as Americans and Mexicans struggle after the Mexican-American War. In this tumultuous era in the late 1800s, Rafael (Rafe) grows into a man who respects both his heritage and embraces life in his new country.

Young Pistolero (Book 1) 2013 Sierra Press
2018 Finalist for Drama TV Series category, by the Latino Books into Movies Awards sponsored by Latino Literacy Now.
#1 Fiction Book for 2015; by The Latino Author, by Corina Martinez Chaudhry

Star of the Young Pistolero (Book 2) 2014 Sierra Press

Death Stalks the Young Pistolero (Book 3) 2015 Sierra Press #1 Fiction Book for 2016; by The Latino Author *Legacy for the Young Pistolero* (Book 4) 2017 Sierra Press #3 Fiction Book for 2017; by The Latino Author *A Reckoning for the Young Pistolero* (Book 5) 2018 Sierra Press

Dangerous Venture (Book 6) 2019 Sierra Press

Justified Vengeance (Book 7) 2019 Sierra Press

The Black Phantom (Book 8) 2020 Sierra Press

Lost Treasure (Book 9) 2024 Sierra Press

Other Fiction

The Jalapeño Republic 2020 Sierra Press
2021 International Latino Book Award Medalist. Insights from the ILBA judges, "It was an interesting book, quite different from most futuristic novels I have read."

Jake Flores Mystery

Just Vanished –2020 Sierra Press
2021 International Latino Book Award Medalist. Insights from the ILBA judges, "From the moment you start reading it, you imagine an action TV series that keeps you involved."

Zia Westerns

Set in the New Mexico and Arizona territories of the Southwest, these westerns draw from the Southwest's unique flavor. Originally part of New Spain and then Mexico, the Spanish settlers and native Indians forged an informal peace until the years after the Mexican-American War brought them into the Wild West. These stories are set during this chaotic time and attempt to paint a realistic picture of the meaning of the Zia symbol.

The Spanish Sword 2020 Sierra Press
2021 International Latino Book Award Medalist. Insights from the ILBA judges, "This book is carefully crafted and felt thoroughly researched."

Valentina 2022 Sierra Press

Spanish Language Books

Este libro constituye la traducción de una obra de ficción realizada por su propio autor. La serie original, galardonada y titulada Young Pistolero, fue escrita en inglés estadounidense y posteriormente vertida al español mexicano por el autor con el apoyo de la herramienta de inteligencia artificial ChatGPT. Cualquier error o imprecisión que pudiera encontrarse en la traducción es fortuito y responde únicamente al uso de dicha herramienta.

Publicación en español de Sierra Press:

Joven Pistolero (Libro 1)
Estrella del Joven Pistolero (Libro 2)
Muerte Acecha al Joven Pistolero (Libro 3)
Legado para el Joven Pistolero (Libro 4)
Ajuste de Cuentas para el Joven Pistolero (Libro 5)
Aventura Peligrosa (Libro 6)
Venganza Justificada (Libro 7)
El Fantasma Negro (Libro 8)
Tesoro Perdido (Libro 9)

PRAISES AND AWARDS

Young Pistolero, Young Pistolero Series
2018 Finalist for Drama TV Series category.
The Latino Books into Movies Awards are conducted by Latino Literacy Now, a 501c3 nonprofit co-founded by Edward James Olmos and Kirk Whisler. The judges for these awards are screenwriters, directors, producers, and others from the entertainment industry. They have deemed these books worthy of consideration for future television and movie production.

Young Pistolero, Young Pistolero Series
#1 Fiction Book for 2015; by The Latino Author
Death Stalks the Young Pistolero, Young Pistolero Series
#1 Fiction Book for 2016; by The Latino Author
Legacy for the Young Pistolero, Young Pistolero Series
#3 Fiction Book for 2017; by The Latino Author

Young Pistolero Series is a great fiction story that incorporates both history and a great story plot of a young man whose life spirals after avenging the rape of his younger sister. It has all the muster of a good western including gun fights, murder, and survival. The author does a fantastic job of incorporating the history of the United States and Mexico during a time when the Wild West was in full swing and struggles occurred on both sides of the border. The descriptions of history add much to the story and make the life of Rafael, the protagonist, really interesting.

Mr. Alvarado weaves a plausible plot and his setting descriptions and actions are right on. His graphic scenarios of land and territories make you feel as if you are right there alongside the rider as he heads through some rough terrain. His characters were exactly what you might expect of people living in the 'rough' west trying to survive the elements and mayhem of that time.

The writer incorporates Spanish words, which allows the reader to identify with the characters; however, he brilliantly illustrates the meaning after each and every word so non-Spanish speaking readers don't miss a beat. The book is filled with so much action that you can't put the book down. It has all the earmarks of a great western series. If you are looking for a good book to read, then this is one to put on your list this year. An excellent read! – Corina Martinez Chaudhry

I know this series will earn many more awards. A wonderful contribution to Southwest Hispano history and culture. - **Rudolfo Anaya, acclaimed novelist, poet, playwright, professor emeritus, 2015 National Humanities Medal Award recipient**

I just completed reading *A Reckoning For The Young Pistolero*. Great book. I've read the entire series and I'm looking forward to the next book. Mr. Alvarado is very skilled at utilizing historical knowledge as well his own personal experiences to keep you captivated from beginning to end. Being from New Mexico, I can personally relate to the language and setting so appropriately used in the book. I highly recommend the entire series. You won't be disappointed. - **Sammy Soto, retired high school educator/administrator Albuquerque, NM**

I am impressed by the historical detail and fast-moving plots. I also like the way he incorporates two very different young men and follows their lives. The author does a good job of developing these contrasting characters so that readers can walk in their boots and see how fate has shaped them. My father was a screenwriter for television when I was growing up in California and he wrote many westerns, including Wagon Train and Gunsmoke. Alvarado's novel could be the basis for one of those television westerns because of its engrossing plot and its clear depiction of heroes and villains. - **Dr. Jennie Nelson, PhD in Rhetoric and Writing, Carnegie Mellon University, post-graduate professor of writing, University of Idaho**

Mr. Alvarado vividly illustrates many rugged times after the Civil and Mexican American Wars through the eyes of a 17 year old peon who comes to the U.S. and adapts and grows into a hero. The Young Pistolero is a great new historical western series!
 – by Richard Golenda, post Secondary and College History Teacher post Chairman of the Pueblo Economic Development Corporation.

JUSTIFIED VENGEANCE

Copyright © 2019 by Robert J. Alvarado

All rights reserved. This book or any portion thereof may not be reproduced or used in any manner whatsoever without the express written permission of the copyright owner, except in the case of brief quotations embodied in critical reviews and certain other noncommercial uses permitted by copyright law, without the prior written permission of the copyright owner.

This book is a work of historical fiction and is not to be construed as real. In all respects, any resemblance to actual persons, living or dead, or descriptions of events or locales is entirely a product of the author's imagination.

The material in this book is for mature audiences only and contains graphic content and language. It is intended for readers aged 18 and older.

A glossary of *italicized* Spanish words is provided at the end of this book, with the exception of words which are equivalent in both languages, such as *importante* = important, *Mamá* = Mama, or words of Latin origin found in the English dictionary. Other words, phrases, and sentences written in Spanish are immediately explained within the text itself.

Printed in the United State of America

ISBN-13: 9780991477777

SIERRA
PRESS

Published by Sierra Press
Phoenix, Arizona
First Printing, June 2019

Young Pistolero Cover design by John Flinn
Graphic art by Lina Luna

DEDICATION

This book is dedicated to my brothers and sister, Manuel, Sylvia, Daniel, Leonard, and Lawrence (deceased).

ACKNOWLEDGEMENT

For my friends and family who have spurred on the story of young Rafe. Thank you always for your support and friendship.

I would like to acknowledge the wealth of historical information which is weaved into this work to depict the places and events of this saga's time period. As a work of historical fiction, where real-life historical figures or actual locations are used, the situations, incidents, or dialogues concerning those persons or places are entirely fictional and are not intended to depict actual events or to change the entirely fictional nature of the work.

DISCLAIMER

In an effort to accurately describe the social fabric of New Mexico during the timeframe of this book, readers should consider the author's transitions from the use of the terms, Spaniards and Mexicans. After the discovery of South America in 1492, New Spain, considered to encompass Mexico and much of central America, was under the control of Spanish Kings and Queens.

Over the next several hundred years, Spaniards emigrated north into what is now the American Southwest. Legions of settlers traveled to spread the Catholic religion and to seek fortunes in gold and silver. For their efforts, the Spanish royalty bestowed land and titles to the adventurous settlers. In New Mexico, Spaniards founded Santa Fe as the capital of the Kingdom of New Mexico in 1610. Industrious, the Spanish settlers created a robust economy and raised their families for generations. Rather isolated, New Mexico remained an extension of New Spain until the Mexican Revolution began in 1820.

After the Mexican Revolution ended in 1821, the country now known as Mexico emerged from under Spanish control. After the Mexican-American War ended in 1848, the border between Mexico and the American Southwest was in dispute. Finally, the Treaty of Guadalupe Hildalgo created the border as we know it today. In the treaty, Articles VIII and IX ensured the safety of existing property rights of Spaniard/Mexican citizens living in the Southwestern territories. Despite the treaty's assurances to the contrary, land grants owned in New Mexico were often not honored by the United States because of interpretations of the treaty and U.S. legal decisions. Fraud and greed by powerful American lawyers and politicians stripped many descendants of original land grant owners of their land.

Because this book is set after the Treaty of Guadalupe Hildalgo, the terms Spaniards and Mexicans are often intertwined. Even today, the descendants of the original

Spanish settlers maintain their heritage as Spaniards. However, Americans who began settling in New Mexico at that time used the term Mexicans for the local population living in the territories.

In today's world, the term Hispanic is often used to describe a diverse population of Spanish-speaking peoples. However, this book attempts to be true to the fundamental use of the terms, Spaniards and Mexicans, as it might have been used by the different characters in the story. In no way does it intend to disparage the people described by the usage of the terms.

CHAPTER 1

"I tell yew, me n Clay Allison scart em greasers up in Cimarron," Kip Donohoe bragged to a group of cowboys at a saloon north of Santa Fe in the New Mexico Territory. A big talker, Kip loved to brag and tell embellished stories of his exploits. The cowboys listened intently, believing everything he said was the gospel truth and Kip loved an audience.

In the saloon, Jerome Westfield sipped a beer and listened to Kip's stories. He was on a trip from San Gabriel to Santa Fe to buy lumber and other building supplies and stopped at the saloon for a drink. Listening to Kip, Jerome thought he was just what the settlers needed to defend their land deeds from the Mexicans. Jerome waited until the cowboys drifted off and Kip was drinking alone at the bar, before he spoke to him.

"I was mighty impressed by your stories," Jerome walked near Kip and told him. The braggadocios man was scruffy with a scraggly beard and untrimmed mustache. Long curly almost blond hair peeked out from under a dusty well-used black Stetson. He was tall and lean and had the look of a rangy cowboy, who spent most of his time in the sun and weather. "I think you are just the man we need up in San Gabriel."

"Who are yew?" Kip asked narrowing his deep blue eyes to slits.

"Name of Jerome Westfield. Me and a group of settlers came from Missouri with deeds to land here in New Mexico. When we got here, they told us the land was owned by some Mexican. They've been trying to get us to leave ever since and causing us a lot of trouble."

"I heerd of such things," Kip responded then turned and studied his whiskey glass.

"They've been harassing me and the other settlers, saying we bought our land illegally. They claim the land belongs to a Mexican named *don* Lorenzo Salazar. They say it was a Royal Spanish Land Grant to his family many generations ago. Fuck the Royal Spanish! It's 1874! What the hell do the Spanish have to do with land in the United States now? We have legal deeds we bought in Missouri," Jerome explained trying to get the gunfighter interested in the settler's plight.

"Why do yew think I cud hep?"

"We're just farmers looking for good land to plant and to raise our families. We're not unwilling to fight, but we need someone handy with a gun."

"What kinda trouble they givin yew?"

"The Mexicans claimed I stole a prized bull from them. They came with guns, lassoed it and tried to take it. My friends and I shot it out with them. We got one of the Mexicans, but the bull and two of my friends got shot up and the bull died."

"Did yew steal that thar bull?"

"Nah, it was just wandering as a stray," Jerome told him.

Kip Donohoe nodded his head knowing how the greasers did not fence in their livestock. Cows, sheep, and other stock often grazed on the large parcels of land the Mexicans claimed as land grants.

"Yew telling me, em greasers came and killed yer bull and shot two of yew? Whadda yew want me ta do? Kill the greaser?" Kip asked.

"We need protection. We'll pay you. Maybe if the Mexicans see a gunman around, they will stop harassing us."

For the past eight months Rafe doted on Ana Teresa, so much she often demanded he stop treating her as if she was going to break. However, it did not deter Rafe's anguish. He feared something dreadful could happen to her and the baby, if he was not vigilantly keeping a watchful eye on her.

"You are driving me crazy, hovering over me this way," she complained.

"I cannot help it *querida*. I promised I would protect you. Remember when Billy tried to kidnap you? And what about the time you were taken in the silver wagon and the man tried to have his way with you? Not to mention how we were run out of Los Angeles by vigilantes," Rafe reminded her of some of the past times she was in danger because of him.

They were on the veranda of their new house overlooking the pastures of his horse ranch north of Santa Fe. Rafe took a lunch break from the GSW foundry and came home to have lunch. It was his normal daily routine to check on her.

"Yes I remember, but I am in no danger now. I am going to have your baby. It is the most natural thing a woman can do. Please stop worrying."

"Well, I am worried about us going to *don* Lorenzo's hacienda in San Gabriel for the wedding," Rafe expressed his concerns. A wedding for *doña* Agustina's niece, Bibiana's cousin, was scheduled for Saturday at *don* Lorenzo Salazar's hacienda. *Don* Lorenzo was Agustina de Soto's father and a well-known bull breeder in San Gabriel. It would be a big affair.

"Why are you worried? It will be a joyous day and they will have a grand fiesta. You will dance with me," she said and went to him. She attempted to embrace him in a close dance position, but her protruding belly would not allow her to get close. They both laughed and Rafe leaned over and kissed her.

"*Querida,* the hacienda is near San Gabriel where there has been trouble with squatters. It was printed in the newspaper several weeks ago. Squatters stole one of *don* Lorenzo's prize bulls. He sent his *vaqueros* to get it back and gunfire broke out. One of his *vaqueros* and a few squatters were shot, along with the bull. Since then, armed squatters have attacked *vaqueros* whenever they see them alone on the range. We should not go. Besides, it is a long trip and it might be hard on you in your condition."

"Don't be ridiculous. We are going Rafael. I want to dress up and be around music and my family. I want to dance with you one more time before we are parents. My mother is excited about going too. She wants to meet people from other haciendas."

After Ana Teresa's father was killed, her mother, *doña* Marcella, chose to stay in Santa Fe after she learned she was to be a grandmother. It surprised Ana Teresa how her mother fussed and doted on her and was joyously awaiting the new life. She was not so doting when Ana Teresa was growing up.

"I hope she meets a widowed *haciendero* someday and will not be dependent on us forever. She is still a young and beautiful woman," Rafe said and chuckled. He did not mind supporting his wife's mother, but wished they had more privacy.

Losing to his wife's demands, they left for the de Soto hacienda Friday morning. Just before noon, *don* Pedro, Carlos, and Rafe mounted up and led the way from the de Soto house. Behind them, a carriage with Agustina, Bibiana, Ana Teresa, and Marcella followed. Marcella held ten-month-old Benicío, Bibiana and Carlos' young son, on her lap. *Don* Lorenzo and *doña* Amalia expected them by evening for the wedding, which would start Saturday morning.

Upon their arrival late in the afternoon, Bibiana retired to her room with the baby and Rafe made Ana Teresa lie down in their bedroom. Agustina and Marcella sat in the parlor with *doña* Amalia. *Don* Lorenzo escorted *don* Pedro and Carlos to the smoking room. A servant poured brandy and gave each a Cuban cigar.

"Tell us about the bull you lost, Lorenzo?" *don* Pedro asked politely.

"My bulls are free to wander the hacienda. One day several of my *vaqueros* were looking for strays and noticed the squatters had one of my bulls corralled in a pen. When they tried to reclaim it, the squatters opened fire. My *vaqueros* had no choice but to defend themselves and try to take the bull. They wounded two of the squatters and a stray bullet killed the bull, or maybe the squatters killed it in spite."

"It is not fair or right these squatters think they own what is not theirs," Pedro griped.

"It is a big problem here, Pedro. Squatters are moving here and settling, saying they bought their land legally. In a way, I cannot blame them. They were swindled. They bought the land unseen, believing it was open territory," he replied with a sigh. *Don* Lorenzo felt no particular malice toward the squatters, however would not allow them to stay.

"I and the other *haciendeross* have tried to evict them, but the sheriff will do nothing. He says it is government business. Now the squatters are fighting back," *don* Lorenzo explained.

"It is happening more and more, mostly here in the northern part of the territory where the haciendas are larger. We have not had as much trouble in Santa Fe, although the *dons* are cautious and vigilant," Carlos interjected.

"Carlos, Pedro tells me you work for a gun maker? If it is true, my friends and I need guns. Will you see if we can buy them from the gunsmith?"

"You can discuss it with Rafael this weekend. He works for George Summers at the foundry," Carlos replied.

"Enough of this unpleasant talk of guns and squatters, please enjoy your brandy and cigars. Tomorrow will be a grand wedding, joining two powerful families. Tonight we rest for the big fiesta planned after the ceremony," *don* Lorenzo said and raised his glass in a toast.

Ana Teresa had a restless night not able to get comfortable on the bed. It kept Rafe awake trying to comfort her. Her restlessness made her nervous thinking the baby might decide to come early. Finally she slept for a couple of hours after Rafe got up, dressed, and left her alone.

In the morning, she felt better and she and Bibiana fussed all morning making themselves beautiful for the wedding ceremony. Ana Teresa had a special dress made just for the occasion, which was supposed to minimize her bulging belly.

"You will be the most beautiful woman at the fiesta," Bibiana flattered her cousin. It was not jealousy by Bibiana, but just a fact.

By late afternoon the fiesta had been going on for several hours. The courtyard was decorated with strands of flower garlands and candles. Long tables of food were set up around the dance floor. Each table had vases of fresh wildflowers. The *dons* and *doñas* were dressed in their finest dresses and *trajes*. A number of younger *caballeros*, sons of the *dons*, stood sipping wine and watching the dancers.

Ana Teresa and Rafe danced the Bolero and the Fandango, as well as she could in her condition. Dancing in the decorated courtyard reminded Rafe of the first time he ever saw her. She had worn a red and black gown and he fell in love with her through her golden brown eyes. After two dances, she asked Rafe to take her to a shady spot where she could sit and rest.

"You should go to our room and lay down," he said.

"No, I would rather stay here and listen to the orchestra and watch the people. Go and talk to the men. I will be fine," she replied.

The music from the small orchestra kept everyone dancing. Even small children danced with each other, making Ana Teresa laugh at their behavior. She noticed a *don* in a brown *traje* danced with her mother several times. While she sat resting, Rafe joined a small group of *caballeros* on the far side of the courtyard. They handed him a cup of wine and continued their animated conversation.

Outside the main entrance to the courtyard, concealed by a high adobe wall, Kip Donohoe, his friends Nat and Jesse, along with three sons of the land settlers arrived at the Salazar hacienda. Inside the courtyard, an orchestra played festive music and they could hear laughter.

"Put on the hoods boys and git yer guns ready," Kip told the group in a whisper. After Jerome hired him, Kip decided they should take the fight directly to the head greaser who claimed he owned the land. Although the man seldom left his hacienda, Kip spent long hours on a hill not far away and knew the man's looks. Killing him should easily settle the dispute about the land Jerome and the other settlers bought in good faith. Kip would collect a handsome reward from the settlers and move on.

Putting on the red hoods with only eyeholes diminished the raider's sight somewhat. Two had rifles and the other four had pistols ready.

"Now!" Kip gave the word. They rode into the courtyard with guns blazing. They shot at everyone – men, women, and even children, but Kip sought out *don* Lorenzo. At first, everyone in the courtyard stood stunned in disbelief as they heard the gunshots and saw the red-hooded raiders. Most of the *caballeros* were unarmed. Some had swords at their sides. Screaming and shouts filled the air as people did their best to protect themselves from the hooded raiders.

"Carlos, take Bibiana, the baby, and Ana Teresa to safety," Rafe yelled. He pulled his GSW pistols and fired back at the raiders. One went down and another dropped his pistol, as Rafe's bullet struck his arm. The few other armed *caballeros* also returned fire and two pulled their swords. The previously peaceful courtyard turned into pandemonium. Gunfire whistled in every direction.

Kip spotted the hacienda owner and took a shot, missing his chest and hitting him in the arm. Several of the Mexicans were armed and returned fire. One in particular had two pistols and was a good shot. One of the young men who came with him lay on the ground and another had his gun shot from his hand. Turning his horse, Kip yelled to the others to go. The raiders headed for the courtyard exit to escape.

"Get to your horses," Rafe yelled out.

It took precious time getting to the hacienda's corral. Rafe jumped to Rayo's saddle and several of the young *caballeros* followed him. They mounted up and ran the horses hard trying to catch up with the raiders. Neither Rafe nor any of the visiting *caballeros* knew the location of the squatter's camp. They rode until it got dark without finding the gunmen.

"We need to return to our families," one of the young *caballeros* told Rafe. He agreed, worried about Ana Teresa.

All was quiet at the main house when Rafe and the others returned. The people had gone home. A dim light shone from the front window of the house and Rafe knocked on the door. *Don* Lorenzo opened it. He looked tired, old, and miserable. His arm was bandaged and in a sling.

"*Señor,* we did not catch them," Rafe reported.

Don Lorenzo only nodded his head as he ushered Rafe into the house.

"Where is my wife? Did she return to Santa Fe with *don* Pedro?" Rafe asked.

Don Lorenzo hesitated, lowered his head, and spoke softly. "*Lo siento Rafael, ellos mataron a tu esposa.*" He expressed his sorrow and told Rafe, they killed your wife.

CHAPTER 2

Rafe's mind reeled. It was not possible. When the masked gunmen came, she was sitting at the far end of the courtyard in the shade, resting. She would not have been in the line of fire.

"Muerta?" he asked dumbfounded. Ana Teresa could not be dead. There must be a mistake. It could not be. When he left to chase the raiders, she was alive and pregnant with their first child. She could not be dead.

"Desgraciados killed four, including *don* Alfonso's five-year-old grandson, and injured six more," *don* Lorenzo tried to explain what had happened, but words failed him and the explanation sounded hollow.

"Lo siento Rafael."

"Where have they taken her?"

"They took the dead and injured to the doctor in San Gabriel."

A creeping emptiness grew inside Rafe as the *don* spoke. The emptiness filled with a surreal numbness. The masked gunman killed his wife and unborn child. Once before he felt an overpowering need for revenge. He shot *don* Bernardo because the *don* raped his fourteen-year-old sister, María. He shot the *don,* although did not kill him. This time he would make sure the masked raiders felt the bark of his pistols.

"Where is the squatter's camp *señor?"*

"About seven miles north along the Rio Chama, north of Arroyo de Presa where the rapids fall along the Chama."

Stumbling down the veranda steps, he jumped to Rayo's saddle, spurring the horse to a gallop. He had not gone far before he realized his mission was futile in the dark. He also had only a few bullets, as he did not bring any saddlebags with him to the fiesta. It was to have been a time of joy, not death. Turning Rayo south, he rode hard toward Santa Fe.

Tears obscured Rafe's vision in the dark half-moon

night, as he rode Rayo home. Only Rayo's keen eyes and senses kept them from injury. He could not face collecting his dead wife's body for burial. He could not think of her in that sense, not her and their unborn child. He tried hard to picture her in the red and black gown she wore the first time he met her. Her golden brown eyes had melted his heart.

Winning her hand in marriage had been difficult. She was a pure blood Spanish *señorita* and he, a *mestizo* of lower class, but God had intervened in their lives allowing them their happiness. She was carrying their first child, which was to be born in May.

His heart pounded in his chest and the rage burst from within, building deep from his soul. He had promised to keep her safe. Now, the life they planned was gone forever. All he wanted was revenge, vowing to himself no rest until he found and killed those who raided *don* Lorenzo's courtyard and killed his beloved Ana Teresa.

It was still dark when he reached the horse barn on his property. His man, Reymundo, was asleep in the bunkhouse. No lights shone in the Summers' house, not too far away. Walking Rayo to a stall, Rafe fed the tired horse, then he headed to the gun foundry where George taught him everything about the business over the past eight years. As he walked into the dark building, he wound through the corridors. Like a blind man, he knew every inch by heart without light. On the finishing table, he found the two pistols he worked on yesterday. He grabbed them and several boxes of ammunition.

Closing the foundry door, he walked up the steep hill to his house. Quickly and doing his best to ignore Ana Teresa's belongings, he stripped his formal *traje* and changed into his casual suit and black Stetson. He grabbed his rain slicker and black suit and rolled them in a wool blanket. Next, he grabbed several shirts, pants, and socks and stuffed them into an extra large saddlebag.

Within an hour after arriving in Santa Fe, Rafe stood in his gray suit and a warm wool jacket. He hung the beaded leather quiver made by Chiwiwi over his back. His short-barrel shotgun nested inside. His gunbelt with his GSW pistols was wrapped around his waist and the small pouch containing the broken pieces of turquoise from the silver star amulet rested in his pocket near his chest. Picking up the bedroll, he walked to the kitchen.

Opening a drawer, he pulled out all the ammunition he kept stored in the house. Looking at the small pile, he wished it was more. He had not been in a gunfight since he joined Big Ed's posse to chase the cattle rustlers last August. Back home here in Santa Fe, he seldom felt the need to wear his guns. In a secret compartment in the kitchen cabinet, he pulled out money and five twenty-dollar gold coins. He knew the money was more than a thousand dollars, which he kept for emergencies.

Then he sat down and wrote a letter to George Summers, his adopted father:

Don Jorge,

> *Ana Teresa was killed yesterday at don Lorenzo's hacienda. Her body was taken to the doctor in San Gabriel. Please go and get her and bury her here at our property. I cannot tell you where I am going. All I can say is those who are responsible for her death will pay. One last thing, please wire half of my money to the bank in El Paso. I may go there, if and when, I need it. Keep Reymundo so he can take care of my horses, especially Rayo. Pay him from my funds. He may continue breeding the horses if he wishes to.*
>
> *Thank you for everything you have done. I love you all,*

Rafe

Ready to leave, he looked around the room and only saw emptiness. He would never share it with Ana Teresa again and this house would never be full of his children. Rage and pain shook him to the core. Walking down the hill to the barn, he strode to Rayo's stall. The large Appaloosa looked at him with dark liquid eyes.

"You cannot go on this trip old friend," Rafe spoke softly to him and ran his hand down his flank. It pained him to leave Rayo behind, but the unique markings made the horse a detriment. Turning to another stall, he saddled and tied the bedroll and saddlebags on a brown gelding sired by Santiago, Carlos' black stallion.

It was still dark at the Summers' house as a rode up and placed the letter under the door knocker. He was thankful the house was quiet, because he did not want to talk to anyone. He did not want to explain nor bear their anguish over Ana Teresa. He knew George would try to dissuade him from his focus to head back to San Gabriel and avenge her.

He spurred the brown gelding down the ranch path until he reached the main road, then turned north. The horse was young and full of energy. Rafe gave it a good heel to a gallop and headed toward San Gabriel.

On Sunday morning, Jerome Westfield found his son, Fred, lying on a cot in his tent. His arm was bandaged and a red stain bled through the white muslin. Fred, shot during the raid at the hacienda, had it tended last night not disturbing his father. He knew his father would be mad at the attempted rout of the Mexicans.

"He did what?" Jerome asked learning of the previous day's events when Fred explained his injury.

"Kip said he wanted to kill the head greaser and put a stop to those Mexicans harassing us. I thought it was a good idea, so me and a couple others went with him. Jimmy Burns got killed and Frankie and I got wounded," Fred told his father ashamed of his actions.

"What about the Mexicans?" Jerome asked.

"I don't know. We shot the place up. I mostly shot into the dirt to scare them. People were screaming. Kip and his friends were shooting at people and when we left, bodies lay on the ground. Kip bragged he killed the head greaser."

"Where the hell is Kip now?" Jerome asked.

"I don't know. He and his friends didn't come back with us. I think they planned on hightailing to E-town after the raid," Fred said.

E-town was the nickname for Elizabethtown, a gold mining town on the western foothills of Baldy Mountain north of Las Vegas, New Mexico.

"The bastard left us to deal with a mess. It was a stupid

thing to do Fred. Those Mexicans will come after us and there are more of them than us. I can't go to the sheriff, because he'll lock you up for murder." Jerome trembled in fear for his son. He knew it would be only a matter of time before the law or the Mexicans found out how his son was involved in the matter.

"You, stay here and don't go anywhere, especially to San Gabriel. I will go see Frankie's father and tell him to keep Frankie hidden. With those injuries, you are dead men if the sheriff or the Mexicans find you."

Jerome quickly walked down along the river to his friend Hank Shelby's home. Without knocking, Jerome pushed open the door.

"Hank, how bad is Frankie?"

"His right shoulder blade is shattered from a bullet. What about Fred?" Hank was sitting at the kitchen table cleaning his shotgun.

"His right arm was hit and the bullet nicked part of the bone below the shoulder. It's gonna take a while for it to heal, but he will be all right."

"Frankie ain't saying much about what he did. What did you get out of Fred?"

"Fred told me, Kip got our boys to go and raid a fiesta the head Mexican was having at his house. They rode in with hoods covering their faces and shot up the place."

"Jimmy Burns got killed," Hank said flatly. "This ain't good, Jerome. What the fuck are we going to do? You hired that asshole and now we're in a hell of a fix."

"We all agreed to hire Donohoe," Jerome reminded him, although he knew he would take the lion share of the blame for the gunman's actions.

"I told Fred he has to stay low. You need to do the same with Frankie. They cannot be seen with those injuries. We got to keep them out of sight until they heal."

"We don't stand a chance if the Mexicans come after us, Jerome. Either we stand and fight or we pack up and move on," Hank said. There was a nervous twitch in his eyes.

CHAPTER 3

George Summers rose at his usual early hour just after the sun lightened the eastern sky. It was Sunday and the family would be going to the ten o'clock Mass in Santa Fe. He did not dress as he usually did on a workday, but rather wrapped a robe around himself and headed downstairs. Josefina stirred briefly. He knew she would sleep most of another hour before rising.

Juanita the cook poured him a cup of coffee in the kitchen and he wandered to the sunroom off the south side of the house. The sunroom was chilly, but George knew the morning sun would warm it shortly. Idly he thumbed through yesterday's newspaper, enjoying the sense of peace around him.

He was just about to go wake Josefina, when he heard the clatter of hooves in the courtyard and a shout. He heard the front door slam before he could reach the entryway. To his surprise, Carlos Zuniga stood holding a folded note.

"Carlos, what brings you to our door at such an early hour and in such a rush?" George asked. Carlos was Rafe's best friend, a man Rafe considered his brother.

"You have not heard?"

"Heard what?" The tone of Carlos' voice and his haggard look struck George in a way which caught his breath.

"There was a gunfight at the fiesta yesterday after the wedding in San Gabriel. Masked gunmen opened fire on the people celebrating in the courtyard."

George gasped. "Rafe?"

"No, he is all right. Is he not here?" Carlos asked.

"I have not seen him. Was anyone hurt?"

Carlos knew George would take the news hard, but there was no other way to say what had happened. "They killed Ana Teresa."

Carlos grabbed George's arm as he stumbled back in shock. Ana Teresa had become part of the family. She and

Rafe were expecting their first child in May and he and Josefina felt as if they were expectant grandparents.

"It cannot be . . . how?"

"*Desgraciados* killed four, including Ana Teresa and *don* Alfonso's five-year-old grandson. Six others were injured," Carlos explained what had happened at the fiesta. He felt personally responsible. Rafe told him to get Ana Teresa and Bibiana to safety. His wife, Bibiana, was alive and Ana Teresa dead.

It was then Carlos remembered the note clutched in his hand. He handed it to George. "Perhaps this will explain."

After George read the note, he handed it back to Carlos. George understood grief. He understood his adopted son's rage and the need to avenge Ana Teresa's death. Perhaps it was not right with God, regardless, the squatters brought the terror to the hacienda and killed innocent people.

"I must go after him. He's going to need my help," Carlos proposed after reading the note. Full of guilt because he did not protect Ana Teresa, Carlos was ready to find Rafe and help him find the killers.

"No Carlos. Your place is here consoling your wife. I will get the law involved," George discouraged him. "I'm sure he will come home after he has time to grieve. Go home and comfort your family."

After George walked Carlos to the front door, he slowly climbed the stairs to the second floor. His heart was heavy knowing he was going to break his wife and daughters' hearts with the news.

George spent the rest of the day in the foundry, working. He knew he should be at the house consoling his family, but he could be of little help while his grief consumed him. He and Josefina lost their first-born, a son, Gregory, to influenza when he was eight months old. Seventeen years later when Rafe came to Santa Fe after saving George's life, he and Josefina welcomed the teenager. Over the years, they grew to think of him as their son. He was not of their blood, but was of their hearts.

When George walked to the kitchen later in the afternoon, he found Josefina sitting at the kitchen table. He could tell she sat there all day crying.

"Why has God done this terrible thing?" she wailed. "Why? Have we done something wrong?"

George walked to her and lifted her from the chair into his arms. "No. It is just life."

"Where is Rafael?"

"He's gone."

"Gone? Where?"

"He will come home when he is ready. In the meantime, he needs to find peace with what has happened," George told her.

Josefina burst into tears. George held her while sobs shook her body. Finally, she quieted and slumped in his arms.

"Come, let me take you to lie down. There is nothing more we can do."

Up in the bedroom, George lay down beside his wife and closed his eyes. At first he could not sleep, then suddenly he was transported into a dream, standing with Rafe and Carlos at the Anaya hacienda.

In the dream, gunfire burst around him. The Isleta Indians were bombarding the hacienda with flaming arrows. He and Rafe were shooting the vaqueros who patrolled the parapet. Inside, Chiwiwi and another young Indian maiden were captives. The dream replayed the events of that day. Then he watched as Rafe carried Chiwiwi's body from the burning hacienda and placed it on the ground near Chief Letoc. Chiwiwi's white shirt was stained with blood and her eyes stared into nothingness.

George turned toward Rafe who suddenly pulled the short-barrel shotgun out of the quiver and growled sounding like a wild animal. Turning he ran back into the compound. George ran to stop him, yelling at the top of his voice to be heard. Rafe raised the shotgun; George yelled for Rafe to stop, but not before Rafe killed two vaqueros standing by the veranda with their hands up.

"George, George," Josefina said shaking him. "George wake up. You were growling," she told him.

Sweat covered his face and he felt damp all over. The

dream was so real it shook him.

"I had a nightmare," he told her. "Go back to sleep. I'm going to the foundry."

Josefina leaned back against the pillow. Sleep evaded her and her mind could not stop thinking about all the happiness Rafe brought to the family. She thought of him as her son and when he brought Ana Teresa home as his bride, the joy in the family doubled.

Rafe was only seventeen when George first brought him to Santa Fe, a young, illiterate Mexican peasant. George glowed when he explained how Rafe saved his life. It was not long before Rafe became like an older brother to their two daughters, Lolo and Lizzy. Rafe learned English quickly and had a fire for knowledge. He worked tirelessly and soon became an asset in the foundry and a part of their family.

After having lost their own son, Gregory, Rafe filled the void with love and pride. She knew George felt the same. Rafe called him Father and her Mother. Life was not perfect for her adopted son. He fell in love with a young Indian girl, Chiwiwi. Josefina never met her. She was killed in Corrales by Carlos' older brother.

Rafe turned his anger against himself and only found solace in tequila. Only love and her faith kept her from going crazy with worry about him, but God finally healed his heart. Then she spent six months believing he was dead in Mexico. Those long months of grief left her with more gray hair and ten pounds thinner.

When he married Ana Teresa and built the home on the hill adjacent to their ranch, it was as if life had finally found a balance. They were just weeks from welcoming their first child. Josefina and the girls spent hours quilting a baby blanket for the crib. Lolo was particularly close to Ana Teresa as they were only a few years apart in age. Lolo shared everything with Ana Teresa – dresses, perfume, secrets, and probably intimate details of Ana Teresa's marriage to Rafe.

Now, Ana Teresa was dead and Rafe was gone. She knew vengeance filled Rafe's soul. Josefina folded her hands and prayed to the Virgin Mary to protect and heal her son's grief. *"Madre de Dios,* keep him in your care."

Later that evening, they gathered at the dining table. Three chairs stood awkwardly empty – Rafe, Ana Teresa, and *doña* Marcella's. The three lived at Rafe's house, although often they took the evening meal at the Summers' home, especially lately as Ana Teresa's term was nearing. Carlos had explained *doña* Marcella returned to *don* Pedro's after the gunfight. She was completely overcome with grief.

"I'm not hungry," Lolo said pushing her plate away.

"We must eat. None of us has eaten anything today," George said.

"Your father is right. We must eat something. There is nothing else we can do," Josefina added.

Clinking of plates broke the otherwise silent meal. Lizzy was finishing a piece of potato when she asked, "Father, can we bury Ana Teresa beside Gregory and baby Bernardo in the back yard. At least then we can make sure to keep flowers growing on her grave. I think she would like that."

"Of course. I will take the wagon in the morning to San Gabriel. Josefina, can you plan a wake for Thursday? We will bury her Friday. Hopefully Rafe will have returned by then."

CHAPTER 4

Rafe rode hard back to San Gabriel not giving the young gelding a deserved break and the horse was well-lathered when he approached the town from the south. His heart burned with rage. Friday, he and Ana Teresa rode here to the fiesta. He could picture her face beaming with joy.

Vengeance demanded swift and total reckoning for the squatters' actions. His soul burned with hate. If he died avenging his wife and unborn child, it would be more the blessing. He did not want to live without them.

It was Sunday morning and the town was quiet as he rode along the main road into San Gabriel. Passing the sheriff's office and the bank, he noticed the sign to the doctor's office and his heart lurched. Someplace in this town was Ana Teresa's body. It would be cold, her eyes unseeing, her heart no longer beating. He tried not to think about his unborn child, but his eyes gushed with burning tears.

He was sure the squatters, who *don* Lorenzo accused of stealing his bull, were at the root of the raid, but which ones? He battled his rage to control his reckless desire to kill all of them. It was not in his nature to kill innocent people, but Ana Teresa was innocent. The others killed or injured at the fiesta were innocent. All the squatters deserved to die.

The spring wind was whistling through the air around him as he rode past the doctor's office. In the quiet of the Sunday morning, it whispered like voices.

"Rafael, come to me," he heard the wind whisper. Whirling around in the saddle, he looked for the source of the voice. Nothing but a few leaves scuttled along the road.

"Rafael," he heard the wind whisper his name again. It was Ana Teresa's voice.

He kicked the gelding to a gallop and rode hard down the main road. Perhaps he was losing his mind. He remembered a time in Mexico when he heard Xihuitl, the Aztec healer's voice in the wind. He heard it clearly, although the Healer was miles away. In explanation, the Healer told him, "There are incomprehensible forces on this earth. Never forget that."

Before noon, Rafe rode into the village of Los Luceros about ten miles north of San Gabriel. Old adobe houses and a few small stores lined the dirt street. It was a small village, one of the original Spanish settlements established by *don* Juan de Oñate's expedition in 1598. It looked unchanged for many years. A sign on one building said Cantina and another Roberto Apodaca's Inn. The inn was located not far east of the Rio Grande.

Stopping in front of the inn, Rafe stepped off the horse. It was Sunday and the town was empty, except for a young boy pulling a mule down the road. It seemed an ideal place to plan his revenge against the squatters.

Hearing Ana Teresa's voice in the wind in San Gabriel forced him to rethink his plans. He resigned himself to not rush into finding the killers haphazardly, realizing he needed to study the area. He needed to locate the squatters, find the guilty raiders, and not kill innocent people.

He had calmed his rage, by remembering the lessons given him by the Aztec healer. The Healer told him, "Never go into danger without knowing what you are up against. Do not leave anything to chance and be aware of everything around you. Death will take you in an instant when you least expect it."

He stuck his hand into the pocket where he carried the small leather pouch containing the fragments of the bent silver star and turquoise amulet given to him by Chief Letoc. He had worn it hanging around his neck on a leather string. The amulet saved his life by stopping a bullet from hitting his heart. Feeling the remnants of the amulet through the pouch and remembering the lessons the Healer taught him, calmed him and gave him resolve.

Rafe tied the brown gelding to the hitching pole in front of the inn and walked up the steps.

"*Bienvenido señor,*" the clerk greeted him.

"A room," he told the man behind the desk deciding to only speak English.

"How long you stay?" the man responded in broken

English.

"Perhaps a week or two. I am looking for land," Rafe lied. He was dressed in a gray suit with a thin black tie and wore a black Stetson.

"The rooms are one dollar. Please sign here."

Rafe signed his name as Ricardo Gonzalez, from Pueblo, Colorado. He placed a silver dollar coin on the desk. "Do you have a stable?" he asked.

"Yes, around back. Abel will take care of your horse." He handed Rafe a key to a room facing the street. "I will have my boy take your horse to the stable."

"No, thank you. I will take him."

Rafe led the horse around to the back where he found a man pitching hay.

"Buenas tardes señor," the man greeted him

"Good afternoon." Rafe handed the man the horse's reins. "Brush him and give him extra oats."

"I will take good care of him *señor?"*

"Much obliged," Rafe thanked him and gathered his belongings before he went to his room.

Once settled, he looked out the window and to his left he saw cottonwood trees. They were beginning to green along the Rio Grande. It was March and this year had a warm start of spring. Rafe settled in a soft chair and relaxed. He had not slept for almost two days and his body was weary.

He dozed fitfully for several hours, but dreams of the red-hooded raiders shook him awake. His entire body was soaked with perspiration. Rising, he changed out of the damp clothes and put on a casual shirt and tucked his hair under the Stetson.

Walking downstairs, he nodded toward the desk clerk and walked out to the street. He needed food and he needed information. He knew he would find both at the restaurant. It was Sunday evening and the room was quiet. Only a few families sat at tables. Two *vaqueros* and one Indian stood at the bar. Rafe sat at an empty table with a view of the door.

"Beer and the daily special," Rafe ordered.

"Sí señor." The waiter hurried off and returned quickly with a glass of beer.

Rafe took several sips and pondered his situation. None of the people in the restaurant were Anglo. He vaguely remembered learning the history of San Gabriel and this area from the tutor George Summers hired for him when he first came to Santa Fe. *Don* Juan de Oñate settled New Mexico for Spain in 1598. It was called the Kingdom of New Mexico and was the northern territory of New Spain. Oñate chose to settle at San Gabriel, which was near the Okhay Owingeh Pueblo, as the Indians were friendly and helpful to the settlers. Oñate set up a military encampment outside of the pueblo and the Indians helped the settlers survive the harsh winter.

The site remained the colonial capital until 1610, when Oñate was replaced by *don* Pedro de Peralta. It was Peralta, who established the Spanish capital at a new location at the base of the Sangre de Cristo Mountains and named it Santa Fe.

The waiter brought a plate piled with tortillas and beef in a spicy gravy. One bite awakened Rafe's hunger. He had not eaten since yesterday afternoon. As he ate, he tried to imagine how it must have been for those first Spanish settlers here in a strange land.

Much like the Anglo settlers now, the Spaniards were looking for land and riches. They were looking for a peaceful place to raise crops and families. At first the Indians helped the Spaniards, but then it turned to bloodshed. The Spaniards were intent on changing the Indians, teaching them Christianity, and dismissing their primitive religion. More colonists from New Spain came and demanded more land. They tried to use the Indians as slaves and hanged a number of dissenters and medicine men who were accused of practicing sorcery. Finally, all out war erupted between the Indians and the Spaniards with the Indians driving the Spaniards south and out of northern New Mexico.

The thoughts brought Rafe back to the present. The squatters were not vastly different. They were looking for land to raise crops and families. The vast lands of New Mexico were mostly open and unsettled. The land provided water, wood, game, and the basic necessities for survival.

Like the clash between the Indians and Spaniards, it had turned to bloodshed.

Rafe shook those thoughts out of his mind. Regardless of history, the squatters had killed and injured innocent people. They killed his innocent wife and unborn child. The dead were not part of this squabble over the land here and did not deserve to die.

When the waiter came to clear his empty plate, Rafe asked him, "I heard there has been trouble with Anglo squatters near here. I have not seen any Anglos in town. Is it safe for me to ride the countryside? You see I am looking for land to buy."

"Aquí hay muchos problemas con los ocupantes ilegales," the waiter told him there was much trouble here with land squatters. He continued relating how squatters raided the fiesta at *don* Lorenzo's hacienda. They killed women and children, then rode out. They wore red hoods.

Rafe tried hard not to react to the retold story.

"You should be careful *señor*. I have heard the squatters have shot at *vaqueros* if they are riding alone," the waiter warned him.

Rafe thanked him for the meal and walked back to the inn. Stars were popping out in the night sky and the temperature had dropped. Rafe buttoned his coat and lowered his hat against the wind.

Back in his room, he sat in the overstuffed chair. He had several problems. First, he wanted to identify the culprits and he also needed to be careful. His initial rage and lack of concern for his welfare had waned. He wanted his revenge, but he wanted to live. He had a horse business, the Summers' family, his mother and sister in Mexico, and his best friend Carlos. He wanted to punish the raiders, but then return to Santa Fe and try to find a way to live without his beloved wife. He wondered if it would be possible to live a life without her.

Pondering plans, he settled on one. Leaning back, he fell sound asleep in the soft chair.

CHAPTER 5

It was still dark when Rafe woke from the nightmare. Ana Teresa lay in his arms with blood gushing out of her chest and he could hear his unborn child crying. He shot out of the chair wanting to scream and kill. At this point, he did not care who he killed. All the thoughts he had last night of returning to Santa Fe to try to resume a life evaporated.

Vengeance tore at his gut and wanted to rip his heart apart. He struggled to calm himself, but his heart would not stop thumping, wanting to burst through his chest. Like a wild man, he sought his pistols. The small room in Los Luceros was unfamiliar and it took him a moment to remember where he was. He splashed water on his face and took deep breaths, asking God to help him. Finally, his rage calmed.

In the distance, he heard the first rooster crow, then another answered the call. A little while later, faint sunlight crept into his room. He took the gun cleaning kit out of the saddlebag and took his time cleaning both his pistols and short-barrel shotgun. It took his mind off the nightmare and focused on getting ready to find his wife's murderers.

Last night he decided on a plan to identify the culprits. However, he had several tasks to do in town before he sought his prey.

He took out a pencil and drew a circle about two and a half inches in diameter with an inner circle, giving it a border of about a quarter inch. Inside he drew a five-point star with each point touching the inner circle. Above the top point he wrote in capitals, MARSHAL, on the bottom he wrote, SANTA FE. In the center he wrote, U.S. Rafe guessed at the dimensions of the fake badge, but on paper it looked about right.

Next, he needed a haircut to continue his disguise. When he walked downstairs, he greeted the desk clerk and then asked, "Where can I find a barber for a shave?"

"Go to the end of the street, you will see Pepe's

Barbería."

As he walked along the dirt street, the small village of Los Luceros was beginning to start the new week. The proprietor of the general store was stacking produce and a wagon was stopped in front. Several children ran along the street carrying books.

Pepe was cutting a man's hair when Rafe entered the barbershop. The barber pointed to a seat with the comb he held in his left hand.

"Creo que fueron los ocupantes ilegales quiénes mataron a su preciado toro. Don Lorenzo ha tenido muchos problemas con ellos," the man in the barber chair said. Rafe listened as the two men discussed the problems at *don* Lorenzo's and about the prized bull stolen by the squatters.

"Sí, estoy de acuerdo," the barber agreed.

"Estas listo," the barber told the man he was finished.

"Gracias Pepe," the man thanked him, handing the barber a few coins, and left.

"I want a short hair cut," Rafe told the barber. He pulled off his Stetson and his dark hair fell almost to his shoulders.

The barber took a look and pointed to the barber chair. "How much do you want cut *señor?"*

"I want it short, above my ears," Rafe told him. The barber began cutting and Rafe, pondered the conversation he heard from the barber and the man.

"You are not from here *señor?"* the barber asked.

"No, I am from Pueblo, Colorado. I am here looking for land to buy. I am told land is cheap and there is plenty to buy," Rafe told him.

"Be careful *señor.* You may be sold land, but it may belong to one of the many Spanish land grants around here. Many people are buying illegal land. There is much trouble and there has been killing." The barber stopped cutting and walked around to look Rafe in the eyes as he told him about the trouble.

"Killing? I want no part of that! Who is being killed and why?"

"It is gringos. They are sold land deeds in the east.

When they arrive they find out the deed is illegal. The *hacienderos* try to drive them off, but the gringos fight back. They killed several people last Saturday at a fiesta. It was very bad. You must go to the *alcalde,* Mayor Ramon Salaz. He can tell you where to buy land legally."

"Where can I find the mayor?" Rafe asked.

"You cannot miss the house *señor.* It is the biggest house in the center of the village," the barber told him.

Los Luceros was a small village and Rafe could see the mayor's house as he stepped to the street. He had purposefully left his guns and saddlebags in his room at the inn.

A woman answered the mayor's door. *"Bienvenido a la casa del Alcalde Salaz,"* she welcomed Rafe to the mayor's house.

"Thank you. I do not have an appointment, but may I speak with the mayor?" Rafe asked.

"Please come in. The mayor is busy, but you can wait if you wish. Please have a seat over there and I will tell the mayor you are here."

Rafe sat and waited, and shortly the woman came with a sweet roll and a cup of coffee.

"Thank you ma'am."

As he ate the roll and drank the coffee, Rafe looked at the paintings in the anteroom. The larger one at the center of the room was a painting of *don* Juan de Oñate on horseback. To the right was a painting of Hernán Cortés, the man who conquered the Aztec Empire. To the left was a painting of *don* Francisco Pizarro González, the man who conquered the Inca Empire. In a way it reminded him of the Palacio Cantina in Santa Fe. The Palacio was adorned with large murals of Spanish conquistadors, including these.

Several pieces of historic conquistador helmets and armor were placed on a table near where Rafe sat. Standing, he picked up the steel chest plate and measured it against his body. It was small and heavy. He put it back and lifted the helmet and it too was small and heavy.

"Those would not fit you *señor,"* a man spoke out and

laughed. "I am Ramon Salaz. How can I be of help to you?"

"I am Ricardo Gonzalez from Pueblo, Colorado. Thank you for seeing me sir." Rafe answered and stuck out his hand. "My brothers and I are looking to buy land here in this area. I was selected to explore what is available here. Can you help me?"

"Yes I can help, but you must know most all the good land here is along the Rio Grande and is part of Spanish land grants. You can buy some of those lands only if the land grant owners are willing to sell," the mayor told him. "Come into my office, I have maps where I can show you what could be for sale."

The mayor pulled out several rolls of maps and unrolled them on a long table. He pointed out the names and areas covered by the land grants. On one of the maps, Rafe saw the land grant owned by *don* Lorenzo Salazar. Finally, he showed Rafe a small hacienda. The man had no heirs and was not able to keep up with his sheep herd. He retired to Santa Fe where his daughter lived.

"Sir, Pepe the barber told me there was trouble and killings by squatters at one of the haciendas. I also heard the same talk at the restaurant last night. Are these just rumors or is it true?"

"I am afraid it is true *señor*. It happened at *don* Lorenzo's courtyard last Saturday before sundown. Masked gunmen killed several people, including women and children, and many others were injured. I know the mayor of San Gabriel has sent a request to the governor to send someone to investigate and find the killers."

"Masked gunmen?" Rafe pretended to be shocked.

"Squatters have taken up arms against the Spaniards. *Don* Lorenzo owns the Spanish land grant, but the squatters do not care. They took one of his prized bulls and there was bloodshed when he sent his *vaqueros* to retrieve it."

"What about the sheriff? Why has he not done something?"

"The squatters believe they have legal deeds to the land. The governor is verifying all the Spanish land grants. I hate to admit it *señor,* but it is a bad situation."

"I will look at the hacienda and the sheep herd, but you must tell me where the squatters are located. I do not want to go near them and get myself killed," Rafe told him. The mayor pointed to the area north and west on the boundary of *don* Lorenzo's land grant. "Stay away from this area. I believe it is where the killers came from. They are homesteading along the river."

Rafe walked back toward the inn from the mayor's home and went to the stable behind it.

"*Buenas tardes señor,*" the man greeted him wishing him good afternoon.

"Do you know where I can get my boot spur repaired?" Rafe asked pointing to the spur on his right boot.

"I know an old Tiwa Indian who makes repairs. His name is Ok'uwapi, but he goes by Red Cloud. You cannot miss him. He lives on the right side of the road north to Taos in a small hut about two miles from here."

It was mid afternoon when Rafe reached the hut of the Indian metalworker. Only the small furnace was burning with a low flame and Ok'uwapi was not there. Rafe made his way to the back entrance hoping to find the old man, but saw no one. He walked around to the front and was headed to a hut nearby when he saw Red Cloud coming out of a grove of cottonwoods and shrub.

"*Buenas tardes,*" Rafe greeted him in Spanish, saying good afternoon, hoping the Tiwa Indian spoke Spanish.

"*Buenas tardes,*" he replied. "*¿Tienes hambre?*" he asked Rafe if he was hungry and lifted two plump quails. Rafe replied with a nod and a smile.

Red Cloud proceeded to clean and dress the birds. He skewered them and placed them over the low burning fire in the forge.

Rafe took out the piece of paper from his pocket with the drawing of the marshal's badge He handed the paper to Red Cloud and asked if he could make it.

The Indian nodded his head. Leaving Rafe to tend the birds, he headed into his shop. While the birds roasted, the deft hands of the old Indian worked a piece of metal. He took a break when Rafe told him the quail were cooked.

Rafe asked the man about his tribe as they ate. "My ancestors were Yunque. They lived on this land for centuries. When the white man with the helmets of iron came, many of my tribe died."

It was a story Rafe knew well. When the Spaniards first settled San Gabriel, they killed or enslaved many Indians, who they thought of as inferior. It was true in Mexico and also true here.

"You do not live in the pueblo?" Rafe asked as a question.

"Hmmm . . . . I married a Spanish woman and the tribe shunned us. We moved here to be alone, then she died a long time ago," Red Cloud answered quietly.

"I'm sorry."

Without saying more, Red Cloud worked on the badge with a smooth rock to grind the sharp edges. Rafe crossed his arms and leaned against the center post of the hut and watched the old man work.

Red Cloud's clear black eyes would glance at Rafe between his movements. In a way, the dark eyes reminded Rafe of Xihuitl, the Aztec healer who saved his life. Red Cloud was older, but had the same assured presence about him. Rafe relaxed and let the old man's company comfort him. For now, he forgot about Ana Teresa and his vengeance. With the pounding of the metal and the soft scraping of the rock, the evil thoughts seemed to leave his mind and body.

A faint red horizon to the right of the trail south guided Rafe back to Los Luceros as darkness fell. He left with a satisfied stomach and a good replica of a United States Marshal badge. It was somewhat crude, but Rafe thought adequate for his needs.

As he rode, it did not take long for the memory of Ana Teresa's death to kindle his revenge. Tomorrow would be the beginning of a new way of life.

He knew he would kill, not because he liked killing, but because vengeance was driving him. He wanted no control over the feelings, as he could not let the murder of his wife and unborn child stand unanswered. It would be justified vengeance.

CHAPTER 6

Monday morning, George Summers took the small flatbed wagon to San Gabriel. It was a grim task to go to the undertaker for Ana Teresa's body. The day was cool and clouds hung gray over the town to match his mood. It was March 23, 1874 and spring was only just starting to melt the snow-capped Sangre de Cristo Mountains, although small wild flowers pushed up through the damp earth announcing an early spring.

Arriving at the undertaker's parlor, George sat on the wagon seat for several long moments. He heaved a long sigh and set the wagon's brake. Stepping down, he reached into the back and pulled at a heavy blanket that he brought to wrap the body.

Pushing in the door, the undertaker looked up at him. "Good morning," George said.

"Buenos dias señor," the undertaker greeted him. George saw two bodies draped in blankets lying on the preparation tables. Several caskets leaned against the wall.

"How may I help you?" the undertaker asked.

"I am George Summers from Santa Fe. I have come for Ana Teresa's body."

"Ana Teresa?"

"Ana Teresa Reyes. She was killed on Saturday at the fiesta. I am her father-in-law."

"Oh yes, the trouble at the fiesta. I did not hear anyone from Santa Fe was killed. I'm sorry *Señor* Summers for your loss. If she was killed, her body was not brought from *don* Lorenzo's."

"Are you sure she is not here?" George knew it sounded dumb even as the words escaped his mouth.

"Of course I'm sure. I prepared *don* Alfonso's grandson, *Señora* Victoria, one of *don* Lorenzo's *vaqueros,* and an Americano. It is said the gringo is one of the raiders. I think they are afraid to come and collect him." The undertaker pointed to one of the covered bodies.

"Do you want me to take the hearse to collect her from *don* Lorenzo's?"

"No thank you. I have a wagon. I'm taking her body back to Santa Fe for burial," George responded. Rafe's note said Ana Teresa's body was taken to the doctor in San Gabriel. George only assumed she would have then been taken to the undertaker. It seemed odd, but it was probably very chaotic at the time.

Walking back outside, George looked at the heavy gray clouds. They threatened rain. Perhaps he should ask the undertaker to retrieve Ana Teresa in the covered hearse. Somehow, the idea seemed impersonal. George jumped to the seat and started the horse. The thought struck him that perhaps *don* Pedro and *doña* Marcella already collected her body. After all, she was their niece and daughter. He decided to check with *don* Lorenzo before leaving San Gabriel.

By the time George arrived at the Salazar hacienda, a light rain was falling. The maid ushered him inside. *Don* Lorenzo was sitting at his desk when the maid led George into the library.

"*Buenos dias.* I am George Summers from Santa Fe. I've come for Ana Teresa's body."

"*Ah, lo siento.* It is a terrible thing *Señor* Summers. Her body is not here. All the dead and injured were taken to the doctor's office in town on Saturday evening."

"That's odd. I stopped at the undertaker, but he thought her body was here."

"Come into the kitchen and I will have Carlita dry your coat." *Don* Lorenzo rose from his desk and walked George toward the back of the house.

"*Por favor,* sit down and have a cup of coffee and a sweet roll. I will gather my coat and go with you."

Carlita, an older woman, poured George's coffee, offered a platter of sweet rolls, and took his coat to hang by the fire.

"Thank you *señora.*" George sat in the warmth of the kitchen and let the hot coffee warm the chill inside him. A few minutes later *don* Lorenzo walked into the kitchen with a coat and two rain slickers.

"It is still unbelievable. What happened?" George asked him.

"A group of squatters moved onto my land last year. I have been trying to evict them ever since. They stole one of my prize bulls and there was bloodshed between the squatters and my *vaqueros*. Everyone was gathered in the courtyard enjoying the wedding fiesta on Saturday when a group of men rode in and began shooting at everyone. They wore red hoods over their heads."

George sensed retelling the story was difficult and remained quiet.

"Most of the *dons* were not armed or only had swords. Some of the younger *caballeros* with weapons defended us. After one of the masked raiders was killed, they turned and rode off. Rafael and several *caballeros* took horses and pursued them. Only then did we realize the carnage the squatters had inflicted. I was shot in the arm, *don* Alfonso's five-year-old grandson and *Señora* Victoria were killed, and six more were injured. During the chaos, Carlos got Bibiana and Benicío to safety and then ran for Ana Teresa. He was leading her into the house when she stumbled. He carried her the rest of the way and took her to where he left Bibiana." *Don* Lorenzo exhaled a big sigh, reliving the chaos and terror was difficult.

"I remember everyone was screaming. After the raiders were chased off, Carlos returned to check on Bibiana and Ana Teresa. He found Bibiana cradling Ana Teresa and sobbing. She told Carlos Ana Teresa was dead. Carlos found blood seeping from her hip. Carlos believes she was shot as he led her to safety. It was why she stumbled."

George was stunned at the depiction of the shooting. Nothing like this had ever happened in Santa Fe. How could the squatters justify their actions over a land squabble?

"Carlos is inconsolable. He thinks she would still be alive if he had left her sitting in the courtyard or that the bullet should have taken him. His grief is crushing him," *don* Lorenzo told George.

"Yes. He told me. What is the sheriff going to do about it?"

Don Lorenzo sighed, then said, "The sheriff said there is little he can do since the men wore masks. No one can identify them, although one was killed here. His body was taken with the others. I had never seen him before, but he was young, still a teenager. The sheriff said he would look into it."

George knew the sheriff would probably do little. In his heart he knew Rafe wanted revenge. George understood, but he would have tried to stop him. Now, hearing *don* Lorenzo's words, he hoped Rafe would be successful.

A short time later, George and *don* Lorenzo rode south from the hacienda toward San Gabriel. It was raining lightly and they both wore the hooded rain slickers. A short way down the road, a lone rider galloped by. His face was shadowed under a wide-brimmed hat and the collar of his jacket was pulled up high against the rain.

By the time they reached San Gabriel the rain had stopped. George drove the wagon to the doctor's office and pulled up. The sign hanging on the stairwell said, Doctor Eduardo Roybal. They climbed the steps and knocked on the door.

"Buenos dias don Lorenzo. Buenos dias señor," a man greeted them when he answered the knock. He wore small spectacles pushed up on his head and his curly hair was gray around the temples. He ushered them inside.

"Buenos dias. We have come for Ana Teresa Reyes," George said.

"Gracias a Dios. I am glad you have come. We did not know how to reach her family," the doctor replied thanking God they arrived. He was smiling broadly. "Follow me."

The doctor walked and pulled open a curtain to a small room in the back. A bed draped in white sheets held a body. A white blanket covered the body up to the face. Ana Teresa's brown hair cascaded on the pillow. Both George and *don* Lorenzo crossed themselves, although George thought it odd her face was not covered. No coins held her eyes shut.

"She is holding on," the doctor said.

"Holding on?" they said almost simultaneously.

"You did not know? I sent a man to your hacienda. I thought it was why you came. She is alive, barely, but she is alive. I've given her a potion to relieve the pain."

"Gracias a Dios!" don Lorenzo shouted. George steadied himself holding onto the edge of the bed.

The doctor then told them how in the chaos after the gun battle, he was overwhelmed by the victims. "Everyone was brought here to me, as the only doctor in San Gabriel. I was told she was dead, but when I finally examined her wounds, she groaned slightly. I did not know who she was."

"And the baby?" George asked.

"The baby is alive as well. However, she needs to gain her strength. The baby is taking all it requires from her and she has not eaten nor had a drink for more than a day. If she does not start responding, I'm afraid she and the baby will die."

CHAPTER 7

George and *don* Lorenzo discussed Ana Teresa's condition with the doctor. He explained the bullet had shattered a bone in her hip and was still lodged somewhere near her spine. He gave her a pain drug so she would not move until he could determine more about her injuries.

"Her condition is too dire to be transported," the doctor told them.

"What can we do?"

"Pray. I am doing everything I can. Perhaps if someone came to stay with her. Where is her husband?" he asked.

"He thought she was killed. He is gone and I do not know where," George replied.

"We must notify *don* Pedro," *don* Lorenzo recommended. George agreed and the doctor sent for a young man to make the trip. George gave the young man directions to the de Soto hacienda.

After the rider left, they waited, hoping Ana Teresa would waken. Several times she seemed to stir when they spoke to her or held her hand. George put his hand on her belly and felt the baby kick and he vowed to do everything in his power to keep them both alive.

Late Monday afternoon a rider came to the de Soto hacienda north of Santa Fe from San Gabriel. The maid ushered the young man into the parlor and found *doña* Agustina in her bedroom. She had not left the room since they returned from the fiesta on Saturday night.

"Why are you bothering me?" she admonished the maid.

"*Perdóneme señora.* A man is here from San Gabriel."

"Go find the *don.* You know I am not up to dealing with this."

"I could not find him *señora.*"

Gathering herself, Agustina walked into the parlor. She

was dressed in black and her face plain without any rouge. Her eyes were puffy from crying and lack of sleep.

"*Buenas tardes,*" she greeted the man coldly.

"*Señora, don* Lorenzo sent me with word for *don* Pedro."

"The *don* is not here. I will give him the message," she said.

"*Don* Lorenzo says to tell you the woman is at the doctor. He says to tell you to come."

"The woman?"

"*Sí,* the woman pregnant with child. She is at the doctor. You must come."

"I will tell *mi esposo* to go collect the body in the morning," *doña* Agustina replied with a sigh, then added. "Perhaps he has already gone, as he is not here."

"*¿Cuerpo?*" the man asked questioning her use of the word body. "The woman, she is not dead *señora.*"

"*¿No esta muerta?*" *doña* Agustina responded shocked at the man's words.

"*No señora.* She is at the doctor's office in San Gabriel."

Doña Agustina's screams were heard all throughout the house. The maids came running thinking the young man had hurt their mistress.

"Go find *doña* Marcella. Quickly! Find *don* Pedro now!" she screamed.

Late in the afternoon, George drove the wagon home to Santa Fe. The drive back was the exact opposite of the earlier ride going to San Gabriel. The dread in his heart had lifted, as had the rain clouds. The sun played peek-a-boo, popping in and out of puffy white clouds.

The doctor warned them against too much optimism for Ana Teresa's condition. He used the term dire. However, nothing could dampen George's spirit. He took a slight detour to the de Soto hacienda. He wanted to make sure the news had reached them. When he drove into the de Soto courtyard, the entire family including Carlos and Bibiana rushed out the front door, laughing and crying tears of joy as they surrounded George.

Agustina held Bibiana's child, trying to relate how they learned the news. Tears spilled down her cheeks and onto the child's blanket. *Doña* Marcella was still wearing her black mourning dress, but her face was beaming with joy.

Carlos grabbed George in a huge *abrazo.*

"Did you see Rafe in San Gabriel?" Carlos asked.

George shook his head back and forth.

"I told *don* Lorenzo to tell his *vaqueros* to keep their eyes open for him. I hope they can find him before he does anything terrible," George whispered.

"I must go find him," Carlos suggested.

"Ana Teresa cannot be moved and the doctor requested for someone to go and stay with her. Perhaps you can take *doña* Marcella tomorrow and then while you are there you can go look for him," George replied.

The following morning, Carlos drove the buggy. Riding inside, *doña* Marcella held several parcels and two hat boxes. Last night she prayed the rosary three times and was filling her time this morning continuing her prayers for her daughter and unborn grandchild.

It was a miracle. After her husband, Bartolo, was killed at the Palacio Cantina in a swordfight last August, Ana Teresa was all she had left in her life. At first, she was unhappy about Ana Teresa's husband, Rafael. However, she was not as rigid about his bloodlines as Bartolo had been. She would rather have her daughter married to an influential *caballero,* but over the months she found Rafael to be kind, generous, and honorable. He welcomed her into their home. She watched how he treated Ana Teresa with love and tenderness.

As the months of the pregnancy continued, Marcella became enthralled in the prospect of becoming a grandmother. She was free from any wifely duties and had no hacienda to run. She quickly found out she had few other skills. Hers had been a life of luxury, tended by maids and servants. Over the past eight months, she helped Ana Teresa in the kitchen and sewed several small items for the baby.

When they arrived in San Gabriel and Carlos stopped

in front of the doctor's office. He helped Marcella climb the stairs and they knocked on the door.

"*Bienvenidos,*" Doctor Roybal greeted them.

"*¿Como esta Ana Teresa?*" Marcella asked on her daughter's condition.

"She is a bit better today. She took a few sips of water. I am glad you are here. I believe it will help rouse her to have someone near to encourage her."

They went into the back room. Ana Teresa lay still against the white sheets and Marcella gasped. She looked pale and deathlike. Carlos held Marcella's arm and led her to a chair near the bed.

"Talk to her. Try to get her to respond," the doctor told them.

"*Mija. Mija,* I am here," Marcella said quietly. Squeezing her hand, Marcella began to talk to her daughter. "Please open your eyes. I am here. You need to live, you and the baby."

"Ana Teresa. It's Carlos. I'm going to look for Rafael. He does not know you are alive. Please hold on so I can go find him," Carlos said. Guilt lingered in his heart, as he felt responsible for her injury. They talked to her for several minutes, but Ana Teresa did not open her eyes.

"Don't give up. She goes in and out of consciousness," the doctor told them.

"I will take your things to *don* Lorenzo's hacienda. I need to see if Rafael has been there. I will return later," Carlos told Marcella and took his leave.

"If you need anything or she wakens, call me. I will be mixing potions in the other room," the doctor said, then walked away leaving Marcella and her daughter in the quiet room.

Carlos drove the buggy north of town to the Salazar hacienda. There was no time to alert them of Marcella's visit, but he knew she would be welcome. *Don* Lorenzo came into the parlor after being summoned by the maid and greeted Carlos.

"*Bienvenido.* We have been expecting you. Did you bring Agustina with you?"

"No. Agustina has responsibilities in Santa Fe. I left Ana Teresa's mother, *doña* Marcella, at the doctor's office. She will stay with her."

"I will make sure she has everything she needs. How is Ana Teresa today?"

"The doctor said she is a bit better."

"*Gracias a Dios.* It is a miracle."

"*Señor,* have you seen Rafael?"

"Not since the night of the fiesta."

"We do not know where he is. He does not know about Ana Teresa," Carlos said.

Don Lorenzo shook his head and looked glum. "I feel terrible. I told him she was dead. It was what we all believed. Where could he be?"

"I think he might be seeking revenge against the squatters. Have you heard anything?"

"No. I reported the raid to the sheriff on Monday morning. He had already heard the news, of course. He thought the squatters' actions deplorable, but when I told him they wore masks and no one could identify the culprits, he suggested we do not retaliate. He warned me the men who came might not be the squatters," *don* Lorenzo finished the last sentence with a grumble.

"Of course it was the squatters. Who else would it be?" Carlos blurted out.

"The sheriff is protecting them trying to keep the peace, but promised to go and talk to them this week. I've directed my *vaqueros* to stay away from their camp, although several are vowing revenge."

Carlos pondered traveling to the squatters' camp himself to seek Rafe. George said Rafe was not riding Rayo. Instead, Reymundo said a brown gelding was missing. George checked the house and Rafe's pistols and short-barrel shotgun were gone. There was no doubt in Carlos' mind, Rafe would find and punish the murderers.

"Can your *vaqueros* scout near the squatters' camp? Rafael will be riding a brown gelding," Carlos asked *don* Lorenzo.

"*Sí.* I will tell them."

Carlos was not a violent man by nature and a devout Catholic, however he believed Rafe was justified in whatever he did. Once Rafe satisfied his vengeance, he would surely go home to Santa Fe. However, the situation had changed drastically. Although the squatters were still guilty of killing and injuring others, Ana Teresa was alive. If Rafe killed anyone, he could be hanged for it.

Carlos left the buggy with *don* Lorenzo and borrowed a horse. The *don* promised to send word immediately if anything happened concerning Rafe or Ana Teresa. *Don* Lorenzo also promised to alert his *vaqueros* to be on the lookout for Rafe.

Carlos stopped briefly at the doctor's office before riding back to Santa Fe. There was no change with Ana Teresa. He told *doña* Marcella someone would come for her later in the evening to take her to *don* Lorenzo's home.

"Send a messenger immediately, if there is a change," he implored the doctor.

CHAPTER 8

The poker players at the Golden Shaft Saloon in Elizabethtown were tired of Kip Donohoe's tale of how he and his gang of red-hooded raiders rode into a courtyard and killed a mess of greasers. Kip embellished the story with each retelling.

"Shud up. Yew dun run that pony ta death, an it probly ain't even half true," Earl groused at Kip.

Since returning to E-town, Kip bragged about his exploits. At first the gang was interested, but now they mostly ignore the braggart. He told the story making him look like a hero for the squatters and reveling in the killing of the greasers. He boasted about killing the head greaser as well as women and children. The gang did not believe him, however Nat Holmes did back up the story.

"Hey Clement, what yew gonna do now that the mines dun got played out?" Kip asked.

"Well, I got nuff money outta my mines. Clay's up in Cimarron. Got hisseff a ranch up near thar. Can you believe that? I might go up thar and git me a place of my own and I heerd they got emselves sum good saloons up thar."

"Cain't imagine yew as a clodhoppin rancher," Roy snickered.

Clement squared his shoulders, whipped out a pistol, twirled it several times, and aimed it directly at Roy's face. "Yew wanna wipe that grin off yer face or do yew want me ta do it?"

"I was just funnin. Yew would be a good rancher," Roy eased back in his chair as he retracted his words.

Kip listened to his friends banter. He found out Clay Allison left Elizabethtown before winter set in. The mines were petering out and the town was a shadow of its former self.

"Clement, what else have you heard about Cimarron?" Kip asked.

"I heerd tell the new owners of the Maxwell Land

Grant be needin gunhands to remove squatters," Clement replied.

"Yea, I hear sumthin is a brewing up thar. It's all bout em greasers thinkin they own the land just cause the King of sumwhere told em they cud have it," Roy said. "That dun sit well with Mericans."

"I'll go an put a stop to em greasers in Cimarron just like I did in San Gabriel," Kip bragged.

Daylight came through the window of Rafe's small room at the inn on Tuesday morning. He had slept fitfully afraid of the recurring nightmare and nervous about what was to come. He did not rush as he gathered his belongings and dressed in his casual suit before he went to check out. After stowing his gear on the gelding, he walked to the restaurant and ordered a full breakfast.

Although he knew he should eat, he could only finish half the meal as he had a nervous twitch in his stomach. He drank two cups of strong coffee, paid for the meal, and walked back to the small stable to get the horse.

"He is all ready for you *señor,*" Abel the stable man said walking the gelding out of a stall.

"Thank you." Rafe flipped him a quarter and mounted.

"I hear you are looking for land *señor.* Be careful on the roads. There is trouble between the gringos and the Spanish. They may not ask who you are before shooting," Abel told him.

"So I have heard. I will be careful."

The map of the town and the location of the squatters was etched in his mind. He rode with purpose, though not in a gallop toward his destination. His senses were on high alert as he rode, wishing he was riding Rayo his trusted Appaloosa. He left Rayo in his barn knowing the remarkable horse was a threat.

He saw smoke lazily drifting skyward before he spotted the squatters' camp. Finding a secluded vantage point in a clump of cottonwoods along the river to hide, he sat on the horse watching the scene. Several makeshift houses stood near the river. Well-used wagons were parked nearby and looked as if they were being used for storage or housing.

A group of young children played a game with a ball. They were laughing and calling to each other. Their childish voices raised the hair on Rafe's neck. He would never hear his child's voice or see him play a game with others. Rage overcame him in an instant, burning in his chest. He could taste the bile in his throat.

They all deserved to die and his instinct was to kill them all. They did not belong here. They came seeking destruction at the hacienda and they warranted his vengeance.

As he watched, a woman came out of one of the houses with a small baby in her arms. She carried a bucket and went to fetch water from the river. Rafe watched her in her task. She and the child were innocent.

Turning the horse and keeping hidden in the trees, he worked his way along the squatter camps. Further down the river, he spotted more smoke rising. Finally, he found a position where he could see several houses along the river. There were three houses and several tents setup in a semicircle. A large coral held several horses and two others held cows. Beside each house, a garden area had been cleared and looked ready for planting.

Across the river, a plowed field of green stretched up a hillside. In the field to the right, three men were working to clear trees for another field. Rafe pondered his task again. He dismounted and tied the horse to a branch of a tree, then settled himself at the base of the tree to ponder his move.

He was alone and obviously outnumbered. The people in town warned him, the squatters would shoot first and ask questions later.

After a while a man came out of one of the houses. He carried a bucket and headed toward the river. The man fetched several buckets of water, taking each to a trough at the corral. Rafe noticed the man was not armed.

A younger man came to the door of the house. His arm was in a sling of white muslin. Walking gingerly, the younger man headed toward the corral.

"Frankie, I told you to stay inside," Hank Shelby said to his son.

"I'm tired of being cooped up. My arm ain't so bad."

After they finished fetching water to the trough, Frankie followed his father back to the house.

"You two sit. I got sandwiches made," Frankie's mother said.

Rafe stood and walked to the horse. He adjusted his gunbelt and checked his pistols. Pulling the quiver, Chiwiwi made for him many years ago from the saddlebag, he strapped it over his back and tucked the short-barrel shotgun in it. The last thing he did before he mounted up on the brown horse was to pin the marshal badge on his suit.

He lowered his black Stetson and spurred the brown horse toward the squatter's house. He sat tall in the saddle, wanting to convey an air of authority as he rode up. Jumping down, he politely knocked on the door.

The older man opened it with a rifle in hand. At first he looked steely. Then his eyes caught the marshal's badge and he lowered the rifle.

"What do you want here?" he asked. Hank let out a long breath. He was not surprised the law had come.

"My name is Ricardo Gonzalez. I am a United States Marshal sent here by the Governor to investigate the murder of women and children at *don* Lorenzo's fiesta last Saturday," Rafe told him. He kept his voice full of authority.

"Why do you think we had anything to do with that? We heard about it, but it was not us," Hank responded with a lie.

"Your son is injured."

"He was hurt clearing trees. A limb fell on his shoulder and broke it," Hank lied again. Rafe could see the uncertainty in his eyes.

"That right, son?" Rafe turned and asked the younger man.

"I . . . I . . that's right Marshal. A tree fell on me."

"Ma'am please remove his shirt," Rafe said to the woman. As she started to move toward her son, Hank raised the rifle. Rafe pulled a pistol before he could get the rifle up and leveled it on him.

"Put the rifle down."

Slowly the woman did as Rafe asked. Rafe felt his stomach flopping with nervous anticipation. When the young man's shirt was off, Rafe walked around to look at the shoulder. "That's a gunshot wound mister. Why did you lie to me?" Rafe growled.

CHAPTER 9

"He's a good boy. He didn't mean to do nothing wrong." The woman began to cry.

"What's your name son?"

"Frankie . . . Frank Shelby. I didn't mean it. I didn't know it would go so far," Frankie sniveled.

"Who was with you Frankie?" Rafe asked.

"It was me and Fred Westfield and Jimmy Burns. Jimmy got killed."

"We were informed there were six men who went to the ranch," Rafe kept his air of authority in his voice.

"It was Kip and his two friends. They made us do it."

"Kip Donohoe is not one of us Marshal and they be gone. They did not come back after the raid," Hank added.

"Where's this Fred Westfield?"

"His house is the second house down the river from here."

"Where's the red hood?" he asked.

Frankie hung his head. The woman opened a drawer in the china chest and pulled out a red hood and handed it to Rafe.

"Ma'am. I suggest you sit here and be quiet," Rafe told her.

"Let's go." Rafe signaled to Frankie and Hank to move.

Rafe walked the father and son at gunpoint to the Westfield house. When Jerome Westfield opened the door, Hank looked defeated. Frankie walked behind him, and then Jerome saw the marshal badge on the third man. The marshal was holding two pistols and some kind of rifle was strapped to his back.

"He's come for Fred," Hank said.

"What do you mean Hank. You know my son was injured when he fell off his horse," Jerome lied.

"The jigs up Jerome. The marshal knows what happened."

"Bring him out," Rafe ordered with a stern voice.

"Ellie, go and get Fred," Jerome told his wife.

Fred Westfield came from the bedroom. His arm hung limply at his side and he stood apprehensively shifting from foot to foot. To Rafe he looked to be no older than twenty years old. As Rafe walked up to him, the young man's eyes shifted from Rafe to his father and Rafe noted a slight trembling of his lips.

"You one of the red-hooded raiders?" Rafe walked up close to him and asked.

"Yes sir. I'm sorry," the young man hung his head.

"Where's the hood?"

"Under my bed."

"Go get it."

As Rafe watched Fred get the hood in the bedroom, his mother begged. "Please Marshal, don't take my son. He's just a boy," Ellie begged.

"I'm sorry ma'am. Your son has a gunshot wound and my report says one of the raiders was killed and some were wounded. It was reported the raiders wore red hoods," Rafe told her. "They will go to trial in Santa Fe. They killed innocent women and children ma'am. Did you know that?"

She nodded and began to cry. "He's no killer. It was that Kip fellow. He was the gunslinger. The boys thought they were just going to scare the Mexicans."

Rafe looked at Hank and Jerome. "Who is Kip?"

"Kip Donohoe. We hired him to protect us from the Mexicans. They have been harassing us ever since we got here. Fred said he had two friends with him."

"Is he here?" Rafe asked.

"No, he and his gang left after the killings at the hacienda," Fred said.

"What will happen to them Marshal?" Ellie asked.

"They will get a trial, but killing is a hanging offence. Now, let's go saddle their horses," Rafe told them.

Tying the two boy's hands, he had them mount up. With the two young men in tow on their horses, Rafe rode out of the squatter's camp. They rode to a spot where he stopped and looked back. He half expected their fathers or others to try to stop him from taking the two killers, but no one was following. All of the horses were still in the corral.

They rode on while Rafe battled within himself. One of these two boys might be the one who killed Ana Teresa. In the chaos, even they probably would not know if they actually shot someone. Rafe could tell the one boy was in pain riding with his shattered shoulder.

Finally, he found a secluded spot with a grove of pine trees not far from *don* Lorenzo's courtyard. He jumped down and pulled the boys off their horses. Getting a rope from his horse, he tied them together at the base of a tree.

"I am a busy man and don't have a lot of patience. I could be back in Santa Fe with my girlfriend instead of chasing killers wearing hoods. You need to tell me who was with you when you raided the fiesta and what happened." Rafe had pulled a knife out and put it on Fred's throat.

"You can't kill us Marshal. You have to take us in. We deserve a trial."

"No, you don't deserve a trial if you killed those innocent people. You deserve to rot in hell," Rafe warned him. Fred wet his pants as Rafe pressed the knife to his throat and he saw the fire in Rafe's eyes.

"I'll tell you. Please don't cut my throat," Fred cried out. "It was that gunslinger my Dad hired to protect us. His name was Kip Donohoe. I thought he was brave. He talked us and Jimmy into taking action against the Mexicans who have been harassing us. He told us we were only going to scare them. Two of his friends showed up. I don't know their names. He made us use those red hoods and then we rode into the courtyard. Kip and his friends started shooting at people. Then everything else is a blur after I got shot." Tears rolled down Fred's cheeks and he was shaking.

"I'm only seventeen Marshal. I don't want to die for something I mighta not done. I didn't shoot anyone, just shot into the dirt," Frankie pleaded.

"Where's Kip Donohoe?" Rafe growled keeping the knife at Fred's throat.

"After the raid, I heard him tell his friends to follow him to E-town. They just rode off east and left us. Our friend

Jimmy was shot down and his parents are afraid to go to town to claim him."

Rafe walked off a little way. One of these two could have shot Ana Teresa. A furious battle raged inside him and killing them would appease his vengeance. Ana Teresa would be avenged, and yet if these two were innocent, then would it not be a hollow victory?

Finally, he walked over and checked their ropes. He walked to the horses and found the red hoods.

"Hey what the fuck are you doing? You said you were taking us to Santa Fe!" Fred yelled out.

Rafe cut a sleeve off their flannel shirts and used the sleeve to gag each of them. He then placed the red hoods over their heads.

"Be thankful for your life and use it for good in the future, if you live. This is your Santa Fe," Rafe told them and rode away.

CHAPTER 10

The following morning Rafe awoke early at a small hotel in the center of Taos. It was late March and spring was showing itself as unusually mild for northern New Mexico in the Taos basin. He dressed and went downstairs for breakfast. Only one other man was seated near him, finishing his food. Rafe ordered and was served coffee and given a folded newspaper.

As he waited, Rafe thought about the two young men he left tied to the tree near the entrance to *don* Lorenzo's courtyard. He wondered what the *don* or his *vaqueros* would do to them. Would they turn them in or take revenge and kill them? He had pondered killing them himself, but decided to go after the ringleaders instead, leaving the decision on what to do with the young men up to *don* Lorenzo.

He took his time eating and when finished he opened the folded newspaper. On the front page the headline was *Spanish Massacre*. He threw the newspaper aside, as the headline tore at his heart. If he would have read it, the article chronicled the events which led up to the attack, then gave an account of the red-hooded thugs who came and shot up the fiesta. The article ran the length of the first page and then continued to the second. Somewhere buried in the text, the miracle of one young woman's survival was heralded.

Finishing breakfast, he took his time gathering his belongings. A little while later after shaving and gathering a few supplies, he left Taos for the easy day's ride to E-town. He headed east into the morning sun following the Rio de Taos. It was more of a large creek, than a river, with only about three feet of snow melt running along the bed.

Riding south of Wheeler Peak, the tallest mountain in New Mexico, the sun warmed his back and seemed to be coaxing the spring grasses and flowers to break ground. The last time he rode to E-town, the nickname for Elizabethtown, was three years ago when George was stranded on a trip to visit his mining friend Bill Moore. It was in the middle of a sudden spring snowstorm, which closed all the passes.

As he rode, he thought about that last trip. When George failed to return home after delivering guns to Bill, Rafe and Carlos set off to E-town to find him. They found the booming gold town rife with outlaws and claim jumpers. The notorious outlaw, Clay Allison, and his gang were methodically killing miners and taking productive claims. When he and Carlos arrived, Clay's gang had Bill, Bill's workers, and George pinned down in a gun battle trying to take Bill's Mystic Lode gold mine. George was wounded in the gunfight. After successfully defending Bill's claim, and getting George medical care, Rafe and Carlos brought George back home to Santa Fe. He still limped slightly from the injury, especially in cold weather.

Rafe alternated trotting and galloping along the trail letting the gelding set the pace. As he got closer to E-town, the trail wound through the foothills of the tall peaks and narrowed. He missed riding Rayo, his large Appaloosa, who was more surefooted than the gelding. Pushing the horse a bit, he wanted to get to E-town before sundown.

The mountains cast the town in a deep shadow by the time Rafe pulled up to the Mutz Hotel. Immediately, Rafe noticed some of the saloons were closed and boarded up along with several other businesses. The last time he was here, constant activity churned up and down the main street. Now, there was only a trickle of miners walking toward town from the mines. Rafe walked into the lobby and noticed it too was mostly empty.

"Good evening sir. How can I help you," the clerk greeted him.

"I need a room. Maybe for the week."

"That will not be a problem. We have lots of rooms. Sign here, please." the clerk turned the registry toward Rafe.

"Last time I was here this town was buzzing. Seems kind of dead out there," Rafe stated.

"Sad thing mister. The mines are playing out. Don't know how much longer the ones still producing will last. Here, room 201, upstairs," the clerk handed him a key.

"Do you know if the Mystic Lode is still running?"

"Yes, Bill is still up there squeezing all he can out of his mine."

"Thank you." Rafe grabbed his belongings and climbed the stairs up to his room.

CHAPTER 11

Josefina, George, Carlos, and Bibiana left early on Thursday morning headed to San Gabriel to see Ana Teresa. According to a message sent from *don* Lorenzo yesterday, Ana Teresa was doing better and the doctor was pleased. The message said she was asking for Rafe. Much to everyone's surprise and grief, Rafe had not returned home. *Don* Lorenzo alerted the San Gabriel sheriff about the importance of finding him. George had made a similar request to the Santa Fe sheriff's office.

Carlos drove the carriage with George beside him. His large black horse, Santiago, was tied to the back of the carriage. "Carlos, we must find Rafe," George repeated what they had discussed many times over the past few days.

There was no doubt in Carlos' mind – Rafe would avenge the attack by the squatters. When they travelled to Mexico last year, Rafe freed a group of condemned *peóns* in Jiménez. Carlos was angry Rafe put them in danger from the *Federales,* however Rafe explained how his experiences led him to believe an inexplicable force controlled his need to defend the weak.

Carlos remembered Rafe's explanation of his actions. "I cannot help it Carlos. Something takes over in me, something I cannot control. The Aztec healer, Xihuitl, who saved my life believed the star amulet which stopped the bullet and left a star shaped scar on my chest was a sign from the Goddess Coatlicue, the Goddess of life and death as taught by the ancient Aztec legends. He told me the Goddess would guide me and protect me," Rafe had told him.

Rafe's reckless actions in Mexico were at a time when he had everything to live for, but he still took action. Now, Carlos worried Rafe's temperament would lead him to his destruction. Vengeance might land Rafe in jail or dead from a bullet, because he believed Ana Teresa was dead.

"I will leave you in San Gabriel with the women and start looking for him. I know his ways better than anyone.

My saddlebags on Santiago are packed and ready to go," Carlos told George.

When they arrived in San Gabriel, Ana Teresa was asleep. Carlos only stayed at the doctor's office a few moments.

"When she awakes, tell her I have gone to find Rafael," he explained to the others.

George walked him to the door. "Be careful, but find him. I will see that Bibiana gets home safely."

Riding north, he pondered his assignment. Rafe could be anywhere, although Carlos was sure he would be seeking revenge on the squatters. No other conclusion seemed plausible. Reaching the Salazar hacienda, Carlos rode into the courtyard. He was escorted into the foyer and waited for *don* Lorenzo to be called.

"*Bienvenido,*" *don* Lorenzo greeted him. He and Carlos shook hands.

"George, Josefina, and Bibiana are at the doctor's office. Have you any word on Rafael?"

"Unfortunately, no. Come sit with me and have a coffee. I do have some news."

After they were seated in the large dining room, *don* Lorenzo explained the new developments. "Yesterday, several of my *vaqueros* found two young men tied to a tree not far from here. They were gagged and had red hoods covering their heads."

"Squatters?" Carlos asked.

"Yes, sons of squatters. They begged and pleaded for their lives. They said a U.S. Marshal came to the camp on Tuesday and found them. They admitted being a part of the red-hooded raiders, but said they had not killed anyone. They said it was a gunslinger named Kip Donohoe and his gang who did the killing."

"What did you do with them?"

"My *vaqueros* gladly would have made them disappear, but I took them to the sheriff in San Gabriel. It is up to the law to discover the truth and to find this Kip Donohoe. Perhaps then the sheriff will force the squatters to leave my land."

The maid poured more coffee and Carlos took a few sips pondering *don* Lorenzo's story.

"I have to find Rafael. He has to know Ana Teresa is alive."

"No one has seen him, but I told my *vaqueros* to look for him."

"Where have the squatter's built their camp?"

"About seven miles north along the Rio Chama, north of Arroyo de Presa where the rapids fall along the river. There may be other groups along the Rio Grande. I've instructed my *vaqueros* to stay away for now. We do not need more trouble."

"Do you have any idea how many are living there?"

"Maybe thirty or forty. I am not sure. If you are planning on going there, you need to be very careful," the *don* advised. He noticed Carlos was wearing a gun belt.

"The squatters are very distrustful of Spaniards. They may shoot you on sight. I can send several of my men with you for protection."

"No, I think it is better if I go alone."

"Go with God then, but be careful," *don* Lorenzo warned.

As Carlos rode north from the Salazar hacienda, he rode carefully keeping in the trees, which lined the Chama River. He looked for signs of a campfire or any other sign Rafe had come this way. In about two hours, he heard shouting and stopped. Stepping Santiago cautiously, he finally reached a spot where he could see the squatter's camp.

A group of men were busy building. Two sides of a wooden house leaned on logs waiting for the other sides to be completed. Children played nearby. A woman was stirring a pot over an open fire. The scene was peaceful. It was hard to imagine these people were the masked gunmen of last Saturday.

Further up the river, Carlos spotted several other houses and wagons. On the far side of the river, fields were cleared for planting. One was gleaming bright green as the newly planted crop caught the sun. A few milk cows were in a pen. These people were farmers.

As Carlos remembered, six men had attacked the hacienda. Sitting on his horse, he pondered whether these squatters were the ones. Had Rafe come here? Obviously, the simple idea was to just ride in and ask. However, if Rafe had come here it would have been with his guns blazing in anger and revenge. Carlos also remembered *don* Lorenzo's warning.

The children's laughter filled the air. He heard a shout as the men raised the third wall of the house. Carlos turned the horse and rode away from the river scene.

It was mid afternoon by the time Carlos rode into San Gabriel. Along the way, he turned the *don's* story over and over in his mind. When he reached the sheriff's office, Carlos tied Santiago to the rail and stepped inside.

"Good afternoon. I understand you have two prisoners here, two young men connected with the killings last Saturday at the Salazar fiesta," Carlos said to the deputy.

"Sure do. Who are you?"

"I'm Carlos Zuniga from Santa Fe. I was at the fiesta. *Don* Lorenzo is my wife's uncle."

The deputy eyed Carlos' gun. This man was a Mexican and only trouble existed between the Mexicans and the squatters. Sheriff Harkins warned him to keep the two young men in the back cell for their safety. It was important they had a fair trial and were not lynched by a mob of angry Mexicans.

"I would like to talk to them," Carlos requested.

"Sheriff said no visitors, except their parents."

"I understand a U.S. Marshal captured them. Can I talk to the marshal?"

"That's what they say, but it is curious. There's no U.S. Marshal within a hundred miles of here. The sheriff sent a rider to the Marshal's office in Santa Fe. They said no one had been sent. Those boys probably made up that story, but then it beats me who tied them up and left them to be found with the hoods over their heads."

"Did the marshal have a name?" Carlos asked.

"That's pretty curious too," the deputy replied. "Those boys said he had tan skin and some Mexican name, like

Gonzalo or Gomez or something starting with a G. I ain't never heard of no Mexican marshal around here. Oh, and he wore a black Stetson hat."

Carlos knew the Mexican marshal was Rafe. There was no doubt in his mind. It surprised him Rafe obviously located the boys, but did not kill them, rather leaving them to face the law. It pleased Carlos' sense of decency and religious beliefs. Hopefully, Rafe would return to Santa Fe now. Carlos reiterated the importance of finding Rafael Reyes to the deputy and why. He told the deputy Rafe was riding a brown gelding.

"We'll keep an eye out for him. *Don* Lorenzo has been here before. I hear that man's wife is doing a bit better," the deputy said.

CHAPTER 12

After checking in, Rafe walked to the Miner's Restaurant for a meal. On the way, he pictured the wild mining town of several years ago. The saloons never closed accommodating miners working all shifts. Music could be heard all night long, with an occasional shooting. At that time, Elizabethtown boasted more than 6,000 residents, seven saloons, three dance halls, five stores, a bank, a school, and two churches.

What he saw now was almost a ghost town. His first thought was it should make finding the man named Kip Donohoe easier.

During the trip here, he tried to formulate a plan on how to find and kill the culprits. He did not think the ruse of the U.S. Marshal badge would work here. These were seasoned outlaws and not gullible squatters. Nothing feasible came to him except hoping he could make contact with Bill Moore.

In the morning, Rafe went to the hotel's livery and saddled the gelding. Without breakfast, he rode up the mountain to the Mystic Lode mine. Three years ago, the trail to the Mystic was treacherous with snow and ice.

Today only mounds of snow clung to the shadowed areas. He passed no one on the trail leading to the mine. As Rafe remembered, Bill Moore was a cautious man, and he wondered why no guards were posted. As he neared the mine shack, Rafe saw smoke rising from the smokestack. He dismounted and knocked on the door.

"Is Bill Moore here?" Rafe asked when a man opened the door. He did not recognize the man as one of the miners working for Bill when he was here last.

"Bill, man here ta see yew!" Rick called into the shack. Rafe stayed outside until Bill came to the door.

Bill Moore saw Rafe's face and was more than surprised. Rafe was his good friend George Summers' adopted son. It was Rafe and his friend Carlos who saved

Bill's mine from determined claim jumpers several years ago.

"Rafe, what the hell you doing up here in this God forsaken place?" Bill asked and took Rafe's hand and shook it, then practically pulled him inside.

"Come on in. We're just starting breakfast."

Lefty and Mike greeted him. Lefty was one of the men Rafe met on his last trip, Mike was another. Bill introduced the third man who had opened the door as Rick Stevens.

Bill handed Rafe a tin cup and filled it from a large coffee pot, coffee flakes floated to the top. Mike shoveled a heaping portion of scrambled eggs, bacon, and biscuits onto five tin plates. Rafe dug in along with the others.

The breakfast filled the hollow part of Rafe's stomach.

"Thank you for breakfast Bill. I left the hotel early hoping I would find you before you went down into the mine," Rafe said.

"What are you doing up here? This is the last place I thought I would ever see you. I was planning on stopping to see George as soon as I close down the Mystic Lode, probably sometime this summer. I've gotten all I can out of her, but now she's just plumb petering out."

"I wasn't planning on coming here, but I'm looking for a man named Kip Donohoe and a couple of his friends. I was told he lives here or came here," Rafe told him and looked for a reaction.

"What the hell you want with the likes of him?" Lefty spoke out first.

"Lefty's right. That man is a mean no account killer," Mike added. "Kip runs with the Allison gang, but I ain't seen or heard about him lately."

"He's been in San Gabriel. He killed my pregnant wife."

The quiet in the room was deafening for several moments as the news sunk in. Bill was the first to respond.

"You're up here looking for him," Bill said. There was no need to exclaim sorrow or outrage. It was something understood between men.

"Yes. I plan to kill him. He had two friends with him."

"That's probably Nat and Jesse. They used to be a gang

out of Cimarron who hung around with Clay Allison over there. They always up to no good. We ain't heard nuthin about them for a while either," Lefty told him.

"Yeah, they be nothing but nocounts," Mike concurred.

Mickey Sullivan knocked on the private poker room at the Golden Shaft Saloon in Elizabethtown. He knew a private poker game was in progress and after knocking twice, he entered.

"Whaddaya want?" Patrick Fitzgerald growled at Mickey.

"Sum new jasper rode into town today, Fitz. He checked into the Mutz and then rode out to the Mystic Lode." Mickey and everyone else in town called Patrick, Fitz.

Fitz was now in charge of E-town since Clay had gone to Cimarron. One of Clay's henchmen, Fitz always wanted to be kept abreast of any news on the mountain. This was his town now and nothing happened here he did not know about.

"Miner?"

"Didn't dress like one, but the clerk over ta the Mutz said he was Mescan."

"Damn greasers are everywhere," Jesse Kincaid grumbled. Cain't git away from their stink."

What was left of Clay Allison's gang had holed up in E-town for the winter. The once boomtown had dwindled to only a handful of mines still producing. Allison and his partners had claim jumped many mines several years ago and played them out. They were not here for the gold anymore, but rather as a safe place without any law. The last sheriff, Danny Robertson, was killed over a year ago.

Four days ago, Kip Donohoe, Nat Holmes, and Jesse Kincaid showed back up looking for Clay. Fitz was suspicious at first, but Kip said they just needed a place away from the law for a while.

After only two days, Kip said he and Nat were riding on to Cimarron to find Clay. "Ain't nuttin goin on round here ta keep a man interested," Kip had complained.

Fitz twirled the tip of his handlebar mustache thinking about Mickey's news. "Keep a tail on im and see what he's up to."

"Yew want us to kill im boss?"

"Naw, just keep an eye on im."

Rafe stayed at the mine most of the day. Bill and the others enjoyed having someone new to talk to after many long winter months at the isolated mine.

Rafe told them of the Governor's decree over the Spanish land grants and how the squatters were moving onto land with fraudulent deeds. He explained it had been happening for many years, but now had escalated into bloodshed.

When Rafe told them of the fiesta and how the red-hooded raiders rode into the courtyard and just started firing, the men cursed.

"Reminds me of the fuckin claim jumpers here," Rick cursed.

"If it weren't for the double-action rifles and pistols George brought here several years ago, we'd all be dead," Bill added.

"Yeah, we've had ta hold em jumpers off more times than I can count," Lefty said.

"We'll hep yew get those jaspers," both Lefty and Mike offered. "They have it comin."

"Thanks, but you don't need to get into trouble. This is my reckoning," Rafe said.

As the long shadows started to cut across the mine, Bill asked Rafe to stay the night. "Be mighty glad for your company," Bill said.

"No I'll go back to town. I'll be here for a few days until I find Kip and the others. I'll come see you again before I leave," Rafe told them.

"He shouldn't be hard to find. Everyone knows the gang hangs out at the Golden Shaft Saloon," Rick told him.

Chapter 13

Josefina, Bibiana, and *doña* Marcella surrounded Ana Teresa as she lay in Doctor Roybal's office. They talked to her and held her hand, although Ana Teresa barely responded.

"She woke several times yesterday and I think she recognized me. She kept mumbling about Rafael," Marcella told the other two women.

"She looks so pale," Josefina said with a grimace.

"Yes, but Doctor Roybal says her heart beat is strong and she is stable."

Marcella showed them how to squeeze water drops between her lips. While the women were managing the patient, the doctor signaled to George. They walked outside and down the stairs to street level. George noticed the doctor looked tired.

"Can I buy you a drink?" he asked.

"I could sure use one," the doctor replied.

Sitting in the restaurant nearby, the doctor sipped at a small glass of whiskey.

"I've never had a case like this. The bullet is lodged somewhere in her hip near her spine," he said. "I'm a local doctor. I deliver babies, treat hives and poison ivy, and set broken bones. I'm not a specialist."

"Are you saying Ana Teresa needs a better doctor?" George asked.

"Yes, she needs someone trained in such delicate matters, not only for her sake but for the baby. I've done everything I can. The closest specialist would probably be in Denver." Doctor Roybal sighed and then continued, "The problem is, if you try to move her, I'm afraid it will kill her. I'm also afraid if she goes into labor with the bullet still in her, both she and the baby could die."

"What about the new hospital in Santa Fe?" George asked. He knew of the Saint Vincent Hospital which had been opened by the Sisters of Charity a few years ago.

"Saint Vincent is mostly an orphanage, although the Sisters do provide a limited amount of medical care," the doctor explained.

It was a dilemma the doctor had been pondering for days. He did not have the expertise the young woman and baby needed.

George only nodded an acknowledgment at the news, not knowing what to say.

"I've tried to stabilize her and keep her from moving, but this cannot go on too much longer. She needs to eat and drink to survive. She needs to move and then there is the baby to consider. It would be a shame to lose them now after all of this."

It was unthinkable to George that he could watch Ana Teresa and the baby die without trying every possible solution.

"You say there may be specialists in Denver?"

"Yes I think so. Denver has a large hospital and I have heard about it."

"Well if we can't take her there, then we have to get one of those doctors here," George said.

Doctor Roybal nodded his head up and down at the idea. "It would cost a lot of money and he will need convincing," he said.

"I'll pay whatever the cost. Can you send a telegram today? If I have to, I'll ride to Denver myself and get him here," George asserted.

Sometime later Bibiana was sitting beside the bed holding Ana Teresa's hand while talking with Josefina and Marcella about the upcoming Easter carnival at the church. Suddenly, Ana Teresa gently squeezed her fingers.

Bibiana cried out to the others and squeezed back. "Ana Teresa, wake up. It's Bibiana," she repeated several times.

Slowly Ana Teresa's eyelids moved as if trying to open. Bibiana kept encouraging her.

Vague forms seem to float in her vision. They looked much like the figures she had been seeing floating around her, except these forms were standing on the ground beside her. Ana Teresa's mind was confused. The floating forms she saw swirled and seemed to encourage her to drift with them. They were sheer white, almost translucent, and yet they appeared to be otherwise human. Once she thought she saw a man who looked like her father.

Several times, she also clearly saw her mother and a short man she did not recognize. Her mother was typically dressed in a blue gown and the man wore a suit.

"Ana Teresa, it's me Bibiana," she heard her cousin say. "Open your eyes and look at me."

Ana Teresa struggled to move her eyelids. They were heavy and it took more effort than she could at first muster. The voices kept encouraging her.

As her eyelids slowly lifted, the first face she focused on was her mother. She was smiling and her eyes were moist.

"Mija, mija," she kept saying.

Ana Teresa moved to another face, the face of her cousin Bibiana. She reached out her hand and touched her forehead. The room was unfamiliar. Confusion bombarded her. Where was she? She could not remember anything, except her house in Santa Fe. The house Rafael built for them.

Doña Marcella dripped water between her daughter's dry lips. More of the room came into focus. Josefina was standing behind Bibiana. The water tasted good. Her throat felt parched. She tried to let the water soothe it.

"Rafael," she whispered. It was barely audible, but Bibiana understood.

"He's coming. Don't worry, he will come," Bibiana replied.

Chapter 14

Rafe rode down the steep narrow trail from the Mystic Lode mine to E-town as darkness fell. The wind picked up and the chill drove through his jacket. The gelding was not as surefooted as Rayo, his Appaloosa, and Rafe kept the horse reined tightly as he made his way toward town. As he rode into town, he noticed the Miner's Restaurant was open and doing a brisk business. He rode to the hotel's stable, left the horse in a stall, and walked to the restaurant.

Pushing in the door, Rafe was pleased the Miner's Restaurant had not changed. The large open area was lined with long tables and benches. Avid chatter and laughter filled the air. Many of the tables were full. Rafe sat down at a table where a few men sat on the other end. They took a quick glance at him and then turned back to their food and conversation. He hoped they had better food than the bear stew they served during that bad spring storm several years ago. Rafe and Carlos had forced themselves to eat it, but only the biscuits were edible.

He sat and a tall blond waitress walked up.

"You're a stranger. We don't get many these days," she greeted him.

"What do you have?"

"Beef stew or fresh trout with rice."

Rafe ordered the trout and drank coffee while he waited. His eyes scanned the room wondering if any of these men were Kip Donohoe. He felt foolish not getting a description out of the two young squatters and now he had no idea what Kip and his friends looked like. Lefty and Rick promised to help him find out about Kip and his two friends, but Rafe did not want to get them embroiled in his vengeance. The men were killers, part of Clay Allison's gang, and no doubt had lots of friends here in E-town, however he now realized he might need help.

As Rafe ate the trout and rice dinner, he let his eyes wander the room. The Miner's Restaurant seemed the only place in town to get meal. Most of the crowd looked to be miners – dusty, dirty, and mostly shabby. Three families with children sat at a table on the other side of the room. Two well-dressed men sat at a table by themselves and another was filled with at least ten armed men. He sat by himself and noticed some of the people curiously looked him over.

The table of ten men talked and laughed. They were not miners and Rafe could easily see their gunbelts. Bill told him a number of Clay Allison's gang were still in town, even though they did not actively claim jump anymore.

Rafe remembered the claim jumpers of several years ago who tried to jump Bill's mine, the Mystic Lode. He and Carlos arrived at the mine just in time to thwart the ambush. Carlos picked off one of the ambushers and they scattered. The following day, they took the body to town when they transported George to the doctor. They explained to the sheriff how the dead man was part of the group of claim jumpers who shot up the mine and shot George Summers.

Later that night, four of Clay Allison's henchmen cornered Bill, Carlos, and himself just outside this restaurant. They wanted to hang Rafe and Carlos for killing their friend. That night ended in bloodshed, but it was one of the claim jumpers who was killed. Bill shot a man named Charlie Peters before the sheriff arrived on the scene.

Rafe took another look at the table of armed men wondered which one might be Kip. He tried to piece together the information he knew. Lefty thought Kip's partners in the raid might have been two men named Nat and Jesse. He said they used to run with Allison's gang. The young squatter said they were headed to E-town. Of course, they could have gone anywhere.

Across the room from Rafe, Clement Bowers sat at a long table having supper with some of his friends. They were part of Clay Allison's remaining gang. Clement studied a stranger sitting across the room. The man was Mexican and wore a black Stetson hat. Something about him looked familiar to Clement.

"Hey Tom, look at that greaser over there. Ain't he that greaser who was with Bill Moore a cuppla years ago?"

Clement leaned over asking his friend Tom. "Yew member, the night Bill Moore plugged Charlie Peters."

"I dun know. Damn greasers all look alike to me," Tom replied.

"Hey Mickey. Yew ever seen that greaser afore?"

"He came in yesterday and rode up to the Mystic Lode mine today. Fitz tole me to keep an eye on him," Mickey replied.

"Iffin he went to the Mystic, its gotta be im. I'll be damned. He and another greaser kilt Jack when we tried to take the Mystic Lode a few years ago. Looks like he's alone. Wonder what the fucker is up too," Clement grumbled.

"He's staying over ta the Mutz. Fitz juss wants im follered," Mickey told the group.

"Fitz is stupid. That Mex deserves to swing fer what he dun. Yew let me know whar he goes," Clement grumbled to Mickey.

"Why dun yew juss take im now?" Earl asked Clement joining the conversation.

"See his guns? He may be a Mex, but if he's the one I think, he's fast. We gotta git im alone without em pistols on," Clement replied.

Rafe enjoyed the fresh trout. He took his time picking the tender meat and making sure not to swallow any fish bones. After finishing another cup of coffee and paying his bill, he decided to walk around town. It was dark, but still early. Music came out of the saloon as he passed by. Curious, he turned back and pushed at the batwing doors.

"What you want. Got beer or red-eye," the bartender asked as Rafe walked up to the bar.

"Beer." Rafe fished a nickel from his pants pocket and put it on the bar top.

"That'll be two bits," the bartender grunted at the nickel.

Surprised, Rafe found a quarter and exchanged it for the nickel. Turning his back to the bar with the beer in hand, he scanned the quiet saloon. Mostly dust covered miners sat around drinking. Saloon girls flirted with them to buy drinks. Rafe smiled to himself seeing the tired older men tolerating the girls, but buying drinks for them. Some of the younger miners danced or were led upstairs by the painted ladies.

CHAPTER 15

As Rafe left the restaurant, Mickey Sullivan quietly rose and followed him. He kept hidden while he watched the greaser, as he had been doing all day per Fitz's instructions. The greaser walked down the street toward the hotel, then turned back and went into the Rich Strike Saloon. Mickey went back to the restaurant.

"He went into the Strike," Mickey reported to the others.

"Come on," Clement grumbled. "Iffin he's the one who kilt Jack, he needs to pay."

Earl and Tom followed Clement and Mickey out of the Miner's Restaurant to the Rich Strike Saloon. They walked in, spotted Rafe at the bar, then casually walked to the far side of the saloon and sat at a table.

"Hey boys, what you doing here? Why ain't you over at the Golden Shaft?" a young saloon girl named Patsy asked when she came to the table to take their order. She knew all of Clay's gang. She knew they were killers. Everyone in E-town knew Clay and his gang were the claim jumpers who killed many successful miners, but no one cared. Now the mines were drying up and the town was drying up too. Even Clay had left town. It was so bad, even the whores were going broke.

"Bring us a bottle of red-eye Patsy," Clement said and swatted her rear.

Rafe stood along the bar watching the out of tune singer entertain the motley crowd. He knew the bartender would know of Kip and his friends and wanted to ask some prying questions. He also knew it would be a fast way to trouble. Bartenders were paid to keep their ears open and to report. A stranger asking questions would surely be reported immediately back to the boss man and Rafe hoped to find Kip without alerting attention.

"You want a refill?" the bartender asked Rafe. He nodded and put another quarter on the bar top.

Clement eyed Rafe. He was holding a beer and watching the singer. Clement studied his prey. It was not so much Rafe's face Clement recognized, but his pistols. The young Mexican wore a two guns. Clement remembered him as a fast draw and deadly accurate. Earl passed the bottle and they each drank a couple of shots of red-eye as they kept an eye on Rafe.

"Hey boys, what yew doin here? Yew usually over at the Golden Shaft," a man asked the group as he walked up to the table.

"Hey Roy. See that greaser over thar. He ain't no miner. Clement thinks he be the one who kilt Jack Braddely up at the Mystic Lode a coupla years ago. We keepin an eye on im," Earl told him as Roy sat down.

"That rat, whaddaya gonna do?" Roy asked pouring himself a shot.

"We gonna foller im an see whar he goes. Iffin he goes up ta the Mystic tomorrow, we gonna bushwhack im," Clement said.

"Why wait. He's an easy target here in town. Jack was a good friend. Besides he's a greaser," Roy suggested.

"He may be a greaser, but he's fast with em pistols," Clement responded.

"Yew scart of some no count greaser, Clement?" Roy pushed him.

"Yeah, Roy's rat. Let's take im tonight. Ain't no sheriff here anymore. What's another dead greaser?" Earl agreed.

While Rafe drank the second beer, Clement and the outlaws discussed a plan. When Rafe finished the beer, he turned from the bar and headed for the door. Drinking beer was not helping him find Kip and his two friends. Walking to the hotel, he climbed the stairs to the second floor hoping to get a good night's rest.

Only Earl followed Rafe from the Rich Strike Saloon. Keeping a bit behind, Earl followed Rafe to the hotel and up to the second floor. Walking by, Earl pretended to open the door to a room on the opposite side of the hallway. Once Rafe closed the door to room 201, Earl quietly snuck back down the stairs.

Clement and his friends waited across the road for Earl. It was a cool but not cold night and they waited near the entrance to the Golden Shaft Saloon. Earl ran from the hotel to where they waited.

"Whaddaya find out?" Clement asked.

"The greaser is up on the second floor. See the light up thar. That be im." Earl reported.

"Awrat, we wait til the light goes out an give im time to fall asleep. Then we go in an kill the fucker," Clement told them.

"I cain't wait ta git my hands on im. Jack was a good friend. Time ta even the score," Tom added rubbing his hands together.

"I'm a goin in with yew fellers. Jack was a good ole boy an my friend. I didn't know he was with yew fellers when he got hisseff kilt," Roy said.

"Yeah, we was up thar trying to run Bill Moore and his boys outta the mine when that thar greaser and another one came up behind us. They shot at us and Jack got it. Member, after we make im pay good, he's mine," Clement huffed. He wanted to be the one who would claim he strung up the greaser who killed Jack Braddely.

In the upstairs hotel room, Rafe sat down at the desk and started a letter to George Summers. He got as far as, Dear George. He sat there pondering what to say. What could he say? He wanted to explain he was hunting the killers who killed Ana Teresa and his unborn child. He wanted to explain the emptiness inside him. He could not find words to express the vengeance boiling in him when he thought about her and his unborn baby.

A week ago, Ana Teresa was alive and happy to be going to the wedding fiesta in San Gabriel. Rafe berated himself for not insisting she stay in Santa Fe. He had not wanted her to make the trip, worried about the baby. She laughed and told him he worried too much.

The dressmaker had made her a new gown to fit her swelling belly. They danced the Fandango and she flashed her golden brown eyes at him, the same way she did the day they met. Now she was dead.

Rafe cursed God for his cruelness many times. Why her? Rafe would gladly give his life in exchange, yet knew she would feel the same as he. Lost. Empty.

Finally, he crumpled the paper and threw it away. Perhaps after he found and killed Kip Donohoe and his friends, he could go back to Santa Fe. About an hour later, he turned out the gas light and stretched out on the bed. Exhausted both in body and spirit, sleep took over.

It was near midnight with only the Milky Way to light up the sky and very little light reached into the Elizabethtown valley. Clement and his friends waited in the damp chill of the night until the light in Rafe's room went out. The only light shining from the hotel was from the lobby.

Stubbing out a cigarette, Clement grumbled, "Let's go." Mickey Sullivan stayed near the door of the Golden Shaft. Clement told him to keep a watch on the street.

They headed across the street and into the Mutz Hotel sneaking past the sleeping desk clerk. Earl led the way to Rafe's room. All was quiet. If anyone was in the other rooms, they must be asleep. Earl tried the door, just in case it was unlocked. On the whisper count of three, Earl kicked in the door and the three thugs rushed in.

A loud sound jarred Rafe and he groggily started to sit up in bed. Several sets of hands grabbed him and held him down as Earl and Roy pushed him back.

"This is fer Jack, yew fuckin greaser," Clement snarled and punched Rafe hard in the stomach twice. Rafe groaned and choked as he tried hard to breathe in badly needed air. In the darkness, he felt the presence of the men, as he could not see anything. The man who hit him reeked of whiskey.

Jack? Jack who? His mind reeled trying to make sense of the attack. Was it Kip and his two friends?

Another set of blows buckled him and he heard a snap. A searing pain tore inside him, still he struggled to get away. Large hands held him down. If only he could reach his pistols. They hung in the gunbelt at the foot of the bed.

"Let me have im," Earl growled.

A fist connected to Rafe's jaw. His teeth cut into his

lips and blood tasted on his tongue. The blows pummeled his face. Helpless he thought about Ana Teresa. He thought how it was fitting he should die and be with her again.

The pummeling continued. Rafe felt like his brains were scrambling in his head. Random thoughts jumped in and out. Suddenly he felt something sharp near his neck. He felt is slice under his ear.

"I'm a gonna gut yew, yew fuckin greaser fer what yew did to Jack," Earl growled.

"Fuck you Earl. Put that knife away. I tole yew he's mine and he's gonna swing," another voice snarled. Rafe could identify three voices, though he could not see the men's faces.

He felt the closest man back off a bit. Rafe struggled to understand. Who was Earl and what had happened to Jack? He wanted to protest and tell these men they had the wrong man. Blood filled his mouth and his tongue did not work.

A set of large hands grabbed him and started to pull him off the bed. Clement Bowers hissed close to Rafe's pulpy face as he pulled him. "Yew kilt my friend Jack Braddely and yew finally gonna swing fer it."

Chapter 16

"What the hell is going on here?" a stern voice came from the doorway. "We're trying to sleep. Go take your fight somewhere else!"

The noise had wakened Trent Bascom and his wife who were sleeping across the hallway. A big man, Trent filled the doorway and the light from his room backlit him into a huge shadow. At first, Trent saw a man with a knife standing over someone helpless in the bed. "Hey, put that knife away!" he yelled.

"Go away mister, this ain't yer problum," Clement yelled at the man and shoved Rafe down. Half on and off the bed, Rafe groaned in agony from his injuries.

"Hell it ain't," the man yelled back and aimed a pistol at Earl. "Get away from that man," he ordered.

Downstairs, the ruckus of the fight in Rafe's room stirred the sleepy clerk and then he heard a loud voice say, "What the hell is going on here?" Quickly he grabbed a shotgun and headed upstairs. He arrived in the hallway to see Mister Bascom pointing a pistol into Room 201. He heard voices inside the room grumbling.

"This is a hotel, not a saloon," the clerk yelled. "What's going on up here?"

"We ain't dun with yew, greaser. We'll get yew later," Clement warned Rafe as they heard more voices outside of the room. "Come on," he growled to Earl and Roy. Pushing the large man aside and passing the clerk, they fled the room.

"You alright mister?" the man asked.

All Rafe could do was groan.

"Go get the doctor," Trent ordered the desk clerk.

"But . . . but it's after midnight," the clerk protested.

"I said, go get Doctor Lowe. Get him over here now," Trent hollered.

Trent walked to Rafe's body and gently lifted him back to the bed. He lit the gas lamp and was appalled at the young man's face. A large gash over his eye bled profusely on his lean, tan face. His lip was swelling quickly and blood covered his lips and chin. A cut under his ear also bled. Welts and bruises blended with the marks of fists turning his face into a pulpy-looking mess.

"You all right?"

"I can't breathe and my side hurts," Rafe struggled to tell the man.

"The clerk is on his way to get a doctor." Rafe nodded a response.

"Why did those men attack you?" the man asked.

"I don't know. They accused me of killing one of their friends, a man named Jack."

As Trent spoke to the young man, his eyes wandered the room. The man was tan-skinned, a Mexican, although appeared to be a traveler or businessman, like himself. A gunbelt with two holsters each holding an expensive looking pistol hung at the end of the bedpost.

"My name's Trent Bascom," he told Rafe and helped him with a glass of water. Rafe struggled to drink, but some mixed with blood and washed down his throat.

"I'm Rafe Reyes. I owe you my life," Rafe said.

"Trent, is everything all right now?" a woman's voice called from the room across the hall.

"Yes Miriam. It's over. Go back to bed. I'm going to stay with this man until the doctor gets here."

"You'd be dead if those men had not been so loud. Must have been when they knocked in the door. Woke me right up." Bascom took a washcloth, wet it, and began patting blood from Rafe's face. "What are you doing here in E-town?" he asked Rafe.

"I was on my way home and stopped to see a friend, Bill Moore. He runs the Mystic Lode mine up the hill." Rafe half lied as he did not want to admit he came here to E-town to kill people.

"You a friend of Bill? He buys equipment from my company. Know him well. I'm here to buy back some of his equipment and sell it to new strikes down west of Socorro. Now that the mines are closing here, I will buy as much as I can."

"Who's hurt?" a voice questioned as Doctor Carson Lowe hustled into the room.

"This man here," Bascom said and stepped aside from the bed. "Oh hello Mister Bascom. Do you know this man?"

"No Doctor Lowe. It was the ruckus over here that woke me and Miriam. They were beating the tar out of him."

"My, my, they did a good job on you young man," Doctor Lowe said not recognizing Rafe from his previous visit to E-town.

"Hello Doctor Lowe. I'm Rafe Reyes. You patched a bullet wound in George Summers' leg a couple years ago. Bill Moore and I brought him to you."

Doctor Lowe looked at Rafe's mottled face. "Oh yes, Rafe, I remember you. Clay Allison's vigilantes pinned Bill and his men down at the mine and a bullet nicked a vein in George's leg. How is he?"

"He's fine, but has a slight limp."

As they talked, the doctor swabbed a stinging fluid on the cuts and wounds on Rafe's face.

"Mister Bascom, can you go ask the clerk to bring some hot water."

"Who did this to you?" he asked turning back to Rafe's purpled bloodied face.

"I don't know, but if Mister Bascom had not intervened they were going to string me up for killing someone named Jack."

"Ah, Jack Braddely I suspect. You remember the trouble up at the Mystic Lode mine. Bill said it was Clay Allison's vigilantes trying to kill him and take his claim. You and Bill brought a dead man back to town. It was Jack Braddely, one of Clay's men."

Suddenly Rafe remembered the name. Actually Carlos killed the claim jumper up on the mountain, although the gang would not know it. All they wanted was revenge for their friend.

"Your face took a bad beating. Just bruises and contusions. You won't look too good for a week or two and might have a few scars. Where else does it hurt?"

"My ribs on my left. It hurts when I breathe," Rafe

told him.

"Here?" the doctor pushed on his side.

"No."

"Here?"

"Yyyeeessss!" Rafe groaned.

The doctor pulled up Rafe's shirt and examined his ribs. Each movement made Rafe flinch and groan. Finally he said. "I can't feel any broken ribs, but that doesn't mean they aren't cracked."

Trent and the clerk walked into the room carrying a pan of hot water and towels.

"Thanks. Set them down here where I can reach them." The clerk set the pan down and left the room, while Trent stayed. He was curious about Bill Moore's friend and it was doubtful he could get back to sleep for a while anyway.

The doctor took one of the towels and soaked it in the hot water. Wringing it out somewhat, he put it on Rafe's ribs. He repeated the heat treatments several times, then took out a roll of bandages and tightly wrapped Rafe's ribcage. As he rolled Rafe over on his side, both the doctor and Trent gasped at the scars on Rafe's back.

"Looks like you've been beat before?"

"Yes. It was in Mexico. I tried to help a dying man," Rafe responded.

"Seems like trouble follows you," Trent said.

"Keep this bandage tight. It will probably take at least a week for those ribs to heal. You won't be able to ride until they do."

"A week Doc! Those jaspers will be back, especially if they know he can't ride," Trent exclaimed. "He can't stay here in town."

"Well, Mister Bascom's right. You got enemies here. You best watch your back. If I were you, I would go and stay with Bill at the mine until you can ride. At least they can protect you."

"Thank you Doctor Lowe. I'll stop by tomorrow and square up with you."

"Don't worry. It's good to see you again. Tell George hello when you see him," Dr. Lowe told him and gathered his bag.

"Thank you again Mister Bascom. I owe you." Rafe put out his hand and Trent shook it.

"Think nothing of it. You can call me Trent. I'm glad you're not seriously hurt. Say, I need to go see Bill. I can give you a lift in my wagon tomorrow."

"Thank you again. You saved my life."

Trent tried his best to shut the broken door and went back to his room. Walking gingerly holding his ribs, Rafe leaned a chair against the doorknob and secured it as best as he could. He stretched out on the bed facing the door with a pistol in his right hand. He did not sleep for the rest of the night. Death almost took him here in E-town before and tonight's encounter shook him to his core.

CHAPTER 17

"Why do you have to go?" Josefina asked George as he packed a satchel early Saturday morning. "Can't you send a telegram or messenger?"

"Doctor Roybal already sent telegrams without any reply. I'm afraid a messenger will be ignored. I must go and convince one of the specialists to come. The doctor is afraid it is our only chance to save Ana Teresa and the baby."

"Well at least you are taking the Overland Stage and not riding alone." Josefina finally relented her worried reprimand of her husband. Of course she wanted him to go to find a doctor for Ana Teresa, but George was in his fifties and Josefina worried more about him now. The stress of the last week only doubled her anxiety.

"Please be careful," she insisted.

"Yes and I must get going. The stagecoach to Denver leaves at ten."

A week after the terrible event at the Salazar fiesta, the dead were buried and Ana Teresa was fully conscious. The ghostly floating figures no longer came in her dreams.

"Good morning. How are you feeling today?" the doctor greeted her when he walked into the room.

"Fine, but hungry."

"That's a good sign. I told your mother to rest today. She has been at your side for many days with little sleep. I've arranged to have a woman who helps me come by and give you a bath. She will be here shortly. Here, I've made some tea for you," the doctor said.

Ana Teresa was following the doctor's orders. She drank broth and tea. She was not in pain unless she or the baby moved.

Yesterday, George and the doctor sat with her and explained the situation. A bullet traveled through her right hip and was lodged somewhere near her spine. By a blessing of God, it missed all her vital organs and also missed the baby. However, she was still not out of danger and most of all going into labor could have serious consequences. Doctor Roybal told her she could not be moved. He needed to arrange for a specialist to come to San Gabriel. Telegrams had been sent to the Denver Hospital, but he had not heard back yet.

George explained to her what happened at the fiesta. Her memory was fuzzy. She remembered dancing with Rafael and then sitting in a chair to rest. Masked riders came into the courtyard shooting. She did not remember anything else.

When she asked about Rafael, George looked glum. "He thinks you are dead. He left with his guns to avenge you. We are looking for him everywhere and the law in Santa Fe and San Gabriel has been notified to find him," George had told her. All of it was unbelievable, yet Rafe's response did not surprise Ana Teresa.

"I'm here to bathe you," a woman came into the room and interrupted Ana Teresa's thoughts. Carefully the woman moved her, rolling her onto her left side a little to wash her back. When she moved, pain stabbed through her. She tried not to cry out. "Be strong," she admonished herself. "Be strong for the baby and Rafael."

Rafe opened his eyes after dozing on and off. The pistol was on his lap and he finally found a position where he could take shallow breaths without stabbing pains shooting into his chest. Light poured into the window as morning came to the Elizabethtown valley. Every part of his body, except his feet, hurt. Slowly he pushed off the pillows and swung his feet to the floor.

Rafe hoped his ribs were only cracked or bruised as Doctor Lowe implied. The doctor told him riding was out of the question for at least a week or more. Gingerly Rafe stepped to the broken door and removed the chair holding it. Then he limped over to the dresser and looked at himself in the mirror. A ghastly face stared back.

Both sides of his jaw were purple and swollen. One eye barely opened and raw red-purple surrounded it. The eye itself was bright red with a brown center looking back at him. A thin cut ran about three inches under one ear. He could not tell if his nose was broken. It was so swollen, as was his face, he looked like an All Hallows Eve monster.

He shuffled back to the bed and sat down. Every movement sent searing pain through his chest. Somehow, he managed to get his pants and boots on and was working on his shirt when he heard a knock at the door.

"You awake?" Trent Bascom called into the room.

"Yes. Come in."

"I brought you a cup of coffee and a biscuit from the restaurant. Figured it best you keep out of sight." Trent came into the room and gasped as he saw Rafe in the light. The obviously handsome face was grotesquely disfigured, with raw oozing scrapes and purple bruises. His nose was swollen and crooked.

"Whew, they sure did a job on you."

Rafe took the coffee and biscuit. Tipping the cup to his swollen lips some coffee dribbled down his chin.

"I'll have my wagon readied out front. When you're ready, just knock on my door, but I suggest we get you out of town sooner than later," Trent told him.

"Thank you for your kindness Mister Bascom." As Trent walked out of the room, Rafe was struck by the man's genuine concern.

Rafe took a small bite of the biscuit. Several of his teeth felt loose as he tried to chew. Luckily the flaky biscuit began to melt into a goo. By alternating sips of coffee and bites of the biscuit, Rafe finished both. Less than a half hour later, he stood at the door across the hallway and knocked.

Trent opened it and smiled. "You ready?"

"Yes, but I could not pick up my bag."

A woman came up behind Trent and peeked over her husband's shoulder. "Oh my!" she gasped at Rafe's face.

"I'll be back later tonight Miriam," Trent said and kissed her cheek.

"Trent, are you sure you shouldn't let the sheriff handle this?" Miriam asked.

"There's no sheriff here. Don't worry. We'll be fine

and I'll be back later this afternoon."

Trent Bascom led the way down the hotel stairs. The town was just starting to come alive. A few other wagons plied along the road as Trent started the horses. The brown gelding was tied to the rear. Even though the wagon seat had metal springs, every bump sent shocking pains along Rafe's left side.

Rafe started a conversation wanting to know more about the kind man driving him to safety. "You said you buy mining equipment Mister Bascom."

"Call me Trent. I heard you call yourself Rafe Reyes. That's a Spanish name?"

"Yes, my real name is Rafael Reyes de Estrada, but I go by Rafe."

"Well Rafe, my trade is in new and used mining equipment. When towns like Elizabethtown are booming, I cannot get enough new mining equipment to sell. Mining has cycles. Sometimes it booms and later it busts. I started buying used equipment from places where the mines busted and I resell it to the next big strike. It helps both sides. I sold most of the big equipment to Bill a number of years ago. Now I'll give him a fair price to buy it back."

"That sounds fair for everyone."

"What are you doing here in E-town? What was all the talk about Jack Braddely?" Trent asked.

"Bill Moore is a friend of my adopted father. He delivered a load of guns here about three years ago. Claim jumpers from Clay Allison's gang had Bill and his men, including my father, pinned down in the mine."

"I remember now. Bill told me the story of how two young Mexicans saved him and his boys from those varmints. They were calling themselves vigilantes, but were really part of Clay's outlaw gang of claim jumpers," Trent interrupted.

Rafe and Trent talked on the ride to the mine. Somehow it seemed to make the painful trip more tolerable. When they arrived at the Mystic Lode's shack, Lefty walked out to greet them.

"Morning Trent. We've been expecting you. Bill is in

the mine gathering some of the equipment. He'll be along soon."

Rafe lifted his head and the sun lit up his beaten face.

"Holy shit Rafe! What happened to you?" Lefty exclaimed when he saw Rafe's mottled face.

"Some of Clay's men thrashed me last night. They recognized me from the fight when Jack Braddely was killed. They took revenge and threatened to hang me. Mister Bascom saved my life."

"Fucking varmints. I'd give my eyeteeth just to give them a taste of their own medicine. Come on in. Let's have some coffee."

CHAPTER 18

It was not long before Bill and Mike came back from the mine to the shack. Bill saw Trent Bascom's wagon outside and walked in the door with a big hearty greeting.

"Trent, you old dog, good to see you." Bill grabbed him in a hearty handshake. Suddenly he noticed Rafe sitting at the kitchen table.

"What the fuck happened to you?"

"Three men broke into my hotel room last night wanting to kill me. Mister Bascom was across the hallway and saved my life."

"You know who they were?"

"One was named Clement, another was Earl, don't know who the third man was."

"Clay's scoundrels. Why would they be coming after you?" Bill asked.

"They wanted revenge for Jack Braddely. Carlos shot him when Clay's gang had you pinned down here at the mine."

"I think I heard them call the third man, Roy," Trent interjected.

"Roy Harvey. He's just like all the rest of that scum," Mike added.

"It's a good thing Trent brought you here. We can protect you until you heal up."

"Thanks Bill. The doctor said it might take a week before I can ride."

"Hey everybody, sit and eat this breakfast I been makin," Lefty called out and set plates around the table with bacon and egg sandwiches. He poured coffee around.

Rick was winding his way back from the Lucky Nugget Mine. The Lucky Nugget was their closest neighbor, run by Jerry Lange. The Lucky Nugget was not fairing much better than the Mystic Lode. Bill sent Rick to tell Jerry about Trent Bascom coming today to buy used equipment.

When Rick rode up to the Mystic Lode's cabin,

Bascom's wagon was parked in front. He jumped from his horse and walked into the cabin. Everyone was sitting the table. Before he said hello to Bascom, Rick saw Rafe's purpled and swollen face.

"What happened to you?" he asked.

"Clement, Earl, and Roy, worked him over good last night," Mike responded.

"Those boys are mean enough to eat off the same plate with a snake. Why in hell did they rough you up? Is it because you're Mexican?" Rick asked.

"No, last time Rafe was up here to find George Summers, he and his friend Carlos got here while Clay's henchmen had us pinned down. Jack Braddely was killed and Clement recognized Rafe. He wanted revenge," Bill answered for Rafe.

"Didn't know that Jack fellow. It must have happened before I came to E-town. I do know Earl. He's a mean sumbitch," Rick added.

"Did you see Jerry?" Bill changed the subject and asked.

"I told Jerry, Trent was coming. He says they are working a small vein and hoping to get some more yellow out. He told me to tell you, he'll see you the next time you come to town," Rick related the information to Trent.

"If you see him again, tell him I'll be back in a couple of months. How about you Bill? Are you ready to sell all the equipment?"

"Mike thinks we are more or less done here. We got maybe a couple of weeks to finish out the last vein," Bill said to Trent. "I'm ready to sell you most of the big stuff and we'll use picks for the rest." Bill needed no negotiations for the equipment. He knew Trent Bascom to be an honest businessman.

Mike gathered Rafe's belongings before Trent Bascom headed down off the mountain. Bill and Lefty rode with Trent to town.

"Rick, I want you to keep a watch on anybody coming up the trail. I don't want Clement and his boys sneaking up on us," Bill insisted before he left.

"Sure thing boss."

Rafe stretched out on the bed facing the door with his guns ready. He was tired from lack of sleep and most of all angry, angry he was laid up and not able to go after Ana Teresa's killers. He was sure Kip Donohoe and his friends were somewhere in E-town. Now, he had other enemies wanting to kill him and there was no way he could protect himself until his ribs healed. The predicament irritated him even more and it fed the rage in him.

On his last trip to E-town, Death stalked him. Charlie Peters and some of Clay Allison's men confronted them outside the Miner's Restaurant. The vigilantes swore to hang him and Carlos for murder. Rafe had all but forgotten the incident. Bill Moore shot Charlie Peters off his saddle and the sheriff stopped the others from their evil intent.

Thinking about the three who beat him, Rafe vowed to reward Death with three more wretched souls, along with the three killers he came after, Kip, Jesse, and Nat. He fell into a deep sleep thinking about revenge.

Bill and Lefty rode into town with Trent to the Mutz Hotel. Along the way, Bill had Trent recall what happened to Rafe. From Trent's memory and descriptions, Bill was sure it was Clement, Earl, and Roy, all part of Clay's old gang, now run by a man called Fitz.

"You go and see what you can find out about Kip and those two others. I'm going to look into what happened last night," Bill told Lefty when they arrived. They split up and Bill went into the Mutz Hotel with Trent.

Bill was taken back when he saw the damaged door to Rafe's room. It would not totally shut and the doorjam was broken. Inside the room was a mess, with blood on the sheets of the unmade bed. He walked across the hallway to Trent's room and knocked on the door.

"Hello Miriam," he greeted Trent's wife.

"Thank you for getting Trent back safe, Bill. I sure hope tonight is quieter," she grumbled.

"Don't worry, dear. Those men will not be back,"

Trent called from inside the room.

"Thanks again Trent, for everything. Rafe's a good young man and does not deserve what happened."

When Bill went downstairs, the desk clerk stopped him. "Bill, where is that young friend of yours. The room is a mess. He needs to pay for that."

"Send the bill to Fitz," Bill grumbled and walked out of the hotel leaving the desk clerk staring at his back.

Bill spent several hours standing at the bar in the Golden Shaft Saloon with a whiskey in hand. He listened to conversations, though no one talked about roughing up a Mexican. Finally Lefty walked up to him.

"Ain't no talk about those three Rafe's looking for."

Bill bought Lefty a drink and they stood at the bar. Lefty sipped at the amber liquid and scanned the room.

"Hey," he nudged Bill, "That's Clement over there playing poker. I'm sure of it."

Clement sat at a table with four other men. A small pile of coins and paper money was in the middle of the table.

"We better get back to the cabin before dark. Nothing we can do here."

"I think I'll stay the night. You know how the fun doesn't start here in town until the moon is up," Lefty told him.

Before sundown, Bill returned to the cabin. He brought several sacks of food supplies from town.

"Lefty is seeing what he can find out about Kip and will come up tomorrow," Bill told everyone.

"What about the ones from last night?" Rafe asked.

"We saw Clement playing poker at the Golden Shaft. Didn't see the others."

"They're probably still sleeping it off upstairs," Mike grumbled. "They do all their dirty work after midnight."

By the way, I stopped and talked to Doc Lowe. He told me to have you put ice on those ribs. He said it will help with the pain and swelling. There's plenty in the small creek just up from the shack."

"Thanks Bill. I owe you."

"You don't owe me nothing. You and Carlos saved our

asses that day you killed Jack. Now, I'll take care of you. It is the least I can do to make sure you get out of E-town alive."

Chapter 19

Patches of ice and snow clung near the shadowed areas on Baldy Mountain where the Mystic Lode mine was located. Using a Bowie knife, Rick chunked off pieces of ice and Rafe wrapped them against his chest. At first he could not stand the cold, but it did not take long for the ice to numb the area where it hurt the most.

Lefty returned to the mine at almost sundown on Monday evening. Rafe was lying on the cot applying the ice to his ribs.

"Holy crap! Your face looks bad. I heard Earl bragging at the Golden Shaft Saloon about working a damn greaser over. He called you a murderer," he blurted out. Rafe tried to laugh, but it hurt too much.

"What else did you find out?" Bill asked.

"Kip and Nat left for Cimarron to join up with Clay. They're all saying Clay's a rancher now, but it could be a lie. Jesse is still here. His mine is yielding some. Clement will probably go to Cimarron to rejoin Clay's gang soon," Lefty informed them. "But, I'll tell you Rafe, those jaspers who worked you over are looking for you and they know you are up here with us. The bartender told me."

"Bill, I can't stay here and put you all in danger," Rafe said.

"You can't go back to the hotel, besides you can't fight with those hurt ribs. You have to stay here. Don't worry we'll keep an eye out for them. We will take turns on guard duty. We're just finishing the last vein, then this mine is played out. You relax and get better and let us worry about Allison's gang," Bill assured him.

Rafe spent several days alternating between napping and applying ice. He could now walk with less pain. The three vigilantes diverted his hate and anger from Ana Teresa's killers for the time being. Although ice numbed the pain in his ribs, rage against the perpetrators at the Mutz Hotel burned bright. He concentrated on getting well as soon as possible.

With the ice treatments, the swelling on Rafe's ribs was subsiding. Since he did not have access to herbs, he remembered a treatment the Aztec healer taught him. He heated a pot of water and soaked a small towel in it, then squeezed the water out and wrapped it in a dry towel and applied it to his side. The Healer had explained the wet heat would draw blood to the injury. The Healer believed blood was the body's healing agent. Rafe alternated the ice and heat treatments.

Whenever he went to spend time at the stream, he always took his pistol. Lefty warned him the three jaspers were looking for him and the next time they would not just beat him.

In the evenings, he and Bill's miners sat around the kitchen table and swapped stories. When Rafe asked what they planned to do after they closed the mine, each one had a different idea.

Bill thought he would retire and go live near his daughter. She was in Saint Louis.

Lefty wanted to go to Silver City. Like E-town, Silver City was a wild and dangerous mining town. Lefty said he had some friends down there.

Mike wanted a house that was warm in the winter and cool in the summer. He said he was thinking about Albuquerque. "I know a bit about cattle and think I might be able to get on a supply wagon team," he speculated.

Rick was the newest member of Bill's team, although he was not young and had worked for several miners in E-town. "I got me a hankering to go to Pueblo Colorado. I hear the railroad is thinking about finishing the tracks from there to Santa Fe. I know a bit about metal work and blasting. I'm thinking I can get on a crew there."

On Wednesday, Doctor Lowe rode up in the afternoon. Rafe was surprised by the visit.

"I was in the neighborhood so I thought I'd check on you," the doctor told him. He seemed satisfied the ribs were not broken and Rafe was healing.

By Thursday, Rafe attempted to ride the gelding around in a circle near the mine. The gait of the horse shot pain through his chest, however Rafe gritted his teeth and bore it. Getting back on a horse was his only way off the mountain.

It took the week for the treatments to work. Rafe was finally able to move without the shooting pain and it allowed him to practice drawing his pistols. He was anxious to get to town and find Jesse, then head up to Cimarron to get Kip and Nat. However, now he might need to deal with Clement and his friends Earl and Roy.

Over the course of the past week, his anger toward the three thugs who beat him had waned. He hoped he could just avoid them, wanting to stay focused on his true mission – kill those responsible for killing his wife and unborn child.

CHAPTER 20

George arrived in Denver late Monday afternoon. He rode the stagecoach to Pueblo, then caught the railroad north. The three travel days made him stiff and tired, but the train was more relaxing. After paying a young boy to carry his luggage, George limped down Larimer Street from the train depot. The leg where he took a bullet which nicked a vein several years ago, was especially bothersome after a long cramped ride.

By the time he reached the Capitol Hotel, his bags were waiting by the lobby desk.

"Ah, you must be George Summers," the clerk greeted him.

"Yes. I see the boy brought my bags."

"Yes sir. I have a nice room on the second floor with a balcony overlooking the square. Do you know how long you will be staying with us, sir?"

"Probably not more than several days. Can you please have a bath drawn?"

It was late and George needed a bath and sleep before figuring out how to meet the doctors at the Denver Hospital.

On Tuesday morning, Doctor Roybal walked into the extra room where Ana Teresa was staying. Like most doctors in small towns, Eduardo Roybal worked and lived in the office. A small sleeping area behind an equally small kitchen was his home. He pulled back the curtain to the room where Ana Teresa occupied the extra bed.

"Good morning young lady," he spoke in a friendly voice. It was unusual for a patient to stay as long as she had and he found her company delightful. Her mother, Marcella, was also a lovely woman.

"Good morning," she replied, but her face was flushed. The doctor quickly moved to her side and felt her face with his hand. There was no doubt she was running a fever.

"How do you feel? Are you in more pain?" he asked her questions.

"I woke up shaking a little while ago. I'm not in pain unless the baby kicks. May I have another blanket?"

"Certainly. I'll fetch it. I have the kettle on in the kitchen. I'll bring you a nice hot cup of tea to warm you."

Doctor Roybal patted her hand and smiled. He did not want to alarm her. A fever in her condition was extremely dangerous, both to her and the baby. If an infection started from the bullet, blood poisoning and gangrene could set in.

Early Tuesday morning, George arranged for transportation from the hotel to the Denver Hospital. Doctor Roybal had given him several names, but he was unsure exactly who to contact. The buggy driver stopped at the main entrance. It was an impressive four-story brick building, larger than any building in Santa Fe. George walked up the steps and into the lobby.

The wood floors were impeccably polished to a shine. Ornate brass oil lights extended down long hallways. In the lobby, well-used leather chairs sat in rows. Several were occupied. It could be a hotel lobby, except for the smell. An overpowering odor of disinfectant tingled his nose. Behind a counter, a burly nurse with a starched white cap was talking to an older couple. George walked up and stood behind them.

"May I help you?" the nurse asked when it was his turn.

"Yes, I need to speak to the head doctor about a very important issue," George spoke.

"Are you sick?"

"No. I am fine. It is about my daughter-in-law."

"You will have to make an appointment," she retorted brusquely.

"You do not understand. My daughter-in-law is extremely ill in San Gabriel. She is eight months pregnant."

"And just where is San Gabriel?"

"New Mexico." George knew this conversation was not going well before the nurse replied.

"New Mexico! This is Denver, Colorado mister."

"Yes, I know. She needs a specialist. The doctor in San Gabriel has been sending telegrams without any reply. Please ma'am, she is gravely ill."

"And so are a lot of the people we treat. If you bring her in, perhaps one of our specialists could see her."

"Please ma'am. Could I see Doctor Sheldon." George spit out one of the names Doctor Roybal had told him.

The burly nurse sighed. "Go sit over there, I'll write a note to Doctor Sheldon, but I doubt he'll see you." She waved a hand at George indicating to go sit in the waiting area.

Doctor Roybal brought Ana Teresa a large cup of hot tea. "Here, my dear. Drink this. I'll check on you in a little while. I need to ride over to *don* Lorenzo's hacienda and redress his arm. I'll bring your mother back with me."

After the doctor left, Ana Teresa sipped the hot tea. It helped to dissipate the shivers. It was completely quiet in the back room of the doctor's office. She could not hear people, wagons, or children on the street below. Only an occasional loud shout or gunshot made its way to her. During the long lonely hours of isolation, she did two things. She prayed, usually the Rosary, and wondered about Rafael.

George and the doctor told her he rode off after he heard she and the baby were dead. It would seem in his character to do so. She was sure he wanted vengeance. However, that was over a week ago and surely somehow he would hear the news or someone would find him. She needed him. She dreamed of him and of their house. In the dreams, she saw him riding a horse, but it was not Rayo, his Appaloosa. It seemed odd to her.

This morning she woke with an odd knot of dread in her stomach. She also woke shaking and the doctor looked a bit concerned when he checked her. She saw it in his eyes behind his smile. Sipping the tea, she started to pray for herself, the baby, and most of all Rafael.

After three hours of waiting, George followed a sign

to a small cafeteria. He ordered coffee and a sandwich. He sat at a table and watched the people waiting in line for food. Some were nurses in their white uniforms, others were men dressed in white pants and shirts. George took them for orderlies. A few were people waiting, such as himself, easily identified by their street clothes.

A short man with a long white coat strode to the head of the line. Everyone gave him respect. A brown bag was handed to him without paying. George saw him nod at the line chef. George immediately knew he was a doctor of high esteem. A busy man, the hospital catered to his needs. George pondered this information while he sipped a second cup of coffee. About a half hour later, another taller doctor walked into the cafeteria and received similar treatment.

"Thanks Joe," the doctor said in a friendly voice, then quickly strode off.

"Anytime Doctor O'Keefe," the cook replied to him.

George spent all day waiting to speak to a doctor. He asked the burly nurse behind the desk several times. She kept telling him to sit and wait, getting more annoyed each time he asked. "The doctors are busy with real patients," she told him.

It was true. The large Denver Hospital was jumping with activity. As he sat and waited, five people arrived with various life-threatening wounds when a carriage overturned. One was a young boy of about eight. A woman helped her husband walk. Blood was oozing bright red down his leg. A frantic father carried a young girl who was limp in his arms. The mother was weeping. So it went all day long.

While he waited, George tried to imagine a way to get Ana Teresa here to the hospital. If she was here, they would treat her. Watching the bustling activity of the doctors and nurses, he could not fathom how he could arrange to take a doctor away from here for probably the best part of a week, even if he could pay the price. As the sun began to dip low in the afternoon sky, George again went to the desk nurse.

"Ma'am, I have been waiting all day to see the head doctor," George said.

"Oh, are you still here? Well I believe Doctor O'Keefe

is still in surgery. Perhaps you should come back tomorrow," she said in a dismissive voice.

George realized the nurse was not going to interrupt Doctor O'Keefe from his work for a man from New Mexico, however now George had a face and a name. "Thank you, I will do that," he said.

George stepped outside and walked down the expansive front entrance steps. Instead of waiting near the front for transportation, he walked left around the large building. He noticed during the day, doctors and nurses did not enter and exit in the front. Finally, he found a back door. Several horses, buggies, and two carriages waited in a row. George stood nearby and waited. Two young nurses exited the door and walked off down the path. Sometime later, several orderlies did the same. George assumed the hospital had dormitories for the younger and unmarried workers.

It was dark by the time George saw the man he waited for exiting the building. Doctor O'Keefe's striking silver hair glinted in the moonlight. Quickly George stepped out of the shadows.

"Excuse me Doctor O'Keefe. My name is George Summers and I need to speak with you about an urgent matter."

"Do I know you, sir?"

"No. I am from Santa Fe, New Mexico. I understand you are the head surgeon here. I am in need of your help."

"It is late. Perhaps if you came back in the morning. Check in at the desk and ask to see me," the doctor said. He was tired from a long day in surgery and his wife would be waiting supper.

"With respect sir, I have been waiting all day. The desk nurse, well, let me say she seems to be a formidable buffer to you doctors."

At that, Doctor O'Keefe laughed. "She can be. Do you have transportation? Perhaps you can share my carriage and we can talk along the way."

"You are very kind sir."

After they were settled and the carriage driver started the horse, the doctor asked George to explain the problem.

He listened politely as George gave him the details of Ana Teresa's condition and the pregnancy. He asked a few detailed questions and otherwise let George explain everything Doctor Roybal had said.

"It is a unique case," he said after George finished. "Doctor Roybal is correct in his appraisal of her situation. We could easily treat her here at the hospital, but I see getting her here could prove fatal."

"I'm willing to pay, whatever the price for you or one of your trained colleagues to come to San Gabriel," George told him.

"I'm sorry. It is not money, it is time. All of my doctors are overworked as it is. I cannot spare anyone for the time to travel to New Mexico."

George's hopes sank. The doctor was friendly and open in his manner. George felt as if he would help, if he could. The carriage driver pulled up in front of a two-story brick home with four large white pillars gracing the front.

"Perhaps, I can help. I have a colleague, an Army doctor, who works at Fort Union. He is highly skilled in bullet wounds. Perhaps you could persuade him to travel to San Gabriel. Come around in the morning after ten and I will leave a letter of introduction with the desk nurse."

"Thank you sir. You have been more than kind."

"Good Luck. Samuel, drive this man to his destination," he called to the driver, then said goodnight to George.

Promptly at ten o'clock the following morning George waited in line at the nurse's desk.

"Oh, I see you are back. Have a seat," she said without greeting him.

"You should have a letter from Doctor O'Keefe for me. My name is George Summers."

"Humpf," she blustered. Reaching under the shelf of the desk, she pulled out an envelope. "Here." George took it and thanked her.

Hurrying back to the buggy he had waiting outside, he directed the driver to take him to the train station. He already checked out of the hotel and the desk clerk told him the last train to Pueblo left at noon.

CHAPTER 21

Clay Allison looked out over the expanse of his ranch stretching off to the far hills. For more than five years, he and his gang jumped claims in the rich Baldy Mountain mining town of Elizabethtown. Knowing the boom would eventually bust, he used the profits of his claims to buy this ranch near Cimarron, New Mexico. Through his brother who had several influential friends, they learned that the Colfax County seat would be moved from E-town to Cimarron after E-town busted. They used the information to buy land at a good rate. Just as predicted, the county seat was moved two years ago.

The son of a Presbyterian minister, Clay was educated and shrewd. Many thought of him only as an outlaw, but he knew how to have others do his dirty work, keeping his neck from feeling a noose. By last fall most of the mines were outplayed, so he moved to his ranch before winter set in. He left Fitz in E-town to cleanup any loose ends and to manage the few of his mines which were still producing.

Clay came to Cimarron intending to lead a quieter life with his new bride Dora. His brother Monroe and his family lived nearby and the weather was more temperate than the cold and windy Baldy Mountain area. He hired local Basque sheepherders to manage his herd of sheep and several Texas cowboys to keep a modest size herd of Texas shorthorns fattening on the good grasses. He was planning on 1874 being a year of new beginnings for him and Dora.

Then in early January he killed Chunk Colbert, a well-known gunslinger. It was stupid and Clay regretted having been taunted by the dangerous man. Colbert came to Cimarron and acted friendly. Chunk told Clay he was looking to be a neighbor and only had respect for what Clay had accomplished. In his newfound generosity, Clay hosted Chunk to the best gambling houses in town, and they talked about racehorses and ranching.

After several weeks, they were at dinner at the Clifton

House, an overnight stagecoach stop on the Santa Fe Trail. Chunk started to give Clay doubts. Colbert bragged he had killed six men and teased Clay that he would be his seventh. To ward off any ideas, Clay laid his pistol on the table. Toward the end of the meal, Chunk made his move. His gun nicked the table's edge as he pulled it up. Clay grabbed his pistol and shot Chunk in the head.

Although he was not charged with murder and it was agreed Clay was acting in self defense, a cloud of doubt swirled around him. Even Dora worried he had not given up his outlawing ways. He could tell people distrusted him. They kept their distance and a number of families refused invitations to dine at the Allisons much to Dora's disappointment.

A little over a week ago, Kip Donohoe and Nat Holmes showed up in Cimarron looking for him. Kip and several of his friends worked for Clay in Texas and also in Elizabethtown. In Texas, they helped rustle cattle and in E-town they rustled claims as part of his vigilante gang. When Kip and Nat found him at the saloon in town, Clay told them he was not looking for hiring guns of any type.

Kip Donohoe stood at the Lambert Inn's bar nursing a whiskey bottle thinking about the events of the past several weeks. He, Nat, and Jesse left San Gabriel immediately following the raid on the hacienda. It had not gone as he planned. When several of the greasers began firing back, all hell broke loose. One in particular was exceptionally skilled and shot one of the young squatters off his horse.

Kip and the raiders started aiming at anything that moved. In the matter of a minute, several greasers, including women and a child were on the ground. Then several of the greasers came after them and he and the gang fled. Kip knew they would swing if the law caught them, so they rode hard up to E-town. He planned hiding out there for a while, but the dwindling town was boring, so he and Nat came to Cimarron to find Clay Allison.

Allison gave Kip no job or encouragement to stay in Cimarron. Apparently, Clay was trying to become a member-in-good-standing in the community after he married last fall. Damn women always corrupted a man from having a good time. It was one reason Kip stuck to whores. After Clay snubbed him, Kip hired on with the new owner of the Maxwell Land Company, an English company. The new owners were hiring gunmen to clean out the squatters, who had built on the mineral rich land. He and Nat spent the last week kicking around the saloons, gambling, and partaking of the painted ladies. Kip thought it easy money using his gun for such work. Hell, he killed the Mexicans down near San Gabriel for much less money.

Kip hired on, while Nat got himself pie-eyed on a saloon girl at the Lambert Inn. Nat had money from his mine in E-town, but Kip's mine went bust. When Kip asked Nat to join him working for Maxwell, Nat declined.

"I'm a lookin fer sum land to start a small ranch," he told Kip. In the meantime, Nat spent most of his time at the Lambert Inn where his girl worked.

"Hey Kip, meet us on the north side of town at sunup," Gil Moran yelled over to him. "We got us a job ta do."

Gil was the head man for the Maxwell Company. He was in charge of the hired hands pushing the squatters off the land. Kip thought of him as a company man. He did more talking than shooting.

"Sure. I'll be there," Kip yelled back.

Kip drank late into the night with nothing much else to do. When the bar closed, he grabbed a bottle, paid for a whore, and headed upstairs. When the light from the coming morning wakened the girl, she pushed him.

"Get off me. You told me you gotta be out of here by morning."

Kip wavered as he put on his pants and boots. The hangover pounded in his head. He grabbed the bottle of red-eye off the dresser. It still had about a third left.

By the time he met up with Gil and the others, the whiskey had helped his hangover, but drinking made Kip mean.

"Remember, we're here to show force, but these

people think they have legal rights to the land. The Maxwell Company does not want headlines, they want results. I'll do all the talking," Gil cautioned the men.

They rode for about an hour before locating several small shacks. Cows chomped hay in a corral and two children played nearby. When a man came from one of the shacks, Gil put up his hand.

"What do you want?" the man asked. He was holding a shotgun, but the barrel was pointed down.

"The Maxwell Company owns this land. You have two weeks to vacate," Gil said.

"That's bullshit. I own this land fair and legal. You need to leave."

Kip listened to the man and Gil argue. His head began to throb from the red-eye. It reminded him of the issues in San Gabriel.

"I'll show you my deed," the man said and turned to go back into the shack. Kip pulled his gun and shot the man in the back.

"What the fuck yew doin Kip? I told yew no shootin unless they pulled their guns. You kilt that man in cold blood," Gil growled at him.

"Hell, he cudda been goin fer his gun," Kip slurred his words. He did not care, he just wanted to kill and go back to town.

"Yew git the fuck outta here, now, and don't ever come back!" Gil yelled at Kip.

"Fuck yew. I dun need yer shit." Kip turned his horse and rode off. He rode back to Cimarron alone. Damn squatters and greasers were nothing but trouble and he was getting tired with their squabbles.

When Gil Moran returned to the Maxwell Land Company, he reported the incident. His boss was angry. "If you can't keep six men in line, I don't need you," the boss said.

"This man was a rogue. It won't happen again," Gil tried to appease his boss.

"It better not. So what do we need to do to make this

go away?"

"I'll handle it," Gil told him.

Kip was coming out of a small cafe when Gil found him. "Hey Kip, the sheriff's comin after yew fer killing that feller."

"Why the fuck is he comin after me? It were a squatter."

"He wern't no squatter after all. He was a legal landowner. The company gave me wrong directions. The family is at the sheriff's office rat now. Yew best turn yerseff in." Gil lied about the whole thing. He knew Kip would run and run fast from the law, far away from Cimarron.

"Fuck no I ain't," he said. "I ain't gonna swing fer yer problum."

"Yew kilt a white man Kip. Ain't like he were an Injun or greaser."

Kip rushed into the Lambert Inn and found Nat talking to his girlfriend near the back entrance. He grabbed Nat by the arm and spun him around. "What the hell r yew doin?" Nat asked.

"We got ta git outta here, Nat."

"What yew talkin bout. I ain't goin nowhere."

"Cum on Nat, we gotta git. I kilt a man by mistake, an the sheriff is lookin fer me."

"Yew know what Kip, yew cud never tell skunks from house cats. Yew got us in trouble down at San Gabriel by leadin us to killin innocent Mescans. Now, yew tell me yew kilt an innocent man. I ain't goin nowhere with yew. I juss bought me some land here and will settle down with my gal. Yer on yer own Kip."

"Fuck yew Nat. When yew git tired of sod busting, I'll be over ta Lincoln whar I got friends and family. Yew can find me thar. Juss go to the L. G. Murphy Company mercantile. My cousin Larry owns it."

Kip wasted no time getting his belongings together. Jumping on his horse, he rode south at a fast gallop out of Cimarron.

Chapter 22

A rider, sent by *don* Lorenzo, arrived at the de Soto hacienda just outside of Santa Fe around noon. *Don* Lorenzo's message contained news from San Gabriel.

Ana Teresa's condition was not much better or much worse. Doctor Roybal reported she was running a slight fever, but the wound did not look infected, however any fever was significant in her case. Emotionally she was concerned about Rafael and it was making her agitated.

The message also stated the two young squatters confessed their role in the raid to the sheriff. They professed their innocence vehemently denying they intentionally killed anyone. They swore they only shot in the air or in the dirt to scare the people. They accused a man named Kip Donohoe and two others as the ringleaders and the ones who shot directly at people. Kip and the other two rode off after the attack saying they were going to Elizabethtown, where they would be safe from the law.

The letter finished by stating Doctor Roybal was asking if there was news from George Summers.

After *don* Pedro read the letter, he summoned his footman and asked for his horse to be saddled. Folding the letter in his vest pocket, he stepped up into the saddle and rode off. He had two places to go – the Summers' ranch and his son-in-law's home. He headed for Carlos and Bibiana's home first.

"Bienvenido," Carlos greeted him. It was an unexpected surprise.

"I come with news," he said. *Don* Pedro handed Carlos the letter and let him finish it.

"Kip Donohoe? Never heard that name before, but if he is going to E-town he may be one of Clay Allison's gang of thugs."

"I thought you would want to know. Perhaps Rafael learned this information somehow and headed there."

Carlos pondered *don* Pedro's words thinking it was

exactly where the pretend U.S. Marshal, who he knew was Rafael, would go if he learned the whereabouts of Kip Donohoe.

"I should go to E-town and look for him," Carlos said just as his wife, Bibiana, walked into the room with their infant son.

"Hello *Papá*. I did not hear you come in."

"Hello *mija*. And how is my favorite grandson?" *Don* Pedro walked over to hug his daughter and grandson.

"He is your only grandson, *Papá*. You are going to spoil him calling him your favorite."

"Well he is my favorite right now."

"What is this talk about E-town?"

"It is possible Rafael has gone there. I need to go and look for him," Carlos told his wife.

"No! You promised me not to go traipsing off again after the trip to Mexico last year. Rafael is a grown man and quite capable of taking care of himself." Bibiana's voice was icy. She respected Rafael and knew her husband considered him like a brother, but Rafael had a wild streak and Carlos promised she and the baby were his only priority.

"But Bibiana, he does not know Ana Teresa is alive. This is not a trivial matter," Carlos protested.

"Send a telegram or tell the sheriff or have George Summers go. Not you," she groused and turned to leave the room. "And I mean it!"

Carlos sighed knowing she was right. He could not just take off over hundreds of miles trying to find Rafe.

"My daughter is right. You must stay here. I am headed to the Summers to find out any news about George. I will stop at the sheriff's office on the way home, alert him of the news, and ask him to send a telegram to Elizabethtown's sheriff," *don* Pedro said.

"I'll come with you."

"No, you better stay here." *Don* Pedro knew his only daughter's temper and Carlos needed to stay here at home and placate her.

Riding the six miles to the Summers' home and gun foundry, *don* Pedro was greeted warmly.

"Have you heard from George?" he asked Josefina, George's wife.

"I received a telegram yesterday. He was going to Fort Union to find a doctor there. I have not heard from him since."

"So he was not able to get a doctor from Denver to come?"

"He did not say anything, but I suppose not. How is Ana Teresa?" Josefina asked.

"About the same." *Don* Pedro did not want to worry Josefina further.

"If you hear from George, please send me a message. I will pass it along to Doctor Roybal. He is quite anxious to have news."

On his way home, *don* Pedro stopped at the office of the sheriff in town. *Don* Pedro told him the news from San Gabriel.

"A Kip Donohoe, you say? Never heard of him."

"Can you send a wire to E-town and tell them of this man and to look for Rafael Reyes?" *don* Pedro asked.

"It would not do any good. E-town has not had a sheriff in over a year. The last one, Danny Robertson, got killed and they never replaced him. I hear E-town is more lawless than ever. I'm not even sure the telegraph still goes there," the sheriff said.

Don Pedro rode home glad Carlos had not come to hear what the sheriff had to say about E-town.

After *don* Pedro's visit, Josefina was more worried than ever. She was sure George was doing his best to find a good doctor and she was not worried about his safety. It was Rafael who filled her thoughts. The young man she considered her son was somewhere alone and heartbroken. He would be capable of anything and desperate enough to risk his own life.

If she were able, she would ride to Elizabethtown to find him herself. Instead, she would settle for a visit to San Gabriel to see Ana Teresa. Josefina called for her maids and daughters. "Be ready to go to San Gabriel in the morning," she told them all.

Carlos spent the rest of the afternoon seething over his wife's behavior. He had made her promises, but Rafe needed to know about Ana Teresa. Carlos had not told her about his suspicion Rafe was pretending to be a U.S. Marshal. No doubt he headed for E-town, if the young squatters told him what they told the sheriff. Carlos thought is probable, as Rafe would have been pointing his pistol in their face wanting information.

"I have to go. I have to make Bibiana understand that," he muttered to himself.

CHAPTER 23

"Bill I need some miner's clothes. Whatever you have and will make me look like a miner. I want Lefty to go to the Golden Shaft Saloon with me and point Jesse out. Once I know what he looks like, I'll go it alone. I don't want you or your men involved in any way. I'm going to do some killing and don't want you having trouble because of me."

"I can't let you go at it alone, Rafe. George would never forgive me if you get killed."

"I hear you Bill, but I have to take care of Jesse before I leave town. You would not like it if your men get killed because of me. Don't worry, I can take care of myself. I just need to know what the man looks like."

"I know you're a crack shot with those double-action pistols. Damn, I should have wired George you were laid up here," Bill responded.

"No, don't wire George unless I get killed. George will only worry or want to come and help. There are some things a man needs to do on his own and this is one." Bill nodded understanding Rafe's dilemma.

Mike gave Rafe some of his old work clothes, as they were about the same size. His GSW pistols were hidden under an old brown coat. Rafe gathered his belongings and stuffed them in his saddlebags. He saddled the gelding and tied down his gear. Lefty made sure Rafe had dust and oil smudged on his face and arms and hands. He especially got the black smudge under Rafe's fingernails.

"Now you look like a miner."

Rafe thanked Mike, Rick, and especially Bill, then he and Lefty rode down the trail Friday afternoon. It was the first time Rafe had ridden the gelding since the beating. Mostly his ribs were healed, but occasionally the horse stumbled a bit on the rocky trail and it jarred his ribs sending a sharp pain into his lungs.

It was mid-afternoon when they reached the east end of town. Tethering the horses a long way down the road, they gathered their lunch pails and walked the rest of the way to the Golden Shaft Saloon, pretending to be just two miners coming home after a shift to get a beer.

Lefty found a table near the entrance and ordered two beers from the saloon girl. Rafe kept his slouchy hat low and sat with his back to the door. Lefty paid for the beers and as Rafe lifted the mug, Lefty told him to look at the third poker table. "He's the one with the tan Stetson. He has a black leather vest over a brown flannel shirt," Lefty identified Jesse Kincaid.

Rafe took another swallow and looked at the man. He got a good look at his face, as Jesse had his hat pulled back on his head. Rafe could not tell if Jesse was armed from where he and Lefty sat.

"Do you think he's armed?"

"Probably. He's one of Clay's vigilante claim jumpers. It's how he got his mines around here. They don't go around unarmed," Lefty said.

Lefty and Rafe watched the players at Jesse's table. One man left and another joined the poker game. Rafe ordered a second beer as they watched Jesse. Casually, Rafe glanced around the saloon. The ground floor was full of tables. The front had a stage where entertainment might be playing, but not tonight. Jesse's table was nearer the stage. A set of stairs rose to the second floor where the whores took men for a roll. A balcony surrounded two sides of the upper floor.

Rafe pondered the surroundings at the Golden Shaft as his mind assessed the odds. Jesse would have friends here to back him up and Rafe had none. The odds were not good. It would be better to catch him in the dark on his way home, but this was personal to Rafe. This man could be Ana Teresa's killer. Avenging her should not be a bullet in the back, but straight up. He wanted Jesse to know why bullets were coming at him.

"How often is he here?" Rafe quizzed Lefty.

"I think he plays poker most nights. He's not a miner. He has a crew finishing the last strike on his mine."

"That's good enough for me. We can go anytime. You

go on back to the mine and thanks for all your help," Rafe said and finished his beer.

Lefty surmised Rafe would corner Jesse later. Even a crack shot would not be crazy enough to confront Jesse here at the saloon. It was almost dark, with just a hint of light still left in the western sky, as Rafe and Lefty walked back to the horses. Lefty tried to get Rafe to tell him his plan.

"You go on back up the hill. There will be killing here and I don't want you involved."

When they got back to where they left the horses, Lefty shook his hand. "Good Luck." Rafe watched as Lefty walked his horse down the road out of E-town toward the mine.

Rafe led the gelding to the small corral behind the Mutz Hotel. He double checked his saddle bags and the horse's cinch. Then he changed into black pants, a black shirt, and a black waist length jacket. No trimmings, just black. He strapped on the arrow quiver across his back and slipped the short-barrel shotgun into it, then wrapped his two-holster gunbelt around his waist. Lastly, he donned his black Stetson and spun the silver rowels on his boot spurs.

Before Rafe left the corral, he checked the cylinders of the two GSW double-action pistols. He shook all thoughts out of his head, except the death of Ana Teresa and his unborn child. He wanted nothing to interfere with what was to come next. In reality, he had no idea what would happen and it was highly possible he would die. The thought only bothered him because if he died here, Kip and Nat would go free.

He tried to focus on the Aztec healer's teachings. "Clear your mind, then you will be able to see." The Healer taught him many mysteries of the ancient Aztec beliefs. He also believed Rafe was blessed by the Goddess Coatlicue, the Goddess of life and death, because of a scar in the shape of a star on Rafe's chest. The Healer believed the Goddess saved Rafe's life for a purpose and now he was bound to help others, especially those in need. It had been so in the past, but tonight was different.

In other instances, it was like hearing the Goddess

calling to him. He felt it deep in his chest beneath the scar. Tonight he felt nothing but the rage in his heart. Tonight it was justified vengeance which pushed him to action and possible death.

In the darkness of the small corral, a set of unknown eyes watched Rafe change into the black outfit. He watched Rafe check the pistols, then holster them. Over his back he slung a beaded quiver and stuck a short-barrel shotgun into it. The owner of the eyes stayed completely still in the darkness until Rafe was gone. The brown gelding was saddled and standing quietly in one of the stalls. A few minutes later, the unknown man untied the gelding and together with another horse walked into the darkness and down the street.

The silver rowels sang from Rafe's spurs as he pushed the batwing doors to the Golden Strike Saloon. No one seemed to take notice of him as he entered. The roulette wheel was spinning and laughter could be heard above the piano. Rafe knew exactly where Jesse sat and strode directly toward the poker table. He stood across from Jesse with his feet spread wide.

"Are you Jesse Kincaid?" he simply asked in a measured voice.

"Ya, who the fuck wants ta know?" Jesse replied. He did not bother to look up while he shifted his poker cards matching pairs and suits.

"The same Jesse Kincaid who murdered women and children down at San Gabriel?" This time Rafe growled loud enough for many nearby to hear him.

"I did'n murder nobody," he grumbled back. Jesse finally looked up at the man accusing him. He was dressed all in black. His face was smeared making his tan skin darker. His brown eyes held hate and anger.

"You murdered my wife. You murdered my unborn child."

Jesse looked up and his blue eyes widened, then narrowed. He pushed back and went for his gun. Everyone at the poker table scattered as Jesse came up with his pistol and fired. The shot went up to the ceiling as two shots from

Rafe's pistols hit Jesse in the chest. Jesse went down on his back hitting the floor with a thud from the force of the bullets. The gunshots reverberated in the saloon.

Earl and Clement were sitting at another table when they heard Rafe's voice and then the gunshots. It was not unusual for gunplay in the saloon, but most often it was one of Clay's gang who did the shooting. Clement looked at the man dressed in black holding two smoking pistols at Jesse Kincaid's table.

"It's that fuckin greaser who kilt Jack," Clement growled to Earl. "We shudda plugged him the other night." He pulled out his pistol and Earl followed.

Roy was on the other side of the room pawing a buxom saloon girl when he heard the shots. He glanced and saw his friends, Clement and Earl, with guns drawn heading toward the commotion. Pushing the girl off his lap, he cautiously made his way to see why his friends had their guns out.

Most everyone in the saloon was ducking for cover. Tables and chairs screeched and crashed as people struggled to get out of the way of the gunfight. The bartender reached under the bar for his shotgun.

"I'm gonna kill yew, yew fuckin greaser," Clement yelled out.

Rafe heard Clement's yell and looked up. He saw Clement and Earl coming at him from his right side. In his momentary relief of besting Jesse, the rest of the saloon had seemed distant. He had not counted on killing the scoundrels who beat him at the Mutz Hotel. He had not come to the Golden Shaft to find them, but now they were coming right at him.

Before Rafe could blink, Clement raised his pistol and fired. The shot caught Rafe's jacket and whizzed by. Two bullets barked out of Rafe's pistols in response. Clement went down in a heap. Earl saw Clement's body buck and then fall.

"We shudda gutted yew that night, but I'm a gonna kill yew now," were Earl's last words before he fell from a well-placed bullet from Rafe's pistol.

Momentarily the saloon was eerily quiet. Although no one knew the young man wearing black, they saw it was a fair fight. Both Jesse and Clement drew first.

Suddenly another gunshot erupted in the silence. A bullet whizzed above Rafe's head and struck the wood banister leading to the second floor. He whirled to his right. Roy Harvey was thumbing the hammer of his pistol. Another shot ripped the quiet. Roy crashed backward knocking over a chair as he fell. He fell down to his knees from the first shot before a second hit him on the side on the head and killed him.

"Couldn't let you have all the fun," Lefty said standing nearby with a gun in hand. He was dressed in a brown suit and brown Stetson hat, not in his miner's clothing.

Rafe recognized him and smiled. "Thank you," he said.

Scanning the room, they looked around for anyone wanting to make more trouble. As they backed away to the door with guns drawn, no one moved.

Lefty had followed Rafe after they spotted Jesse in the Golden Shaft. He knew what Rafe was planning and thought he might need help. Rafe had saved Bill's mine from Clay Allison's gang and Lefty wanted to repay the debt. He circled back after making Rafe believe he left town. He watched Rafe in the corral dress in black. After Rafe walked off to the saloon, Lefty followed with their horses in tow. The brown gelding and Lefty's mare were tethered to the hitching post outside the Golden Shaft Saloon.

"Get out of town, now. Fitz will probably send men after you. They have lots of friends," Lefty told Rafe.

Rafe jumped on the gelding and reached down a hand. "Tell Bill what happened here. Thanks for the help." The bright moon in an otherwise clear sky lit his way as Rafe rode out of E-town. He rode as hard as he could down the moonlit path heading down the mountain away from Elizabethtown. He was headed to Cimarron. There he hoped to find Kip Donohoe and Nat Holmes.

Killing Jesse abated his vengeance a bit, but two more must die before he could head home to Santa Fe. Home to what? The image of his wife and unborn child tore at his heart. He could never live in his house again without them.

He had killed in anger before, however the rage inside him now was deeper. In the past, he raged against injustice. His rage drove him to want to kill *don* Bernardo for raping his fifteen-year-old sister María. The same rage was there when he killed the Reynolds' boys for hurting him and his uncle's family in El Paso. Now the rage drove him to kill three men and stalk two more.

Was he a killer? Was this his fate, his destiny? The Aztec healer would call it his *tonalli*. He would say one's fate or destiny could not be changed. It was something the Gods gave a child, based upon the Aztec calendar. He told Rafe how in the ancient world of the Aztec, the Gods were supreme. In those days when a boy child was born, the father would wrap the boy's umbilical cord around a small carved shield. If the father wanted the Gods to give the boy the *tonalli* of a warrior, the shield was then given to an Aztec warrior to have it buried at a battlefield. The Aztec believed the *tonalli* was part of a person's soul.

The Aztec healer believed Rafe was connected to the Goddess Coatlicue. The scars in the shape of a star on his chest was her mark and protected him. Rafe wondered if he still had her protection or had he crossed over the line from guardian of the defenseless to a broker of vengeance. All he knew was he had two more men to kill.

CHAPTER 24

On Friday morning, Josefina, Lolo, and Lizzy took the buggy. They were cramped, but Josefina chose to drive the buggy herself. She asked Esteban to remain at the ranch in case George returned home.

It was the third day of April and spring had come into its full glory in Santa Fe. Small wildflowers of purple, pink, and yellow dotted the sides of the path. The only remnant of winter was the snowcap still showing on the upper peaks of the Sangre de Cristo Mountains.

Josefina kept the horse at a quick pace arriving in San Gabriel at about ten o'clock. She drove directly to Doctor Roybal's office. He received them with gracious pleasure.

"She needs some diversion. The hours of lying here unable to move around has been hard on her. Your visit will be good medicine."

Josefina and the girls surrounded Ana Teresa. Lolo gave her a big hug and Ana Teresa grimaced. "Oh, I'm sorry. I forgot you are not supposed to move."

"It's fine. The pain will go away in a minute."

"Do you have any word from Rafael?" Ana Teresa asked hoping they brought good news.

"No my dear. We have not heard from him yet, but all the sheriffs have been notified and surely he will be found soon," Josefina replied.

After a momentary look of defeat, Ana Teresa gave them a broad smile. "Well at least you are here. I have been so lonely. Mother has been coming every day, but it is so good to see you. What is happening in Santa Fe? I want to hear everything," she queried the girls for news.

Lolo and Lizzy had grown to think of Ana Teresa as more than a sister-in-law. Only a few years older than Lolo, they shared happy talk about the parties and dances. Lolo had an ardent suitor and while Lizzy loved to tease her about it, Ana Teresa was Lolo's confidant.

"Did you see Victor at the church Easter social?" Ana

Teresa asked Lolo about the young *caballero*, Victor Archuleta, who professed he was smitten by Lolo's beauty. Ana Teresa knew Lolo was interested in the young suitor, but had been toying with him.

"Of course. He tried to occupy my time, but I brushed him away several times," she replied and they giggled.

Josefina stayed for a little while, then told the doctor she would drive to *don* Lorenzo's hacienda and tell Marcella to take a day of rest. Leaving her daughters, she climbed up onto the buggy seat and headed north, following the directions the doctor told her.

Don Lorenzo welcomed her when she arrived and the maid ushered her to the veranda. "Go summon my wife and *doña* Marcella. Tell them Josefina is here," the *don* told the maid.

"Have you heard from George?" was the *don's* first question.

"He is going to Fort Union. The doctor in Denver suggested the Army doctor there could come. They are highly trained in bullet wounds. I do not know anything more."

"And Rafael?"

"Nothing. I am fraught with worry. Carlos wanted to go to Elizabethtown to look for him after he received your message. *Don* Pedro asked the sheriff to send a wire."

"Our sheriff already tried to do so. The lines to E-town are down and nothing can get through."

Josefina was disheartened by the *don's* explanation. If only George would get home. He would know what to do.

"Josefina, what a pleasant surprise," Marcella said joining them on the veranda.

"I brought the girls for a visit with Ana Teresa."

"What a wonderful idea. I go see her every day, but she is growing bored with me." Marcella laughed.

Doña Amalia joined them a few minutes later and *don* Lorenzo excused himself and left the three women chatting and laughing. He thought it good medicine for all of them. The past two weeks had been nothing but frustration and anger. The two young squatters were still in jail, but claiming their innocence of the murders. The squatter family of the dead boy finally came to town and claimed their son's body. The sheriff reported his conversation with the squatters about their land rights and the events of the raid. The sheriff told Lorenzo the family was heartbroken to have lost their only son in such a terrible matter. They did not blame *don* Lorenzo or his men. They all blamed someone name Kip Donohoe.

Four Spaniards were dead, including *doña* Victoria *and don* Alfonso's five-year-old grandson, and one squatter. *Don* Alfonso threatened the sheriff with more violence, if he did not act. How dare the squatters suggest any blame on him? They were entirely to blame for the deaths of his friends and the death of their son.

Don Lorenzo's *vaqueros* reported the squatters posted guards near their homesteads. The guards always carried rifles or shotguns. The situation was increasingly volatile, while the sheriff did nothing to prevent more bloodshed. The old *don* sighed thinking all he really wanted was for peace to reign over the San Gabriel valley once again.

George Summers disembarked the stagecoach at the stage stop in Wagon Mound, New Mexico, as darkness was overtaking the sky on Friday. It was the village closest to Fort Union. The stagecoach went on south, while George checked into the stage stop's small guest quarters.

"Last room on the left, Mister Summers," the proprietor told him. "Outhouse is out the back door."

"Thank you. Can you waken me early as soon as breakfast is ready?"

"Certainly sir."

George limped down the hallway and found the small bedroom plain, but adequate. The small bed had two heavy quilts and two feather pillows. George bent wearily to remove his boots and stripped off his suit, hanging it carefully over the bed rail, then crawled under the quilts. Although his body was weary of the traveling, his mind was not quiet.

Tomorrow would be a week since he left Santa Fe on

his quest to find a doctor for Ana Teresa. A week was a long time in her condition. Determined to keep his faith, at times doubt crept in. Perhaps she was worse; perhaps Rafe had come home; perhaps the baby came; perhaps she was dead. He had wired Josefina from Denver, upon his arrival, and then to tell her he was going to Fort Union.

George quietly prayed as he did each night before sleep. He prayed for Ana Teresa's survival. He prayed for Rafe to return so he could be by her side. She needed him now more than ever. Exhausted, sleep overtook him.

CHAPTER 25

A crowing rooster stirred George awake. It was still dark. Dressing, he headed down the hallway and found the proprietor in the kitchen with his wife starting a fire in the large stove.

"Good morning," he greeted them.

"Good morning sir. It will be about an hour before breakfast is ready. The coffee will perk quickly."

"Thank you. I need to get to Fort Union today. Might I rent a buggy or a horse?"

"Going to the fort? You got business there?" The man's attitude was not suspicious, but rather the tone of his voice was curious. George doubted many civilians went to the fort.

"I need to find a doctor there, a Doctor Spencer."

"I see. He's a good man. We get soldiers through here after he's fixed them up. He came to town and treated Mister Chester when he cut his arm almost clean off."

"He also helped Amy Breck when she had so much trouble with the birthing of that last baby. You remember Alvin," the wife chimed in.

George was pleased to hear the glowing reports of Doctor Spencer. He sounded like a man willing to help.

"We don't have a buggy, but you are welcome to one of the horses in the barn. Any of them which ain't one of the team horses," Alvin told George.

George arrived at the fort around nine on Saturday morning. Soldiers were busily performing the morning routines and chores. A young soldier greeted him and took the reins of the horse as he rode up to the building marked Headquarters.

"Good morning sir."

"Good morning private. I've come to see Doctor Spencer. Where might I find him?"

"Captain Spencer would be in the dispensary, over there." The private pointed to a long building across the expanse of the internal courtyard of the fort.

"Much obliged," George thanked him, leaving the horse in the private's care.

When George entered the dispensary, rows of tidy beds stretched down one side. Only three were occupied. A tall man was bent over one of the patients. George waited until he was finished.

"Sir, I assume you are Captain Spencer?"

"Yes I am. Who are you?"

"My name is George Summers. Doctor O'Keefe in Denver suggested I talk to you. Here is a letter he wrote as introduction."

The doctor took spectacles from the pocket of his white coat and moved to a brighter spot in the tent. When he was finished reading, he lowered the letter. "Come to the back. We can sit and talk about your problem."

The doctor led George to his personal quarters. He poured two cups of coffee and asked George to sit. His manner was easy and friendly. George explained the nature of Ana Teresa's situation and everything he could remember Doctor Roybal told him. The doctor asked George where San Gabriel was located, as he had not traveled in New Mexico, except near the fort and to Cimarron a few times.

"It has been over a week since I've been traveling and two weeks since she was shot," George told him. "I've not had news, but when I left she was strong."

The doctor leaned back in his chair and seemed to ponder the situation quietly.

"Professionally, the case sounds very interesting and Lord knows I could use a break from this isolated place. However, the Army disapproves of its doctors treating civilians, unless they are brought to the fort."

George's shoulders visibly slumped. It seemed his problem was not much changed. "Alvin at the stage stop said you treated some people in Wagon Mound, because you were the only doctor nearby. I thought you . . . " George could not finish the sentence.

"Yes, that is true. I made an excuse to go to town. However, I cannot be gone for any extended time. If I were needed here, . . . well I cannot go." The doctor tapped his pencil on the desk then continued, "I do have a young associate doctor. He recently graduated from the Medical School in Philadelphia. He is on his rotating assignments."

The doctor went on to explain how recently graduated doctors were sent to the field to get additional training. They spent three or four months at different Army forts to gain field experience. His young assistant had graduated with high honors and trained in modern medical techniques. Things had been unusually quiet at Fort Union and Doctor Spencer thought Ana Teresa's case could be considered field training, since it involved a bullet wound.

"I believe I could send him with a special waiver," he finished.

"Thank you, thank you. Where is he? When can we leave?" George practically stuttered as he responded to the doctor's offer.

"He is out on maneuvers with a regiment. They should be back later today and we will speak to him, although I expect him to agree."

"I will ride back to town and gather my things and arrange to buy a horse," George said.

"I assumed you would be taking the stagecoach to Santa Fe, then traveling by buggy or carriage?"

Not knowing the stageline's schedule, George was sure riding directly west to San Gabriel would be faster, even if more difficult. George estimated the direct route was half the distance.

"If your assistant agrees, we can make the ride in a day from here. By the way, what is his name?"

"Lieutenant Charles Hapwell."

CHAPTER 26

Saturday morning, the small mining village of E-town was buzzing with questions. Last night, four men were gunned down by two men in the Golden Shaft Saloon. One killer wore black and accused Jesse Kincaid of murdering women and children at a place called San Gabriel. When Jesse protested and went for his gun, the man in black shot him point blank. It was said the man in black was damn fast on the draw.

Someone heard Clement accuse the man of killing Jack Braddely. When Clement went for his gun, the man in black's pistols barked and Clement fell dead to the floor. Fitz heard the same story from several of his men.

Earl's last words according to one of the witnesses made little sense. Earl shouted at the killer, "We shudda gutted yew that night, but I'm a gonna kill yew now."

No one was quite sure about how Roy Harvey was shot, although a few men said it was a second man in a brown Stetson hat. Neither man was dressed like a miner.

After the shootings, the killers disappeared into the night. Fitz ordered his vigilantes to search everywhere in town. He ordered his men to spread out through the mines and search thoroughly. E-town had no sheriff and Fitz was the only local person with enough authority and men to send search parties. Besides, Clement, Earl, and Roy worked for him and he wanted the killers found.

"Especially check at the Mystic Lode. Bill Moore must know something. That stranger was here last week," Fitz directed his gang. "If yew find im, I want im brought back here alive. We're gonna hang im for everyone to see."

When Fitz's vigilantes rode into the Mystic Lode mine, they pushed Bill aside. They searched every part of the mine and cabin for the stranger. The only people in the mine were Mike and Lefty. Their faces were covered in dirty bandanas and grime. Rick was in the cabin cooking lunch.

"Where is that stranger Bill? Fitz wants to know,"

Mickey Sullivan demanded.

"He was a businessman and left with Trent Bascom. You know Trent's no killer and the Mexican was helping him. They went down south to Socorro, I think," Bill lied to throw the gang off Rafe's trail.

Finally satisfied the man in black was not at the mine, Fitz' men left. Bill Moore rubbed his chin thoughtfully. Lefty told him of the events at the Golden Shaft last night and Bill thought the killings were justified.

Rafe rode hard all night, stopping near a large lake in the early hours to let the gelding rest. Mike had packed a bit of jerky and a few biscuits in his saddlebag and Rafe devoured them as the sun began to rise. He followed the lake to the east end where the Cimarron River trailed off east.

"Rafe, it's about forty miles to Cimarron if you keep following the river. When you get there, find Alexander P. Sullivan, at the Cimarron News and Press. Alexander can help you find Kip and Nat. If not, he will know someone who knows them. I know him from social gatherings in Santa Fe and he spent time here in E-town reporting on the mines. Alexander is a good newspaperman and a law and order advocate. Here, I wrote an introduction letter to him for you." Bill had given him the instructions and the letter before he left the mine.

Cimarron was new territory for Rafe. He knew little about the town, except it had a notorious reputation. Bill Moore told him it was mostly run by Texans, similar to the Allison gang's strangle hold on E-town.

As he rode into the morning sun, he tried to formulate a plan. The reckless vengeance he initially felt had been mitigated by the events of the last several weeks. His rage tempered to a measured revenge.

His problem was how to find the other two murderers without causing suspicions. The letter from Bill to Alexander would be a big help, if the newspaperman could be trusted. He had been lucky in E-town. Perhaps, he could use the U.S. Marshal ruse again and arrest them. He thought it could work. Random thoughts jumbled in his weary brain.

Rafe arrived in Cimarron just after noon. The town was alive with activity as would be typical of a Saturday. Supply wagons lined the street in front of the mercantile. Women with children in tow walked the sidewalks, while cowboys lounged outside of the saloons. No one took notice of a lone stranger riding a brown gelding wearing a black Stetson hat.

Rafe rode slowly looking for the newspaper office and found it on the north end of town not far past the Lambert Inn. The shades were up on the windows and as Rafe got to the door, he heard the clanging of what he thought was a running printing press. Opening the door, he walked into a large front room stacked with folded newspapers and filing cabinets. A door led to another room in the back, where he could see two men operating the press.

"Hello. Is Mister Sullivan in?" Rafe asked the man sitting at the front desk.

"I'm Sullivan, what can I do for you young man?"

"Mister Sullivan, my name is Rafe Reyes from Santa Fe. My friend, Bill Moore of E-town, suggested I look you up when I got to Cimarron. Here, he gave me this letter of introduction." Rafe handed the letter to him.

While the man read the letter, Rafe looked him over. To Rafe, Sullivan looked to be in his late forties with thinning not yet gray hair. He had blue eyes under thick eyebrows and rosy cheeks. Rafe waited until he finished reading the introduction letter.

"Says here you were at the massacre at the Salazar hacienda in San Gabriel?"

"Yes sir."

"Terrible, terrible. I heard about it from one of my suppliers. I've met *don* Lorenzo several times over the years at bull auctions. You know, we've had similar problems up on the Baca land grant north of here, but nothing as blatant as that attack. In the letter, Bill asks me to help you in any way I can. Why are you here?"

Rafe swallowed hard. Bill trusted Alexander Sullivan, but Rafe had no such feelings. The newspaperman could as easily turn him over to the sheriff as he could help him.

"I am after two men who organized that raid. I was told they came here from E-town. Their names are Kip Donohoe and Nat Holmes," Rafe reluctantly told him.

Alexander looked Rafe over. He was a young Mexican dressed in black. His face was streaked with grime and his black clothes dusty from the trail. He wore two pistols in his gunbelt.

"Son, you should go to the sheriff and tell him about this. Besides, Kip is no longer here. I heard he left after he killed an innocent man who they thought was a land squatter. He was riding with the men from the Maxwell Company. He is a very dangerous man and so is Nat Holmes. They have both ridden with Clay Allison and are murderous thugs."

"Is Nat still here?" Rafe asked.

"I have not heard to the contrary, but then I don't keep up with those sorts."

Alexander looked at Rafe, not believing the unkempt young man was capable of taking on killers, certainly not ones such as Clay Allison's henchmen. Alexander wanted no part in any scheme to murder Nat Holmes nor any blood on his hands for the death of this young man.

"I'll tell you again son, go to the sheriff. Let him handle this. These are dangerous men."

"This is personal Mister Sullivan and I can take care of myself. All I need from you is cover and a way to identify Nat. I'll make him tell me where Kip went. You see, Kip was the leader of the raiders who shot up *don* Lorenzo's fiesta and killed women and children. My wife and unborn child were killed there."

The newspaperman leaned back in his chair shocked at the information. Alexander Sullivan had no moral respect for any of Clay Allison's men. Over the years he reported their crimes, which never seemed to get punished. "What will you do when you find them?"

"I'll take them back to San Gabriel to answer for their crimes." It was one idea, but Rafe knew in his heart he would kill them and leave them for a buzzard's meal.

"Very well, you can work for me cleaning the place up and delivering papers. You can sleep in the back room. I'll make some inquires about Nat Holmes."

CHAPTER 27

George had secured a horse and returned to the fort to wait for the young Army doctor to return. As the day wore on, the waiting became difficult. He had no news of Ana Teresa's condition and could only pray she was still alive. Perhaps all this effort was futile.

Lieutenant Charles Hapwell and the Army regiment rode into the courtyard of Fort Union late in the afternoon. The young doctor looked barely old enough to be in the Army, let alone be a trained doctor. George gave him a few moments to brush the dust from his clothes and to turn the horse over to a private, before he walked toward him.

"Good afternoon, Lieutenant," George greeted him.

"Do I know you?"

"My name is George Summers. I have already discussed a problem with Doctor Spencer. He suggests you are the man I need to see. Can we go to the dispensary and discuss it more with him?"

"Certainly sir."

As they walked to the clinic, the young doctor noticed George walked with a limp and asked about it.

"I took a bullet through the leg that nicked a vein several years ago. I was lucky the doctor in Elizabethtown was able to save the leg."

"Ah, I see you two have met," Doctor Spencer said as they walked in. "Come to the back so we can talk."

As George explained Ana Teresa's condition to Lieutenant Hapwell, he listened intently.

"I have no expertise in something so tricky," he said looking at Doctor Spencer. You are the one who would be best suited for something like that."

"Yes, but as captain, I am supposed to stay at the fort at all times. You know Army regulations." The two doctors argued back and forth for several minutes. Finally, Doctor Spencer relented.

"All right. It has been quiet here lately. You can man

the dispensary and I'll go to San Gabriel," he said to the young doctor. Then he turned to George and said, "I cannot be gone longer than four days, three is better."

George shook his hand profusely. Unfortunately, darkness had overtaken the fort and it was agreed they would leave at first light.

As daylight crept over the eastern sky, George and the captain rode due west to La Cueva, along the La Cueva Canyon, and then into Tres Ritos. A well-used path followed Rio Pueblo, a narrow river running at the bottom Sipapu Peak. Tres Ritos was an ancient place, originally settled by the Pueblo Indians. A small Catholic Church made from adobe stood at the end of the pueblo village.

They had been climbing in altitude for the last hour and through expanses of fir trees and open meadows, where shallow creeks twisted and turned. At one point, the incredible mountain vistas shimmered in the sun.

"Where are we? This is beautiful country," the doctor asked not having traveled in this part of New Mexico.

"New Mexico is richly varied in terrain. In the north, it is graced with the tail end of the Rocky Mountains. The land was originally occupied by Indians, now called the Ancients, long before the Spaniards came, Captain."

"Please call me Regis," he said with an easy grin. "Tell me more about the history of New Mexico. I was born and raised in Pittsburgh, Pennsylvania and know little of this area."

They continued on, following the streams through the canyon lands south of Taos. Regis absorbed the history of New Mexico, asking questions, and trying to understand. It was foreign in many ways, having been raised in the East. All of the history of the United States he learned in school discussed the Pilgrims and the settlements of the original thirteen colonies. He had never learned the rich history of the Southwest and the Spanish influence of New Spain.

It was a long exhausting day's ride into San Gabriel and they arrived late, making the last part of the trip from Truchas in the dark. The closer they got to the town, George's stomach riled in anticipation. He hoped they had not made this trip in vain. When they reached Doctor Roybal's office, a light shone in the window.

George knocked on the door. Captain Spencer stood behind him carrying his medical bag.

"George, it is good to see you, come in," Doctor Roybal greeted him and the man standing behind him.

"Doctor Roybal, this is Captain Regis Spencer. He's a doctor from Fort Union."

"Welcome Doctor Spencer. Come this way. Ana Teresa is in the back." George heaved a sigh of relief. Ana Teresa was alive.

When the curtain opened, Ana Teresa recognized George Summers and gave him a huge grin. Standing with him was a taller man she did not know.

"Ana Teresa, this is Doctor Spencer. He is an Army doctor from Fort Union."

"How are you my dear?" Regis Spencer greeted her. She was a beautiful young woman. Her brown hair curled on the pillow and her golden brown eyes caught the light of the candles. Her extended belly proved she was very pregnant.

"How do you do, Doctor?" she said. "Hopefully you can get this bullet out of my hip so I can walk again."

"I certainly hope so. Let's have a look."

Doctor Roybal stayed with the Army doctor, while George left the room and let them examine Ana Teresa. Finally, they came out. George thought they both looked rather glum. Doctor Roybal led them to his small personal backroom area.

"What's the matter?" George blurted out. The long week of trying to find a specialist and the day's journey to get here had put him at the end of his patience.

"She's obviously strong, but the bullet wound is tricky, even without the baby on the way," Spencer replied.

"We know that," George's voice hinted of exasperation.

"I think the only choice we have is to open her up and then take the baby and the bullet out at the same time. The wound shows a slight bit of infection and Doctor Roybal said she has been feverish on and off the last several days.

We cannot risk a full-fledged infection setting in."

George understood infection. The body would try to fight it, but like his eight-month-old son who got influenza, it could overwhelm the body's natural defenses quickly. His son died within two days. What he did not exactly understand was the doctor's reference to the baby. "What do you mean, take the baby?" George asked.

"It is technically called a surgical birth. The womb is opened and the baby cut out. Sometimes the baby can survive and other times not. I think it is her only chance. I agree with Doctor Roybal, if she goes into labor in her condition, she will die, as will the baby."

"Can you do the surgery?"

"Of course, I'm a trained surgeon, but still it is a tricky operation."

"And what are the chances of success?"

"Probably fifty-fifty, maybe more for the baby. She looks to be late in her eight month. The baby would be slightly premature."

George wished Rafe was here. Only her husband should have to make a decision of this magnitude. "Did you tell her?"

"No, not yet. I wanted to discuss it with you first."

CHAPTER 28

George and the two doctor's returned to Ana Teresa's room. George was the one to explain the risks to her and Doctor Spencer explained the operation.

"I'm ready," she said without hesitation. "Just promise me to save the baby. If it is a boy, name him Rafael Bartolo Reyes, a girl Alicia Marie," she told George.

"We will start in the morning. Get some sleep young lady and don't worry." Doctor Spencer took her hand and squeezed it.

After they left her, Ana Teresa felt relieved. She knew her condition was dire. She had known from the beginning, although Doctor Roybal told her she was fine. All she wanted was for the baby to survive. Someday Rafael would return and that piece of her would be here for him. He would be a wonderful father and their child proof of their love.

George and Doctor Spencer checked into the small hotel in San Gabriel. They agreed to meet in the lobby at seven in the morning.

Early Sunday morning before he met with the doctor, George sent messengers to *don* Lorenzo's and *don* Pedro's hacienda. He left instructions for *don* Pedro to notify Carlos and Josefina. In the messages, he explained about the operation and told them all to come to San Gabriel immediately.

Doctor Roybal prepared an operating table, as such, to the best of his ability. He brought extra lamps to the room and clean towels and bandages. He cleaned and set out his instruments on a table nearby. He had two large pots of water simmering on his stove. By the time George and Doctor Spencer arrived, Roybal thought he was ready.

Spencer looked around and nodded with approval. Roybal was ready to be his assistant.

"Do you have a woman nearby, a midwife perhaps, to assist with the baby?" he asked.

"George, go quickly and ask the desk clerk at the hotel

to send for *Señora* Zamora."

George was happy to have something to do. The waiting and worrying had left him sleepless most of the night. As he left, the doctors went to talk to Ana Teresa. They explained to her how Doctor Roybal would pump a gas into her nose. The gas would make her sleepy.

"Will it hurt the baby?" she asked.

"No, the baby will be safe."

"I'm ready doctor." Doctor Spencer was touched by the young woman's quiet resolve. Her lovely golden brown eyes smiled at him.

"All right. Let us say a prayer, " Doctor Roybal said.

After the prayer, the doctors carefully moved her to the bed in the front room, which had been prepared for the operation.

"Where is George?" she asked. "I need to tell him something before you start."

The messenger arrived at the de Soto hacienda around nine in the morning. *Don* Pedro quickly went to tell his wife, Agustina, they were not attending Mass this morning, but to get ready to go to San Gabriel. Quickly, he had a horse saddled and rode to Carlos and Bibiana's home, a short distance away.

"I'll ride to the Summers, while you take Bibiana and Agustina in the carriage," Carlos insisted after he read the message. *Don* Pedro agreed. "Hurry Bibiana. Get Benicío ready and your mother will be ready when we get to the hacienda."

Carlos quickly saddled his black stallion, Santiago. His mind swirled with thoughts of the pending operation and with Rafe. He should be here. Carlos felt guilty he had not disobeyed his wife's demands and gone to E-town to find him. He rode at a gallop and reached the Summers' ranch around ten-thirty.

"The family left only a short time ago. They are headed to church," Esteban told him as he rode into the courtyard.

"*Gracias* Esteban. I will find them."

Carlos whirled the horse around and rode hard down

the road toward Santa Fe. The sleek black stallion responded to Carlos' urging.

"Mother, there's someone coming up fast behind us," Lizzy said to her mother. Lolo was driving the buggy at a good clip. "Perhaps it is Rafe!" she said excitedly.

Lizzy never stopped believing Rafe would one day ride home to them. She prayed every day, sometimes several times, to bring her adopted brother back.

Lolo eased up on the reins and Carlos quickly closed the gap between them.

"Carlos! What is the matter? Is it Rafe?"

"No, it is Ana Teresa," he replied. Relaying the message, Josefina instructed Lolo to turn the buggy around and they followed Carlos to San Gabriel.

When George returned to Doctor Roybal's office, Ana Teresa asked for a few minutes alone with him.

"George, I know the risks today. You must tell Rafael how much I love him. Tell him the baby is my gift to him."

Tears welled in George's eyes and he could not stop them. "Ana Teresa, you are going to tell him yourself. God will see us through this day."

"God has his own plans. It will be his will, not ours. Promise me you will keep the baby and raise it as your own until Rafael returns."

George noticed her eyes were clear and looked more joyous than scared. He had never noticed how the gold glinted in them as the light caught her face.

"I promise." They held hands for a few moments, then George called out to the doctors, "She's ready."

Just as Doctor Roybal was administering the first dose of nitrous oxide, a knock sounded at the door. *Don* Lorenzo, his wife, and Marcella stood nervously and Marcella rushed to her daughter's side. George tried to explain who they were to Doctor Spencer.

"They must leave. I need complete quiet," Spencer said with a tone of authority, yet with compassion. "Only let in the midwife, George. Tell the others to stay downstairs or at the cafe."

George sent the family to the cafe and stood as a guard outside the door. A few minutes later, an older woman climbed the stairs. George let her in. It seemed hours, although not that long before he heard a newborn baby's wail. A rush of breath, which seemed to come deep from his soul, escaped his lungs. The baby wailed again.

"God be praised," he said under his breath.

A little while later, *don* Pedro's carriage drove up the street. Bibiana, her mother, and the baby sat inside. George walked down the steps to meet them.

"You will have to wait in the cafe with *don* Lorenzo. They are in the middle of the operation. The baby has been born."

"Gracias a Dios," Agustina crossed herself and kissed her thumb.

"That is all I know at this time. Where is Carlos?"

"He left to find Josefina and your daughters. I'm sure they will be here soon."

George resumed his guard duty as *don* Pedro turned the carriage around and drove down the street to the cafe.

"Lolo drive faster," her younger sister urged.

"No. We will get there when we get there. Lolo is pushing the horse as fast as she should," Josefina responded.

"But mother, Ana Teresa needs us."

"What she needs is our prayers, *mija.*"

George spotted Carlos riding ahead of a buggy about a half hour later. He walked to the street to greet them.

"How is she?"

"I don't know. You need to wait at the cafe," George told them.

"I'll stay here. You go to the cafe," Carlos replied.

Chapter 29

"There, I see the bullet," Doctor Spencer said. "Give her more gas. The baby is out of danger and I need to make sure she won't move," he ordered Roybal.

The midwife had tied the cord and washed the baby boy. He was smaller than many, but seemed to possess everything in good order. He had a cap of unruly dark hair. His tiny fingers and toes wiggled. She wrapped him after the bath and cuddled him while the doctors worked on the mother.

Doctor Roybal pumped more gas into Ana Teresa's mouth and listened to her heart. Her breathing was shallow, but steady.

Doctor Spencer had removed several small bone fragments from the wound as he probed. The main part of the hip socket was intact. The bullet was lodged between the sacral canal and the tailbone. It was a precarious place, so close to the tip of the spinal column. Pushing it further as he probed might possibly paralyze her. He stopped for a minute and wiped his brow.

"What's wrong?"

"Just a bit of nerves. You were right not to move her."

"What can I do?"

"Hold a lamp closer. I need as much light as possible," he responded.

The two doctors worked in unison. Very carefully Doctor Spencer probed for the bullet near the tailbone. She was bleeding profusely from the afterbirth and the incisions. Every time Doctor Spencer wanted to make a move, blood seeped and obscured his view.

"Pinch off that vein," he ordered Roybal.

Finally, his clamp reached the lead slug. He pulled ever so slightly, but it did not move. He pulled harder and finally it backed out of the hole it made. Two more seconds and the bullet was completely free. He dropped it into a metal dish with a clink.

"Now give me as much light as you can while I close the wound." He carefully cleaned any inflamed tissue and closed the wound with sutures. Doctor Roybal checked her steady breathing. When Doctor Spencer was done, he took a deep breath and went to wash his hands.

"The next twenty-four hours are critical. We must pray the wound does not get infected."

"Do you think she'll walk again?"

"Certainly. The hip joint is fine. If she lives, she'll walk."

Doctor Roybal opened the door and found Carlos waiting.

"Go tell the family the baby boy is healthy and the operation went well," Doctor Roybal explained.

Sunday night Rafe woke from a dream soaked to his skin. At first, his surroundings were foreign and he fought to regain his senses. He was in a small, dark room with no window. It could be midnight or noon, he did not know which.

The effects of the nightmare subsided, leaving him only with the feelings of vengeance in his soul. He had two more souls to send to the depths of hell, Nat and Kip. Hopefully, Nat was still in Cimarron. However, Cimarron was not E-town. There was a sheriff and law in the town, although Mister Sullivan warned him it was also a dangerous town and had weathered more than the typical run of outlaws.

Clay Allison owned a large ranch north of town. Sullivan said the outlaw came last fall with a wife and settled into what appeared to be a normal life. Then in early January, he killed a gunslinger named Chunk Colbert in the Clifton House. Sullivan showed Rafe several newspaper articles he had written about the incident. People were divided about whether Clay was guilty of murder or had rid Cimarron of a dangerous criminal. Clay was acquitted.

CHAPTER 30

Monday morning Alexander Sullivan came to the shop earlier than usual. Rafe's dilemma put him in a quandary. He knew the callous Allison gang had gotten away with murder in the past, but abetting Rafe in his task to waylay Nat Homes left him troubled. Rafe was only one man against the ruthless gang.

"Good morning Mister Sullivan," Rafe greeted him. He worked hard to keep his demeanor friendly and calm. The dream came again last night, a bit different, but the dream only fueled the fire in his belly for vengeance.

"I want you to go the sheriff about this matter. You can't go up against the Allison gang by yourself. It is foolish of you to think you can," Sullivan warned Rafe.

"I appreciate your concern Mister Sullivan. I assure you I will not go directly at Nat. I only want to find a way to get him alone. I have to know where Kip has gone. He is the leader of the raiders who killed my wife. I need Nat to lead me to him."

"You understand I am a man of reputation here in Cimarron. I cannot get involved personally in this matter. I will help you, but you must promise to keep me above any suspicion."

"Yes sir. I understand and give you my promise. Anything that happens will not involve you in any way."

For two days, Rafe had worked at the Sullivan print shop, sweeping floors, carrying paper and supplies to the printers, and setting type. He was keeping close and not making his face known in town. He was thankful for the few days of rest, as his ribs still stung when he picked up the heavy paper bundles.

On the third morning, Alexander Sullivan took Rafe on the wagon to deliver stacks of newspapers to the mercantile, several saloons, and the hotels in Cimarron. When they got to the Lambert Inn, Sullivan introduced Rafe to Henri Lambert, the owner of the establishment.

"Henri, I'd like you to meet Rafe Reyes. He's helping me for a few weeks," Alexander said when he greeted Henri.

"Glad to know you. Stack those papers at the corner of the bar," Henri said in a slight French accent.

As Henri and Alexander talked, Rafe carried bundles of newspapers and stacked them as he was told. As he did, he scanned the room. The long bar reflected the light from constant waxing. Behind the bar, a huge mirror was graced by ornate wooden pillars. The dark mahogany of the pillars reached the stamped metal ceiling. Tables around the restaurant part of the room were covered in white tablecloths and set with dishes and cut glass. Even the Palacio Cantina in Santa Fe was not this elegant.

It was just before noon and only a few cowboys leaned at the far end of the bar. Rafe walked back to where Alexander and Lambert were talking.

"You have a very nice place here Mister Lambert," Rafe commented.

"Best restaurant and hotel in New Mexico. You must come and eat here while you are in town."

"I will do that," Rafe said.

"See you later Henri." Alexander tipped his hat.

"Good to meet you Rafe," Henri called to them as they walked out.

Alexander led Rafe out the door and back to the wagon. "Believe it or not, Henri was the personal chef to President Lincoln and then later for General Ulysses S. Grant. He came west looking for gold after the Civil War and tried his hand at mining in Elizabethtown. When that failed, he opened a saloon in E-town. Several years ago, the Maxwell Company enticed him to come to Cimarron and open this place. Henri has rued his decision at times."

"Why?" Rafe asked.

"The Lambert Inn has a reputation of violence. I've done a number of headlines about who was shot at Lambert's last night. People in town ask each other every morning, "Who was killed at Lambert's last night or say Lambert had himself another man for breakfast," Alexander said.

"I would not expect that at such a fine place," Rafe said remembering the large mirror and bar and the white tablecloths.

"I'll tell you, Clay Allison's men hang out there and there is where you will find Nat Holmes. You need to be careful, but especially if you go there at night. They don't like strangers much and definitely don't like Mexicans," Alexander warned him.

"I understand and I appreciate your help. How can I find out what Nat looks like?" Rafe asked.

"We will come back later and see if he is here. Albert, the printer, told me Nat is smitten with a saloon girl named Gloria."

They finished delivering the morning's papers and returned to the print shop. "You clean up the shop and wait till I get back." Sullivan told him.

As Rafe cleaned the shop, he pondered about how he would approach Nat Holmes. His rage tempered over the last two weeks, and although he still wanted his revenge, he did not want to die. Besides, he made a promise to Alexander.

He needed to take Nat Holmes alive, at least long enough to find out the whereabouts of Kip Donohoe. He thought about using the marshal's badge trick, just as he arrested the young squatters in San Gabriel. However, Cimarron had a sheriff and Nat might not be as gullible.

Alexander wanted him to go to the sheriff. "Let him handle Nat," Alexander told him several times, but Rafe wanted Nat alive and talking. It was the only way to find Kip. If what Alexander told him about the Lambert Inn being a rough place where men were killed nightly, he could get killed just trying to get close to Nat. A better plan might be to study Nat's habits and get him when he was away from the saloon, however that might take days or weeks. They were precious days Kip Donohoe would be further from his grasp.

His mind wandered to other ideas. He could stalk Nat at the Lambert, and draw him into a gunfight. He would try to get him talking about Kip before he killed him. If what

Alexander told him about the Lambert Inn was correct, the gunfight would be just one of many. No one would care as long as Nat drew first. Even if he killed Nat in a draw, he wondered whether Alexander would turn him over to the sheriff and just how far Alexander's friendship would go.

Each plan had questions and drawbacks. Cimarron was not familiar turf and he had only one friend in town, Alexander Sullivan. Rafe appreciated Alexander's help, but people would now connect Rafe to Alexander. People like Henri Lambert and it might bring trouble to Alexander's door.

It was getting near sundown and Rafe was waiting for Alexander to return when he heard gunfire. Peeking out the front window, he saw five men on horseback shooting up into the air and at buildings. It reminded him of the Sutton Texas cowboys shooting up San Marcial. Rafe wondered if one of the men was Nat Holmes. As quickly as the gunfire started, it stopped. Rafe stuffed one of his pistols under his shirt, went out and locked the door behind him.

Music and shouting blasted out of the several saloons and the Lambert Inn down the street. Rafe presumed the desperados who shot up the street had gone inside and started drinking.

"Hey! Told you to stay inside. Those boys might have shot at you," Alexander told Rafe as he rode up.

"I stayed inside until the gunfire stopped. Who is that gang?"

"Probably from the Triple Bar X. They're the rowdiest bunch, mostly Texans. Help me get the afternoon papers loaded."

Rafe loaded the wagon with the papers finished by the printer. He put his pistol back in a drawer. So far, he had not worn his guns when in town. To the public, he was simply a Mexican errand boy.

"Hop in. We'll deliver these and then we'll go see what's happening at the Lambert," Alexander told him.

A noticeable change in the atmosphere of the saloons was evident. While it was quiet and subdued this morning, now the tables were full and music filled the air. Painted up saloon girls worked the floor. Cowboys and locals sat playing poker at many tables and each saloon had a roulette wheel and Faro tables.

As Alexander and Rafe approached the Lambert Inn, Sullivan took his time tethering the horse. "Rafe, stick close to me. Do not go off on your own. You will be safe as long as you stay with me. If Nat is in there and I point him out, do not, and I mean it, do not go after him. You will be dead before you get to him," he warned Rafe sternly.

Rafe nodded in agreement and followed Alexander into the Lambert. He found them a spot at the bar and ordered two beers. "Alexander, what brings you here at this late hour?" Henri spoke out as he approached the bar.

"Hello Henri. I'm showing young Rafe where not to go after dark." The two men chuckled.

"Alexander is right about that young man. Someone will die of gunfire before sunup. You can count on it."

"What about the law here?" Rafe asked, acting naive.

"Ha! Clay Allison is the real law around here. He's pretending to be a rancher, but he has his finger in everything. Keep your hat low. There'll be a lot of his cohorts here and they do not like Mexicans. You could be the dead one before sunup. Take my advice and do not come here alone. Isn't that so, Alexander?"

"Henri is right, Rafe. I only brought you here to see for yourself."

Henri left them at the bar to attend to several other guests. The saloon was packed with men, mostly Texas cowboys. Rafe could tell by the way they dressed with overly large bandanas and tall cowboys hats. Waiters with plates of food circulated the room.

"Compliments of Henri," the waiter told them setting two plates in front of Alexander and Rafe.

"Dig in. Henri is an excellent chef," Alexander said.

The plate held a fillet of trout, with green beans and potatoes. It was covered with a thin, slightly tangy sauce. It was the best meal Rafe tasted in a long time.

A singer took the stage while they ate. Her voice was loud and the song rowdy. The cowboys began to yell and whistle. She worked the room and men threw coins her way. A young girl quickly snatched the money off the floor.

Alexander nudged Rafe. "Over there. Look at the table near the end of the bar. See the girl, the one in the green and black lace dress and bulging bosom. Her name is Gloria and she just sat down on Nat Holmes' lap."

Rafe could not tell how tall the man was. All he saw was a man wearing a black leather vest over a light blue long-sleeved shirt and denim trousers. He had on a well-worn black Stetson. Long stringy brown hair curled out from under it. Rafe could only see the right side of his face. He had a shaggy reddish mustache and a small beard. It was enough for Rafe to recognize, if he saw him again.

While he watched, Nat pawed Gloria, although she seemed to like it. Several times he pawed at her breasts and kissed her roughly. She only pushed his hand away when he reached under her skirt. However, she laughed as she pushed it away.

As Rafe studied his prey, gunfire erupted from the far side of the room. The shots disrupted the noisy room and heads ducked low. Rafe saw a cowboy with a smoking pistol in hand looking down on whoever he shot. He pulled up his pistol and waved it, daring anyone to challenge him. No one made a move, so he holstered his pistol and sat down to continue the poker game.

"See what I mean?" Alexander said.

CHAPTER 31

Rafe was haunted by the dreams. Often he wakened in a sweat, only to fall back again into the dream.

Each dream started peacefully. He saw Ana Teresa's smiling face and other times he saw blurry images of gray floating beings. It felt like the most peaceful place he had ever known.

Then suddenly he was being torn apart. Blood covered him from head to toe, dripping, dripping. His peaceful place was shattered before his eyes. He wanted to fight, but was helpless. All he could do was wail.

Out of the blood he would find himself holding a baby in his arms. It was so tiny and helpless. It had a swath of dark hair. He knew he was holding his baby. His son. The baby looked peaceful, quiet. He touched the baby's face and stroked his tender cheek. The baby opened his eyes and his face transformed into a hideous face. It was twisted and angry. Sometimes the face was Jesse Kincaid's. Last night the face was Nat Holmes.

It was everything Rafe could do to control his temper. Around the print shop, he assumed a courteous and helpful disposition, while inside he seethed. Nat Holmes and Kip Donohoe were constantly on his mind.

Two days later, Rafe drove the wagon to the front of the printing office and unloaded two stacks of fresh paper. He was on his way out the door to pull the wagon to the back when a young woman almost ran into him. She was dressed in a simple spring flower patterned dress and a flat brim straw hat tied under her chin with a red ribbon.

"Uh, uh . . . excuse me," she said holding on to Rafe's arms so she would not fall.

"I'm sorry, Miss. I didn't see you coming," Rafe apologized.

"Who are you and where is my father?"

"My name is Rafe Reyes. Who is your father?"

"Mister Sullivan. He owns this shop."

Rafe was surprised, as Alexander never told him he had a daughter. In fact he knew nothing of Alexander's family.

"Oh, he is out making his rounds. I guess he is looking for news and getting advertisers."

"Well, my name is Nellie Sullivan. My father didn't tell us he hired another man."

"Pleased to meet you, Miss. Your father was kind enough to put me on and I am very grateful for his help." Rafe slightly bowed to her as he explained her father's kindness.

Nellie took another look at the well-spoken young man. He was tall and tanned, with black hair and melting dark brown eyes. He was clean-shaven and although dressed in working clothes, he was not the typical cowboy lout who used Cimarron as their playground. Her heart skipped a beat and she tried hard not to show it.

She stood for several seconds staring at Rafe. "Uh, oh please tell my father I will be at the mercantile and that I need a ride home."

"I don't know when he will be back. I would be happy to drive you home," Rafe quickly responded, but did not know why he said it.

The young woman was beautiful. Her deep blue eyes and pink rosy cheeks reminded him of a clear fresh spring day. The hair trailing out from under her hat was deep reddish blond. After offering her a ride, he became awkward and shifted from foot to foot.

"If my father is not back, you may drive me home. I have some shopping to finish first." Nellie Sullivan turned and walked out the print shop door, leaving Rafe staring at her back.

As she left, Rafe shook his head wanting to erase the image out of his mind. Her beauty momentarily stunned him and his heart skipped a beat. Distracted from the sudden interaction, he tried to keep himself busy around the print shop.

"What's wrong with you boy?" Dan the printer called out to Rafe and laughed. Dan had seen the encounter between Rafe and Nellie.

"Wha . . . what . . do you mean?" It was all Rafe could reply.

"She's a pretty little gal, ain't she? I don't blame you getting all flustered. Gotta tell you, Alexander's very protective of her," Dan continued.

"I can see why."

"Yeah, you're right about that," Dan agreed.

Rafe shook Nellie from his mind. He had no future here. His only future was killing and Nellie Sullivan deserved better than that. Rafe forced himself to focus on Nat Holmes. Over the last several days, Alexander allowed him to make the deliveries on his own. He had been keeping a sharp eye out for Nat or his girlfriend Gloria. He spotted her several times in the Lambert Inn, always later in the day when he delivered the evening papers. He had heeded Alexander's warnings and did not go to the Lambert at night alone.

Later this afternoon, he planned on being near the Lambert about the time when Gloria came to town. He wanted to see what direction she came from. He stacked the fresh paper for Dan and began to sweep the back room. It needed swept often as the paper created lint, which was bad for the printing press, or so Alexander told him.

After noon, Nellie returned with her arms full of packages. "Is my father back yet?' she asked after she placed the packages on the front desk.

"Not yet," Dan told her.

Rafe came out from the back and nodded a hello at her.

"Rafe, would you be kind enough to drive me home?"

"Ah . . . yes, certainly."

She started to gather the packages, but Rafe went and took them from her and led the way to the wagon. He held her elbow to help her up to the seat, then climbed up beside her. He snapped the reins and barked, "Giddy up," to the horse.

"Tell me how to get to your house."

Instead of replying, she asked him a question. "I've been thinking about you. Have you ever been in Santa Fe?"

Rafe visibly recoiled a bit from the question. Why was she asking? Bill Moore told him Alexander Sullivan lived a brief time in Santa Fe before he moved to Cimarron or perhaps she saw his picture in the newspaper when he was facing the charge of murdering Diego de la Torre. He felt he had to lie to her. "I grew up in Albuquerque."

"Oh, I figured you came from a large town. You speak very good English," she complimented him.

"Thank you. I was taught by a man I worked for. He was from Boston."

Nellie sensed Rafe was nervous answering her questions. He was definitely Hispanic. His darker skin and features were a testament to his heritage. His English, however, was impeccable, better than most anyone outside of her family and a few others in town, like the mayor.

His face was lean and tan. He usually had a melancholy expression, but once he smiled at her and his dark brown eyes glittered. He was tall, maybe six feet, with broad shoulders. The cowboys in town disgusted her and the only real marriage prospect in Cimarron was Jack Borden. Jack was a rancher's son, polite, but certainly did not light her heart with fire.

"What did you do before you came to Cimarron?" she asked.

"Oh, I've had several jobs. I've worked in a foundry and helped in a horse breeder's barn. Last summer I helped a friend track down some cattle rustlers. I guess you would say I've done all types of jobs." Rafe's brain could not make lies quick enough, so he used whatever he could to appease her question.

"There, turn right. My house is just over that rise."

Rafe turned and followed the Cimarron River past several houses until they came to a place where the river made a right turn. She pointed to a modest white house facing the passing river.

"You can tether the horse there," she said pointing to a single pole to the right of the house. "Please help me take my packages in."

Rafe gathered the packages and followed Nellie into the house.

"Mother," she called out when they entered. A

beautiful woman dressed in a neck high beige dress came out from the parlor. "Who is this, Nellie?"

"Mom, this is Rafe Reyes. He works for Dad and was kind enough to drive me home."

"Welcome to our home, Rafe."

"Thank you kindly, Missus Sullivan."

"Nellie, there is fresh tea in the kitchen. Go fetch some for Rafe. I'm sure you two are thirsty." Missus Sullivan showed Rafe a table to deposit the packages and then took his arm.

"When did you start working for my husband?" she asked.

"I was on my way to Pueblo, Colorado, last week and stopped to give him a message from Bill Moore. Mister Sullivan, I mean your husband, gave me a job to clean up the shop and deliver papers. I won't be here too long."

"Well you are welcome. We so seldom get visitors."

"Here Rafe, come sit with me on the veranda." Nellie brought a tray with a small pitcher of tea and two glasses. Rafe took the tray from her. He was feeling deceitful and his nerves were on edge. Taking a few deep breaths, he followed Nellie to a table and chairs. In his mind, he just wanted to focus on Nat Holmes, not make up lies to Nellie Sullivan.

CHAPTER 32

Doctor Spencer left town the day after the surgery. Ana Teresa thanked him profusely and promised to send Rafael to give personal thanks when he came home.

"It was my pleasure, my dear. I will remember this trip always," he told her.

He also refused any payment from George. "It was a nice break from my duties at the fort. Besides, it has been a long time since I was able to deliver a baby and save a life at the same time," he said. George shook the doctor's hand heartily.

Doctor Roybal tended the surgical wound twice a day, making sure it did not get infected. *Señora* Lovato came and helped Ana Teresa with the baby, as did her mother who continued to live at *don* Lorenzo's hacienda.

A week later, Ana Teresa sat in a carriage wrapped in a blanket for the ride back to Santa Fe. Her mother held a tiny bundle in her arms, well protected from the breezy spring air. It had been over a week since the operation, which saved her life and the life of the baby. Her joy was overwhelming, except Rafael had not been found.

Spring had come to the Santa Fe valley and Easter had already been celebrated while Ana Teresa languished in the back room of Doctor Roybal's office. She still had some pain and walking was extremely difficult, but she was going home.

When they arrived at the Summers' ranch, the family, including Carlos and Bibiana, spilled from the front doors. Josefina and the girls had made one bedroom ready for her mother and another for Ana Teresa and the baby. It had been decided she would stay at the Summers' home until she was stronger or until Rafe returned.

"*Hola*, welcome home," several voices called out in unison. As the family encircled her, cries of joy and happiness abounded.

"Lolo, take the baby. George, help them down," Josefina ordered taking charge. Marcella handed the tiny bundle to Lolo, then stepped down from the carriage. Carefully George and Carlos carried Ana Teresa from the carriage seat, up the steps and into the house.

"I need to rest," Ana Teresa told everyone. "I'm exhausted from the trip." Carlos swept her into his arms and carried her to the upstairs bedroom. When he placed her on the bed, she turned to him and caught his arm. "Carlos. Where is Rafael? Have you not heard anything?"

"You know he thinks you are dead?"

"Yes, but why has he not come home?"

"He could be anywhere. I need to talk to George about him. Now that you are home, we need to find him. Don't worry, just rest," Carlos told her.

Carlos found George in the parlor, while all the women had gone to the kitchen with the baby. Carlos had not seen George since the day they all waited for the outcome of the operation. His teaching job kept him busy and he expected George was equally as busy catching up on orders at the foundry.

"George, we need to find Rafe," Carlos insisted. George nodded as a reply. "What can we do? Hire a detective?" Carlos asked.

"I've been thinking on it for several days. My prayers for him to come home by himself have not been answered."

"Nor mine, but Bibiana is right that I cannot go riding off helter-skelter looking for him. We have to have a plan or at least an idea where he might have gone," Carlos replied.

"We know he was bent on seeking revenge on the masked raiders. Two of them were caught and are sitting in jail in San Gabriel, but the sheriff has heard nothing about Rafe."

"I think he went to E-town. Remember I told you one of those two identified a man named Kip Donohoe and said he went to Elizabethtown," Carlos said.

"And *don* Pedro asked the sheriff to wire E-town and the lines are not working," George replied. "I wish I had known. Elizabethtown is very near Fort Union. I could have stopped there when I was fetching Doctor Spencer."

"Is Bill Moore still in Elizabethtown? How can we

reach him?"

George walked to his desk and pulled out a sheet of paper. "Let's make a list of everyone we can think of, anyone or anywhere he might have gone. If we cannot send a wire, then we'll send a letter."

For the next hour, George and Carlos discussed people to contact. Big Ed Seeley, in San Marcial, Bill Moore in E-town, Rafe's uncle in El Paso. "And the padre at the mission there," George said.

"Certainly. What about some of the people you and he sell guns to? John Grady in Albuquerque, the sheriff in Las Vegas, and Chief Letoc?" Carlos reminded him.

"What about people in Mexico? We need to write his mother and sister," George said. It was a long shot, but he might be prone to going to see his family at the hacienda in Torreón.

"Don't forget the banker in El Paso. Rafe's letter said to send money there," Carlos added.

In the end, the list contained twenty-two names. George and Carlos split the list and agreed to begin a written campaign to find Rafe. If telegraphs were available they would send a telegram, otherwise they would write letters. They both seemed satisfied with the plan.

Later that evening, the entire family stood around the large Spanish table in the Summers' dining room. George gave the blessing, praising God for returning Ana Teresa and giving thanks and welcoming the baby, Rafael Bartolo Reyes, to the family. His last prayer asked God for Rafe's safe return. Everyone said "Amen."

CHAPTER 33

For three afternoons, Rafe drove the print shop wagon to scout the area around Cimarron, watching for Nat Holmes. Pretending to be working for Alexander was good cover. Yesterday, Rafe saw Nat riding back to the Lambert Inn from the northeast. Alexander told Rafe he heard Nat was looking at buying a small ranch near French Lake. It was enough for Rafe to go on and it was time to make his move.

Nellie Sullivan came again to the print shop and asked Rafe to drive her home. Rafe sensed her interest in him and he found her beautiful and intelligent. Dan the printer teased him about it. They knew nothing of his broken and vengeful heart. Rafe needed to move on, and felt bad he would disappoint Nellie.

He slept fitfully that night anticipating the next day and worried the dream would haunt him. One of the sleepless hours, he wrote a letter to Alexander Sullivan thanking him for his help. He added at the end, "If I die, contact Bill Moore. He will know what to do."

When he closed his eyes, he could picture Ana Teresa's face. It was a face he would never see again. Life had been cruel and now he was ready to follow life's path and seek revenge. He tried hard not to think about the consequences, whatever they might be in this life, or when God assessed him. Rafe packed his gear and left before daylight. He left the letter inside Alexander's desk drawer.

Later that morning, Rafe tethered the gelding in a patch of cottonwood trees not far from a trail to French Lake. After he ate a cold breakfast, he checked his weapons. He was dressed in his gray suit. The U.S. Marshal badge was pinned on his lapel. The short-barrel shotgun nested in the arrow quiver slung over his back. His double-action pistols were holstered around his waist. The Bowie knife Lefty gave him was stuck down his boot. He adjusted the black Stetson lower, to cover his eyes, then patiently waited for Nat Holmes to come by.

Several scenarios ran through Rafe's mind on how to get Nat to tell him where to find Kip Donohoe. What he did not want to happen was a shootout before he got the information. The hours wore on slowly as the sun rose high in the sky. Finally, his thoughts were interrupted when he saw two people on horseback riding his way. A woman was riding along with Nat.

He had not considered this situation. The woman was no doubt the saloon girl, Gloria. Although she was not a threat, she made this encounter more difficult. She was innocent of Nat's wrongdoings and Rafe would not hurt her.

He pondered for several minutes as he watched them approach. For Rafe, this could not wait. He rode up to them with a pistol in hand.

"Nat Holmes?"

"Yeah, who the fuck r yew?" Nat's eyes focused on the pistol pointed at him. The unfamiliar man, wearing a gray suit, wore a badge. Nat could not see the man's face in the shadows of the trees and the man's black Stetson was purposely covering his eyes.

"I'm Ricardo Gonzalez, a U.S. Marshal from Santa Fe. You are under arrest for the murder of women and children in San Gabriel."

"What's he talking about Nat?" Gloria asked alarmed. She knew Nat was not an angel, but killing women and children seemed impossible.

"This man is full of shit. I did'n kill no women an childrn," Nat lied to her.

"Ma'am, you have nothing to do with this. I'm taking this man to Santa Fe to stand trial for his crimes. You may go," Rafe told her sternly. He deliberately wanted her to think he was headed to Santa Fe.

"Gloria, go and get Clay!" Nat commanded. "Get him back here quick."

Gloria turned her horse and rode back the direction they came. She spurred her horse to a gallop heading to Cimarron.

"Unbuckle your gunbelt and hold it by the buckle, then hand it to me with your left hand," Rafe told him. "Don't try anything foolish. I would like nothing better than shooting you on the spot and saving me the trouble of getting you to Santa Fe," Rafe warned him.

"Now ride, that way," Rafe told him pointing toward the east side of the lake.

"Hey, yew said we was goin ta Santa Fe. It's thataway." Nat pointed west.

"You just go where I'm telling you."

"Yew ain't gonna git far before Clay and his men cum fer me. They'll make yew pay fer this," Nat said trying to scare Rafe.

Gloria rode quickly back to Cimarron. She rode directly to the Lambert Inn. Breathless, she found Ben Matthews and told him what had happened to Nat.

"I'm telling yew, it was a U.S. Marshal," she repeated. "Yew gotta git Clay and some men and go after em. He said he was taking Nat to Santa Fe to stand trial for killing women and children someplace." Gloria could not remember the name of the town the marshal said, but she clearly remembered Santa Fe.

"I ain't heard of no marshal around these parts. If I get Clay and this is some kind of a hoax, there will be hell to pay," Ben said.

"Please Ben. Yew gotta git Clay and a bunch of men and go after em," Gloria whined.

Ben Matthews rode into Clay Allison's ranch within the hour after Gloria found him in town at the Lambert Inn. Ben believed Gloria's story, even if it made little sense. Nat was no angel and possibly there was a warrant for his arrest.

"The law's got Nat. Gloria and Nat were headed to French Lake and a lawman arrested Nat," Ben told Clay after he found him in the barn.

"What for?"

"It was a U.S. Marshal from Santa Fe. He arrested Nat, saying Nat killed women and children, and he was taking im to Santa Fe for trial. He let Gloria go."

Clay nodded at the news. Kip Donohoe told him about the ruckus in San Gabriel, and how it got out of hand after some of the greasers were armed and fired back.

"That's his problem. He probably deserves what he gets."

Ben momentarily looked at Clay with a questioning look. Clay was not a man to back down. He kept control over his gang by protecting them from the law and eliminating the lawmen when necessary.

Clay wanted little to do with either Kip or Nat, but people in Cimarron looked to him for protection. Responding to Ben, Clay knew it was his reputation he was protecting, not Nat Holmes.

"Where is that marshal now?" Clay asked.

"I don't know. Gloria said he is taking Nat back to Santa Fe. She left em near French Lake."

Clay let out a sigh. The last thing he wanted was a wild goose chase after Nat Holmes and a U.S. Marshal, but he had no choice. It was important the gang believed he was in charge.

"Let's go. Round up the boys and meet me on the road south of town as soon as yew can."

Ben whirled his horse around and headed back to town. Clay stuck the pitchfork he held in his hand into a pile of straw. After saddling his horse, he headed to the house to find his wife.

"Dora," he called several times.

"Yes?" he finally heard her voice from the upstairs.

"I've got to go out fer a while. I might be late."

Clay grabbed a jacket and mounted his horse. About forty minutes later, he met up with Ben Mathews and seven other men. Clay led them southwest toward the trail to Taos, as it was the most direct route to Santa Fe.

CHAPTER 34

Rafe pushed Nat east around French Lake keeping a pistol pointed on him. He found Ponil Creek and followed it. The dense trees along the creek gave him cover and shade from the bright sun.

"Yew ain't no U.S. Marshal," Nat complained. "Who the fuck r yew?"

"Shut up and keep riding," Rafe replied.

Finally after several hours, the creek fed into the larger Cimarron River. Rafe followed the river until long shadows began to cover the river valley. He found a wide spot lined by shrub and tall cottonwood trees. Rafe figured they were some fifteen to twenty miles from Cimarron and it was complete wilderness.

Along the trip, Rafe practically shook from anticipation. His hatred for the man riding near him grew with each mile. It might have been a bullet from Nat's gun, which killed his wife and child, or not. He wondered if it mattered. Others at the fiesta were killed and injured, no doubt by Nat's involvement.

His brain toyed with ways to kill him. Shooting him as he did Jesse Kincaid seemed too easy and did not appease his rage. He wanted Nat to suffer, but not until Nat told him where to find Kip.

A little while later, they reached a treed grove near the river and Rafe barked at Nat to stop.

"Dismount here," Rafe told him. Rafe always had his pistol pointed at Nat. He would take no chances. Nat was nervous and shaky, but still belligerent.

"Yer a dead man when Clay finds yew," Nat whined.

"Up against that tree," Rafe ordered and pushed Nat. He tied Nat's hands behind the tree, and then tied his legs, just above the ankles to the tree.

It was the first time Nat Holmes got a good look at the man in the gray suit and black Stetson. His tan skin and dark eyes met Nat's. Nat realized the man was a Mexican. He was probably one of the greasers from San Gabriel.

"Yer not gonna git away with this yew fuckin greaser. Yew ain't no fuckin law. Clay will find yew and kill yew," he growled at Rafe.

"You are right about that. I am not the law, too bad for you. You and your gang killed my wife and unborn child."

"I did'n kill no woman or kid. Yew plum crazy. I dun even know what yew talkin bout."

"You remember Nat. You and your gang rode into a wedding fiesta in San Gabriel. You wore red hoods. You shot up the place killing innocent people."

Rafe saw the flicker in Nat's eyes. He remembered all right. Nat twisted in the tight ropes.

Rafe pulled out the Bowie knife and stuck it into the tree next to Nat's right ear. Then he got close to Nat's face and snarled, "I'm going to cut your balls off and make you eat them. Next, I'm going to cut your ears off, before I start to whittle away other parts of you." He could smell Nat's rotten whiskey breath.

"Why dun yew shoot me an git it over with yew fuckin crazy Mescan?" Nat sneered.

"No, I want to see you suffer and cry for your life. You can scream as loud as you want out here. No one will hear you. Why did you raid the fiesta in San Gabriel?"

"It wern't my doin, I juss went along," Nat lied.

"What? I was told by Jerome Westfield in San Gabriel, you were the leader of the raiders. Was he lying?" Rafe got close and spit the words into Nat's face in a harsh voice.

"Yeah, he lied. I was not the leader."

"Who was the leader?" Rafe asked still face to face with Nat.

"I cain't tell yew. He'll kill me."

"I don't think that's your problem right now." Rafe took the large knife from the tree and tested the sharpness of the blade on his finger.

"All right. All right. It was Kip Donohoe. He was the leader. He asked me and Jesse to ride along. He took sum of em squatters along, but they was juss boys."

"Where can I find Kip?" Rafe asked, wanting to test Nat.

"He's usually at the Lambert Inn. Take me thar and I'll point im out ta yew," Nat lied, hoping the dumb greaser would fall for it. Clay and his friends would take care of this greaser, if only Nat could get him back to Cimarron.

"You're lying Nat. I was told Kip left Cimarron." Rafe took the knife and cut Nat's pants at the crotch. With the back of the knife, he pulled out Nat's manhood and testicles.

"No, no, please don't," Nat cried out and pissed himself down his pants leg.

"Tell me where Kip went and I won't cut your pecker off."

"He went to Lincoln. I swear, he went to Lincoln." Nat's voice pleaded and Rafe knew he was telling the truth.

"Why did he go there?"

"I dun know."

Rafe turned the knife and with the point he nicked Nat's testicle. "Don't test me. Why did he go there?"

"He's got family thar. His cousin Larry owns the mercantile. He said it was safe fer im thar."

"This is for my wife and child," Rafe snarled. With a swift slice of the knife, Nat's manhood and testicles flew out in front for him to see. Rafe mounted up and galloped off east until he could not hear Nat's screams.

CHAPTER 35

Clay and his men rode the thirty some miles at a good clip and reached the village of Taos at sundown.

"Spread out. Check the livery, hotels, and cantinas," Clay told the others.

Clay and Ben rode to the sheriff's office. Clay was not anxious to talk to the sheriff, but he was the most likely person to know about a marshal in town. Relating a portion of the story, Clay asked if the sheriff had heard about a marshal from Santa Fe around the area."

"No marshal checked in with me," the sheriff told Clay.

"Said he was a U.S. Marshal from Santa Fe. Yew know anybody down there it might be? I was told he had a Mexican name."

"Sorry, don't know any Mexican marshal from Santa Fe."

The other men checked all the hotels and inns and found no U.S. Marshal or Nat. It was dark before Clay was sure they were not in town.

"We'll spend tonight here. Ben, yew go to Santa Fe tomorrow morning and check at the U.S. Marshal's office. The rest of us will go back to Cimarron," Clay ordered the gang. Clay saw Ben Mathews stop himself from voicing a complaint, realizing Clay was blaming him for this wild goose chase.

Rafe rode as far as he could away from where he left Nat Holmes before the night made traveling dangerous. Making a cold camp, he pulled a piece of jerky from his saddlebags. He rubbed the gelding down with the saddle blanket and tethered him near a patch of grass, before finding a flat spot for himself. Around him, the symphony of the night critters filled the air.

Wrapping himself in his bedroll, he leaned his head against the saddle. In the quiet, he could still hear Nat's screams. It was not in his conscious nature to be so vicious, but these men deserved to suffer and die. All of them were guilty, not just the one whose bullet pierced his wife's body. Exhaustion finally overcame his burning rage and Rafe fell into a deep sleep.

The dream was real, as real as if he was there. He saw Ana Teresa sprawled naked on the ground bleeding from a bullet wound in her stomach. Between her legs, their dead baby lay face down covered in blood and dirt. Rafe tried to go to them, but something stopped him, some force was holding him back. It was the screaming that woke him, his screaming.

He sat up in a cold sweat, shaking to the bone. The vision of the dream would not leave him and he could not stop shaking. All he could do was scream at the hurt and loss. He screamed until the pain in his ribs was unbearable. Like Nat Holmes, there was no one to hear.

It was still dark when he started a small fire. He added several small sticks and stacked larger ones to get it going. Still shaking, he managed to start a pot of coffee. The image of the dream would not leave his mind. It ignited the fury in him. He had killed Jesse Kincaid at the saloon in Elizabethtown and left Nat Holmes to die, tied to a tree in the wilderness where no one would find him.

He had felt rage before. It drove him to shoot *don* Bernardo for raping his sister. It was there when he confronted the Reynolds brothers and killed them for hurting his uncle's family. He had no rage when he killed the Texas cattle rancher, John B. Sutton. Sutton drew on him and Rafe fired first. Diego de la Torre taunted Rafe and although Rafe responded to his challenge, it was not this type of rage.

His vengeance against the trio who killed Ana Teresa and the baby was beyond measure. It turned his soul blacker than black. He knew vengeance would drive him until Kip Donohoe felt his retribution or it drove Rafe mad.

Rafe wanted to ask God to forgive him, but he could not. God would never forgive him for these killings. It was a mortal sin and there would be no forgiveness. Still, he believed he was justified.

He wished Xihuitl, the Aztec healer was here to help take the rage and hate out of him. Xihuitl would know how to make him whole again. He thought about Carlos and wished he was here. Carlos was devout and had a better grasp of spiritual matters. He told Rafe he felt vindicated from killing his murderous brother, Benicío. It was a small comfort. If God could forgive Carlos for killing Benicío, then perhaps it was not too late for his redemption.

Suddenly the quiet and desolation he felt sitting by the creek made him miss Carlos, George, and the family. He wanted to get on the horse and ride home to Santa Fe. He wanted to feel their arms around him, giving him comfort. They would want him to stay, to forgive, and start anew.

They were no doubt mourning Ana Teresa. She was part of the family since they married. They treated her like a daughter and were like expectant grandparents awaiting the birth of the baby. Even in their grief, they would not condone his quest to avenge Ana Teresa's death.

No matter how hard he tried, he could not get the image of Ana Teresa and the dead baby in the dream out of his mind. The image smoldered in the dying morning fire. He would find Kip Donohoe and kill him. He hoped it would calm his rage, seeing Donohoe's soul sent to the depths of hell and then perhaps Rafe could return to Santa Fe.

When Alexander arrived at the print shop the following morning, it did not somehow surprise him to find Rafe and his belongings gone. In his desk he found a letter. It emphasized, "If I die, contact Bill Moore. He will know what to do."

Later that day, Alexander had two people stop by telling him of Nat's disappearance. Gloria's story about a U.S. Marshal arresting him for crimes in San Gabriel solidified Alexander's belief as to what may have happened to Nat – Rafe Reyes avenged the death of his wife and unborn child. Nat deserved his fate. Whatever Rafe may have done to Nat was justified and Alexander would never write about what he knew and true to his word, Rafe did not implicate Alexander in any way.

In preparation for the large weekly edition of his newspaper which would be printed on Friday, Alexander Sullivan wrote an article about the disappearance of Nat Holmes:

April 17, 1874: Cimarron News
Nathaniel Holmes, known in these parts as Nat Holmes, was arrested by a U.S. Marshal on Wednesday. He was accused of participating in a raid at the hacienda of don Lorenzo Salazar in March, where innocent women and children were killed. Nat will be returned to the local authorities in Santa Fe for trial.

CHAPTER 36

Rafe kicked out the dying fire and with a purpose tried to eliminate any evidence of his camp. Packing up and mounting the gelding he rode south, keeping the morning sun on his left side. He purposely avoided any towns and villages and kept a fast, but elusive pace. His gray suit was folded in his saddlebags, along with the marshal's badge. The woman, Gloria, could possibly identify him, if Clay's men ever found him. His brain toyed with the notion the sheriff of Cimarron might circulate a WANTED poster of a U.S. Marshal wanted in the disappearance of Nat Holmes. Nagging thoughts about loose ends invaded his mind as he rode.

Near the third day of his travels south to Lincoln, Rafe reached Lake Sumner. Reaching Lake Sumner brought back memories of last summer. A gang of Texas cowboys rustled some of Ed and Cynthia's Seeley's herd taking them to Wyoming. As a coincidence, Rafe and Carlos were in San Marcial a few days after the heist and Rafe joined Big Ed's posse. They had traveled northeast following the cattle rustlers, passing this big lake on their way. It was only nine months ago, yet seemed like a lifetime.

A long day later, he arrived at Fort Sumner. His food supplies were exhausted. Finding a small inn west of the fort, he tethered the gelding to the rail.

"Good evening," the clerk greeted him.

"Good evening. I need a room and a bath," Rafe said to the clerk. He then asked about where to wash up and about the restaurant. He signed the register as a Samuel Soto from Pueblo, Colorado.

When Kip Donohoe arrived in Lincoln, his cousin, Larry Murphy, was dubious of his story. Larry could tell Kip was on the run, but he was family. "Yew kin work fer me out at the ranch, but keep yer nose clean. Yew kin hep with the cattle," Larry had offered. Kip hated cattle punching, although he had little choice and agreed.

"Git along, yehaa," Kip Donohoe shouted at several strays. It was Kip's second cattle delivery to Fort Stanton. When he arrived in Lincoln several weeks ago, it was the only job his cousin, Larry Murphy, would give him.

A rangy cowboy riding nearby slapped his chaps with a lariat and yelled. The small herd moved slowly over the rocky desolate terrain toward the fort.

"Keep em critters movin!" Kip yelled. His cousin Larry had a contract with the fort to supply beef to feed the Mescalero Apaches who were under the jurisdiction of the government facility. Owning the local mercantile, his cousin controlled much of the market to the government. Kip thought it was quite a crafty move by Larry to control the supply routes to the isolated Army in the area.

It was a day's trip there and back, if the stupid beasts would keep moving and it was a job Kip detested. He did not like trailing the nasty dusty critters, but it was the only job his cousin Larry would give him. He believed it was Larry's way to keep him out of trouble in Lincoln. Being treated like a kid or a criminal pissed Kip off big time. As soon as he had enough cash, he would leave Lincoln for good.

"Hey Kip! There's Fort Stanton," one of the cowboys yelled to him a little while later.

Kip lifted his gaze. In the distance, a row of two-story whitewashed buildings stood out against the foothills. The buildings were the officer's residence houses. At the end of the row, was a stone church and a large building where the Army taught school to Mescalero Indian children. In the foreground, hay bales were stacked high.

"Keep that herd in line!" Kip yelled and spurred his horse. By the time they drove the cattle into the fort's corral, Kip was in the lead. Several Army soldiers helped the cowboys get the herd into the corral while Kip headed to the headquarters office.

"Good morning Kip," the young corporal greeted him.

"Nother herd fer ya," Kip said.

"How many?"

"Fifty-four," Kip replied.

"Are you sure. The last delivery was three short. Captain Howard said I'm to dock you for the shortage against this herd."

Kip bristled at the corporal's comments. Of course the corporal was right. Kip had lied about the number to pocket some money and now realized the Army was not as stupid as he thought.

"Ah . . . I am sorry bout that corporal. I guess it's hard to count em critters when they are movin. I mightta counted one or two twice, but today I'm sure I put fifty-four in your corral."

The door swung open and the corporal came to attention. Captain Tom Howard walked into the small room and returned the salute from the corporal.

"Hello Donohoe. Saw the herd. They look a bit on the scrawny side, but they will do this time. You tell Larry I can get better from Mexico, if this is the best he can do," the captain said.

"Yes sir. Yew know it's spring and these were the best we had," Kip responded.

"Tell Larry this should do us for the next month. Corporal, pay Mister Donohoe." The captain walked into his private office and closed the door. The captain's comment surprised and angered Kip. No cattle deliveries for a month meant no money in his pocket.

The corporal turned and counted out the payment and handed it to Kip. "If there is another shortage, it will be deducted from next month's shipment."

"Well, you make a good count. Iffin there's more, I want ta know," Kip replied in a surly tone.

Kip tucked the money into his shirt pocket. Turning, he walked from the headquarters office back out into the bright sunshine. The cows were all safely milling in the corral and his men were talking to the privates and smoking cigarettes.

"Cum on, we gotta git back ta Lincoln," Kip yelled to them. They mounted and followed Kip along the Rio Bonito around the high hill terrain back to Lincoln. On the way back, Kip mulled his situation over in his mind. He needed money and needed it now. He did not want to wait another month or two driving cattle and doing odd jobs for Larry. He pondered trying his luck again at poker, but last week he lost four hundred in a big pot.

The ten mile trip without the cows to slow them down passed quickly and they got back just before sundown.

"I'm headed to the Lone Star. Yew'll wanna go, I'm buying?" Kip yelled out to his crew. Pulling his pistol, he fired it into the air while spurring his horse the short distance down the street. All the others followed his lead, announcing their arrival with gunfire. All but three, followed him to the saloon.

Kip paid for a round of beers for the men, while he downed a couple shots of red eye. The fiery amber liquid calmed his frustration. The Lone Star was unusually quiet, but then it was Wednesday evening. Poker was the game at two tables, while six men surrounded a Faro table near the back. Kip knew things would get busier as the night progressed. In a little while, Julie would start singing. He liked her low sultry voice and liked to dream of bedding her, but she was no whore.

"Say Kip, r we gonna git paid taday?" Buster pushed in at the bar beside Kip. A shorter man than Kip, Buster had a lopsided grin from a bar fight and a broken jaw. Although he was not a handsome man by any accounts, Buster always seemed to have a saloon girl on his arm or waiting nearby. Today was no exception. Carol Ann was waiting for Buster to get paid and head upstairs.

"Awrat, yew boys go on ahead and have another round. I'll go git our pay frum Larry." Kip put another quarter on the top of the bar and headed for the door. He walked to the mercantile where he found Larry in his office.

"Hey Kip, everthin go awrat at the fort?" Larry Murphy looked up from his desk as Kip walked in.

"Yeah, we got em critters thar with no problems. I dun like herding em fuckin cows, Larry. Ain't yew got sumthin else fer me ta do round here?" Kip complained. Larry could smell the liquor on Kip's breath and the slight slur in his words.

"Hell Kip, yew need to stay outta town. After what yew dun up at Cimarron, I'm surprised the law ain't cum after yew by now. That's why I have yew workin the ranch ta keep yew outta sight fer awhile til things blow over," Larry admonished him.

"Fuckin squatter deserved it. I dun nuttin cept what they hired me ta do," Kip groused back.

"I'm telling yew, yew gotta stay low."

"The law ain't gonna cum after me. I'm tired of workin the ranch. I need to be round people and em gals at the Lone Star," Kip responded with a sly grin. "Here's the take fer the cows. Now, give me the money fer the boys. They be waitin at the Lone Star fer me."

Kip waited impatiently while his cousin counted out the money Captain Howard gave him at the fort and began to separate the pay for the cowboys. Kip hoped Larry would not notice the wad of bills was short.

"Captain Howard thought the cows were a bit skinny. Asshole said he cud git better cows frum Mexico. Said he dun want nother shipment fer about a month," Kip told his cousin.

Larry Murphy bristled at the comments. He knew Captain Howard was tiring of his stranglehold on the supplies for the fort. The captain told him the Army needed to use many suppliers and thought competition was a good thing.

"Yer fifty dollars short." Larry looked up from his counting. "Hand it over Kip."

"I gave yew evrythang. Asshole corporal said we shorted em last time and he subtracted fer that. Ain't my fault," Kip groused.

Larry wanted to believe Kip, but knew his cousin's outlaw nature. It was only because he was family that Larry helped Kip at all. He believed Kip might be skimming off the top, but he thought better of riling him. He finished counting the money and handed a stack of bills to Kip.

"Here's the pay. Dun stay too long in town. Git yerself

back to the ranch early, yew hear," Murphy told him.

When Kip strode back into the saloon he put a dollar on the bar and ordered, "Set em up barkeep."

Buster pushed to the head of the line, then the other cowboys wasted no time spending their money on whiskey and women. Kip turned his attention to drinking.

CHAPTER 37

Believing he was far enough away from Cimarron for safety, Rafe rested at Fort Sumner using the assumed name of Sammy Soto from Pueblo. Instead of concealing his identity, he made a point of talking to the hotel clerk, the waiter in the restaurant, had the liveryman check the gelding's shoes, and even chatted with a few soldiers. He wanted everyone in Fort Sumner to remember Sammy Soto from Pueblo, Colorado, and not a pretend U.S. Marshal or Rafe Reyes from Santa Fe.

The rest was good for both he and the gelding. From his conversations, he learned the majority of the fort's Army regiment had been reassigned and only a small detachment remained after the Navajo and Mescalero tribes signed treaties. The town of Fort Sumner was now a major stop on the Goodnight-Loving cattle trail from Texas to Wyoming. After the three days of rest and resupplying his food sacks, Rafe left Fort Sumner and followed the winding Pecos River toward the small settlement of Roswell.

Spring in New Mexico brought warmer daytime temperatures, but the nights were still cold. Spring also brought winds to the high desert terrain. It blew the silty soil and stung his face. When the wind howled, he rested the gelding and swam in the river to rinse off the dust.

In places, the river widened and created small lakes of water. In other parts, the river narrowed and tumbled over rocks creating small rapids. All along the river cottonwood and desert willow grew, except where the rocky escarpment came to the river's edge.

The river afforded Rafe plenty of small game to eat and he was often lucky to catch a trout. He saw many deer, but only shot at rabbits and grouse. He had no methods to carry a deer carcass and did not want to kill a deer for a small meal. Twice he saw small brown bears catching fish in the river and he gave them wide berth. At night he built up a large fire to fend off predators. He wished he was riding

Rayo, his trusted Appaloosa with more sensitive ears. Rayo would alert him to any four-legged dangers.

The days were long and lonely, full of anguish and regret. At night he slept lightly, waking often to night sounds or when his sleep was interrupted by horrific dreams of Ana Teresa and the baby. As he headed further south, the landscape became more barren. The juniper and pine forests of northern New Mexico were replaced with scrubby bushes and cactus of various types. Rafe thought without the river, the land would be very inhospitable.

About a week later, he reached an area where the river supported a *bosque* and shallow swampy estuaries. Egrets and other water birds were abundant. The soil near the water was sandy, showing the history of when the area was a large land-locked sea.

Finally, he reached the tiny town of Roswell, consisting of two buildings, a general store, a large corral, and post office. The general store had sleeping quarters for paying guests, so he rented the space for the night, registering as Sammy Soto. Once again, Rafe used his alias. He stripped the gelding and was directed to a small corral behind the store where a boy promised to feed the horse well and give him a good brushing.

That evening he sat for dinner with Van C. Smith and his partner Aaron Wilburn. Smith and Wilburn owned the general store and post office. The men were good natured and glad to have a visitor. Rafe asked how the two arrived in Roswell.

"I guess you could say Van and I own the town, what there is of it," Aaron told him with a laugh. "We came here six years ago from Nebraska. Captain Joseph Lea thought it a good spot and built a small trading post, cause the Chisum Trail goes near here. We bought it from him and built what you see."

The two men talked about cattle drives, Texas cowboys, the sometimes harsh weather, and especially the lack of water in the area.

"The Hondo River runs just yonder. When a big rain comes it runs like a torrent, but in late summer, it's mostly dry. Weather ain't like in Nebraska," Aaron said.

"We sunk a well, and it filled with this damnable silty soil," Van grumbled.

"Why do you stay?" Rafe asked.

"It's home and someday we'll be on the map. You have to see the night sky. You've never seen anything like the stars here," Van told him.

"Yeah, the moon's so big you can almost touch it. And occasionally we see shooting stars streak across the sky."

"Do you play poker Sammy?" Van changed the subject and asked.

"I'm not good at it. Man on a stagecoach ride from California to Tucson, Arizona tried to teach me the game," Rafe replied.

"Too bad, I was hoping to take some of your money." The men laughed easily and Rafe found their company relaxing.

"Don't do it young man. Van is a professional gambler. He likes to take on them rangy cowpokes who come off the Chisum Trail. They think they are good at the game, but Van always comes out ahead."

"Aw, come on Aaron. You know that ain't true. Those boys get me once in a while," Van bantered.

"What is your business?" Van asked.

"I'm a gunsmith from Pueblo, Colorado," Rafe told them.

"What are you doing way down here?" Aaron asked.

"On a sales trip. I'm headed to Lincoln. My boss got a letter from a Larry Murphy at the mercantile saying he wanted to buy our weapons," Rafe lied to them.

"What's so special about your weapons?" Van asked.

Rafe pulled out one of his pistols and emptied the chambers, then handed it to him. "This is a double-action pistol. All you have to do is squeeze the trigger and it will fire."

Van picked it up and looked it over then pointed it at the wall and squeezed the trigger rapidly, three times. "I'll be damned," he said and handed the pistol to Aaron.

"GSW? What does that stand for?" Aaron asked

noticing the insignia on the handle.

Rafe was tongue-tied for a moment, then replied, "Just the brand name."

Aaron pointed the pistol at the wall and clicked three chambers. "What about the kick, seems like it would throw your aim off for the next shot?"

"You have to practice till you get used to it," Rafe told him and took the gun back.

"I know Larry over at Lincoln. Not real well, but I have to tell you that man is a tough one. You watch yourself when you deal with him," Aaron warned him.

"I've been around many wild towns selling these guns. I can take care of myself," Rafe told him confidently.

"I suppose you can young man, still, you best watch yourself over at Lincoln. Lots of Mexican hating Texans there," Van warned him.

They talked after dinner for several hours. The two proprietors were happy for the educated company Rafe offered. Their usual guests were cattle drovers, Texas cowmen, or the occasional military troop. Finally, Rafe said goodnight and headed for the comfortable bed in the guest room.

For the first time since Ana Teresa's death, Rafe got a solid night's sleep without any nightmares. A crowing rooster nearby claiming his territory, brought Rafe out of a deep sleep. Stretching, the aroma of coffee hurried him to get up and get breakfast.

As he packed his belongings and checked the loads in the pistols, he turned the GSW pistol handle in his hand. It was the signature of George's foundry, the George Summer Weaponry Company, and as such it nagged Rafe. Aaron noticed the insignia and asked questions about it last night. Searching in his saddlebags, he found the two pistols he took from foundry the night he left. The handles were smooth and the insignia had not been etched on them. He replaced the GSW pistols in the holster with the plain ones, and tucked the GSW ones away with his clothes.

With all his belongings packed, he headed to the sink out the back door and to the outhouse. When he arrived in the kitchen, Smith greeted him.

"Good morning. Bacon and eggs suit you?"

"Sure sounds good," Rafe replied. "I'll get an early start."

"So you said yesterday. I got the stableboy to get your horse ready."

Rafe wasted no time on the meal, thanked Van and Aaron for their hospitality, and rode out of Roswell as the sun sparkled over the eastern peaks, painting an orange, pink, and gray vista.

CHAPTER 38

Rafe pushed the gelding and the young horse was willing. It was sired by Santiago, Carlos' black stallion. Santiago was bred on *don* Bernardo's hacienda in Torreón, Mexico, where the *don* bragged his horses were decedents of the first horses brought to the new world by the conquistador, Hernán Cortés. Regardless whether *don* Bernardo's claim was true, Spaniards introduced the horse to the new world, which helped them conquer the Aztec empire.

The gelding was a good strong horse, but Rafe wished he was riding his Appaloosa, Rayo. The Appaloosa had extraordinary instincts and had helped Rafe out of numerous dangerous situations. The brown gelding was smart and was learning Rafe's actions, but did not have Rayo's innate perception.

The trip from Roswell wound over many small canyons in rough, dry, rocky terrain. About half way to Lincoln, he found the Rio Hondo as it cut through the canyons. He stopped at the river and let the horse wade in the water. While the horse rested and grazed, he stretched under the shade of a cottonwood tree and relaxed.

His mind vacillated on how to find and kill Kip Donohoe. It seemed simple enough to find him at the mercantile, however he was nagged by his own oversight. He still had no idea what Kip looked like. He should have forced Nat Holmes to give him a description while he had the knife at Nat's throat. Now, he could pass the killer on the street and be naively unaware.

Pushing these thought out of his mind, he tried instead to focus on keeping to a plan. The good night's sleep last night helped to rest his weary body, while he did his best to keep the image of Ana Teresa and his unborn dead child from peaking his rage. The Aztec healer Xihuitl's lessons made him ponder his next move. "Do not fight in anger. Be aware of everything around you," Xihuitl had taught him.

Besides not knowing how to identify Kip, he was going into a dangerous unknown. Kip had family in Lincoln and Rafe supposed Kip also had friends. Rafe had no one.

All he knew about Lincoln was it was renamed after President Abraham Lincoln in 1869 and was named the county seat. Originally, it was called *Las Placitas del Rio Bonito* by the original Spanish settlers, which meant place by the pretty river.

Late in the afternoon after clearing a small rise on the trail, Rafe got his first view of Lincoln, New Mexico. He stopped the horse and looked at the small town below him.

Nat told him Kip was going to his cousin's store. He knew Nat was telling the truth, but wondered if Kip had already moved on. Van and Aaron warned him that Lincoln was run by Texans who disdained Mexicans. The thoughts rumbled in his brain as he sat on the knoll.

He knew no one in Lincoln to help. His only idea was acting as a gun salesman while scouting the mercantile for Kip Donohoe. If it came to a showdown, he had a big advantage with his expertise and the double-action pistols. He hoped it was enough to keep him alive.

So far, everyone who knew Kip said he was mean and ruthless. Nat said it was Kip's idea to lead the raid. The image of his nightmares flared up again and it made him curse loudly, almost spooking the horse. He breathed deeply to control himself, patting the horse's neck, and spurred the gelding to a slow trot.

He rode down the main street of Lincoln dressed in his gray business suit and black Stetson imposing what he hoped was an impressive figure. He rode tall in the saddle and could tell he did not go unnoticed as he rode into town. A set of three cowboys took a second look at him and one pointed. He kept the Stetson low shadowing his face. He wanted Lincoln to see a well-dressed rider, with a fine horse, and supplies tied to the back of the saddle. He wore his two guns in the gunbelt where they would be readily visible.

He passed the L. G. Murphy Mercantile. A bit farther, there was a small saloon across the street named the Lone Star. It had a single star painted red above the door. Up the road, he found a small inn where he stopped hoping they had a room for him. He tethered the horse in front and went into the lobby.

"Hello," he called out. No one was at the front desk. "Yes," a young woman with long light brown hair came out from the back room. She was younger than he thought at first glance, a teenage girl in fact. "My mother isn't here right now. She'll be back soon." she said with a fresh smile.

"I was hoping to get a room for a few days," Rafe told her. The young girl acted shy and did not look Rafe in the eyes.

"I can't give out rooms. You'll have to wait til my mother gets back. She should be here any minute," she told him and returned to the back room.

Rafe stood looking around the front room and admired pictures of what he thought was the owner's family. Out the front window and across the street an American flag waved in front of the post office. To the right stood the unfinished shape of a chapel in only freshly cut two-by-four lumber. It stood on a completed wooden floor.

As he stood looking to the street, a woman rushed by the window and the bell on the front door jingled. Rafe turned as the woman rushed past him and placed packages on the counter. She was an attractive woman, dressed in a high-neck blue dress with long sleeves. Both the neck line and sleeves had white ruffles. Blond hair with some light brown streaks fell to her shoulders and was pulled back with a silver clasp.

Alice Baker turned and saw a well-dressed young man looking at her. A saddlebag hung over his shoulder and the gunbelt wrapped around his waist held two pistols. Taken back a bit because his black hair and tan features did not fit her initial image, she stammered on her reply, "Ahh . . . ah . what can I do for you?"

"Hello. I told your daughter, I was hoping I could get a room here for a couple of days. I have business here," Rafe told her with a smile. He had removed his black Stetson and held it in his hands in front to him.

"Ah, well I do have a room. Are you a Mexican?" she asked.

"Well, no. I'm an American. Why do you ask?" he responded knowing fully why she asked, but keeping a pleasant demeanor.

She blushed. The young man's English was flawless. In fact, it sounded more Eastern and certainly not Texan or Mexican. His face was tan and his smile showed a full set of straight white teeth. He stood tall and rather handsome, but the black hair and tan complexion was a dead giveaway. He looked Mexican, although not like the typical poor Mexicans here in Lincoln.

"What are you doing here?' she finally asked.

"I'm a gun salesman from Pueblo, Colorado. Is there a problem?"

"Well, I'm not supposed to rent to Mexicans."

"I'm not Mexican. As I told you, I'm an American. I don't see the problem," Rafe said keeping his boyish smile.

"Well . . . okay," she said hesitantly. "But you best be careful here in Lincoln. There are many Texans here and I could get in trouble. Here, sign the registry." She turned it toward him.

Rafe signed his name as Sammy Soto.

"My name is Alice Baker. Ruthie, come and show Mister Soto to room four," she called out to her daughter and handed a key to Rafe.

"Do you have a place for my horse?" Rafe asked.

"No, but you will find a livery stable down the street. Ask for Slim. Tell him you are staying here. He will take care of your horse."

Rafe followed Ruthie to his room thinking about the exchange with Alice. Mexican hating Texans was nothing new to Rafe, however it was something else he needed to worry about here in Lincoln.

Ruthie took the key from Rafe and unlocked the door.

"Hope you like the room sir," she said and smiled.

"Thank you Ruthie. It looks fine."

"If you need anything just ask me or my mother."

"Ruthie, what did your mother mean about not renting

to Mexicans?"

"Well, just like she said. We were told not to rent to Mexicans. It's the order by the town council. I'm surprised she let you have the room."

"Like I told her, I'm American."

"Sure do look like a Mexican, only you don't dress or talk like one," she said and laughed.

"I'm an American, just like you. Where were you born Ruthie? Here in Lincoln?"

"No, my mother and father came here when I was six. Papa got shot three years ago and now I help Mama with the inn."

"I'm sorry. What happened to you father?"

"One night a drunk came late and was trying to break down the front door. When Papa told him to move along, the drunk shot him down, leaving Mama and I alone. This house is all we have."

"Let's hope I don't cause your mother any trouble," Rafe said and gave Ruthie a silver dollar.

Ruthie turned the silver dollar over in her hand. Most customers gave her at most a nickel for showing them to their rooms. Sometimes they gave her nothing but a thank you. A whole dollar was a fortune and she knew she should give it to her mother. Ruthie tucked the dollar in her pocket and curtsied slightly.

"Thank you sir."

Chapter 39

After putting his saddlebags in the room, Rafe walked the horse to the livery stable. It was not a large place, but he was surprised to see eight stalls when he walked in.

"Hello," Rafe called out.

A man came out from one of the stalls. "What can I do for you?" he said with a thick Hispanic accent. The man was tall and skinny. His hands, wrapped around a pitchfork, had long slender fingers and his dirty pants hung on his frame. He was not dark-skinned, but Rafe could see obvious Spanish features in his face.

"I'm looking for Slim," Rafe said.

"I'm Slim," the man said with a slight easy grin.

"Alice over at the inn said I could bring my horse here. She said you would take care of him."

Slim set the pitchfork against a stall wall and walked over. He ran his hands down the brown horse's flanks.

"Yes, you came to the right place. That's a fine animal. You won't find any horse that fine around here. I've seen some like this down in Mexico. Where did you get it?"

"My friend in Pueblo, Colorado, breeds them. He sold me this gelding at a good price."

"Too bad he's a gelding. I'd of paid handsome to stud him out for me. Don't worry *señor*, I will take good care of him."

Rafe relaxed thinking Slim was both an experienced liveryman and not a Texan. Digging in his vest pocket, Rafe found a fifty-cent piece. He pressed it into Slim's hand before he handed him the reins.

"Thanks Slim. I'd appreciate if you give him extra feed and he needs a good brushing."

Slim turned the coin in his skinny fingers. *"Gracias señor."*

Rafe thanked him again and walked out of the livery into the sunshine thinking at least one person here in Lincoln was not a Mexican-hating Texan. Returning to the inn, he stayed in his room after he bathed and took his meal in the dining room. Heeding Alice's warnings, he stayed inside the hotel rather than walking the streets or going to the saloon. Later in his room as he stretched out on the bed with his back against the bed's headboard, his mind wandered with ideas and trepidation. He thought finding Kip Donohoe might not be too difficult. He was sure Slim knew him. Liverymen knew everyone in a small town like Lincoln. Rafe had almost asked Slim earlier, but decided it might seem odd and raise concerns. It was better to bide his time and learn more about the town before he made any move.

Daylight came in through the curtains sometime after Rafe heard the rooster calls the next morning. He woke often throughout the night worrying and did not get a good night's rest.

Three things worried him. First the Texans – he would try to stay out of their way, but he knew it would be impossible. Rafe had dealt with Texans before. They hated Mexicans and stuck together. Second – how to identify Kip Donohoe and somehow get him alone. Third – how he could take him without getting himself killed by Kip's relatives and friends or hanged by the local sheriff.

From somewhere downstairs, the smell of frying bacon wafted into the room. Rafe dressed and pulled on his boots. At the breakfast table Rafe was the only guest up early.

"Good morning. I have bacon, eggs, and biscuits," Alice told him as she poured a cup of coffee for him.

"Sounds good to me."

"Scrambled or sunny side up?" Alice asked.

"Scrambled please."

After breakfast, Rafe washed up and wrapped his gunbelt around his waist. He put the two unmarked double-action pistols in the holsters and threw his saddlebag over his shoulder. He walked out of the hotel into bright sunshine. The sky was a clear teal blue. Rafe knew it was May, but had lost track of days. They did not seem to have a meaning anymore.

Walking to the livery to get his horse, he found Slim

was cleaning out the only empty stall.

"Good morning," Rafe greeted him.

"Up early I see," Slim replied.

"Yes, I usually rise early. Can you saddle my horse?"

Slim grinned and leaned the pitchfork against the back wall of the stall. He walked across the barn to where the gelding was standing quietly.

"This sure is a good horse mister. Too bad they cut off his best feature," Slim said and laughed. "You said you got the horse in Pueblo. You from there?"

"Yes, I grew up there," Rafe lied.

"What are you doing way down here?" Slim asked. He looked at Rafe again in the morning light of the livery. The young man was an anomaly. He definitely looked Hispanic, but spoke perfect English and dressed impeccably. He had a two-gun gunbelt around his waist and wore it low. Slim wondered if he was a gunfighter.

"I'm a gun salesman, name of Sammy Soto. I've been working my way north from Las Cruces and my next stop will be Albuquerque." Rafe deliberately convoluted the story and the direction of his wanderings as he did with his name.

"What kind of guns do you sell?"

"Here let me show you." Rafe took one of the pistols out of the gunbelt.

"This is a double-action pistol. All you have to do is squeeze the trigger and it will fire. You don't have to thumb the hammer each time."

Rafe emptied the chamber and handed Slim the pistol. He looked it over and tentatively squeezed the trigger several times. With each click the chamber moved. Slim shook his head as he handed it back to Rafe.

"Sure is a beaut. Wouldn't mind owning one myself," he told Rafe.

"I can put in an order," Rafe said, not quite knowing what to respond.

"Naw. I'm just dreaming. I can't afford a pistol like that. Besides, the town council don't like Mexicans wearing guns around here."

"That's the second time I've heard the town council

has rules about Mexicans. I thought New Mexico is a territory of the United States?"

"Maybe, but the Texans around here don't like Mexicans and they run the town. They ain't over their defeat at the Alamo, I guess. I'm surprised Alice rented you a room."

"I'm not Mexican. I'm an American, just like you."

"Say, you're right. I was born here, not in Mexico. Don't matter much though. The Texans hate you just cause you're brown and speak Spanish," Slim groused.

Slim's manner was friendly and open. It was obvious he had no great love for the Texans in Lincoln. Rafe heard it all before. General Santa Anna's bloody victory at the Alamo was a rallying cry of Texans against all Mexicans.

"Say Slim, I imagine you know just about everybody here in town."

"Yep. Know all their horses too. I'm the local blacksmith."

"I was up in Cimarron and met a man named Kip Donohoe. He told me I should come to Lincoln and see his cousin Larry Murphy who owns the mercantile here. He thought his cousin would be interested in the guns. Do you know Kip?" Rafe took a chance hoping Slim would know the killer.

"I know that *cabrón,*" Slim responded with a hiss calling Kip an asshole in Spanish. "He came here a couple weeks ago from up north. You stay away from him. He's meaner than a pissed-off rattlesnake. He didn't pay me for putting up his horse for a couple of days, because he said I did a bad job. Then I heard how he bragged about stiffing a greaser."

Rafe shook his head back and forth. "Yeah, I got that impression when I met him up there. Word was he killed a man in Cimarron for no reason. They said it was why he left town. Where does he hang out, so I can avoid him?" Rafe asked.

"If he's in town, he's usually over at the Lone Star. That's one place you better never show your face. Mostly Texans there and you know how they feel about Mexicans."

"Thanks for the warning."

CHAPTER 40

Rafe rode to the L. G. Murphy & Co Mercantile to put the first step of his plan in motion. On the wooden front of the mercantile just below the name was a sign advertising: Work Clothes, Boots & Shoes, Dry Goods, Farm Equipment, Tobacco, Coffee, Guns & Ammo. The mercantile was the largest building in town, even larger than the Lone Star Saloon. Along the sidewalk, barrels and crates of fresh vegetables and fruits were displayed. Near them shovels, rakes, and other hand tools leaned against the wall. A variety of ropes hung on hooks. Barbed wire and fencing equipment was stacked on the far end of the building.

Rafe pushed in the swinging doors. Inside, the place was abuzz with people. Around the large main room were more barrels and tubs full of rice, grains, seed, and crackers. Large flour, sugar, and grain sacks were stacked one on top of each other. Behind the counter were rows of cans, jars and whisky bottles. A second room had clothing, hats, blankets and all kinds of dry goods. In fact, the store was jam-packed with goods as advertised on the sign outside.

Rafe patiently waited for the clerk to address him. He had dusted off his gray suit this morning and brushed the black Stetson to look his best. He also wore a white shirt with a narrow black tie at the neck.

"Hello, I'm looking for Larry Murphy. Is he in?" Rafe asked the young man.

"He's in the back. Can I help you?"

"I was told to see Larry. I'm a gun salesman," Rafe replied to the clerk.

"Oh. Foller me, I'll take yew to im."

The young man opened a door behind the counter and called, "Uncle Larry! Man here ta see yew."

A few moments later, a middle-aged man poked his head from the door. He wore a dark suit and a blue shirt with a tie. It was obvious Larry Murphy was a working proprietor of the business. Rafe breathed a sigh of relief. He knew from the many gun selling trips with George, that working proprietors took a keen interest in the quality of the goods they supplied. He stepped up toward the door.

"Hello Mister Murphy. My name is Sammy Soto and I am a gun salesman from Pueblo, Colorado. I'd like to show you our newest line of pistols. These are the latest double-action models we make," Rafe spoke right out as he shook Murphy's hand.

"Well, come on in," Murphy said opening the door to the back office wide and then closed the door behind them. Rafe removed his Stetson and placed it on the desk.

"I already got me a gun supplier. What's so special about yer guns?" Murphy asked gruffly as he got a better look at Rafe. The gun salesman from Colorado was a well dressed Mexican. As a member of the town council, Larry believed in the town's rules about greasers. They were allowed to buy his goods, but the town council frowned upon buying from Mexican farmers or suppliers. Larry adhered to the policy, although he had a few Mexican and Indian suppliers he used anyway.

"Well, these are special made double-action pistols. To fire each round, you do not have to thumb the hammer. You just squeeze the trigger. If you have a place where we can shoot, I'll show you how it works." Rafe handed one of the unmarked pistols to Murphy, who turned it over in his hand several times.

"I heerd of em double-action guns, but I never seen one. Let's go out back, I wanna see it in action." Murphy unlocked the back door and led Rafe outside. Behind the mercantile, several wagons filled with goods, waited to be unloaded. Behind the wagons, an empty area faced a forest of short junipers and several large boulders. Rafe checked the chamber and took careful aim at a small boulder. Three quick squeezes of the trigger ricocheted bullets off the rock.

"Holy shit!" Murphy exclaimed. "Let me try that thing," Murphy said and took the pistol from Rafe. Pointing it, he squeezed the trigger twice. One shot hit the target, the other fired high. He re-aimed, fired again, and the bullet ricocheted with a distinct sound.

"It takes practice to get used to the kick for the second shot," Rafe assured him.

"Reload it. I wanna to try it again," Murphy said excitedly.

This time Murphy took his time and held his aim on the secondary shots. A huge grin spread across his face as his sixth shot hit the target with a distinct sound. "Hot dang. I like em. How much do yew want fer thisin?" he asked.

"Well, I can't sell you my demonstration models. All I can do is take an order and have them sent to you. I need these pistols on my sales route," Rafe told him.

"How long yew stayin? I want yew to show em to sum of my men." Murphy's excitement with the pistol pushed any notion the gun salesman was Mexican from his mind.

"I'm staying at Alice Baker's Inn. I can stay around a while, if you give me an order for some guns. I'm in no hurry, but have rounds to make on my way to Albuquerque," Rafe told him.

"Cum back tomorrow. I want sum of my men to see this gun. Be here after I close the store and meet us out back here. Can I keep this here pistol over night?"

"No, sorry, I can't let it out of my sight. It is my livelihood," Rafe said hoping the man would not challenge him, thinking his plan was falling into place and it could be the way to finally get a line on Kip Donohoe.

After they said goodbye, Larry Murphy counted his blessings for not turning the Mexican salesman away as he might have done. The guns were magnificent. Not only the cowboys around here would want one, Larry thought about the Army regiment at Fort Stanton. Captain Howard and all his officers would be mighty happy to own one of those pistols.

CHAPTER 41

Kip had spent the best part of the last week at the ranch. He noticed the ranch foreman kept a sharp eye on his whereabouts and gave him the shittiest jobs. It was no doubt by Larry's request.

Today he and a few other cowboys were rounding up the stays. He hated the stinky stubborn beasts. Larry's ranch was not fenced and the cattle wandered in all directions. Larry explained the unfenced cows foraged for wild grasses, reducing his dependence on hay for feed.

"Hey Kip, I'm gonna git these doggies back to the ranch. Yew comin or goin up yonder?" one of the other cowboys asked him.

Kip casually let his eyes scan the horizon. He made it look like he was scanning for strays, but really he was checking to see if anyone else was in eyesight.

"I think I see sumthin up thar." He pointed toward a ridge not too far away. "I'll go check it out. See yew back at the ranch in a little while."

Kip rode off and crested the ridge. Looking back, no one was in sight. Spurring the horse southeast, he headed toward the town of Lincoln at a fast pace.

Kip reached Lincoln before the sun went down. Keeping off the main street, he worked his way behind several buildings until he was well past the mercantile. He did not want to chance Larry catching him in town.

A couple hours later, he sat alone downing red-eye at the Lone Star. He had started with several beers, then switched to the hard liquor. The more he drank the more irritable he felt. He knew Larry would be angry he came to town, but he just did not care.

Drinking always fueled Kip's discontent. He was tired of the whores here at the Lone Star. He had paid them all and none were worth anything in his mind. He hated this shitty little town of Lincoln, and moreover his cousin Larry's attitude. He wanted to be back in Cimarron, where there was real action led by his friend Clay Allison. So what if he killed a no good squatter. In fact, he was not sorry about killing the women and children over at San Gabriel. Hell, all fucking greasers should be run out of the territory.

"What yew doin all alone, Kip?" Buster Thomas asked rousing Kip from his thoughts. He took a seat across the table and helped himself to a swig of the red-eye.

"Aw fuck. I hate this shitheel town."

"Why? Lincoln ain't so bad. It ain't hot like Texas and the Lone Star's a nice place," Buster said.

"This fuckin place? Now Cimarron, that's a fun place ta be. They got pretty women up thar and the Lambert has a singer with a voice like velvet," Kip boasted.

"I ain't never been thar. Fact I ain't be no where much," Buster replied.

Kip sipped the whiskey and told Buster of his adventures. He painted each story with colorful people and places. He bragged about the murders he committed, especially against greasers. With Buster sharing the bottle of whiskey, it was already two-thirds empty. Kip did not mind giving Buster the drinks, since Buster was attentively listening to his stories and it stroked Kip's ego.

"Yew shur dun a lot of killin." Buster grinned thinking Kip was the most interesting man he ever met. "Yew gonna stay here in Lincoln?"

"Naw. Thar tain't no action here and I dun like herding cattle over ta Fort Stanton fer my cousin. As soon as I git me sum money, I'm outta here," he groused.

"Whar yew gonna go?" Buster asked.

"I heerd tell, silver and gold got discovered over ta Silver City. I might go thar and try my luck. Hell, I had me a gold mine over ta E-town, but it fuckin ran out. Juss my shitty ass luck or I'd not be here in this shitheel place," Kip continued complaining. Buster listened and poured himself and Kip another shot.

"Damn, iffin yew go ta Silver City, I'll be a goin with yew. I'd like to try my hand at minin."

Kip and Buster finished the bottle blustering about gold mines. Kip was feeling no pain when the batwing doors swung open and three *vaqueros* walked in with their spurs jangling. They left a trail of dust as they walked across the room. All were armed with one pistol in a single gunbelt and a *bandolier* stuffed with bullets across their chests. They went straight to the bar.

"Tequila por favor," one of the *vaqueros* ordered.

"¿Eres de México?" the bartender asked if they were from Mexico. The bartender was not Hispanic, but having been raised in Lincoln, spoke some Spanish.

"Sí, trajimos una manada de ganado a la hacienda Sandoval y necesitamos tequila," the head *vaquero* answered saying they brought a herd of cattle to the Sandoval hacienda and needed tequila.

The bartender shook his head, *"Vayensa a la cantina. No servimos Mexicanos."* The bartender made no move to serve the three telling them to go to the cantina as he did not serve Mexicans.

"Tequila," the *vaquero* said again with a growl pulling his pistol and pointing it at the bartender.

The bartender put a bottle and three shot glasses on the bar for them. One of the painted up whores passed near them and one of the *vaqueros* grabbed her arm. *"Oye, chica, toma un trago con nosotros,"* he said telling the girl to have a drink with them. She did not understand, smiled, and tried to pull away.

"Otro vaso," the *vaquero* told the bartender to set up another glass.

Kip signaled the bartender for another bottle. "Who are those Mescans?" Kip asked him when he delivered the bottle to the table.

"They're from Mexico. Said they delivered a herd of cattle to the Sandoval hacienda."

"Sandoval! That's the fucker who's tryin to undercut my cousin at Fort Stanton with shitass Mescan cattle," Kip slurred to Buster.

The alcohol was taking over Kip's faculties. The three *vaqueros* stood at the bar. They had taken off their large pointed hats. One had long dark hair pulled back and tied with a strand of leather. The leader had a large handlebar mustache, fringed leather chaps, and a knife tucked in the top of his boot. The third man had his arm wrapped around the saloon girl.

"Those fuckin Mescans are taking r gals, Buster. I ain't gonna let that happen," Kip growled. He filled his shot glass and downed it quickly, then poured another shot.

Without saying a word, Kip got up and pulled his pistol. He was unsteady on his feet and swayed, but the bullet from his pistol found its mark. The *vaquero* facing the bar got it in the back slumping over the bar top. Shocked, the others went for their guns.

"That's rat yew fuckin greasers. Git yer guns," Kip yelled.

Everyone in the saloon quickly scattered for cover. The girl near the *vaqueros* screamed and ran away quickly.

Buster jumped up and joined Kip in the gunfight. He had no specific hatred for the Mexicans, but Texans stuck together. If they were coming after Kip, then Buster would have his back.

The two *vaqueros* nearly cleared their pistols when they both got hit by bullets from Kip and Buster's pistols. In an instant, all three *vaqueros* lay on the floor dead or dying. Kip and Buster walked up and stood over them with smoking pistols.

"What the fuck, Kip!" the bartender yelled at them.

"I hate fuckin Mescans, specially iffin they take r gals," Kip slurred.

"Yew two git the hell outta here, now! Jerry, go git the sheriff!" the bartender yelled excitedly.

CHAPTER 42

Yesterday after meeting Larry Murphy, Rafe kept a low profile in town. He returned early to the inn and took supper with Alice and Ruthie. They talked about the weather and life in Lincoln, small talk. Later he retired to the his room and slept well until awakened by Alice's crowing rooster. Cleaning up, he went downstairs for breakfast.

"Good morning Mister Soto," Ruthie said and poured a cup of coffee for him.

"Good morning Ruthie."

"We have flapjacks, eggs, and bacon this morning," Ruthie told him.

"Sounds real good. I'm starving. Do you have a newspaper?" Rafe asked.

"Yes, but it's last week's. We should get the latest tomorrow," she said bringing the paper for him.

"Would you like more coffee?" Ruthie asked him.

"Sure. I'm not in a hurry," he said and set the paper down.

"Did you hear about the big ruckus in town?" she asked him.

"No. What happened?"

"Some cowboys shot three *vaqueros* over at the Lone Star last night. Killed all three." There was excitement in Ruthie's voice and Rafe wondered if she was happy the *vaqueros* had been killed and not the cowboys.

"That's too bad," he replied trying to keep calm and reserved. It was not his town and not his fight. His fight with Kip Donohoe was the only thing pressing his mind.

Rafe finished his breakfast and took his time scanning the newspaper. The most significant stories pertained to land grant issues near Rincon. He thought it was not far from the place where *don* Juan Dionisio Anaya's *vaqueros* found he and Carlos camped for the night last July. The men warned them of trouble brewing in the area with squatters. "Nothing changes," he murmured to himself. As he was in no hurry, having all day before going back to the mercantile, Rafe leisurely sat reading the newspaper and drinking three cups of strong coffee.

Back at his room, Rafe set out his guns and began a thorough cleaning process. Larry Murphy told him to come back late this afternoon, near closing time, so Rafe had all day to kill. As he worked, he kept thinking how close he was to finding and killing Kip Donohoe.

Then what? He did not want to go home, not yet. He was not sure he could face a life without Ana Teresa. His adopted family would welcome him back, but Rafe wondered how they might feel about his violence. Would they understand it as justified vengeance or now see him as a killer? Methodically, he cleaned and polished the guns until he was satisfied, then carefully put them in the saddlebag.

Four cowboys arrived at the mercantile late in the afternoon. Larry sent a message to the ranch for the men to come before sundown. They tied their horses and walked through the back door to Larry's office.

"Where's Kip," Larry asked.

"Dun know boss. He and Buster had a dustup at the Lone Star last night and they was gone this mornin," Jackson replied.

"Yew mean that ruckus with the Mexican cowboys? Kip was part of that?"

"Way I heerd it, he shot one of em in the back."

Larry Murphy grumbled. He hoped Kip was long gone. His asshole cousin was trouble, the kind of trouble a businessman like himself did not need.

Before sundown, Rafe left the inn carrying a saddlebag containing the double-action pistols. He walked to the mercantile and made his way around back where he met with Larry Murphy yesterday. Larry and four other men were there waiting for him.

"Hey there, glad yew came. I tol these fellers bout em special pistols of yers and they are anxious to see em," Larry said. Rafe looked at them wondering if one was Kip.

"Name of Sammy Soto," Rafe said and stuck out his

hand and each one said their name as they shook. None of them were Kip Donohoe.

Disappointed, he took the pistols out of the saddlebag and loaded only one of them. After explaining how the double-action worked, he fired three consecutive shots at a large boulder about twenty paces away. Smiles greeted Rafe from all the men watching. Each one of them tried the pistol and Rafe walked away with an order for twelve pistols from Murphy. They would never see them.

Rafe walked back to the inn in the twilight. He had counted on Kip coming for the demonstration. After all, he was Larry Murphy's cousin. He was so sure he would meet up with the killer for the first time today and tomorrow he would find a way to kill him. "Now what do I do?" he muttered to himself.

The next day, Rafe woke up depressed. Eating a quick breakfast, he went to get his horse.

"Hey Slim, get my horse ready," he said as he walked into the livery.

"Yes sir." Slim went and saddled the gelding and brought it out to Rafe who was waiting out in front of the livery.

"Hey, did you hear about your friend Kip Donohoe?"

Rafe perked up "No, I haven't seen him since I got here. What about him?" Rafe asked.

"Two days ago he killed three Mexican *vaqueros* at the Lone Star Saloon. Killed one in cold blood. Shot him in the back."

"What! Is he in jail?" Rafe asked suddenly concerned he would not be able to get to him, if the law had him in jail. He wondered if killing a Mexican in cold blood in this Mexican-hating town was a hanging offence. If so, it would solve his problem.

"No, he and his friend Buster ran off after the killing."

"Anybody know where they went?" Rafe asked.

"A couple of cowboys came to town yesterday from Murphy's ranch. One of them said Kip and Buster might be headed to Silver City. Kip had been bragging about owning a gold mine over at E-town and how he hated working as a drover for his cousin Larry. He bragged to them how Silver City was a booming place. I think that's where he went."

"Well, I didn't get to see him. I'm headed to Albuquerque, so it's too bad. Sounds like the law will catch up to him one day," Rafe said.

"How much I owe you?"

"Dollar a day and I fixed a loose shoe. Three fifty should cover it," Slim said. Rafe handed him four dollars.

"Thanks for everything Slim."

Mounting the gelding, Rafe rode to the inn and gathered his belongings. He paid Alice and said his goodbyes quickly.

"Good luck on your trip to Albuquerque Mister Soto. If you come back, you will always be welcome here."

"Thank you Alice," Rafe said. "I appreciate your kindness and hospitality. Tell Ruthie goodbye for me."

When everything was stowed on the horse, he saddled up and rode out of Lincoln, to where he was not sure. He needed time to think about his next move.

CHAPTER 43

Once far enough away from town, Rafe turned southwest winding his way between the steeper mountains and finally following a flowing creek. The creek was deep in spots and had rose-colored reeds growing along the banks. He stopped several times to allow the gelding and himself a drink. The quiet of the desolate area was only broken by the calls of birds attracted to the creek and croaking toads.

Near sundown, he was relieved to see a small village ahead. As he approached, he stopped an old Mexican man pulling a donkey with a load of firewood strapped to its back.

"Hola. ¿Cuál es el nombre de este pueblo?" Rafe called to him and asked what was the name of the village.

"Tularosa," the man responded politely.

Rafe nodded not surprised at the name. Tularosa was a Spanish description for the red or rose-colored reeds growing along the banks of the creek and Rafe had heard the name Rio Tularosa somewhere along his travels with George Summers.

"¿Hay una posada en este pueblo?" Rafe asked the man if there was an rooming house or inn at the village.

"No señor, no hay habitación, pero podría quedarse en la misión de Saint Francis de Paula," he answered there was nowhere to rent a room, but he could stay at the Saint Francis de Paula Mission.

"¿Donde esta la mision?" Rafe asked for directions. The man pointed down the road and told him he could not miss it.

Tularosa could barely be called a village. At the end of several ramshackle buildings and adobe houses, he found the mission. The spire of a fairly new white-washed chapel pointed into the sky and a small compound was circled by a low adobe wall. After tethering the horse, he took off his hat and entered the chapel. Dipping his fingers in the holy water, he made the traditional sign of the cross, then kneeled at the back pew.

The chapel was small and dark. Candle sconces lined the side walls and in the front two larger candles burned to illuminate a cross. The adobe walls kept the room cooler than the outside air. Rafe knelt and folded his hands over the wooden bench seat in front of him. The chapel appeared to be empty, quiet, and the feeling around him peaceful. It was a peace he had not felt since the day before the fiesta at *don* Salazar's hacienda – the day before Ana Teresa and his unborn child died.

Before he recited his prayers, Rafe reflected on what brought him to this small mission in this small village, so far away from what was his good life in Santa Fe. It would be easy to be angry at God and blame all his troubles on the Almighty, but he could not. Now, there was blood on his hands. How could he ask God to forgive him? The sixth commandment, 'Thou shalt not kill' weighed heavy in his heart. He had killed Jesse Kincaid and left Nat Holmes to die in the wilderness. It was not his nature to be vicious, but the image of Ana Teresa's death overrode the guilt. He was about to start his prayers, when an elderly woman dressed in black with a black veil, the traditional dress of mourning, walked out of the confessional.

A padre dressed in a brown robe walked out of the other side of the confessional. A wooden crucifix hung at the end of the shorter strand of rope tied around the padre's waist. After a curious look at a well-dressed young man kneeling in the back, the padre made his way to the last pew where the stranger knelt.

"Welcome to Saint Francis. I am Padre Simón de Burgos. You are new here?"

Rafe looked up at the padre. Unlike Padre Antonio at the mission in El Paso, this padre was young and thin with a thick fringe of sandy hair cut in the tonsure style. Rafe thought he was probably not much older than himself.

"No padre, I am Rafael Reyes de Estrada. I am just passing through and was told I could find a bed to sleep here at the mission," Rafe told him using his real name.

Crossing himself Rafe stood up. The padre saw the gunbelt and two pistols wrapped around his waist.

"Yes, you may stay the night, but we do not allow guns here. Get your belongings and I will show you to the guest quarters."

"Where can I put my horse?" Rafe asked.

"Leave it where it is. I will ask Lucas to tend to the horse and your weapons."

Rafe went outside and gathered his gear, stowing the weapons. The padre followed him and waited by the door. Following the padre to the back of the chapel, they walked down a corridor and the padre showed him into a small room.

"I will send someone to get you for the evening meal. You will find soap, water, and towels in the communal room at the end of the hall," the padre told him and left.

Rafe shrugged out of the gray suit. It was beginning to look shabby after hard travel on the trail. He shook it to release the dust and draped it over a small chair. After a refreshing washing of his face and body with a soapy towel, he returned to the room and reclined on the bed. As always, she was there when he closed his eyes.

He struggled to get the nightmare images of Ana Teresa and his dead child from his mind. He tried to replace them with dancing the Bolero at *don* Pedro's home the first time they met. Slowly he put the anger aside, enjoying the daydream of dancing with his wife. It was not hard to focus on her golden-brown eyes, as it soothed his heart and put him to sleep.

A knocking at the door brought him out of a light sleep. "Yes." he called out.

"Padre Simón said to bring you for the evening meal," a voice called through the closed door.

"Yes, I am coming." He got up quickly, donned his suit coat and opened the door to find an older padre waiting. He followed him to the dining hall.

"Welcome Rafael," Padre Simón stood up and spoke to the small group. "Everyone, this is Rafael Reyes de Estrada. Rafael, this is Padre Gaspar, Sister Angelina, and Sister Emma," the padre introduced the small group. Rafe was surprised how few people resided here. Padre Gaspar was the older priest who brought him to the dining room. *"Buenas tardes,"* Rafe greeted them and they returned the greeting before Rafe took a seat next to Padre Gaspar who then started a prayer.

"Tonight we raise our thanks to you oh Lord for bringing Rafael into our midst during his journey. We ask your blessing oh Lord on these two plump chickens and fresh vegetables from our garden, which have been prepared for our sustenance. Thank you for your bounty and your grace. We ask these blessings oh Lord. Amen." he finished the prayer and opened his eyes.

"Padre Gaspar used his skills to broil the fowl in his special way," the Padre Simón said to Rafe.

The smell of the broiled chicken made Rafe's stomach grumble and it filled him with joy to be welcomed at their table. Unlike the mission outside of El Paso, the nuns and priests joined in happy conversation as they dug into the broiled chicken, with fresh squash, carrots, turnips, and fresh made tortillas. It was Rafe's first Spanish meal since he left Santa Fe and he devoured his helping with gusto.

"Rafael, where is your home?" Padre Simón asked after Rafe's plate was clean.

"Ah . . . Santa Fe," he answered. He almost said Pueblo, Colorado, but something about being in the mission and with the priests made him want to tell the truth.

"What brings you to our small village?"

The Padre's second question was more difficult to answer truthfully. He did not want to lie, so he used half-truths. "I am a gunsmith and on a sales trip. I was in Lincoln and just happened to come by Tularosa," Rafe answered. "What about you Padre? This mission looks new. How did you come to be here?" Rafe asked quickly trying to change the subject. Padre Simón did not look Mexican, definitely not a *mestizo*. He was light skinned and had gray-blue eyes and sandy hair.

"My family comes from Burgos. It is in the province of Castile, in the north of Spain. I was born in Mexico City. Padre Gaspar comes from Michoacán and the sisters both come from Sonora, Mexico," Padre Simón explained.

"I was born in Torreón in the state of Coahuila," Rafe told them.

"How is it that you now live in Santa Fe?" Padre Gaspar asked.

"Padre, it is a long story. Surely you have other chores to do." There were parts of his life history he thought he would rather not share with these strangers, especially priests.

"We have nothing but time and you are our welcomed guest. Please entertain us with your life's story."

CHAPTER 44

"Well, I was raised a *peón* on a hacienda in Torreón. My father died at the battle with the French in Puebla in 1862. When I was seventeen-years old, I came home to our *jacal* for lunch one day and found my fifteen-year-old sister had been raped and battered by the *haciendero*. I took my father's flintlock pistol and went to the main house. There I shot the *desgraciado* in revenge. I took a horse and escaped north to my uncle's rancho in El Paso."

"Oh!" both of the sisters reacted to what Rafe said with a gasp. It did not surprise him and then he continued. "On my way north I came upon a grisly scene. Indians had attacked a small wagon in the desert east of El Paso. One man was killed and the other gravely injured. I did what I could to ease the man's suffering and removed an arrow from his leg. I managed to right the wagon and find the team horses, then took the man to El Paso to find a doctor. The man was a gunsmith named George Summers from Santa Fe."

Rafe looked at the eyes intently staring at him and took a breath. There was so much more to the story, but he decided to cut it short.

"George appreciated my help and realized my situation. He took me to Santa Fe and taught me English and the gun business. He said he owed his life to me, but really I owe him my life."

"God works in mysterious ways, my young friend," Padre Simón said. The priests and nuns crossed themselves and nodded in agreement.

The conversation amongst them turned to chores and the weekly schedule as they finished the meal. Padre Gaspar and the sisters rose and began to stack the dirty dishes and clear the table.

"Rafael, come with me. I have a jug of a fine wine made by Gaspar," Padre Simón said. Rafe followed him into a courtyard surrounded by a flower garden. They sat at a wooden table. From a clay jug, the padre poured wine into two clay cups. *"Salud,"* they raised the cups and drank. They drank the first cup and the padre poured another.

For the first time since he left Santa Fe on his quest for revenge, Rafe relaxed. Being at the mission was like a salve for his soul. He liked the young padre who was talking ardently about how God brought him to Tularosa. As Padre Simón spoke about how he gathered his flock here in this small village and how the people helped to build the chapel, Rafe's mind wandered to better times in his life.

"I have noticed something in you since you came here. What is troubling you brother?" Padre Simón asked suddenly changing the subject. Startled, Rafe sat up and stared at the padre.

"What do you mean? Troubled?" Rafe replied.

"Your soul is heavy. You may do your confession. Whatever it is that is troubling you stays with God."

"I am reluctant to confess, Padre. So much has happened in my life and I am not sure God has me in his favor. Perhaps it is better to accept my fate," Rafe told him looking down at his hands holding the clay cup. He raised the cup and took a sip.

"Everyone is in God's favor, Rafael. As you must know, God the father gave his only Son to be sacrificed for all our sins, past, present and future. I am a good judge of character and you do not strike me as a man who would willingly sin against your fellow man."

"I have, Padre. I am not the man you think I am."

"Then tell me about the man you are."

"Padre, I explained how I grew up on a hacienda in Mexico. Like most working people, my family and I were *peóns*. After I shot the *haciendero* for raping my sister, I fled north and ended up in Santa Fe as I told you. I was educated by my adopted father and taken in by his family like a son. However, I am still a *peón* in the eyes of Spaniards, because I am a *mestizo*."

"I am aware of the Spanish *casta* system. It is not of God's making, but of people. It is slowly changing."

"Yes, slowly, and not without a fight. I was shunned

by the Spanish aristocracy in Santa Fe and harassed because I fell in love with a Spanish woman. Because of my feelings for her, I was attacked and almost killed by the young Spanish *caballeros*. They tried to stop our courtship because according to some ancient Spanish caste rules, they believed I was not allowed to even talk to a Spanish *señorita* because I am *mestizo*. I fought for my rights as an American and a man died because of that fight when his horse fell upon him. The Spaniards tried to hang me, but the American justice system prevailed and I was found innocent." Rafe finished the story about the incident with Diego de la Torre and the fateful events in Santa Fe.

"And did this woman love you in return?"

"Yes Padre. We married. Her name was Ana Teresa."

"Was?"

Rafe stopped and raised the wine cup and drained it in one swallow.

"She was killed by squatters in San Gabriel. We were at a wedding fiesta for her cousin and six masked men rode into the courtyard firing at everyone. She and several others were killed. She was eight months pregnant with our first child." Rafe broke down and sobbed. It was the first time he allowed himself to let the grief pour out.

The padre waited patiently, allowing Rafe's grief to run its course. It was a sad story, not unlike many the padre heard over his time as a priest. Life was difficult. Any number of pestilences, diseases, hunger, childbirth, animal attacks, accidents, and plain stupidity of the human race could snap a life in an instant.

Finally, Rafe collected himself. "I have broken the commandments, Padre. I have killed. Not willingly in the past, but I have been hunting the men who killed my wife and unborn child. God will not forgive me."

"And you have killed these men?"

"I have killed two. Two others I left for the *don* in San Gabriel to deal with. Now I am hunting a man who was the leader. I tracked him to Lincoln, but missed him. I was told he might be headed to Silver City. When I find him I will kill him, Padre."

Padre Simón leaned back after hearing Rafe's confession. He was a bit stunned by what he heard and slowly brought up his cup to his lips and drank from it. "Rafael, vengeance cannot be the answer. We must learn to forgive, because you must not become a killer like the man you seek."

"I have already killed two, Padre. I am already just like them. The only difference is I have not killed innocent women and children. I have killed in retribution."

"Our Father teaches us a killing is a killing. You must pray to God to forgive you. Only he can wash you of your sins. You must stop this and go home. Vengeance cannot bring back your wife and unborn child. They are with God in heaven now."

"I hear your words padre, but I have conflicting feelings. I have blood-thirsty Aztec blood flowing in me that pushes me and Spanish blood that believes in God's commandments and forgiveness. The Aztec Gods push me forward to spill the blood of these killers. How could God let this terrible thing happen and go unpunished? Sometimes I believe God has abandoned me."

Rafe's words came tumbling out. God had sent him more than his fair share of grief. At each turn of his life, it seemed his life was full of strife and hardship. Only George Summers and the Summers' family remained a shining beacon of unconditional love for him. He had planned to build on that for Ana Teresa and his children. He planned to give his children all his love and to raise them in a world full of opportunity. Then that dream was shattered by a bullet fired from the gun of deranged killers.

Padre Simón sat silently thinking and looking at Rafe. "You fascinate me, Rafael. Never before have I met a man quite like you. A so-called *peón,* a *mestizo,* educated, and a man of two worlds – the old and the new. It is sad the priests who came with Hernán Cortés and other Spaniards destroyed the Aztec libraries. We would have learned so much of that world. Still, I beg you, stop this vengeance. You must go home and atone for the sins you have committed. Ask God to forgive you and do not kill anymore."

"I am torn, Padre. I want to go home, but I swore this vendetta. I do not believe I can face the memories of my wife without avenging her. The Aztec side of me is pushing to kill."

"Do not let the dark side win, brother. You are a better man listening to your Spanish side. God loves you and will give you strength." Padre Simón spoke firmly, but with compassion. He genuinely liked Rafe and wanted to save him from leading a life directly into Satan's kingdom.

"Stay here, Rafael. Stay until you rid yourself of the evil which is pushing you. I can help you."

Rafe looked at him. The padre's kind face was full of concern.

"I will think on it, Padre. I thank you for your advice. I know it is good, but like I said there is a force pushing me to find and make the murderer atone for his sin," Rafe said in strong terms. Tears came to his eyes as the image of Ana Teresa filled his subconscious and would not go away. "I am tired Padre. I need rest."

"Yes, it is late, you rest, and we will speak again tomorrow," Padre Simón said after he saw the tears. He stood and walked with Rafe back to the small bedroom.

Rafe awoke long before sunup in a cold sweat from a nightmare. In the dream, Ana Teresa was calling to him, motioning to him with one hand. In her other arm, she held a bundle. It was a different nightmare than the ones where he saw her covered in blood and their baby dead in the dirt. She looked happy and smiling. Rafe woke believing she was calling him to join her in heaven.

Padre Simón's kindness and words were also on his mind. He should give up this quest and go back to Santa Fe. Nothing could bring them back. Nevertheless, he had gone too far and God would never allow him to unite with Ana Teresa and their child in heaven. Rafe knew he was going to hell. Well, if he was going to Satan's palace, then Kip Donohoe was going with him. Frustrated, he got up and got dressed.

It was still dark outside and he had trouble finding the

small stable. Quietly he saddled the brown gelding and loaded his gear. Pulling the reins and leading the horse out of the courtyard, he saddled up and headed south out of Tularosa. After a little while of riding in the darkness, Rafe slowed and treaded carefully as he saw a whiteness to the right of him. The trees and even the small brush had disappeared. He rode carefully and as the sun started to lighten the eastern sky, he discovered he was riding near a vast white sand desert. For hours he skirted the desert, riding southeast away from the rising sun.

By noon, Rafe was still passing the white sand desert and following a trail he hoped led to Las Cruces. He rested the horse, but found no shade trees or any water sources. He poured water from his canteen into his hat and let the horse drink from it. The heat of the desert pushed him on and he hoped he could reach Las Cruces by sundown.

CHAPTER 45

"Look how he's holding onto my finger," Lolo said to Lizzy. The baby had grown over the past several weeks to be almost full-term size. The doctor estimated he now weighed over six pounds. His cheeks had definitely puffed out and his cherub looks were delighting the entire Summers' family.

It had been over three weeks since Ana Teresa and the tiny baby arrived home. Both were doing well. The Summers' teenage daughters were enthralled with the baby's every accomplishment. They spent many long hours walking, cuddling, and helping in every way with him. Marcella, Ana Teresa's mother, had to fight them to get a chance to hold her grandson.

Doctor Roybal warned Ana Teresa to limit her activity until she was totally healed. He warned her against heavy lifting and certain other movements. She could walk, but with pain and did not venture far. In the first weeks, George or one of the foundry men carried her up and down the stairs to supper and back to the bedroom. Now she was carefully navigating the stairs by herself. Most sunny spring afternoons found her sitting in a rocking chair on the veranda.

Today, she was sitting enjoying the sun when a buggy drove into the courtyard. Carlos was driving. Bibiana and her mother *doña* Agustina holding Benicío stepped down.

"Bienvenidos," she welcomed them.

Ana Teresa was surprised when *doña* Agustina set Benicío on his small feet. The toddler held her hand and took uncertain steps, but he was walking.

"Look at him!" Ana Teresa cried out.

Bibiana rushed up the steps and gave Ana Teresa a hearty *abrazo.* "He started walking a couple days ago."

"He's young. Isn't he too young to be walking?"

"Carlos says every baby is different. Some walk earlier than others, some talk earlier. Mother says I didn't walk until I was almost fifteen months and then I started running."

Carlos walked up and gave his respects to Ana Teresa, then asked for George. "He's in the foundry, of course." Carlos nodded and walked down the front steps and headed across the courtyard in front of the house. The large foundry was well off to the side and behind the house. Carlos found George working at a long table. Gun parts were spread out on the table in various stages of completion.

"Buenas tardes," Carlos greeted him.

"Oh, Carlos. I'm glad you have come. Let's go to my office where it is quieter."

Carlos thought George looked weary. No doubt running the foundry without Rafe's help was tiring and Carlos knew George was a perfectionist when it came to the guns. They reached the office and George closed the door.

"I received some responses to my letters," George said. He picked up two envelopes.

"Has anyone seen him?"

"Yes. Here read this letter from Bill Moore," George handed a folded piece of paper to Carlos.

George,

Good to receive your letter. Rafe was here over two months ago. He was seeking the men who killed his wife. You can imagine how shocked we all are to learn she is alive and well. He found one of the men here, a Jesse Kincaid, and confronted him. Of course Rafe outdrew him. Lefty says Rafe headed for Cimarron, where he believed the others were hiding. Contact Alexander Sullivan at the Cimarron News. I gave Rafe a letter of introduction to him. If he went to Cimarron, Alexander would know. Elizabethtown is almost dead and we will be pulling up stakes soon. I will write to you when I reach Saint Louis.

Your friend,
Bill Moore

"He was probably in E-town or Cimarron when I rode near there getting Doctor Spencer at Fort Union." George pursed his lips as he spoke in frustration.

"You could not know," Carlos responded. "I could have ridden off to E-town after we learned Kip Donohoe was headed there." Both men shook their heads in personal reproach.

"Who is the other letter from?" Carlos asked.

"Padre Serrano, from the mission in El Paso. He sees Rafe's uncle Jose every Sunday and no one has seen him there. He has the brothers at the mission saying special prayers for Rafe's safe return."

"That's the mission where Rafe funded the school?" Carlos asked.

"Yes, and the padre who married Rafe and Ana Teresa. I thought it might be a place Rafe would go if he was near El Paso, or to his uncle's home."

Carlos took the letter and scanned it himself. It ended by saying the padre was in declining health. Carlos set the letter from the padre on the desk and picked up the one from Bill Moore.

"What about this Alexander Sullivan?"

"I already sent him a wire two days ago, but have yet had a response."

It was little to go on and Carlos was as equally frustrated as George. "Well, I suppose it is something. He has to be somewhere."

"I still find it hard to believe he has not come home, even though he thinks Ana Teresa dead. His horses and life are here in Santa Fe," George said.

"Yes, I agree. Perhaps we should go to Cimarron immediately and see if he is still there," Carlos suggested.

"We can wait until I hear from Alexander Sullivan. I am doubtful Rafe is there."

"What else can we do?" Carlos asked.

"When Bill said Alexander Sullivan is a newspaper man, it gave me an idea. We can contact local newspapers and have them run articles about Rafe – man is missing, or wife of missing man is alive, something that would catch people's eye. Hopefully his."

"That's a great idea. Rafe likes to read newspapers. Surely he will see it. We should have thought about this before."

George patted Carlos' shoulder. "We'll find him."

CHAPTER 46

Kip Donohoe and his friend Buster Thomas arrived at Silver City after five hard days on the trail. They had some money, about enough for another week. Kip cursed himself for not going to his cousin for more money before they fled Lincoln. Although, he doubted Larry would have given him any. In fact, all they really had were the clothes on their backs. Their horses were pretty much done in and they limped into Silver City walking the last several miles, leading the helpless animals.

They found the livery stable and pulled the horses in. "Em hosses cud fall any minute," the stable man said and laughed.

"Yew got that rat. Feed em good and git em rubbed down," Kip told him.

"Dun yew worry. I'll fix em up or they'll be dead by mornin."

"Yew know if a man named Harvey Whitehill is here in Silver City?" Kip asked.

"Harvey Whitehill? How do yew know im?" the stable man looked quizzically at the two dirty cowhands. Mister Whitehill was the most upstanding citizen of Silver City. He was running for sheriff in the election next week.

"I knew im when he was in E-town," Kip blustered. "Knew im well up thar."

"Yew can find im down at the end of Main Street. He has the biggest and best house in town. Yew cain't miss it."

"Much obliged." Kip led Buster to find Whitehill's house.

"Do yew really know this Whitehill feller," Buster asked.

"Yep. Met im a coupla times up in E-town. He had a mine up thar, but it ran out. He tole everyone he was gonna go ta Silver City and try his luck thar. I'm thinking he can hep us git a job," Kip told him.

Whitehill's house was impressive. A sign stretched

across the front stating, "VOTE FOR WHITEHILL."

A maid opened the front door of the Whitehill house when Kip knocked. "Yes?" she asked. She was a young Hispanic woman and gave Kip and Buster a concerned look. "I'm a friend of Mister Whitehills. Tell im Kip Donohoe would like ta see im."

"You wait here," she said in a Spanish accent and left them on the porch.

Road dirty and weary, Kip and Buster sat on the porch rail and waited. It was almost sundown and the evening was turning cool. The door opened. "Please, come in," the maid told them and led them down a long hallway to Harvey Whitehill's office.

"Kip, what are you doing in Silver City?" Whitehill asked, but did not get up from his chair behind his desk. He was a bit uneasy over Kip's appearance. It looked like Kip and the other fellow had slept in a rainstorm and then rolled in a mud puddle. His hair was matted and his clothes dirty.

"My mine gave out like yers up thar at E-town. Went and tried ta make it up thar at Cimarron. Dun like pushing cows, so me and my friend Buster here thought we'd try our luck at minin here in Silver City," Kip lied. "I membered yew was cumin here, Harvey. I was a hopin yew might hep us git goin on a mine," Kip continued.

Kip shifted from foot to foot. Harvey Whitehill had changed since the days in E-town. Harvey was dressed in a white ruffled shirt and satin smoking jacket. The furnishings in the house were expensive. When they were in E-town, Harvey was a miner. He had a good claim and had workers, but he was not the Harvey Whitehill now sitting in the chair in this fancy room.

"Glad to know you Buster. I guess it is your lucky day and mine too. I could use a couple of men on a new find I got going. Can you start tomorrow?"

Kip was disappointed, however held his tongue. He had hoped Whitehill would help to set them up on a mine of their own, not working at his mine. Well, it was a start anyway.

"Yeah, we can start tomorrow. Rat now we need a

place ta stay," Kip responded.

"Not a problem. We built a mine shack up there for anyone who wants to stay there. Here take this note to Ma Barker's Boarding House. Get yourselves cleaned up, fed, and get a good night's rest. Come by at sunup and I'll take you up there." Whitehill wrote a note and handed it to Kip. "By the way Kip, I heard Henri Lambert moved up there to Cimarron?"

"Yes, the Frenchman opened a hotel, restaurant, and saloon. Called it the Lambert Inn. Mighty fine place, Harvey, and a rowdy place too. Jaspers git emselves kilt most every night."

"That so? Henri didn't strike me as one who would tolerate that kind of behavior at his place," Whitehill said.

"He ain't got no choice. Cimarron is a wild place, anybody kin git kilt thar," Kip said with a slight grin.

"I'm going to tell you now boys, I'm running for Grant County Sheriff and I'm going to win. So stay out of trouble. I'm going to clean up Silver City and make it a respectable place. This is not Elizabethtown," Whitehill gave them a warning. Whitehill knew Kip ran with the Clay Allison gang and had a reputation as a troublemaker. Here in Silver City the claim jumping gang boss was Candy Boggs. He had a hideout up near Silver Creek and had the current sheriff in his pocket.

Whitehill had his reservations hiring Kip, however he needed workers badly and Kip knew the mining business. He also knew how to use a gun when necessary.

CHAPTER 47

Rafe welcomed the long shadows as a break from the hot sun when he rode into Las Cruces. He had frequented Las Cruces on gun selling trips over the past six years and knew the town well. The first time he came to the City of Crosses was with George Summers when he was seventeen. While trekking across the white sand desert, he pondered whether to stop, as he would be recognized. Here he could not use his made-up names and aliases as he had been doing along the way. Finally, he decided to stop in a usual manner, pretending he was on a sales trip. He needed a bath and a good night's rest.

Riding in from the east, Rafe followed the dirt road until he could see the steeple of Saint Genevive's Catholic Church. Unlike Lincoln, Las Cruces was an old Spanish town, settled originally by Mescalero Apaches and then by Spanish settlers along the Rio Grande. The snaking river gave sustenance to the Indians and the settlers and later to travelers along the El Camino Real, the King's Highway and also called the Chihuahua Trail.

At the north end of town, Rafe passed the Catholic Church and cemetery and turned southwest onto Main Street. He directed the tired horse to the El Camino Inn. It was where he usually stayed on his trips here. After settling the horse in the small corral, Rafe walked into the inn.

"Bienvenido Señor Reyes," the desk clerk greeted him by name.

"Buenas noches. Necesito una habitacion y un baño," Rafe told him he needed a room and a bath.

"¿Cuántos días?" The clerk asked how many days he was staying.

"No lo sé," Rafe replied he was not sure.

Later, after languishing in a warm bath, he dressed and walked to a small cantina. A plate of beef simmered in robust red chili sauce and tortillas filled his empty belly. After drinking a second beer, he walked back to the inn.

Loud talking in the hallway woke him late in the morning of the next day. Stretching, he stayed in bed for a bit thinking about what to do next.

The only sure thing he knew, he was headed to Silver City. There he hoped to find Kip Donohoe and kill him. Silver had been found in the hills north of what was a small settlement and it was now called Silver City. Rafe heard the silver boom there was in full swing. He knew it would be much like Elizabethtown was several years ago, where the discovery of ore brought thousands of hopeful miners. A hastily built town would be surrounded by a bustling tent city.

The boom and bust mentality of miners and hustlers meant Silver City would also be much like Elizabethtown, where killings and claim jumping would rank high in the crime rate. If Kip Donohoe was there, Rafe thought he would be up to no good. This played in Rafe's favor. Killing a claim jumper would probably not be a hanging offence.

He tried not to ponder what to do if Kip was not there. He would have to back track and just hope to find his trail. Could be the killer was at any of the small villages from Lincoln to El Paso. Perhaps Kip might even have gone into Mexico. Even that thought did not dissuade him from his task. If Kip escaped into Mexico, Rafe would follow. It was his home turf and there they spoke his native language. Kip would be the outsider and at a disadvantage.

He shook the thoughts from his brain and got out of bed. Dressing in work clothes, he went to a small cafe for lunch and then checked on the gelding. Deciding to take a ride, he saddled the horse and headed south. The late spring day was glorious, with a teal blue sky and puffy white clouds scuttling along in the spring breeze. The Organ Mountains rimmed the Mesilla Valley floor. The Rio Grande flowed at the base of the mountains creating a swath of dark green.

The Organ Mountains were steep and rugged as they rose high into the sky. Studying the peaks, Rafe thought they still sported a bit of snow, but then decided it was just granite gleaming in the bright sunlight. Away from the river, the terrain was sparse with creosote bushes, native grasses, and a variety of low growing cactus.

Winding his way along the river, he finally arrived at the stagecoach waystation south of town. The El Camino Real was dotted with waystations to provide security and rest for travelers. Most caravans stopped here south of Las Cruces before they headed north or west.

Rafe rode into the waystation's barn and jumped off his horse.

"Good afternoon," the liveryman greeted him. "You stopping for the night or just getting some food?"

"Just stopping to rest my horse and get a drink. You can keep him saddled, but give him some oats, please."

"Sure thing mister. Just go on inside and I'll take care of your horse."

Rafe walked through the door of the main building and sat at an empty table. The smell of food cooking made his stomach suddenly growl.

"Good afternoon. I got stew or steak and potatoes," the waiter said.

"The steak and potatoes sounds good and a beer, please."

"Sure thing. Coming right up."

Several others were in the room eating. Waystations were mostly quick stopovers for stagecoach drivers to get a fresh team of horses and the passengers to get a meal. Wagon caravans also used the waystations to rest and eat. A three-wagon caravan and a team-hitched wagon were parked in the yard. Seeing the wagon gave Rafe an idea.

When the waiter returned with his food, Rafe asked, "Do you know if any wagons are headed to Silver City?" he asked the waiter.

"Well, I can ask the station master."

The waiter placed a broiled T-bone steak on an oversized plate on the table. Steam rose from the freshly cooked steak. Rafe's eyes widened a bit at the delicious sight and he wasted no time going after the inviting dish. In between bites, he took swallows from a glass of beer. After finishing the steak and potatoes, he picked up the bone and chewed clinging bits of meat.

When the waiter came to check on him, Rafe ordered a piece of apple pie.

"There is a caravan going to Silver City tomorrow. See the man over there, the one with the brown floppy hat and mustache. He's the wagon master. His name is Elmer Goggins and the station master says he's a crusty old coot, so be careful when you approach him," the waiter whispered, then turned to retrieve Rafe's piece of apple pie.

Rafe took his time savoring the apple pie, while he studied the man named Elmer Goggins. He looked to be in his fifties, although it was hard to tell. Stringy brown hair poked out from under the floppy brown hat. His face was covered by a wild, graying beard. Rafe could tell the man was short and stocky. He wore bib overalls under a rough weave wool coat. Rafe thought about buying the man a beer, but a half full glass sat on the man's table. Rafe stood up and walked over.

"Mister Goggins, I understand you are taking a wagon caravan to Silver City tomorrow?"

"Yeah, what's it ta yew?" he answered gruffly, then took a drink of beer leaving foam on his long black, graying mustache.

"Well, I'm a gunsmith going there to sell guns. I'm a good shot and could help protect your cargo in case of trouble."

Old Elmer Goggins looked Rafe over. "What's yer name young feller?"

"I'm Sammy Soto from Pueblo, Colorado."

Elmer looked up at the young man, a Mexican by his tan complexion and dark features. He wore two pistols around his trim waist. He did not look or talk like a gunman and something about his manner put Elmer at ease.

"I'm leavin at sunup, if yew ain't ready ta go, I'll leave without yew," he told Rafe still holding to his gruff manner.

"Thank you sir. I won't be any trouble to you, but like I said I am good with my guns. I'll be here at sunup," Rafe said, tipped his hat, and left.

Elmer agreed to allow the young man to go with him against his better judgment. In his business, he could not afford to trust anyone, especially a Mexican. Knowing greasers were a lazy lot, Elmer thought the young man probably would not show up in the morning.

Rafe returned to Las Cruces and readied his gear. Keeping to his room at the El Camino Inn, Rafe asked the desk clerk for an early wake up. He slept deep and restful, with the nightmares haunting him only twice. Sometime in the not yet light morning, he was awakened by a tap on the door.

The desk clerk had the gelding saddled and waiting. Rafe arrived at the waystation before sunup. True to his word, Elmer Goggins had the wagon caravan ready. Six sturdy mules were hitched in front. As soon as Rafe got there, Elmer started the team and headed west.

"Did'n think yew'd be comin, Sonny," he said grinning at Rafe.

"Would not miss this for the world," Rafe said and laughed. "Let's go."

CHAPTER 48

After the first few days, Kip and Buster found the work in Whitehill's mine hard and dirty and the pay was not what they expected.

"Hey Kip, fuck this minin shit. I'd rather be herdin em stinkin cows. Let's git on back ta Lincoln," Buster complained.

"We cain't go back, the law'll git us. I'd rather go back ta Cimarron, but the law'll git me thar too. We gotta stay here," Kip said in a depressed voice. They were riding back to town for the weekend and heading to the Silver Lady Saloon.

Later they sat at a table near the stage where a voluptuous woman sang a cowboy love song:

I struck the trail in seventy-one,
The herd strung out behind me;
As I jogged along my mind ran back
For the gal I left behind me.
That sweet little gal, that true little gal,
The gal I left behind me!

If ever I get off the trail
And the Indians they don't find me,
I'll make my way straight back again
To the gal I left behind me.
That sweet little gal, that true little gal,
The gal I left behind me!

Kip and Buster sipped on their beers and listened to the singer. At the end of the song, a loud voice interrupted the din of the saloon.

"I'm lookin fer anyone wanting to join up as a deputy. I need three men. I'm paying a hunderd dollars a month. Iffin yer interested cum on up to the bar." Kip noticed the man wore a tin star on his chest. He turned and strode to the bar and the bartender quickly poured him a beer.

Kip noticed no one hurried up to the bar to join the sheriff. A hundred dollars was not a fortune in a mining town. Some of these miners probably dug a hundred dollars a day out of their mines or more.

Buster got up. "Cum on Kip, we'r gonna be deputies."

"What the fuck, Buster. I cain't be no fuckin deputy. I'm wanted by the law."

"Hell, they cain't find yew down here. Yew tole me yew ain't seen no wanted posters out on yew. Cum on let's go. I dun like em fuckin mines. Ittid be better bein a deputy," Buster grumbled and rose from his chair.

The killings in San Gabriel and Cimarron seemed thousands of miles away. No doubt if anyone pursued the red-hooded killers, they had given up long ago. A hundred dollars a month was a good amount of money. Buster was right. The pittance they were making hauling heavy rocks at the mine, was barely enough to scrape out basics in overpriced Silver City. Besides, Kip hated being down in the darkened mine shaft with the stale air and creaking timbers. It always scared the shit out of him. As Buster walked up to the bar, Kip followed.

Kip and Buster signed up with the sheriff as deputies. Kip expected the foreman at Whitehill's mine to be mad when he told the man he and Buster were quitting. The foreman just shrugged and paid them what they were owed.

The current sheriff was an older man named Fred Jenkins. After the first week, Kip suspected Fred was on the take from the local claim jumpers. Kip knew all the signs from his time in E-town where Sheriff Danny Robertson had been on the take from Clay Allison to look the other way. Kip also suspected the sheriff only hired a handful of new deputies to look good for the upcoming election. His opponent Harvey Whitehill was running on a Law and Order ticket, promising to clean up the town and make it safe.

The hundred dollars a month Sheriff Jenkins promised them would not be paid out until the end of the month's term, so Kip and Buster were broke. They spent what little money they had on overpriced food, drinks, and whores and they were quickly realizing even the salary of one hundred dollars a month would barely keep them alive in Silver City.

After paying for a room with a bed at Ma Barker's Boarding House during the first week, they had been sleeping under the stars in a makeshift lean-to made of tree branches and a canvas tarp. It leaked in the rain and gave them little shelter, but Ma Barker threw them out when they could not pay the one dollar each a night for room and board. Tonight, they sat in the Silver Lady Saloon nursing a beer.

"I'm almost busted," Buster complained.

"I hate these mining towns. They overcharge for everything," Kip replied.

"What r we goin do? A fuckin plate of food at that miner's camp is fifty cents." Buster took a sip of the beer. He thought if they stayed much longer in Silver City they would starve.

"We gotta git us a claim and quick. It's the only way to survive in these boom towns," Kip told him. Kip had been pondering ideas since they arrived. He hated the hard work of mining and knew the only way to make good was to jump a claim. Working in E-town with Clay Allison had taught him well. "Easier to take it than to find it," Clay used to always say.

However, Clay had over two dozen men in Elizabethtown backing his plays. He had the sheriff bribed to look the other way. In Elizabethtown, Clay had the bartenders, saloon whores, and even the bankers were bribed to sell him information. Nothing went on in E-town Clay did not know about. That especially included which miners had made a good strike.

Kip had run with the Allison gang and knew the methods. After a good strike was found, the gang intimidated the miner to sell out. If that did not work, then the miner met with an unfortunate accident. Of course it was cold-blooded murder. The next day, Clay or one of the men filed on the claim and became the new owner. Clay's gang in E-town had safety with their numbers along with the well placed bribes.

Here in Silver City it was no different. Rumors of claim jumping were rampant and several dead miners had been brought back to town over the last week. Kip heard a man named Candy Boggs was the man running the claim jumpers. He heard rumors about a hideout up off Silver Creek. Kip noticed the sheriff talked a good talk about stopping the jumpers, but never had any of the deputies actively pursuing them. Instead, Kip and the other deputies mostly put on a show at the saloons and later at night patrolling the town.

"Buster, been talking with the other deputies. They tell me a man named Candy Boggs is the Big Bug here in Silver City. We gotta git ta know the man and maybee join up. If the sheriff loses the election, we're gonna be outta of a job. If Boggs is anything like Clay Allison, we kin work fer im and git us our own mine."

"I dun know Kip, I dun like that dirty mine work. I think we shud go back ta Lincoln," Buster complained.

"I tole yew Buster, we cain't go back. It's safer fer us here. Yew wait an see. We'll git rich if we join up with that Candy Boggs feller," Kip said wanting to assure Buster.

CHAPTER 49

Candy Boggs sat on his horse high above the valley leading to the Mother Lode Mine owned by Alberto Chavez. It was rich with silver and one Boggs wanted to take before the election for the new sheriff happened on Saturday. Damn election was going to change things here in Silver City. He believed Whitehill would win and at least for some time follow his slogan to clean up the town. Candy doubted Whitehill would be as easy to bribe as Jenkins. He might have to meet with an unfortunate accident instead. But for now, Candy focused on getting the Mother Lode Mine.

He and the gang had been scouting the mine for more than two weeks. It was one of the larger mines, with seven or eight men working for Chavez. It would not be as easy as the typical one or two miner sites they harassed often. These miners would be armed and ready to fight.

Art Baker, Candy's right-hand man, sat his mount next to Candy. They had discussed the plan and Candy sent two of the men in the opposite direction to flank the mine. A little while later, he saw a signal from Texas Bob that he and Boone were in place.

"Go on. Take it," Candy said to Art. Candy rarely participated in the raids, keeping his hands clean of blood. Art spurred his horse and rode with three other men down toward the mine.

The Boggs' outlaws rode into the mine clearing. Art's first shot took an unsuspecting miner to the ground in a heap. Bullets flew at the opening of the mineshaft sending men running for cover. Several found a little cover and fired back. One of Candy's men on horseback went down. It was a lucky shot.

Alberto Chavez and three of his miners were deep in the tunnel. Shots rang outside. First one or two, then more. The sound resonated off the tunnel's rock walls.

"Jumpers," Chavez yelled. He and his men grabbed their rifles and headed toward the tunnel entrance.

Candy's men worked quickly and efficiently, killing the miners trapped outside the tunnel before Chavez and his men reached the mouth of the shaft. They kept well inside, firing sporadically.

"Johnson, the rest of em are in the mine. We gotta go in and git em," Art Baker called out, as he dismounted.

"That'll be rough going, Art," Johnson warned. "They're armed."

"There can only be three for four of em in thar. We killed four here and from our scouting we only spotted seven or eight of em," Art said. "Let's go."

Up on the ridge hidden by the tree line, Candy Boggs heard the echoes of fierce gunfire below. After the first wave of gunfire outside the mine ended, he saw Art and Johnson heading toward the mine tunnel with their guns drawn. Candy picked his way through the trees closer to the Mother Lode. Gunfire sounded out of the mineshaft, then after a long while, dead silence hit his ears. He nervously waited in the shadows. Anything was possible in a dark mine tunnel. Old Chavez would know the best places to ambush his men. Finally, Art signaled with his hat, meaning success. Boggs turned his horse toward town to file on the Mother Lode Mine. Meanwhile his men would bury the bodies a good distance from the mine and clean up the mess.

Kip and Buster were working as deputies for Sheriff Jenkins, but the election was in a couple days and Kip suspected Whitehill would win easily. Harvey presented a prosperous and intelligent persona and people wanted to believe his slogans.

A saloon girl strode up near their table. "Yew fellers looking fer some fun tonight?" she purred at them. The Silver Lady had the best looking whores in town, but still they looked overused. Even the excessive face paint makeup could not hide the years of hard work.

Kip waved her away. He had no money to waste on whores even though he was horny as hell. He heard Buster grumble about money again under his breath. A few moments later, a ruckus started on the far side of the room at a poker table.

"Yew heard me. Yer a cheater! Yew dun dealt off the bottom of the deck" a voice yelled.

Chairs squeaked against the wooden floor as people quickly tried to move away from the potential violence.

"I dun no such thing. Yer just a poor loser," another voice yelled back. A chair crashed to the floor in the background of the yelling.

"Yew been cheatin me all night."

"Yew won a coupla pots. How's that cheatin?"

Kip rose up to view the confrontation, but Buster stayed in his seat staring at his almost empty beer glass. He saw the bartender grabbing for his shotgun under the bar. Kip was a deputy now and the sheriff had hired them to stop this type of disturbance. He walked over to the table, with the bartender right on his heels.

Pulling his pistol, he stood sternly near the glaring poker players.

"Put the guns down," Kip barked the order.

"Yew heard the deputy. Knock it off Smokey. Yew too Sam. I dun allow this kinda shit in the Silver Lady. Yew know that," the bartender's loud and booming voice announced to everyone he expected them to behave. He was a large man, tall and heavyset. Kip thought he could manhandle almost anyone with his large frame without any help, but the shotgun was an added reinforcement.

"He started it, callin me a cheater," one of the men whined.

"Well I said knock it off now," the bartender growled.

Slowly the saloon returned to normal. The poker players went back to their game, the music restarted, the chairs were righted, and new drinks poured.

Kip returned to the table.

"Yew shudda backed me," Kip grumbled at Buster.

Rafe kept to himself riding slightly behind the lead wagon. Elmer Goggins was indeed a master in keeping the mules moving steadily. Three wagons where hitched together, each with a canvas cover over the contents. The road west from Las Cruces was mostly flat, leaving the tall Organ Mountains disappearing well behind them.

Rafe had traveled this road with George Summers on one business trip when they stopped in Las Cruces and they then took this road to Lordsburg. He remembered it as flat, dusty, and barren. The mules plied the dusty road in a steady, but Rafe thought slow pace. It was high noon by the sun before Rafe rode up next to Elmer.

"Say Mister Goggins, I was wondering why you use mules instead of horses," Rafe tried to start a conversation with the wagon master.

"Yew must be a greenhorn, Sonny," he replied.

"Why do you say that?"

"Well now, yew wooden ask that question iffin yew ever been to Silver City afore."

"No, I've never been to Silver City."

"Well yew see, this here road is nice an flat now, but the road up into Silver City is narrow, steep, and rocky. It gets flooded out regular and will be hard goin. Mules is better," Goggins explained. He grinned at Rafe and his demeanor seemed a bit friendlier.

"I guess you've made this trip often. What can you tell me about Silver City?"

"I've been makin this run once a month for the past three years. I'm the main supplier for the miners up thar and I take care of em good."

"So that's what you're carrying in the wagons, mining supplies?" Rafe asked it as a question.

"Yeah and mail, supplies for the general store and food supplies. I carry just about anythin they need, especially candles and Tommy stickers. Even carried a coupla whores last year. Yeah Sonny, I take em just about anythin." Rafe laughed and Goggins grinned.

"Hey, what the hell's a Tommy sticker?"

"Yeah, yew wooden know about em. They're an iron candle holder they stick into the mine wall. They cain't use lanterns down there cause they could blow the place up."

"I heard Silver City is booming."

"Used ta be a sleepy little Spanish village called

sumpthin San Vicente."

"*La Ciénega de San Vicente,*" Rafe responded in Spanish. "It means the Oasis of Saint Vincent."

"Yeah that Spanish name. Anyway, then silver ore deposits were discovered at Chloride Flat. It were up on the hill just west of the farm of Captain John M. Bullard and his brother James. Think it were 1870, maybee 71. They renamed it Silver City that summer, instead of that Spanish name yew said," Goggins explained what he knew about Silver City.

"So it was the Bullard brothers who struck it rich?" Rafe asked.

"Well yes and no. After the Bullards found silver, another man name of Harvey Whitehill came to Silver City from E-town and struck it big, real big. Now he owns most of the mines and town. He's a good man though. Why yew goin to Silver City? Yew ain't tole me."

"I'm a gunsmith from Pueblo, Colorado. I heard Silver City was a wild place and thought maybe I could make some sales."

"Well Sonny yew probly could at that. The miners need protection frum claim jumpers and the claim jumpers need . . . well they need guns ta do their jumping, I reckin."

"Sounds a lot like E-town used to be," Rafe commented.

"Yew been to E-town?"

"Several times. Helped my friend Bill Moore save his mine from jumpers. I spent some time in E-town several years ago and I might have met Mister Whitehill. If not, I'm sure he knows Bill Moore."

"Yew might want ta look im up when we git thar. He's a friendly type feller. I heard tell Whitehill's running for county sheriff. Says he wants ta clean up Silver City. If so, he's got a tough job," Elmer said.

"That sounds like a good idea Mister Goggins. I may do that."

"I ain't that important to call me mister. Call me Elmer." Elmer was beginning to like the young Mexican. He was not one of those wild outlaw types that were overrunning Silver City. There was a killing almost every day. Elmer had become very cautious, especially after delivering his goods. The outlaws in Silver City knew after he dropped his load, he was paid in cash. It made him a target.

"I haveta tell yew Silver City is a wild town, with em claim jumpers and killers. They say it's a man name of Candy Boggs who runs em claim jumpers. Yew best stay away frum im. Maybe yew cud stick along with me until I drop this load. I cud use some extree protection."

"I'd be happy to Elmer."

CHAPTER 50

The election was Saturday, May 16, 1874. Harvey Whitehill won in a landslide. Harvey threw the town a huge party, with free food and free drinks at all the saloons. Kip and Buster took full advantage of the offer and stayed in the saloon until the wee hours of the following morning.

Kip was unsure what Whitehill's election meant to his position as deputy, but assumed it meant he was again out of a job. On Monday morning, Kip and Buster turned in their badges to ex-sheriff Jenkins and he paid them the portion of the month's pay they deserved. It gave them enough to buy a bed a Ma Barker's and to get a shave, bath, and Buster even bought a new shirt at the mercantile. Kip thought the money would keep them about a week before it ran out.

Harvey's election posed two problems for Kip. First, he was unsure if Harvey was mad he and Buster quit at his mine and second, claim jumping would probably get even harder. Kip thought about going back to Cimarron and wondered if the ruckus he caused there had died down. Stuff like that usually was forgotten pretty quickly.

Several days later Kip saw a WANTED poster on the bulletin board outside of Sheriff Whitehill's office. It had become routine for Kip to view the posters, just in case his face or name was on one of them. This WANTED poster was different. It read:

WANTED: HONEST MEN FOR JOB AS DEPUTY – PAYS $200 A MONTH

He read the poster and kept on walking, chuckling to himself. So, Whitehill wanted deputies to keep the peace, just like Sheriff Jenkins, but he upped the pay. As Kip continued down Main Street, he saw a group of bystanders standing in the middle of the street. He could see Whitehill's head sticking up in the middle of the crowd. He was yelling for the people to move aside. By the time Kip reached the scene, two men were carrying a body up the steep embankment from the Big Ditch as the creek was called. The Big Ditch ran the length of the town, fed by runoff from the mountains.

The men carried the body to where Sheriff Whitehill stood and gently laid it down on the ground.

"It's Hershel West, Sheriff. Been shot through the chest," one of the men reported to Whitehill.

"Oh my God," one woman gasped. "Poor Edna. What will she do, and she's about to pop a fourth baby," another woman lamented.

"Give these men room," the sheriff yelled again.

"What about yer law and order, sheriff. Looks like it ain't workin so good," a man in the back yelled.

"Shut up Tom," Sheriff Whitehill hollered. "Nothing to see here folks. Go on home or about your business."

Kip hung back watching the scene, standing in the shade of the covered walkway across the street. The dead man was carried off and the crowd dispersed. Whitehill carefully walked the area between the two buildings and then carefully stepped down the embankment into the ditch. Kip could see his head and then it would disappear below the deep ditch, only to reappear in another spot.

About a half hour later, Whitehill struggled up the side of the ditch. He carried something in his hand. Kip strolled across the street and met him.

"Good morning Sheriff Whitehill," Kip addressed him formally by his new title.

"Oh, hello Kip."

"What was yew doin down in the ditch?"

"Looking for clues. I found some shell casings, but they are not hard evidence."

"That's too bad. Why would anyone want to kill that man?"

"Hershel just got lucky last week up at his mine. Found a nice vein and stupidly bragged about it at the saloon. These greenhorns never seem to learn."

"Tough luck."

"Damn claim jumpers. Hershel was a good man. Had a wife and three kids. He wasn't a gunhand and the jumpers knew it. No doubt they killed him after he had a couple drinks at the saloon."

Harvey Whitehill looked over at Kip. He knew Kip ran with the Allison gang up in E-town, but he knew Kip joined up as a deputy for Sheriff Jenkins. Whitehill believed in the old idiom, 'leopards don't change their spots.' He had a hard time believing Kip had turned his guns to a useful purpose instead of outlawing. However, he needed men and he needed them fast.

"Kip, I need some good men. Job pays $200 a month and a bonus for bringing in claim jumpers. Ma Barker will put you up for half price. What do you say?"

"Well I guess that sounds purdy good," Kip drawled.

"Tell you what. Come by the office later this afternoon and I'll get you sworn in again. I have to go talk to the widow. I should be back in the office by two o'clock."

"Just one thing Harvey, I need an advance up front," Kip said.

"How much?"

"Say fifty and what about my friend Buster Thomas? He was deputin with me fer Sheriff Jenkins."

"I can use both of you. Come to the office this afternoon and I'll swear you both in," Harvey replied.

"I'll see yew after two."

As the sheriff walked off, Kip wondered why he had agreed to be a deputy again. He usually was on the wrong side of the law. Over the last several weeks, Kip's limited funds had kept him from his drinking habit. In a more sober mood, he found he liked Silver City. The town had a beautiful spot nestled close to the mountains and he was tired of running and sleeping on the hard ground.

Kip strolled back up the hill to the lean-to looking for Buster. The lean-to was really just sticks and a canvas cover. Buster was nowhere around.

"Damn," Kip muttered.

He folded what few belongings of his were strewn around the site and stuffed them into his saddlebags. Putting the saddle on his horse, he looked around. Ma Barker's sure beat this hellhole. Climbing onto the horse's back, he rode back down the hill into town.

"Yew did what?" Buster almost choked when Kip found him at the Silver Lady Saloon and told him the news.

"I joined yew up too."

"Yew gotta be kiddin me. What if the Whitehill finds out about yew? He ain't like Jenkins. I think Whitehill means what he says about law and order."

"I figure if a wanted poster was out on me an Nat an Jesse, it would already be hanging up."

"You swear to uphold the law?" the sheriff asked each of them as they stood in his office later that day.

"Yes sir," they each responded.

Whitehill handed them badges and gave them instructions. "Okay boys, I got a complaint from Albert Dunne about some men scouting his claim. Told me he filed a complaint to Sheriff Jenkins and he did nothing about it. It's up on the northwest trail. You'll see the sign to the Lucky Judy Mine. Albert said he put up a new sign, so you can't miss it. Stay clear of the mine and see if anyone is watching the place. It may be Bogg's men and if so, they will be extremely crafty. Keep a sharp eye out, but don't go after them unless they attack the mine or the men."

As they walked out of the office, Whitehill shook his head slightly. He wondered if Kip had turned a new leaf and he had no idea about Buster's background. He wondered if perhaps he was letting a wolf into the hen house.

CHAPTER 51

As Rafe rode along with Elmer and the mule wagons, the going got a lot tougher and the mountains loomed ahead of them. The trail up the foothills was worse than the trail to E-town. It was rutted and washed out in areas. Finally, they clanked into Silver City mid afternoon.

"Over thar, Ma Barker's Boarding House is just about the only place to stay. Ma serves good meals and the rooms r quiet and the beds r soft."

"I'll go arrange for two rooms while you pull down there to the mercantile. I'll be along shortly."

"Nah Sonny, yew dun nuff. I'll be alright."

Elmer called Rafe, Sonny. It was fine by Rafe, as he had used one of his aliases, Sammy Soto. The less people who knew his real name and real intentions the better. Over the past four days, Rafe learned a lot about the old muleteer. He was born in Canton, Ohio and came west when he was twenty. Elmer tried his hand at mining and cattle droving, until he got shot in the thigh. It made both of those jobs impossible. He started driving a regular supply wagon four years ago when Silver City began to boom.

"I'll have your back Elmer, just like we talked about," Rafe replied.

While Elmer drove down the road to the mercantile, Rafe tied the gelding to the hitching rail in front of Ma Barker's Boarding House. On a simple sign near the front door was written, FOOD AND ROOMS. Inside he found the boarding house to be fresh and homey. Several people loitered in the living room. A large heavyset woman bustled around in a dining room.

Rafe walked toward her. "Excuse me. My name is Sammy Soto, are you Ma Barker?"

"Sure am. You wanting a room?" Ma Barker looked at the slim well-armed young Mexican man. He was well dressed, although his clothes were dusty. He had a several days growth of a dark beard on his face. She did not particularly like the gunslinger look of him.

"Yes Ma'am. Two rooms. One for me and one for Elmer Goggins."

Ma Barker's face immediately changed from a bit of a scowl as a huge grin spread across her face. "You with Elmer? Well why didn't you say so? Elmer always stays here when he's coming through. He takes special good care of me. Brings me special things I can't get no place else. Come with me."

Ma Barker showed Rafe to a room at the end of the hall on the second floor. Elmer can have that one," she told him.

"Thank you kindly ma'am."

"Don't ma'am me. Call me Ma. Everybody does. Supper is from six to eight and breakfast is early. Outhouse is in the back. I expect you to keep your room and yourself tidy and quiet. I don't allow no parties and no women."

"I understand," Rafe replied.

After securing the two rooms, he unloaded his belongings, especially the extra guns and short-barrel shotgun. Taking the saddlebags to his room, he splashed his face with water.

The face staring back in the mirror was unfamiliar. The months on the trail left him gaunt both inside and out. His dark brown eyes were somewhat sunken. They held no joy and stared morosely at the rest of his face. His cheekbones protruded more than usual. A week old beard covered his chin. His oily unruly hair had grown longer again and stuck out oddly from where his Stetson covered his head.

He tried hard to remember his face when there was joy in his heart. The man he used to be was gone, replaced with this monster before him. He used to be a son, a brother, a husband, and almost a father. He bred blooded horses and made guns in George's foundry. Now he was a killer.

Just several months ago, he had everything to live for. His life was full of joy and anticipation. Now he cared little if he lived or died. He only wanted to live long enough to kill Kip Donohoe. Splashing his face again, Rafe patted it dry with a towel and turned to leave.

As he walked down the stairs, Ma called his attention.

"Mister Soto, I forgot to ask how long you will be staying?"

"I'm not sure, possibly a week. It depends on how well my business goes," Rafe told her. Ma did not ask about Elmer. He usually stayed only a few days on each trip.

Rafe walked out into the sunshine of Silver City. He could see the town had been hastily built, with rough-sawn lumber buildings and canvas roofs. Up the road leading to the mountain, canvas tents dotted the landscape for as far as his eye could see. He untied the gelding and hopped aboard. Keeping the horse to a slow walk, he headed down Main Street to find the mercantile.

Elmer's wagons were not parked in front, but Rafe was sure they could not be unloaded already. Kicking himself for not staying with Elmer, he pushed in the mercantile doors and strode in.

"Hey Sonny!" Elmer called to him. Elmer was seated on a barrel smoking a pipe.

"Where are the wagons?"

"Out back. A couple of boys are unloading them and doing inventory. Did yew see Ma?"

"Yes, I got us two rooms. She was excited you were back in town. She said you bring her special things," Rafe told him with a sly grin.

Elmer's eyes glinted. "She likes sweet treats, so I bring her chocolates, raisins, and dried apricots. Iffin I kin find em, I bring her pecans, but that's usually in the fall."

"Well she certainly likes you," Rafe said with a grin.

A short stocky man came from the back room and broke into their conversation. "Well everything looks good Elmer. I'll get it all tallied and Roger will give you your money tomorrow. He should have a list of what we need for the next trip made out by then too. Come by after noon," the clerk said.

"Much obliged. Come on Sonny, let's go git those beers we been dreamin about."

After several cold beers at the Silver Lady Saloon, Elmer walked and Rafe rode back to Ma's Boarding House.

Ma greeted Elmer with a big hug and a bigger hug when he gave her the brown paper packages he was carrying. She grinned a wide smile and kissed him on his cheek.

"Ah sucks Ma. Yer gonna embarrass me."

"Excuse me Ma. Do you have a place for my horse and a hot bath for me?" Rafe asked.

"Take the horse around back and I'll get the hot water started. Evening meal is in about two hours. I'm makin fried chicken and biscuits."

"Yew know that's my favorite," Elmer said and gave her a swat on her ample behind. Ma Barker giggled like a young girl.

After a bath and a shave, Rafe dusted the gray suit and brushed the black Stetson. The rest of his clothing, he stacked in a pile, having decided to ask Ma if there was a laundry in town. The aroma of fried chicken filled the air when he opened the door and he followed it to the dining room.

"Help yourself. Biscuits are in the bowl, cool tea and water in the pitchers on the table, and the chicken is coming in a minute," Ma told him.

Before the chicken made it to the table, Elmer walked into the dining room. Rafe did a double take. Elmer was clean shaven and dressed in a plaid jacket and brown pants. His hair was clean and slicked back on his head. Rafe noticed his blue shirt picked up the blue in his eyes. It was as if he changed from a grizzly bear into a dapper man.

When Ma Barker walked into the dining room with the platter of chicken, Elmer took the heavy dish from her and put it on the table. Ma blushed.

"Now you all help yourselves."

"Thank you ma'am." Rafe wasted no time as he took several pieces of chicken and two biscuits. Ma had placed a large jar of jam and a dish of butter on the table, and Rafe smeared his biscuits with both. He poured a glass of cool tea.

Two other men strolled into the dining room and joined Rafe and Elmer. James Jeffries was from Oklahoma and Pete Lauflin was from Missouri. Both were hoping to make a strike. Pete left a wife and four children in Saint

Louis.

With his hunger satisfied, Rafe excused himself from the table and told Elmer he was going to take a walk through town.

"Yew be careful now. Member what I tole yew bout this here town, Sonny," Elmer warned him.

Rafe strolled along the boardwalk of Silver City. Long shadows were overtaking the town and gaslights illuminated the buildings. The length of the main road through town was not long. He passed a bank, the darkened mercantile, two saloons, the sheriff's office and jail, a Chinese laundry, two cafes and the assay office. Down a side street, he saw three houses with red lights signaling sin.

As night fell over the city, the mountains and the road dotted with canvas huts disappeared, leaving the small town surrounded by only darkness. Rafe continued along the road, which started to climb steeper toward the mountains. Further past the main part of town, small wooden houses dotted both sides of the road. Wooden signs announced their occupants – doctor, lawyer, dressmaker, land office. As the road ended, a large two-story house with pillars stood like a guard to the mountain. The house had a view back over the entire town. Across the porch, a banner flapped in the wind. It was too dark for Rafe to read it, but he assumed the house belonged to Harvey Whitehill. Rafe saw notices in town about the recent election.

Turning at the end of the road, he headed back. Rafe was satisfied that if Kip Donohoe was in Silver City, he could find him. As he walked in the darkness back to town, a group of men were laughing and hollering coming toward him. Talking loudly, the men obviously had their fill at one of the saloons. Rafe was heeled with his two double-action pistols and unafraid. In his mind he thought if Elmer was right about Silver City being a wild place, he would need to be ready for any trouble.

The group of miners walked on by Rafe without any acknowledgement. Rafe relaxed and walked the rest of the way back into town.

Chapter 52

Rafe heard the piano music and a woman's voice before he got to the batwing doors of the Silver Lady Saloon. Surprisingly, the piano was tuned, unlike most tinny pianos in other saloons he had been to. No one noticed when the batwing doors swung back and forth, as Rafe stepped in and made his way to near the end of the bar.

"Beer," he ordered.

He took the mug and turned to face the woman singer and three frilly dressed young women who danced behind her while flashing their dresses up above their knees. Most of the patrons watched the show, while most all the poker and Faro tables were full with gamblers. If Silver City was like E-town, the gamblers were miners spending their hard-earned profits. Among them would be shysters and cheaters looking to turn a quick profit.

Rafe watched and listened to the woman's smooth but powerful voice. A tremendous roar erupted when she finished the song and left the stage. Only the piano man stayed and continued playing.

Rafe looked around, wondering if Kip Donohoe sat at a poker table or was one of the men sitting at a table near the stage. How he wished he knew what the killer looked like. His brain flicked to images of taking the killer as he had Jesse Kincaid in E-town. He would confront him, calling him a murderer of women and children, and shoot him on the spot.

"Hey thar, Sonny." Elmer's voice shook Rafe out of his thoughts. "Huh, oh, hey there Elmer. I thought you might stay at Ma's," Rafe responded.

"Time fer that later. Right now I need a shot and a beer."

Rafe signaled the bartender and ordered for Elmer and another for himself. "How long you staying in Silver City?" Rafe asked.

"I'll spend a few days here and rest the mules. How

bout yew?"

"Don't know yet. I'll go to the mercantile tomorrow and show the proprietor my guns and I think I'll take your advice to go see Harvey Whitehill."

"Just found out Whitehill was elected as the new sheriff. Cud be he will buy those fancy double-action guns of yours. He's the richest man in town." On the trip to Silver City Rafe told Elmer about the guns and demonstrated them to him.

"I kin introduce you to Roger who owns the mercantile. He's a good sort," Elmer offered.

"Thanks. I will go with you tomorrow when you get paid. Remember I promised to have your back until you get out of town," Rafe told him.

"Yew an me make a good team. Say, maybee yew'd consider being my partner. We cud move double the supplies and yew being good with a gun, well, yew cud keep us safe like," Elmer said with a grin.

"That's a good offer, Elmer, and I appreciate it, but I've got other business. My gun selling business takes me in all directions and you need somebody steady."

"Well, it were juss a thought. I'll still introduce yew to Roger tomorrow. I'll tell him yew are alright and em fancy guns are alright, too."

"Tell you what, Elmer. I'll make sure you get one. I sure do appreciate you letting me tag along with you. I had no idea how to get to Silver City."

"Well, I thank yew, Sonny. That wud be rat nice of yew."

A ruckus caught their attention from one of the poker tables just a couple of tables away from where Rafe stood. Chairs skidded and a table was tipped over, scattering chips, bottles, and glasses.

"Yew scum sucking pig! Yew ain't gonna cheat me," a loud voice yelled.

"Don't be crazy Sombrero Jack. I ain't no cheater. You're drunk right now. Put that gun away," a gambling man demanded. He was dressed in black with a white ruffled shirt and a thin black bowtie. His eyes stared wide open looking at the pistol pointed at him by George "Sombrero Jack" Schaefer.

"He's rat Jack, Hank ain't no cheater. Put the gun away," the bartender growled. When the shouting started, the bartender rushed from behind the bar and held a short-barrel shotgun pointed at Sombrero Jack's ribs.

"Awrat, awrat, I'll put my gun away."

"Now git outta here until yew sober up!" The bartender pushed Jack with the point of the barrel of his shotgun. The man nicknamed Sombrero Jack grumbled something to a young teenager standing awkwardly not too far away.

Rafe and Elmer watched the show. It was a small ruckus and since the players knew each other well, it probably would not have turned into real trouble. A teenager moved and followed Sombrero Jack toward the door.

"Who is that kid going out with that man? Is that his son?" Rafe asked.

"That snot-nosed kid been hangin round with Sombrero Jack for some time now. People say Jack is a bad influence on that boy. I think his name is Billy or Henry McCarty, or sumthin like that," Elmer told Rafe.

Rafe watched the skinny young teenager follow the gambler called Sombrero Jack out of the saloon. He looked no older than thirteen or fourteen, with shabby clothes, light brown curly hair, and a worn gunbelt wrapped around his waist.

"Billy! Yew git on home to yer mama!" the bartender yelled at the kid, but the teenager scooted out the door.

Elmer shook his head. "That kid Billy has had it hard. I seen the other kids pickin on him causa he's kinda small fer his age. One time I seen him with a black eye, but Sombrero Jack is juss no good. That Billy will turn out a no good, iffin his mama can't keep him away from Jack," Elmer groused.

CHAPTER 53

Kip Donohoe and Buster Thomas were sitting in the Silver Lady Saloon when a ruckus on the other side temporarily stopped the roulette wheel dealer from spinning the giant wheel. Shouting and furniture crashing to the floor ended quickly without gunplay.

Buster was ready to jump up and make his way to the commotion, but Kip put a hand on his arm. Whitehill had specifically assigned them to the mining camps. They were to look for trouble up in the mine area and stop any attempts to jump a claim. The business in the saloon was not their problem. Whitehill had others doing that job.

Off duty, Kip had stripped his shirt of the deputy badge and it rested in his pocket. Working for the law gave him mixed emotions. The pay was good and Whitehill even gave them each an advance, but being on the right side of the law was new for Kip.

Across the room, Kip heard the bartender shout at Sombrero Jack and the kid named Billy who always hung around with him. Sheriff Whitehill said Sombrero Jack was a bad influence on the teenager. He asked all the deputies to watch Billy for misdoings, but to go easy on the kid.

"Ain't his fault. That momma of his is sick and his step-father don't give a damn," Whitehill told them.

Soon the ruckus died down when Sombrero Jack strode out the front doors with Billy trailing behind him.

"We sure got it easy now," Buster gloated to Kip. "I gotta thank yew fer talkin me into signin up with Whitehill."

"Whadda yew mean?"

"Well, we got rooms and grub over ta Ma Barker's and a soft bed ta boot, and she's a damn fine cook. All we do all day is ride up in the mountains. Compared to shovelin ore, it's a rat easy job."

"Yew think we gonna get rich on two hundred a month?" Kip grumbled. "Even if it's easy, we're goin nowhere bein deputies and Whitehill knows it. Sum day a gunhand or one of Candy Bogg's men will put us in our graves and Whitehill will juss hire sumone else."

"Yer handy with a gun Kip. It would take a damn fine shot to beat yew. Yew much better'n me," Buster praised his partner.

"Yeah, I'm good. Still we need to git us a claim. Silver is the ticket in this town. We gotta git it before its all gone like up in E-town," Kip groused.

"How we gonna do that? I don't know how to find silver."

"We let sumone else find it, then we jump the claim," Kip said with a grin.

"We're supposed to be catching claim jumpers, not doin the jumpin."

"First we'll catch us a coupla jumpers and then we'll know which mine to take. I've been thinkin on it a lot. It's easy as pie," Kip gloated.

"Easy! And what about the Sheriff? Yew plannin on doin that right under his nose?"

"Dun worry about that, Buster. I got it all worked out."

The following morning, Rafe rose a bit later than usual at Ma Barker's Boarding House. Last night he spent several hours cleaning his guns to perfection. By the time he walked downstairs, the large dining room table was covered with dirty dishes. He thought it odd.

Walking to the sideboard, he poured himself a cup of coffee and piled a plate with three biscuits and bacon. Cutting the biscuits open, he put a large slab of butter and spoon of jam on each piece.

Suddenly he heard laughter from the kitchen. "Stop that Elmer. You are such a devil."

Rafe had to chuckle to himself. Apparently Elmer and Ma had a thing going on. Elmer sweetened her up with sugar treats and chocolate on his trips and Ma reciprocated in turn.

Rafe coughed loudly as he pulled a chair out from the table and sat down. Ma hurried into the dining room, but her hair was untidy and her apron askew.

"Good morning Mister Soto. I'm sorry I was busy in

the kitchen and did not hear you come down."

"It's quite all right. I helped myself."

"I have some eggs keeping warm in the kitchen. I'll be right back with them."

As Ma hurried out of the room to the kitchen, Rafe heard Elmer's voice. He could not make out the conversation, but a few minutes later Elmer followed her through the kitchen door.

"Mornin Sonny. Beautiful day ain't it?" Elmer had a grin from ear to ear.

"Good morning Elmer. Sleep well?" Rafe could not help but ask the ridiculous question.

Elmer sat down and Ma scurried to pour him a cup of coffee.

Down the hall at Ma's, Kip dressed and donned his deputy badge. Pulling on his boots he buckled his gunbelt. The room was a mess. His clothes were thrown haphazardly. He knew Ma would disapprove, but she could not throw them out this time. They were Harvey Whitehill's deputies. Turning, he closed his door and walked across the hall. Knocking, he called out, "Buster, yew ready?"

Buster opened the door and stepped out. "Sure. Let's go"

They walked down the hallway toward the dining room. They had both eaten earlier. As they passed the large opening to the dining area, they saw Ma standing by two men at the table. One was an older man and the other a Mexican.

"Have a good day deputies," Ma called to them. "Would you like an apple for your pocket?" she asked.

"Thank yew kindly Ma'am," Buster said. He walked into the room and Ma handed him two red apples.

"Cum on," Kip said gruffly and turned making the last few steps toward the front door.

"Who were they Ma?" Elmer asked.

"Two of Sheriff Whitehill's new deputies. Whitehill is paying me half their rent to allow them to stay here. It's good money and I feel safe with them in the house," she responded.

CHAPTER 54

After breakfast at Ma's, Rafe drank a third cup of coffee while Elmer went to his room to change and wash up. Idly, Rafe thumbed through an old newspaper from El Paso.

The newspaper was full of advertisements for boots, ladies dresses, hats, farm equipment, baking powder, and an assortment of other wares, both large and small. Rafe folded the newspaper and put it on the table when Elmer walked into the room.

"I'm ready ta go, Sonny."

Rafe stood up and adjusted the gunbelt on his hips. Elmer had promised to introduce him to the owner of the mercantile. They walked out into the bright sunny day and headed up the street. Most of the stores in Silver City were quickly built wooden structures. Crude simple signs with painted letters hung above the doorways – BARBER, BANK, BLACKSMITH, GENERAL STORE, JAIL, AND ASSAY OFFICE. Only the Silver Lady Saloon and Ma Barker's Boarding House had more ornate signs.

Rafe was sure the owner of the mercantile would know Kip Donohoe. Surely Kip needed supplies if he were here. As they walked the short distance, Rafe's mind swirled with anticipation.

"Hey Roger," Elmer called to the man behind the counter. The store was mostly empty of customers, except for two women looking over the hat selection.

"Hello Elmer. I've got your money ready. The supplies were all in order and I thank you."

"Glad ta hear it."

"Doc Warner was mighty happy to get his supplies, too. He told me to give you his thanks," Roger said.

"Roger, I'd like yew to meet a friend of mine. He came up with me from Las Cruces as sorta a bodyguard. This here's Sammy Soto from Pueblo, Colorady. He sells guns. Mighty fancy guns. Yew shud take a look at em," Elmer explained introducing Rafe to the owner.

"Glad to meet you." Roger held out his hand.

"Hello sir. I'd like to show you my guns. Do you have a spot outback where I can demonstrate them?"

Roger looked around the store. He was the only clerk and the two women the only customers. "Say Elmer, keep an eye on the till fer me while Sammy and I go out back."

Roger and Rafe walked out the front door and then around to the back. About twenty feet behind the store, the creek called the Big Ditch cut a deep path, and then beyond was only trees. Rafe took out one of the pistols and began his sales pitch and demonstrated it.

Roger was excited and shot the pistol through three loaded rounds of bullets with a big smile on his face. It was a typical response to the guns and Rafe was expecting the man to make a large order.

"They sure are beauts. I've only heard about them. You say you make them in Pueblo?"

"I don't make them, but the foundry where I work does. They make pistols and rifles."

Roger handed the pistol back to Rafe. "I'm guessing they carry a fancy price, too?"

"Well, yes they are more expensive than a single-action model," Rafe replied.

"Well Sammy, this is how it is here in Silver City. Most people come here with only a couple nickels to rub together in their pockets. They spend everything they have trying to find silver. Many go hungry. I've got a whole case of used guns that miners hawked trying to just get a meal in their belly or replace a broken pick axe. The only person I see being able to buy your guns would be Sheriff Whitehill."

"Oh, I see."

"Go see Whitehill. He's the richest man in Silver City and now the sheriff. I bet he would want one for himself and maybe his deputies. He's swearing to clean up this town."

"Roger, I assume you know most everyone in town? I have a message from Larry Murphy over in Lincoln for his cousin Kip Donohoe. I need to find him before I leave," Rafe lied, hoping Roger might know the killer.

"Kip Donohoe?" Roger rubbed his chin. "Don't

recognize that name. I don't give credit, so there's lots of miners here I don't know by name. What does he look like?" Roger asked.

Rafe almost laughed at the question. If he knew what Kip looked like, his life would be much simpler.

"Well, I really don't know. Larry just told me he was here and to give him a message," Rafe replied.

"Why don't you come back sometime and ask my clerks. They might know him."

"Well thanks anyway and thanks for the tip about Sheriff Whitehill. I'll show him the guns before I leave Silver City." Rafe tucked the pistol in his gunbelt and followed Roger back into the store.

Rafe left the mercantile without a gun order and without any information on Kip Donohoe. Roger paid Elmer for the supplies and Rafe walked with Elmer back to Ma's. Elmer carried a package under his arm.

"How long did you say you are staying? Remember, I promised to keep you safe," Rafe told Elmer. The words triggered a memory. Rafe had promised to keep Ana Teresa safe and had failed miserably. He promised himself to avenge her death and was failing at that, too.

"I'm gonna stay nother day, Sonny. Yew run along. I gotta go see Ma. I bought her a present and I think she'll be right grateful." Elmer chuckled and it made Rafe smile.

Rafe walked to the small corral behind Ma's and saddled the gelding. Jumping to the saddle, he rode the horse onto the main street of town. Frustration, anger, and remorse filled his soul. Rafe decided to ride north of town and spurred the horse into a gallop. He wanted to have a look at the countryside and the mines. Tomorrow he would see the sheriff and casually ask about Kip.

Kip and Buster left Ma Barker's and rode north up the mountain as they did each day. Dotted along the numerous creeks and crevasses were lean-tos, canvas tents, and a few more solidly built shacks. As they rode, a large blast of dynamite in the distance resonated off the mountains. It was a normal sound heard many times each day. The effort to blast and then dig into the mountain to find a vein was dangerous and backbreaking work.

"I sure am glad we dun have ta do that work nomore up at Whitehill's mine," Buster said hearing the blast. "We got it easy peasy now." Buster had his right leg looped over the pummel of the saddle as they plodded along.

For the past week, they had seen nothing but grimy miners working their claims. Violence in Silver City had paused after the new sheriff was elected. It was as if the town, miners, and outlaws all took a collective breath and were holding it. Kip knew it would not last. Another blast reverberated in the distance. This time they could tell it was closer.

"Sounds like it's comin from the Lucky Judy." Kip and Buster had been riding the ridges over the past week learning the layout of the mines, which dotted the crevices of the ridgelines. They especially watched the Lucky Judy as Sheriff Whitehill instructed. They had seen no evidence of claim jumpers scouting the area, but Kip knew it was probably only a matter of time before Candy Boggs began his operation again.

"Let's go on up thar. We can hide in the clump of tall juniper," Kip said and pointed to a grove of trees not too far ahead. Dismounting, they sat in the shade watching the mine. Dust from the blasting shot out of the mine tunnel three more times as they watched. After each blast, three men dumped wheelbarrows of rock into a pile.

A little while later, Buster nudged Kip's elbow. "Look up thar, I bet its em jaspers the sheriff was talking bout." Buster pointed to the outline of three men on horseback. The sun was catching their outlines and they appeared gray against the blue sky.

"Yeah, yew may be rat. Let's keep an eye on em. Iffin they attack the mine, we wait till they kill the owner, then we move in and git em," Kip said. This was exactly the chance he was hoping for to put his plan into action. Instead of stopping the jumpers, they would let them attack the Lucky Judy. Then he and Buster would swoop down on the claim jumpers while they were cleaning up the evidence. The unsuspecting claim jumpers would never suspect they would be jumped. Once they killed or captured the claim jumpers, he and Buster would brag to Whitehill of their worth. Whitehill would pay them a bonus. Meanwhile, Kip would go and claim the Lucky Judy at the land office. The plan was a sure bet.

After about an hour, the three gray forms turned from their lookout spot and rode off. Kip cursed, "Fuck! I was hopin em jaspers would attack. Let's wait a bit longer. Cud be they'll cum back with more men."

Rafe urged the gelding up the rocky slopes. The horse nervously skittered and tried to buck Rafe after hearing each blast of dynamite reverberate in the air. "Shhh boy, it's all right." Rafe would stop and rub the horse's flank with his hand to calm him. Slowly Rafe continued climbing the path along a ridgeline. Below his path, numerous tents and shacks denoted the mining claims.

The mining districts of Silver City reminded Rafe of the mountains surrounding Elizabethtown. Small cabins or canvas tents were erected near the mouth of the tunnel. The miners used local timber from the tall pines to shore up the shafts as they blasted into the mountain. The dynamite loosened rock and then the miners cleared it to create a tunnel. Rafe remembered the men at Bill Moore's mine. They were looking for gold, but Rafe assumed mining silver was similar.

The mines dotted the landscape along the crevices of the mountain created by the retreating ice age. As Rafe rode higher, the temperature distinctly dropped. Snow still clung in shadowed areas.

The mountains reminded him of the Sangre de Cristo Mountains north of Santa Fe. He rode Rayo up into the foothills often and sometimes up to the tree line. Rayo was more sure-footed than the gelding and finally Rafe turned and headed back. From high up on the mountain, he could barely see the buildings in Silver City below.

On his way down, three riders passed him. They seemed to come out of nowhere and were riding fast down the mountain. They said nothing to him.

CHAPTER 55

Kip and Buster waited hoping the claim jumpers would come back to the Lucky Judy Mine.

"They ain't comin," Buster complained after another hour of waiting. "My butt is sore juss sittin here."

"The sheriff tole us to watch this mine in particular and that's what we're gonna do," Kip growled back.

They watched the three men go in and out of the Lucky Judy shaft. After numerous trips with full wheelbarrows, they ran from the tunnel opening and hid behind several small boulders. In a few minutes, a small explosion blew rocks and dust out of the shallow shaft. Then the miners resumed their job of clearing the rock debris.

"Looks like backbreaking work ta me," Buster grumbled. "Why do yew want to own a mine anyway."

"Oh, quit yer bellyaching or I'll cut yew outta the deal," Kip warned.

The two kept to the shadows and patiently watched. The men working the Lucky Judy labored with the heavy loads. Off to the far side of the tunnel opening, a large pile of rock spilled off down the gully. After many hours of labor, one of the men wearing a checkered shirt popped out of the mouth of the tunnel. He wore a dusty cap on his head and a bandana wrapped around his nose and mouth. As he reached the outside air, he pulled down the bandana.

Kip and Buster stayed well hidden in the trees watching the man near the tunnel. Shortly, another man exited and held a rock in his hand. Kip could see the two men talking and holding the rock up into the sunlight.

"Look, they're checkin that rock. They mustta hit sumthin," Buster said excitedly.

Kip thought the body language of the miners was happy. The one man slapped the other on the back. The two men returned to the tunnel several times, exiting with wheelbarrows of rock. Kip noticed they piled the more recently wheeled loads into a new pile.

A blast in the distance caused Kip to change his view to the far ridgeline. Something was moving, creating a shadow, and then disappearing for a moment and then moving again. It looked like a lone rider.

"Look Buster," Kip said and pointed across the small valley. He caught a reflection of something shiny flashing in the sun. Kip pointed at the movement in the distance.

"Maybee they've come back," Buster said.

"Or maybee they've been watching like us. Those miners have found sumthin and the jumpers will be wantin it."

"Get ready. If they go down to take this mine, we'll jump em," Kip continued.

"Let's go circle around and juss git em now," Buster suggested.

"Yew are loco. Yew cain't arrest sumone for sittin on their horse. They ain't dun nuttin yet."

It was not long before the movement on the opposite ridgeline disappeared. Long shadows started to stretch off the western peaks making visibility harder.

"Hey, where'd they go?" Buster whined.

"Cum on, we gotta catch up to em." Kip spurred his horse and headed to the other ridgeline. Finding no one in sight, he and Buster headed down the mountain path.

Somewhere north of town, Kip spotted a lone rider on the path ahead. Kicking his horse, he caught up to the rider and called out, "Yew there. Stop!"

Rafe had enjoyed his ride in the mountains and it had calmed his spirit. The sun was still bright in the blue sky, but the mountains created long shadows and Rafe did not want to get lost. He knew darkness came to the mountains early. When he heard the voice yell, he jerked the reins and the gelding went up on its hinds legs then settled down. Turning in the saddle, he saw two men riding up.

Kip saw the rider was dressed in a gray suit wearing a black Stetson. He was riding a fine brown horse. When the man turned, Kip saw he was Mexican.

"Hey Mex, what yew doin up in those mountains? Yew ain't no miner dressed like that," Kip groused suspiciously.

"I was taking a ride," Rafe responded.

"Yew seen three riders?" Kip asked.

Rafe looked and saw the two men were wearing badges. From the shadow of their hats, he could not see their faces. "Yes, three men passed me back up on the mountain more than an hour ago. Why do you ask?"

"None of yer bidness why I'm askin, Mex. I'm askin yew, what were yew doin up there on that mountain?"

Rafe did not like the lawman's attitude. They stopped their horses close enough for Rafe to recognize them as the two deputies from Ma's Boarding House.

"I suppose there is no law here in Silver City against someone taking a ride?"

"Ain't no law. I'm juss askin yew what yer up to, Mex."

"I was taking a ride on a beautiful day, deputy," Rafe said controlling his anger against the rude lawman. He did not want to cause any trouble with the law. He just wanted to concentrate his energy on finding Kip Donohoe and killing him.

Kip turned without replying and spurred his horse. Buster followed. Rafe watched them as they rode ahead of him toward town.

After the evening meal at Ma's Boarding House, Rafe and Elmer sat out on the veranda. Elmer lit up a pipe. "I'll be a leavin tomorrow, Sonny. How long yew stayin?"

"I didn't get to see Sheriff Whitehill today, but I hope I can see him tomorrow."

"How'd yew do with Roger over at the mercantile?"

"Not good. He has many guns the miners sold back to him and told me those same miners could not afford my guns. He recommended I go see Sheriff Whitehill. After I see him, I'll move on to Tucson," Rafe lied.

"Sorry it didin work out, but sometimes I get the same answer from Roger. Once, I brung a load of nice shoes and black suit coats. Brung a coupla fancy lady dresses, too. Roger juss looked at me and laughed. He asked me who up here would buy such stuff."

"Mining is a tough business. Miners need sturdy and

warm clothes and shoes," Rafe responded remembering the men at Bill Moore's mine in E-town.

"Dun I know it."

"Let's go get a beer at the Silver Lady," Rafe suggested. He wanted to go just in case someone called out Kip's name or he could think of a way to nonchalantly ask the bartender.

"Naw, I cain't go Sonny. Ma's got sum chores fer me ta do," he said and winked at Rafe.

Rafe was about to get up and go to the saloon, when two men strode toward the front door. They were the two lawmen he met up on the north trail. They said nothing to either he or Elmer, passing them by on the veranda. Their boots clunked and their spurs jangled as they strode down the hallway and then Rafe heard two doors slam shut.

"I'll see you in the morning, Elmer," Rafe said as he got up and left for the saloon.

CHAPTER 56

After a restless night, Rafe got up early and walked downstairs to the dining room. Ma was bustling to get the place settings put on the table for the morning meal.

"Good morning Mister Soto," she said to him. Rafe was sure she blushed and her hair was a bit disheveled.

"Good morning Ma."

"It's supposed to be a nice day. Coffee will be ready in a jiffy," she said and continued her hurried work.

"I'll go see to my horse while you get the rest of breakfast ready," Rafe told her.

Rafe saddled the brown gelding and strapped a saddlebag containing the double-action pistols. Elmer was in the kitchen pestering Ma, when Rafe went back into the boarding house.

"Sonny, I'll be a leavin this mornin, soon as I have me sum breakfast. Yew sure yew dun want to join up with me?" Elmer asked.

"Well Elmer, I do appreciate the offer. I'll ride with you out of town and make sure you get away from here without any trouble. I have to head to Tucson next on my rounds. Someday I'll get back to Las Cruces. Maybe I'll find you there."

"That's all right, Sonny. Yew go on and sell sum of em fancy guns of yers," Elmer said with a smile. "Remember ta bring me one on yer next trip this a way."

"Where yew off to this mornin?" Ma asked.

"I'm hoping Sheriff Whitehill will be in his office, then I'll be heading to Tucson. Wish I was going back to Pueblo. Guess I'm getting a little homesick, but I still have a long way to go before I go home," Rafe lied.

"Wish yew luck, Sonny."

"Thanks Elmer, you have a safe trip," Rafe said. "Ma, you take good care of this old coot when he gets back," he said with a grin. Walking out into the sunshine, he went to get his horse.

Elmer sat and Ma refilled his coffee cup. Elmer needed to be on his way, but languished over the comfort of Ma's place. She was a damn fine cook and lovely woman. Her husband died over six years ago leaving her this house. When the boom started, she built it into the boarding house it was today and did all the work – cooking, cleaning, and fixing.

While Elmer ate a second helping, two deputies sat with him and were served by Ma. Elmer kept to himself and the deputies said nothing to him. When he finished he called to Ma to say goodbye. As she walked out with Elmer, the deputies were leaving. She called out to them, "Have a good day, Deputy Donohoe."

Elmer saw them ride off to the north before it registered. "Say Ma, was that Kip Donohoe?"

"Yes, why?"

"Sonny, tole me he was lookin fer a feller named Kip. Yew tell im when he gits back, that's the man he's lookin fer."

"Sure will. You be safe going back to Las Cruces and get back soon," she told Elmer and grabbed him and hugged him. Elmer gave her a light playful slap on her rear end.

Kip and Buster rode north toward the Lucky Judy Mine. Kip was hoping today was the day the claim jumpers would attack to take the mine. They got to the secluded spot in the tree line and dismounted. The mine was quiet, but a thin ribbon of smoke blew from the chimney of the small cabin.

Kip wondered if they were too late. Perhaps the jumpers had already taken the mine. He was relieved when a plaid-shirted miner exited the tunnel pushing a wheelbarrow. Soon another man joined him.

"Say Kip, I think we shud git back ta Lincoln. Shurly the law dun care no more bout em greasers yew kilt. I sure do miss the Lone Star Saloon and that big-titted, Susie."

"I ain't takin no chances goin back thar, Buster. I tell yew we kin do good here. If it all works out, we gonna be the new owners of our own mine. Stick with me boy, I'll make us rich."

They waited for several hours without any sign of the jumpers. Buster was leaning against a tree eating an apple. He spotted the riders first. It was just after noon when the sun was high in the sky. Three men on horseback swooped down from the opposite ridge of the valley. When they reached the mine, they rode in with their guns blazing.

"Let's go git em," Buster shouted out excitedly jumping to his horse.

"No. Wait." Kip told him and held his arm.

"Iffin we don't go now em claim jumpers will kill those men down thar," Buster protested.

"That be rat. I want em to kill the owner, then we go down thar and git em. Once we take em to jail, we go and claim the mine fer ourselves. It's all legal like and the sheriff will give us a reward."

Rafe finally found Sheriff Whitehill in his office around noon after several attempts to find him earlier that morning. The sheriff was sitting at the front desk when Rafe walked in.

"Sheriff Whitehill, my name is Sammy Soto. I am a gunsmith from Pueblo, Colorado," Rafe introduced himself removing his black Stetson.

"Yes, what can I do for you?" Sheriff Whitehill asked looking up from his desk. Standing in front of him was a well-dressed Mexican. The man was about six feet tall and trim in stature. His face was clean shaven and his eyes brown and clear. Not only did he present a refined man in his dress, he spoke English without a Spanish accent. He wore no guns, but had a saddlebag flung over his shoulder.

"I'd like to show you a new kind of revolver my company sells. It is a double-action. Are you familiar with that type of weapon?" Rafe asked as he pulled one of the pistols out of the saddlebag and put it on top of the desk.

"Well, I've read about them, but have never seen one," Whitehill said. His eyes widened as he picked up the weapon. Gripping it in his right hand, the smooth polished handle fit perfectly in his palm. The metal of the barrel gleamed from polishing. "How does it work?"

"Do you have a place we can go where I can demonstrate?"

"Yes, let's go out back." Whitehill got up and led Rafe out the back door.

Rafe loaded the pistol with six rounds, pointed at a tree, and fired three bullets by only pulling the trigger all within five inches apart. Bark from the tree sprayed each time a bullet struck.

"Each squeeze of the trigger releases a bullet. There is no need to thumb the hammer," Rafe explained.

"Let me try," the sheriff said and took the pistol from Rafe.

Taking his time, he pointed at a tree to the left of the one Rafe shot and fired twice. The first bullet hit, but the next went wild and missed.

"Sheriff, it takes some practice to get used to the kick, but once you feel it you will know how to fire the next shot. Here, let me reload it for you. Now, fire the first shot and take your time after the kick and fire again. After a while, it will become automatic. You will react to the kick and be confident for the next shot. Like I said, it takes a little practice."

Whitehill aimed and fired and hit the target, let the pistol settle a moment, then fired the next shot and hit the tree. He fired the next too quick and missed, then shot the remaining three bullets with fair accuracy all hitting their intended mark. His face lit up with a smile.

"I see what you mean. What I like about the pistol is how smooth the trigger works. So, how do I get a pair of these?"

Rafe noticed he did not ask about price.

"All you need to do is sign the order and I will wire it to Pueblo and they'll be shipped to you," Rafe lied. The sheriff asked for another round of bullets and Rafe was surprised when all six hit a tree in succession.

"You learned to handle it quickly," Rafe complimented him.

"Come back inside and I'll give you an order for ten of these. I want all my deputies to be carrying one," the sheriff said. Whitehill was pleased thinking his deputies would have the upper hand over any claim jumpers and it would give them the edge to take a real bite out of the lawlessness here in Silver City.

When they got back inside the office, two deputies stood in the front room, each guarding a man in wrist irons.

"Howdy Sheriff. We got em claim jumpers I tole yew about yesterday. They shot at us, but they ain't too smart. While I kept em busy, Buster was able ta git round em and shot the third man dead. After that, these two gave up purdy quick," the taller deputy said.

The sheriff looked at the two. He recognized them as men who worked for Candy Boggs and was not surprised. Candy's gang had been quiet lately, no doubt waiting to see how Whitehill was going to change the lawless attitude here in Silver City.

"What about Albert Dunne and his men?" the sheriff asked.

"Well sheriff, we didin get a stranglehold on these here varmints before they killed em miners."

Sheriff Whitehill shook his head in disgust. "Well, these two will make a good spectacle when they dangle from a rope. You did well, Kip. Both of you. Take the chains off and put them in the first cell."

Chapter 57

Rafe froze as the sheriff called the taller of the two deputies, Kip. The deputies were the two who stopped him on the north road yesterday and were staying at Ma Barker's. Rafe's mind swirled. How the hell did Kip Donohoe become a deputy sheriff? As the deputies pushed the criminals toward the back cell, Whitehill resumed his conversation with Rafe.

"Now, young man, let's get that order worked out. I like those pistols. Any chance I could buy one of these now?"

Rafe could not respond. He was thunderstruck realizing Kip Donohoe had been slipping through his fingers for the last several days.

"Mister Soto, are you all right? I'm asking about your pistols."

"Oh . . . sorry Sheriff. I can't sell them. I have lots of stops on my way to Tucson and up to Phoenix, before I head east again."

Rafe stammered over his words. Inside, his body was shaking. His heart pounded as adrenaline coursed through his veins. It took every amount of self-control not to pull his pistol and shoot Kip in the back right here in the sheriff's office. He'd be hanged, of course, but his vengeance would be satisfied. Thankfully, he was not wearing his guns and Sheriff Whitehill held the empty demonstration one. It kept him from doing anything overly stupid.

Kip and Buster returned from the back cells putting the men's wrist irons on the sheriff's desk.

"Thank you deputies. Take the rest of the day off. You've earned it," Whitehill told them.

Kip smiled and jerked his head at Buster to leave. "Let's go git a beer."

Rafe stared at their backs as they walked out the door. His mind swirled with jumbled thoughts of Ana Teresa and his dead baby. The killer just walked out the door wearing a deputy badge.

"Sheriff, I'll get this order wired as soon as I can. Depending on how long it takes to ship from Pueblo, you'll get the pistols in probably about a month."

"Thank you Mister Soto. I'll be waiting for them."

Rafe left the sheriff's office with his head spinning and his heart pounding out of his chest. He tried to calm himself, tried to think straight, and not allow his emotions to control the situation. He had seen his prey. Kip was here in Silver City and Rafe now knew where to find him. The killer was a deputy sheriff. It still seemed impossible and Rafe knew killing Kip in cold blood in town was a sure way to a rope around his neck.

Rafe saw Kip's face. The man was scruffy with a scraggly beard and mustache. Long curly almost blond hair spread out from a dusty well used, black Stetson. He was tall, maybe an inch taller than himself. A single pistol hung from a holster not from Kip's right hip, but from in front of his right leg. Kip called the other deputy, Buster, and they were no doubt in the Silver Lady Saloon celebrating their efforts to catch the claim jumpers. Rafe assumed they would be there for a while.

His mind spun with indecision. All the ideas, which had rumbled in his brain about killing Kip, evaporated. Not only was Kip a dangerous man, he was a deputy sheriff. Killing him as he had done Jesse Kincaid would not be acceptable and using the phony marshal badge would definitely not work. Rafe climbed onto the gelding and spurred the horse down the street.

He had not gone far when he spotted Kip and Buster coming out of the Land Office. It surprised him, thinking they had gone directly to the saloon. Rafe tipped his hat low and rode on by toward Ma's. He left the horse tied to the front rail and did not see Ma when he when upstairs to pack his belongings. In a hurried manner, he stuffed the saddlebags and rolled his other possessions in the bedroll. His gunbelt he wrapped around his waist putting the two GSW pistols in the holsters. Today he wanted his personal pistols to be the instrument of Kip's death.

Looking about the room, he made sure everything was packed. He grabbed the short-barrel shotgun in his hand and walked out and down the stairs. The boarding house was unusually quiet. Checking the kitchen, Ma was nowhere to be found. Rafe took a piece of paper, wrote a note and enclosed a twenty dollar gold coin for his payment. After loading the gelding, he rode to the mercantile.

"Hey, yew leaving?" Roger asked when he spotted the gun peddler gathering food provisions.

"Yes. I met with Sheriff Whitehill and got my order. I'm headed west to Tucson." Rafe had lied to his new friend about his real dealings here in Silver City while acting as a gun salesman.

"Well, yew have a safe trip. I'll be here iffin yew ever git back this way," Roger told him.

Rafe paid for the provisions and packed them onto the horse. Mounting up, he rode to the back of Silver Lady Saloon and tethered the horse near the back door. Walking casually down the side alley, Rafe walked to the front and into the saloon.

The Silver Lady Saloon was busy. It was not the only saloon in Silver City, but was the largest. Rafe was pretty sure it was where he would find Kip Donohoe. Rafe walked up to the bar and put a quarter down. The bartender filled a glass of beer. While he sipped on it, Rafe looked around the room. Kip and the other deputy, Buster, sat at a table near the stage. A bottle of whiskey sat between them.

"Hey Buster, I tole yew to trust me. That mine we took frum em claim jumpers is ours now," Kip said smiling at Buster and downing a shot. After they left the sheriff's office, Kip and Buster headed directly to the land office and filed on the Lucky Judy Mine.

"An when Sheriff Whitehill finds out, he'll put r asses in jail," Buster complained.

"He ain't never gonna know. That mine belongs to us now, fair and square. Em jumpers killed the owners, not us. He cain't do nuttin about it. In fact he'd be right proud, I spect."

Kip remembered when Harvey Whitehill was in E-town. He had several large mines and Kip suspected Whitehill became the owner after just this type of underhanded move.

"I ain't shur, Kip."

"Dun yew be a chickenshit, Buster. I dun want ta be a low life deputy all my life. That mine is gonna make us rich. Have nother drink." Kip poured them both another shot.

Rafe turned the beer glass in his hand. Looking past the piano player, Rafe spotted the back door. His plan was simple. He would walk up to Kip, call him a killer of women and children, kill him, then rush out the back door. It was a similar plan to how he confronted Jesse Kincaid in E-town. If Buster reacted, he would die too. Rafe thought about that night and remembered Lefty covered his back killing Roy Harvey. Tonight, if Kip and Buster had friends in this town, Rafe had no one giving him cover.

He knew the plan was probably foolhardy. It was the dark side of vengeance, even though justified. His heart beat hard with adrenalin giving his mouth a taste of acrid metal. He was ready to be done with this chapter in his life. He had nothing to remember and nothing to go back to. If he died here in Silver City, then Satan could have his soul.

Rafe finished the beer, took a deep breath, and pulled his suit coat away from his guns. The bartender was serving a man standing close to his left side.

"I gave yew a quarter. Yer tryin to cheat me outta a beer, asshole," the man grumbled.

"You paid for the last beer. Now you owe me a quarter for this one," the barkeep said.

"Fuck yew," the man gabbed for the glass of beer, pulling it hard and some splashed on Rafe as the man bumped him. Instinctively, Rafe jumped aside.

The man beside him was drunk, swaying, and arguing with the bartender. Rafe brushed the drops of beer from the sleeve of his coat.

"Yer in my way, greaser," the drunk grumbled at Rafe.

"Sorry mister. Do you need a towel," the bartender said to Rafe.

"No. Just give the man a beer," Rafe said and flipped

a quarter on the bar top.

When he turned back toward his prey, Kip and Buster were not sitting at the table. Wildly Rafe scanned the room, but they were nowhere in sight.

CHAPTER 58

Realizing Kip and Buster were gone, Rafe hurried to the back of the saloon, exited the back door, and mounted the gelding. When he reached the main street in front of the saloon, Kip and Buster were not in sight. Both Ma's Boarding House and the sheriff's office were north of the saloon, so Rafe instinctively turned north.

"Yew shur the sheriff cain't hang us fer takin that mine? Remember I'm the one who kilt that jumper up there, not yew," Buster complained.

"No one was ever hanged fer killing a claim jumper," Kip responded.

"How about fer jumping a jumper?" Buster whined still worried about his part in Kips' scheme.

"Yew juss worry too damn much," Kip grumbled.

They had just turned west onto Silver Heights Street from Main Street. "Cum on, let's go check out our new mine," Kip said and spurred his horse to a gallop.

Rafe rode at a quick trot up Main Street. He was scanning everywhere and just passed the Bank when he spotted two men on horseback riding west on Silver Heights Street. He recognized them and turned to follow. He spurred the gelding, but stayed far back.

"I'm still not shur, Kip. What r we gonna tell the sheriff?"

"Well the way I have it figgered, first we gotta make shur this mine is producing enough to keep us goin. Then we juss tell im we got us a mine and we cain't be lawmen anymore."

"What iffin em jumpers blame us? What if they say we dun kilt the owners?" Buster continued to fret.

"Yew juss ain't all that smart. Who yew think the sheriff is gonna believe? His deputies or the jumpers?" Kip groused getting tired of Buster's complaining and worrying.

"Cum on, we need ta git goin while we still got light enuff to check out that mine," Kip urged him and slapped the reins of his horse to go faster.

Rafe followed the pair, but far back. They were riding hard, but going straight to a destination. Apparently they felt no threat, as neither looked to their back trail. After an initial disappointment for not confronting Kip in the saloon as planned, Rafe decided catching him somewhere here in the woods was a much better idea.

The going was getting steeper and rockier as they worked up the mountain. Rafe kept pace, but also kept along the trees, keeping the pair always in his sights.

It took Kip and Buster over an hour to get to the mine. Only small juniper covered the landscape below the small hill where the mine entrance was located. As they reached the Lucky Judy Mine, Kip stopped and turned to Buster.

"Told yew we wooden have no trouble. We gonna be rich, Buster. I tole yew to leave it ta me. Yer gonna have a good life once we git that silver mine workin," Kip appeased his worrying partner.

They tethered their horses to a post in front of a small wooden shack. Kip opened the door of the shack and took inventory. It was sparse, but tidy. Pots and pans hung on nails and a black potbelly stove was in the corner. Two beds were made and stood along the far wall. It was not as nice as Ma's, but would be reasonably comfortable. The way Kip had it figured, they would continue to be deputies until the mine proved its worth.

Rafe stayed near a thick patch of junipers and spied on the two who rode down toward a shack. A mine tunnel entrance was not far away. Jumping off the horse, Rafe pulled out the beaded quiver and slung it over his back. He tucked his short-barrel shotgun into it. Spinning the chambers of his two pistols to check the loads, he was ready.

"Cum on. Let's go into the shaft," Kip said. Buster followed Kip out the door and toward the mine tunnel. At the entrance, Kip lit two candles and started inside. Buster hated the cold, damp, dark tunnels, but followed.

Rafe watched the two go into the shaft. He waited a few minutes, then mounted up and quickly rode toward the mine. Wasting no time, he jumped off, pulled his guns, and cautiously made his way to the mine opening. He stopped at the entrance, then only went in as far as he could see in the daylight. From somewhere inside, he heard voices.

"Buster, go git that box of candles. I seen it back in the shack."

Rafe recoiled, retreating against the tunnel wall and waited for Buster to come by. "Put your hands up," he hissed quietly to Buster as the man walked past him.

"What the fuck? Who r yew?" Buster cursed. His hand moved for his pistol. Rafe was close enough to clunk him on the head with the butt end of his pistol, but somehow Buster's gun went off.

Kip did not bother to know what happened. He pulled his pistol and fired three shots toward the entrance of the tunnel. They ricocheted as they hit the sides of the walls. After the first volley, Rafe crouched and waited. Buster's still form was in front of him.

"Who the hell is out thar? Buster, yew alwrat?" Kip hollered from inside the mine.

"You killed Buster," Rafe shouted into the shaft. "You killed him just like you killed those women and children in the courtyard in San Gabriel," Rafe yelled back at him.

"Who the fuck r yew?" Kip bellowed.

"I'm the one who is going to send you to your father in the depths of hell, where you will burn for eternity," Rafe replied. He wanted to shake Kip to the core, if he had any bit of religion in him.

"Fuck yew. I'll shoot the fuckin Devil when I see him," Kip yelled back with a sinister laugh. Rafe lay behind Buster's body. Taking three quick shots into the mine, he heard the bullets ricochet several times. Kip's gun responded as two shots whizzed above Rafe's head.

Rafe was well schooled in firearms. The reports of his shots and Kip's return fire, told him the shaft was not long. He estimated Kip would be less than one hundred feet from the entrance. When he saw Kip at the sheriff's office, he wore only one gun. His gunbelt had not been full of bullets, and Rafe estimated Kip perhaps had a total of fifteen shots. Knowing he had more, Rafe contemplated playing this cat and mouse game until Kip was out of ammunition, then taking his justified revenge up close and personal.

Rafe fired off three more shots and then reloaded his pistol after Kip responded with two shots in return.

"You starting to remember killing those innocent women and children in San Gabriel, Kip? You remember the day you wore a red hood and shot up a wedding celebration at the Salazar hacienda."

"Em fuckin greasers had it comin. They were harassin rightful landowners and I took care of the problum."

"Problem?" Rafe's hands shook uncontrollably as rage overtook him. "You killed my wife and unborn child. They never did a thing to hurt anyone in this world and you took them away from me forever."

While Rafe kept Kip talking, he realized bullets were not effective and he remembered seeing a box of dynamite to the side of the shaft entrance. Keeping close to the tunnel wall, he backed his way out as he fired two shots.

Two shots whizzed in return near his head. Ducking low, he took three more rapid shots. The speed of the shots would confuse Kip and then he ran out of the mine's entrance. Reaching inside the box of dynamite, he wrapped his hand around three sticks.

"Come out now and give yourself up or I'm going to blow the place up with you in it," Rafe warned him.

"Fuck yew. Cum an git me. I'm glad I kilt em people in the greaser's courtyard. If I kilt yer wife and kid, then I'm glad and now I'm gonna kill yew. I hate fuckin greasers," he cursed and took two shots toward the faint light he could see near the tunnel's entrance.

Rafe searched his pockets for matches and found none. *"Mierda,"* he cursed.

He could throw the dynamite and shoot it, but was likely to miss in the dark shaft. Knowing he had matches in his saddlebag, he pondered going to get them. It might give Kip a chance to escape. Two more shots came above his head, this time a little closer. Keeping low, Rafe crawled back to the entrance. Ruffling through Buster's pockets, he found a tobacco pouch, but no matches.

Two more bullets whizzed out of the tunnel and near Rafe's head. He returned the fire with three shots into the shaft, heard the ricochets, and then a grunt.

"Got you that time. You better come out. I have plenty of ammunition and one of those ricochets is going to kill you if I don't get to you first," Rafe warned him.

"Fuck yew, greaser. Come in an git me."

Buster groaned and reached a weak hand up to Rafe's arm. Instinctively, Rafe raised the butt end of his pistol and hit Buster again above his ear. Buster slumped back on the ground.

Rafe felt the tobacco pouch and opened it. Inside he found several stick matches.

"I'm only gonna ask you one more time to come out, before I blow this place up," Rafe yelled out.

"Yew fuckin liar. Yew ain't got no dynamite. Come in an git me."

"This is for my wife and unborn child. You're going to hell Kip!"

Rafe struck a match and lit the three sticks and waited until they were half burnt before he threw them in as far as he could into the mine tunnel. He grabbed Buster by the shirt and dragged him away toward the opening, then only had time to throw himself to the side of the tunnel. Debris and smoke flew out of the entrance covering parts of Buster's body when the dynamite exploded.

Rafe got up and shook his head trying to clear the ringing out of his ears caused by the concussion of the explosions. After the dust settled, he looked into the tunnel. The entrance was collapsed with timbers and rock sealing Kip Donohoe in his tomb.

Checking on Buster, the man was still alive. Rafe looked down at him. He had no idea how Buster was connected to Kip and he was wearing a deputy badge. Rafe could not kill him. To his knowledge, Buster was innocent of anything except being here with Kip.

The reverberations of the blasts and the smoke had subsided. Rafe walked over to the gelding and climbed up on the saddle. Spurring the horse to a trot, he turned south down the mountain. His work was done.

CHAPTER 59

Rafe turned the horse back down the path away from the mine and toward Silver City. His work was finished and a giant weight lifted from his soul. Justified vengeance took the last evil soul to the depths of hell and Ana Teresa and his unborn child were avenged.

By the time he reached Silver City, the sun was dipping low in the western sky, but he kept riding directly through town. All he wanted was to go home. The thought of living in Santa Fe without Ana Teresa had always enraged him, but now suddenly he believed he could find peace.

His horse breeding business and the gun foundry needed him. The Summers' family was probably frantic with worry over his whereabouts these last months. He missed Carlos and their close friendship and although the gelding had performed well, he missed riding Rayo. The magnificent Appaloosa was the pride of his horse business. Riding south from the town, he wished he could waken in the morning in his house on the hill overlooking his pastures.

He made camp somewhere southeast of Silver City later that night. Building a small fire, Rafe listened to the vocalizations of the night critters. Scurrying of tiny feet and then a squeal reached his ears as a nighttime predator found dinner. Building the fire up as the embers glowed red hot, Rafe settled himself against his saddle . He placed one of his GSW pistols in his lap and allowed himself to doze off.

The call of a coyote close by wakened him in the dark. The fire had burned down. Stirring the embers and adding more wood, it burst back to life. Rafe kept the fire going the rest of the night, sitting in its glow planning his trip home.

His first desire was to ride directly to Santa Fe. He estimated he could be home in a little over a week. He had made the trip from Las Cruces to Santa Fe many times on gun selling trips. Once he reached the El Camino Real, the trip would be easy. This main pathway through the center of New Mexico had been established by Spaniards as a trade route centuries ago. It was well used and towns as well as stage stops dotted the route.

The El Camino Real was east of Silver City and even though he did not know the terrain and his exact location, it seemed an easy idea to follow the morning sun east to find his way. Finally, the sky began to lighten and Rafe saddled the horse and kicked out the fire. He rode toward the coming of the morning sun.

Clarence "Butch" Fredericks was making his morning rounds of the mining camps as he did twice a week. On his packhorse, he had candles, coffee, sugar, flour, rice, bacon, and an assortment of other staples often needed by the miners up in the hills. His path took him along Bushy Tail Creek, where many mines dotted the steep path. Passing the sign for the Lucky Judy Mine, Butch rode down toward the small shack. Two horses were tethered to a post.

Jumping off his horse, Butch called out to the shack without response. Calmly he walked to the horses. They were saddled and the saddlebags were still full of provisions. It was odd and Butch cautiously looked around and strained his ears, but heard nothing. Claim jumping was rampant up here in the mountains and although they would have no cause to hurt him, Butch remained alert.

Walking toward the mine shaft, he saw a man sitting with his back against the side of the tunnel entrance covered in debris. The mine tunnel behind the man was completely caved in. Rocks closed the opening and timbers were strewn like matchsticks. Butch walked over to the man.

Buster Thomas looked up in a dazed stare at an unfamiliar face.

"Yew okay feller? What happened?" the man asked.

"Water," Buster replied.

Quickly, Butch grabbed his canteen and then helped Buster take a drink. Then again, he asked what had happened.

"Yew git caught by jumpers?" he asked.

Buster was not entirely sure. He and Kip were checking out the mine and then a Mexican came and started shouting at them.

"Kip. Did you find Kip?" Buster asked the man.

"Kip? Who's Kip?" Butch replied and looked down seeing the deputy badge on the man's shirt. "I ain't seen nobody here, but yew."

"He was in the mine," Buster told him.

"That mine's collapsed. If he was inside, he ain't coming out. Kin yew stand?"

Butch helped Buster to stand up and climb onto a horse. Taking it slow, they rode back down the mountain to Silver City.

The ringing in his ears from the blast at the mine yesterday had dissipated as Rafe rode east. The morning sun warmed the air quickly and before long Rafe stripped his jacket. It was not long before his stomach growled loudly. Jumping off the horse, he searched the saddlebags for the provisions he purchased at the mercantile. His canteen was already half empty. The reality of his situation struck him.

He was probably two or three days from reaching a town or the El Camino Real and he might be in Apache country. Although the Apache had signed a peace treaty several years ago, rumors circulated that Cochise often raided ranches or caused trouble in the southern parts of Arizona and New Mexico.

Moreover, he had little cash and only enough provisions for a few days. Santa Fe was too long a trip to make without more provisions. He needed to stock up before heading north. Remounting, he decided water was his first priority and then he needed to head south to find a quick route to Las Cruces. Santa Fe could wait a little while longer for him to arrive home safely.

Following his instincts, he skirted the foothills. Finally, he found a creek running with clear water. Letting the horse drink his fill, Rafe did the same and filled the canteen.

Helping Buster keep upright on the horse, they made a slow trek back into town. Butch continued to ask questions. Buster seemed confused and kept talking about

Kip. He rambled about taking the mine and about working for Sheriff Whitehill, remembered the Mexican man's face, but little else.

"Yew need a doc," Butch told him. "I think sumthin hit yew hard on yer head."

Buster could not do more than nod in agreement. When they reached the center of town, Butch helped to half carry Buster up the stairs to the doctor's office.

"He needs help, Doc."

"What happened to him?" the doctor asked.

"Found him outside of a mine tunnel. It looked like it had blown to bits."

"You better go get Sheriff Whitehill. It might have been claim jumpers."

Butch left Buster with the doctor and headed to the sheriff's office. Whitehill was not there, but one of his deputies said he had walked home for supper.

"Tell him to go to the doctor's office when he gets back. One of his deputies was injured."

The doctor gave Buster a potion to help with the pain and dressed his wounds. Buster's breathing was labored, as if the blast had damaged his lungs. He had a large gash on the side of his head. The doctor put a salve on the scrapes on his arms and face and made Buster take sips of water. More than an hour later, Sheriff Whitehill opened the door and walked in without knocking.

"Heard you had a hurt deputy here, Doc."

"Yes. I've patched him up."

Whitehill took a longer look at the injured man. "Buster, that you? What happened? Where's Kip?"

"Dun know Sheriff. He was still in the mine. Dun know if he got out," Buster worked hard at getting the words out.

"What mine?"

"The mine em claim jumpers kilt the owner, the Lucky Judy. Yew member those two jumpers we brought in yesterdee. Kip claimed it, sayin he wanted to try makin a fortune in silver."

"What happened?"

"We went there to check it out. I was comin outta the tunnel a man wearing a black Stetson came up. I thought he was a jumper and tried to pull my pistol. Then things went black. I member shootin and yellin."

"Then what happened?"

"I dun member Sheriff. I heard a loud boom and it rained dirt and rocks. When Butch found me, the tunnel was closed by an explosion."

"And where was Kip when the shooting started?"

"He was inside the tunnel."

"Anything else you can tell me about the other shooter?"

"He was a Mexican and he looked like that feller in your office when we brung em jumpers in," Buster said.

CHAPTER 60

Three days later Rafe reached Las Cruces. He was tired, dirty, and hungry. The provisions he purchased in Silver City ran out yesterday. He could tell the gelding was just as tired. Directing the gelding to the El Camino Inn, he settled it in the small corral, then walked into the inn.

"Bienvenido Señor Reyes," the desk clerk greeted him by name welcoming him back.

"Gracias." Rafe told him he needed a room and a bath.

"Certainly. Will you be staying long this time?"

"No, I'll be leaving tomorrow morning for Santa Fe. Can you have someone tend to my horse? He needs a good brushing and oats."

"I will have Pepe attend to him *señor.*"

Rafe climbed the steps to the room on the second floor. Dropping the saddlebags on the floor, he stretched out on the bed. He closed his eyes and was instantly asleep. A little while later a knock on the door awakened him.

"Your bath is ready *señor.*"

"Gracias. I will be down in a moment."

The bath revived him and Rafe dressed and walked downstairs and up to the desk clerk.

"Do you know when the stagecoach for Santa Fe will be leaving?" Rafe asked. He had decided after the months of riding horseback, he would appreciate the comfort of going by coach.

"Eleven o'clock tomorrow morning," the clerk replied.

"Can you make me a reservation for a seat?"

"Certainly. I will take care of it."

Rafe walked out into the late afternoon sunshine. The weather in Las Cruces was much warmer than it had been up in the mountains of Silver City. Sweat popped out on his brow. He walked to the local cafe down the road and stepped inside. The aroma of roasted meat greeted his nose and made his mouth water.

An hour later he had eaten his fill. The roast pork in a green chili sauce was served with warm tortillas. A large helping of Spanish rice filled the plate and Rafe devoured every bite. When he paid the bill, he noticed his money belt was getting thin. The thousand dollars he took from his kitchen cabinet months ago was almost gone. Carefully he counted the money and thought he had enough to buy the stagecoach ticket and to pay his way home. If he ran out, he could sell the gelding for a good price.

The sun had dipped behind the horizon and taken some of the heat of the day with it. He decided to stretch his legs by a long walk through the town. The center of the town of Las Cruces had been built in a typical Spanish style with a large central plaza. Many small shops lined both sides of the square. It was alive with activity. Minstrels played music, children played as their mothers' watched, street vendors hawked their wares, and young lovers walked arm in arm.

Several weeks ago, the scene would have put him in an uncontrollable rage. Today, he was able to see life being lived and appreciate it. He sat for a while listening to a man playing a guitar, then continued on his way.

He was on his way back to the inn when he walked in front of the Las Cruces sheriff's office. On the bulletin board in front, several WANTED posters were nailed up. Rafe barely glanced at the signs, but then something caught his eye.

WANTED FOR MURDER:
Name: Sammy Soto
Wanted for the murder of Deputy Kip Donohoe in Silver City
Identification: Mexican gun salesman
Description: 6 feet tall, dark hair, brown eyes, riding a brown gelding
Reward: $500 dead or alive

The poster was signed by Harvey Whitehill, Sheriff of Grant County, New Mexico. Rafe's brain reeled. He was wanted, not him exactly, but him posing as Sammy Soto. He stood staring at the poster, trying to believe it was real. Over the past several days, he lamented to himself about not killing Buster. He left Buster injured but not dead at the mine, as he could not bring himself to kill an innocent man. Now he knew it was a mistake.

Buster could identify him. He would lie to Sheriff Whitehill about what happened at the mine. He also knew nothing about the events in San Gabriel. From what Elmer Goggins told Rafe about Harvey Whitehill, he knew the sheriff would not let the killing of one of his deputies stand unanswered.

Hurrying back to the inn's corral, Rafe saddled the gelding. He rushed back to his room and quickly gathered his belongings. Walking down the stairs as calmly as he could, he told the desk clerk he remembered he had an urgent appointment in El Paso in the morning. He would not be able to take the stagecoach to Santa Fe. Dropping a dollar coin on the counter, he bid the clerk a good night.

"Have a good trip. See you on your way back," the clerk said to him.

Rafe tied his bedroll and saddlebags onto the horse and mounted. Keeping the horse to a walk down the main street, he waited until he was to the edge of town before spurring him hard into a gallop.

Chapter 61

He rode through the night forced to keep on the main road. All night his brain churned with regret and fear. He did not want to hang for Kip's death. He had made a stupid and costly mistake in confronting Kip at the mine. He should have waited until he could have found him alone.

The reality of his situation quickly forced him to make a new plan. Going to Santa Fe was no longer possible. Even though the WANTED poster was for a man named Sammy Soto, it might not be difficult for Harvey Whitehill to learn of Rafe's real identity. The double-action pistols were unique and might eventually lead back to George's foundry, even though he only demonstrated with the unmarked ones.

By daybreak he was nearing El Paso. Across the border was Mexico. It seemed his only choice at this point – go across the border and stay in Mexico. He was a wanted man here in the United States and Mexico was his homeland. He saw no other option.

Riding on, he saw El Paso in the distance and let the horse trot south while thoughts swirled in his mind. Rafe had come to El Paso often, not only to see his family, but on sales trips. It was a place he had both friends and family.

He thought about his uncle and family's ranch. It was the ranch he bought and paid for after the sheriff evicted Henry Reynolds. Briefly, his mind flicked to hiding out there for a while, until he could determine if there was a posse chasing him. There he would have support and family to help protect him. He shook his head knowing he could not bring trouble to their doorstep.

He thought about the Mission north of El Paso and Padre Serrano. The padre had nursed him back to health and protected him once many years ago. Rafe repaid the mission with enough money to build a school. He would be safe there. He could join the brothers and ask God to forgive him. Shaking his head back and forth, he knew it was not for him.

Nathan Peters was the sheriff of El Paso now. Nathan had helped him several years ago when he was a deputy. With Nathan's help, Rafe shot Roy and Eldon Reynolds after they tried to kill the former sheriff. Rafe knew Nathan would be fair and believe his side of the story. He wondered if it would be enough. However, it might not matter what Nathan thought, as it would be left up to a jury. From the law's point view, he was a killer. As he rode into El Paso, Rafe kept a watch on his back trail. No posse was chasing him, at least not yet.

As he rode slowly into the town, Rafe felt as if all eyes were staring at him. His skin crawled and his stomach was full of bile. It was the bitter taste of his own stupidity. Justified vengeance led him on his quest to avenge Ana Teresa and their unborn child. Now it was going to put a noose around his neck.

Rafe rode into El Paso from the north. The town was familiar – Hastings Livery owned by Charlie Hastings, the Stratton Hotel where he usually stayed, Lilli Jean's Saloon, the El Paso National Bank run by his friend Terrence Howard, all places he knew well. It was familiar and he had lots of friends here, but now all was changed.

Further on he turned south down Piedras Street toward the Mexican side of El Paso and tried to calm himself. He rode until he could see the Rio Grande. Across the river was Mexico, less than a half mile away. Although he considered himself an American now, Mexico was home. The hacienda he inherited, the Reyes hacienda, belonged to his sister and her husband. His mother and Billy lived there and would welcome him with open arms.

Sitting on the gelding, he stared south. It had been a long and hard fought eight years since he rode north from Mexico and started his new life in the United States. He considered himself an American, a Santa Fe horse breeder, adopted son of George and Josefina Summers. Now he was a killer on the run, even if in his mind the vengeance was justified. He saw no other course of action. Tears momentarily blurred his eyes.

He urged the horse toward the river, and then

something stopped him. He needed money. His provisions were gone and he only had a few coins in his pocket. The only way he could get money was from his account at the El Paso National Bank, hoping George had transferred the money he asked for. He turned the gelding around and rode back toward the center of the town, knowing he had to take this chance.

Rafe rode slowly, nonchalantly, back into the main part of town. He made no moves to call attention to himself. At the bank, he tied the gelding to the rail near several other horses.

Opening the door to the bank, he saw Terry Howard's office door was closed. Terry was the bank manager and personally took care of Rafe's accounts here.

Two people stood in line at the teller. Rafe waited his turn. The young teller was new, not the older man he had met numerous times. When it was his turn, he stepped up and spoke.

"Hello, is Mister Howard in? I would like to make a withdrawal from my account."

"I'm sorry, but Mister Howard has stepped out for lunch. I can help you make the withdrawal. What is the name on the account?"

"I'm Rafael Reyes de Estrada."

"Ah yes, the Reyes account. Here it is." The clerk inspected the account card.

"It shows both you and a Jose Ortega can take withdrawals."

"Yes that is my uncle Jose. A deposit of approximately three thousand dollars would have been made in March. Is that so?"

"Yes, I see a deposit for three thousand, three hundred on March twelfth. How much would you like to withdrawal?

"Three thousand."

The clerk looked momentarily surprised, and then nodded his head. "Just a moment then, I'll get the money ready for you."

"Excuse me. Can you make a couple hundred of that in coins?"

Three people had lined up behind Rafe waiting for their turn. He expected Terry Howard to return from lunch and greet him. What could he say to Mister Howard? He was a killer on the run and needed his funds to live. He could not tell Terry about seeking vengeance and killing those who were responsible for killing Ana Teresa. Finally, the teller returned with a cloth bag.

"Two hundred in gold and silver coins as you asked, and the rest in paper money. Is that everything?" the teller asked politely.

"Yes, thank you."

Rafe tucked the cloth bank bag under his shirt and walked from the bank. Untying the gelding from the rail, Rafe rode east. As soon as he was well out of El Paso, he rode hard toward the Mexican border. He crossed the shallow Rio Grande ten miles east where no guards patrolled, and then circled back to the Mexican city of Juárez.

For two days he relaxed in a hotel in Ciudad Juárez. He was safe here and unknown and after pondering his options, he decided on a plan. Gathering his suit and other clothes, Rafe went to a mercantile store. The clerk helped him fit into two sets of *vaquero* pants and a leather jacket. The brown jacket was embroidered with small stars and silver buttons adorned the sleeves.

His choice would be considered plain and nondescript by many standards. Picking up a flat-crown black hat and fitting it on his head, he finished his new look. Looking into a mirror, Rafe was satisfied he could pass for a typical *vaquero*. Selecting a blanket and other provisions, Rafe paid the man in coins.

"*¿Conoces a alguien a quien le gustaría esta ropa?*" he asked the clerk if he knew anyone who would like to have his old clothes.

"*Yo los tomaré,*" the clerk replied he would like to have them.

Next, he went to a leather shop and bought two sets of Mexican boots, the type worn by *vaqueros,* and leather chaps. As he was about to leave, he noticed a table of Mexican spurs sitting near the door. Mexican spurs had longer and spikier rowels than Texas spurs. He picked up an ornate pair and took a few minutes to strap them to his new boots.

With his transformation complete, Rafe took his new belongings to the hotel. He had decided traveling through Mexico as a *vaquero* would be safe and gave him the cover he needed to travel armed.

He ate a light dinner before he went to his room for the night. Still tired from lack of sleep and the events of the past several months, he allowed himself one last night of rest before starting on his next journey. He had decided to travel south to visit his family in Torreón, then to find his friend, Xihuitl, the Aztec healer. With Xihuitl's help and council, he hoped to get past the hurt and guilt. The hidden city of the ancient Aztecs in the wilderness of the Sierra Madre Mountains was a permanently safe haven, a place he could find peace.

Chapter 62

George Summers received a letter on June eighteenth with the insignia of the El Paso Republic Bank on the outside. The bank manager, Terry Howard, was one of the many people he had notified about Rafe's disappearance. He tore at the envelope hoping for good news.

Dear George,

In regards to your several letters about Rafe, he stopped last Friday and collected three thousand dollars in cash. I was out of the office at the time and the transaction caught my eye during my nightly review. Unfortunately, my normal teller had been ill for several days and I had a temporary teller filling in. I failed to give him instructions in regards to the account and thus Rafe came without notice.

As soon as I discovered the transaction, I checked at the local hotels and saloons looking for him. I rode out to Jose's ranch on Saturday morning and asked if he had stopped by, but to no avail. I have also notified Sheriff Peters to be on the alert for him. I am truly sorry to say, we have not been able to find him anywhere here in El Paso.

The teller described him as rather shabby with several days beard growth, but otherwise alive and well. I will keep diligently looking for him and my tellers have been instructed to double check anyone answering Rafe's description.

I can only hope this letter brings you a small comfort knowing he is alive.

Best Regards,
Terrence Howard

George laid the letter on his desk in his office at the foundry. Terry was correct to say it was a comfort to know Rafe was alive. It had been almost three months since the fateful fiesta and since Rafe left Santa Fe. George and Carlos had been corresponding with the numerous people and places they thought Rafe might go. The El Paso Bank was one of those places, as Rafe had a fairly large account of money in the bank. The account supported his uncle's ranch and family.

In Rafe's departing letter, he instructed George to wire half his funds here in Santa Fe to the bank in El Paso, so it would be a place he would go if he needed money. George sighed again looking at the letter on his desk. In a swift movement, he raised a fist and slammed it down on the letter.

"Damn," he cursed under his breath. To have searched so long and to have missed him by a simple coincidence of the teller's illness was maddening. Nevertheless, Rafe was alive. It was the first positive news in the long months of waiting and dread.

Picking up the letter, George left his office and headed to the main house. He tried to encourage himself this letter brought good news.

Reaching the kitchen, he found Lizzy busy helping Juanita.

"Lizzy. Go find your mother, sister, and Ana Teresa. Ask them to join us. I have some news." Her father was holding a letter in his hand.

"*Papá.* You've found Rafe?" she almost screeched. Her father looked somewhat somber and Lizzy suddenly realized the news might not be good. Turning from her work, she ran from the kitchen. Tears stung her eyes.

George read the letter to the family after they gathered in the kitchen.

"*Gracias a Dios*" Josefina crossed herself and praised God for the news.

Lizzy and Lolo jumped up and down hugging each other. Only Ana Teresa seemed quiet and perturbed.

"He's alive and well," Lizzy squealed.

"Yes, we should be pleased at the news," George said.

Finally Ana Teresa spoke. "Three thousand dollars is a lot of money, George. Why do you think he needed that much? Surely he would not have taken the money, if he planned on returning here to Santa Fe."

Unfortunately George agreed with her. It bothered him since he read the letter. Rafe would only take that large amount of money out of the bank, if he was not planning on being near El Paso or Santa Fe again for quite some time. The only other thought which occurred to George was Rafe might be planning on buying a parcel of land or some other large purchase. That seemed unlikely, but possible. Perhaps he was thinking of starting afresh somewhere else.

"We must focus on the good news. He is alive and well. Although our efforts to locate him have failed so far, eventually we will find him or he will return on his own accord. We must continue our prayers for him," George told them.

Later alone in her room, Ana Teresa clutched the baby in her arms. He looked up at her with liquid dark eyes, much like his father's. Dark hair covered the crown of his head.

"Your father will come home," Ana Teresa whispered to the baby. "He will come. He loves you even if he has not met you yet." The baby cooed at her as if he understood.

She was joyous at the letter's news. Rafael was alive and had been seen in El Paso. It was more than they had known in months. Each night she prayed and said a Rosary for his safety. Each morning she prayed for some news and today her prayers were answered.

"Rafael, please hear me. Please come home," Ana Teresa spoke to the empty walls of the room and tears pooled in her eyes. Clutching the baby tighter, she rocked him in her arms.

FIN

Please continue reading a preview of the next Young Pistolero Series adventure by Robert J. Alvarado, *The Black Phantom* (Book 8) 2020 Sierra Press.

CHAPTER 1

For several weeks, Rafael Reyes de Estrada felt safe and secure at a hotel in the heart of Ciudad Juárez, the Mexican border city across the Rio Grande from El Paso, Texas. He was a wanted man across the border, accused of killing a deputy sheriff in Silver City, New Mexico. It was true, he was a killer, but it was justified vengeance against the men who killed his wife and unborn child.

Yesterday at the cafe, he read a newspaper from El Paso. The article claimed the killer stalked and deliberately dynamited a mineshaft, burying Deputy Kip Donohoe. Buster Thomas, claimed Kip was inside the shaft. In his eyewitness account, a Mexican man hit Buster over the head and began arguing with Kip. Sheriff Whitehill was calling for a manhunt for the killer of his deputy sheriff throughout the Southwestern Territories. The killer was identified as Sammy Soto, from Pueblo, Colorado.

Whitehill was the newly elected sheriff for Grant County. New Mexico. He no doubt had a reputation to create and if what Elmer Goggins told Rafe was true, Sheriff Harvey Whitehill would not rest until he brought the killer to justice.

Rafe had been hunting Kip Donohoe since the fateful day last March when Kip and several others rode into a wedding celebration at the Salazar hacienda in San Gabriel. They wore red hoods and shot indiscriminately at anyone. It was retaliation against *don* Lorenzo Salazar for defending his land rights against squatters. Rafe and his wife, Ana Teresa, were in attendance. She was eight months pregnant with their first child and killed by a stray bullet.

Unable and unwilling to control his blind rage, Rafe hunted down and killed Jesse Kincaid, Nat Holmes, and Kip Donohoe for their crimes. He sent them all to hell and felt no remorse. During his quest for justice, Rafe used a number of aliases. The one he used in Silver City was Sammy Soto. However, he made two fatal mistakes. Posing as Sammy Soto, he met with Sheriff Whitehill and demonstrated the double-action pistols, pretending to be a gun salesman. He also could not bring himself to kill Buster Thomas the day Rafe confronted them at the mine, leaving a witness. Now there was a manhunt and a five hundred dollar price on his head.

After killing Kip, Rafe felt released from his vengeance and he planned to go home, back to Santa Fe to resume his life as a horse breeder. It would have been difficult without Ana Teresa, but he had family and friends there. Now he could not go back and was in Mexico, headed to Torreón. His sister, María and her husband Rodolfo, ran the Reyes hacienda there. His mother and Billy Swanson also lived there and he would be welcomed. It was the place he grew up as a *peón,* but it was not where he considered home.

Rafe had discarded his American clothes and bought clothing fitting a *vaquero.* He was dressed in an embroidered short leather jacket and soft leather chaps. The clothing was used, although he purchased new boots and Mexican silver spurs. His gunbelt was wrapped around his waist with the two unmarked double-action pistols in the holsters. Putting on the flat-crowned hat finished his transformation. He had decided traveling as a *vaquero,* a Mexican cowboy, allowed him the safest disguise. He would be ignored and able to blend into the fabric of rural Mexican society. *Vaqueros* were not a target for wealth nor abused like *peóns.*

He was delayed at the border town trying to buy an ammunition loading kit, but the ones he found were not up to the standard he need for the double-action pistols. Two days ago he was directed to a man who loaded his own ammunition, by a clerk at a gun shop. Rafe went to the man, but learned he did not have the equipment.

"I know a place in El Paso. They have the kit you are

looking for," the man told him.

Rafe hesitated, not wanting to go to El Paso himself. "*Señor*, I got in trouble in El Paso and I'm afraid I cannot go there. I will pay you, if you go there to buy the kit for me." Rafe told him.

"I can do that. I was planning to go there to buy supplies. Come back later this afternoon and I should have the kit for you," the man assured Rafe.

Rafe gave the man money to buy the kit and some for his services. In the meantime Rafe went looking for a packhorse. True to his word, the man had the kit for him that evening.

After a hardy breakfast the following morning, Rafe paid his tab, saddled the brown gelding, and set out south on the Chihuahua Trail. He estimated it was a week's ride to Torreón. The June weather was pleasant, not overly hot and the summer thunderstorms had not started. Only a few caravans heading south were on the trail and Rafe passed them without an acknowledgement as he rode at a good pace.

Four days later, he rode out of the city of Chihuahua, cheerful for making good time on the trail. If he pushed the brown gelding, he could be home in three days. By late afternoon, Rafe steered the horse to a grove of cottonwood trees having spotted a clear creek. He had been on this trek before, several times, so he remembered certain landmarks and camping spots. His last trip to Torreón, Rafe and his best friend Carlos were headed to the hacienda for his mother's wedding to Billy Swanson.

Thinking of Carlos and the Summers' family he left behind in Santa Fe pained him. They probably thought him dead. When he was hunting the killers, he kept from any contact, but now he thought he would write a letter once he reached Torreón and let them know he was alive.

Rafe jumped from the horse and it stepped into the cool water of the flowing creek. Well trained, the gelding would not run. He tied the packhorse nearby. Tired, Rafe stopped early, finding a clear spot to camp for the night. He began to clear a spot for a fire. Both he and the horses were tired, as he rode hard the last several days wanting to get to Torreón.

He started a small fire and added two larger pieces of wood. The horses were eating grass near the stream and Rafe was leaning against a tree relaxing, waiting for the fire to catch. Above him in the dark blue sky, several large birds soared on the currents. From this distance, Rafe could not tell if they were eagles or hawks or simply vultures.

His solitary journey allowed him to reflect over the events, which led him here. It had been more than three months since the death of his beloved wife and their unborn child. Although she was avenged, his mind still fueled hate for their loss. He had wanted to return to Santa Fe and resume his former life, but fate apparently had other plans. Perhaps it was God's punishment for his violence.

Leaving the United State forever, he returned to his home country of Mexico seeking refuge. As a start, he needed solace and nourishment, the kind he knew only his mother could give him.

Suddenly, a man's voice across the creek interrupted his thoughts and the quiet solitude.

"*¡Levántate, imbécil!*" a man's voice yelled out, telling someone to get up and calling him an asshole.

Rafe sat up, seeing a man on horseback pulling a rope with another man at the other end. The rope was tied in a loose knot around his neck and his hands were tied behind his back. The tied man was a *peón*, dressed in a simple dirty white *camisa* and *pantalones*. His dark hair fell around his tan face. As Rafe watched, the *peón* stumbled and fell.

"*¡Levántate!*" The man on the horse pulled at him and yelled again for him to get up dragging the *peón* along the ground.

"*Por favor señor, ten compasión,*" the *peón* begged for the man to have compassion.

"*No hay compasión para ti, ladrón. Mi padre te colgará cuando te lleve a la hacienda,*" the young *caballero* replied telling the *peón* he had no compassion for him, a thief. My father will hang you when I get you to the hacienda.

Rafe took a better look at the horseman and saw he

was a young *caballero,* dressed in a black *traje.* Silver stars the size of a quarter ran down on the outside of his pants, down to where they flared out at the boots. Large rowels on his spurs emphasized how he controlled the horse. A black waist-length jacket had silver trim across the man's chest and down the sleeves. A flat crown hat with a thin silver band completed the look of a prosperous Mexican gentleman.

It was an image Rafe knew from his youth and of the young *caballeros* in Santa Fe. The Spanish gentry disdained *peons,* treating them as slaves or worse. It was the old Spanish *casta* system. Spaniards of pure Spanish bloodlines maintained superiority over people of mixed Spanish and Indian bloodlines. Rafe was one of those people. Born to a mixed blood peasant woman and fathered by the *haciendero,* *don* Bernardo Reyes. Although dressed as a *vaquero,* here in Mexico Rafe was a *mestizo,* a mixed blood *peón,* no better than the man on the ground.

Rafe was raised a *peón* on *don* Bernardo Reyes' hacienda, indentured to him. In Mexican society, *peóns* were used as slaves. Rafe was not sure why the *caballero* was dragging the man, but it did not matter. Hate and venom for the Spanish caste system churned the bile in his empty stomach.

"¡Oye, suelta a ese hombre!" Rafe yelled at the *caballero* to turn the man loose as he quickly stepped across the shallow creek.

"Esto no es asunto tuyo," the *caballero* told Rafe the matter did not concern him. He waved his leather quirt at Rafe in a motion of dismissal.

"Turn him loose," Rafe growled in Spanish.

The *caballero* went for his pistol, but Rafe had his out and pointed at the man. "Drop it on the ground," Rafe told him.

The horseman's wide eyes stared back at Rafe in shock. *Vaqueros* did not confront a gentleman in such a manner, but he obeyed and dropped the pistol.

"How dare you interfere? Who are you *vaquero?*" the *caballero* asked him.

Rafe did not answer him. Adrenaline and rage flowed

through his veins. He thought the rage, which had driven him to violence in New Mexico, had declined with Kip's death. Instead, his fury at the arrogant *caballero* intensified.

"Get down and untie the man," Rafe ordered him while he held the pistol aimed at him.

"You will pay for this. My father will send many men to find and kill you," the *caballero* warned Rafe as he untied the *peón* on the ground. The *peón* was dressed in frayed peasant clothing, which looked brown from the dust covering him from head to toe. He was barefoot. As he was untied, he spit dirt and had a coughing fit.

"I have no respect for your father, if he has a son who would drag a man by the neck. What kind of a man are you? What has this man done to deserve this kind of treatment from you?"

"This *peón* is a thief and must be punished."

"What did he steal?"

"He took one of our calves."

"Did you take one of the hacienda's calves?" Rafe asked the *peón*.

"*Si señor,*" the *peón* said, lowering his head expecting Rafe to beat or punish him.

Instead Rafe asked, "Why did you take the calf?"

"To feed my family and the others *señor*. His father, the *haciendero,* drove my family out from his hacienda and left us to die from starvation," the man answered.

"You were thieves, you and your family, and all the others. You deserve what you received, which was nothing." Again the *caballero's* tone was haughty and arrogant. After he untied the man, he pushed him back down to the dirt.

"Go wash yourself," Rafe told the *peón,* pointing to the creek.

"You have no right in interfere, *vaquero*. This is my father's business."

Rafe toyed with killing the young *caballero*. Vengeance was calling to him again. He had turned into a killer and the thought of killing no longer nagged him much. Satan already had a place prepared in hell for him.

"Take off your clothes!" Rafe demanded of the young

caballero.

"*¡Jódete, no haré tal cosa!*" the young *caballero* cursed retorting to Rafe, fuck you, he would do no such thing.

"Take your clothes off or I will start shooting. First your fingers, one by one. I warn you I am a very good shot," Rafe warned him and fired once near the man's hand.

The *caballero* quickly took off his clothes and threw them at Rafe. Setting the clothes aside, Rafe tied the *caballero's* legs, then his hands behind his back. He took the man's *traje,* folded it, then forded the creek returning in a few minutes with his horse and the packhorse.

Looking the *peón* over, and seeing they were about the same size, Rafe pulled out one of the *vaquero* outfits he bought in Juárez from a saddlebag and handed it to the man. "Put these on and take the man's boots." Rafe told him.

"*Desgraciado,* do not take my boots. I will find you and kill you!" The *caballero* tried to kick the *peón,* but his boots were taken.

While the *peón* dressed and put on the boots, Rafe took a look at the young *caballero's* horse. It was a beautiful black horse, strongly built, compact yet elegant. It had a thick mane and flowing tail which almost reached the ground. Rafe recognized the breed. It was an Andalusian. Liquid black eyes looked at Rafe as he walked up and whispered into its ear. The horse responded to Rafe with a snort and lifted its head up and down.

"Can you ride a horse?" Rafe asked the *peón.*

"*Sí señor.*"

"Mount up, we must get out of here." Rafe helped him up on the brown gelding then went and had no trouble mounting the *caballero's* black horse. Rafe led the way as they rode off west toward the foothills of the Sierra Madre Mountains, leaving the screaming barefoot young *caballero* on the ground, wearing only his underwear.

SPANISH GLOSSARY

Italicized Spanish words used repeatedly throughout the series which do not have an English counterpart, such as important = *importante* or Mama = *Mamá*. Other infrequently used words, phrases, and sentences written in Spanish are immediately explained within the text itself.

abogado: a lawyer, attorney at law
abrazo: a hug
abuelo; abuela: grandfather; grandmother (m;f)
adios: goodbye
alcalde: the mayor of a town or city
amigo(s); amiga(s): friend (m;f)
anglo(s): a word to mean a white man, an American
ayúdame: help, asking for help
baboso(s): drooling idiot (a slang or curse word)
bandido(s): a bandit or outlaw
bueno: good
buenos días; tardes; noches: good day; evening; night
bienvenido(s): welcome
cabrón: asshole or bastard (a curse word)
caballo(s); caballero(s): horse; horseman or gentleman
cállate: shutup or be quiet
cálmate; cálmese: be calm or calm down
camisa: a blouse or top
casita; casa: small home, home
chaqueta(s): jacket or suit coat
chico(s); chica(s); chiquita: young boy or young girl (m;f)
chingado: shit or fuck (a curse word)
cojones: slang for a man's testicles
compañero(s): companion, friends
criollo(s): Spaniards born in the New World
ciudad: a town or city
culón: a chickenshit (a curse word)
desgraciado(s): a miserable wretch or terrible person
Dios: God
don; doña: title for nobleman/woman
gachupín(s); peninsulares: Spaniards born in Spain
garrancha: means sword, slang for penis
gracias; muchas gracias: thank you; many thanks
grandee: Spanish nobleman, aristocrat (i.e. dandy)

hermano; hermana: brother; sister (m;f)

hacienda: a large plantation or estate

haciendero(s): the nobleman owning the hacienda

hola: hello greeting

Indio(s); India(s): means Indian (m;f)

jacal(s): small ramshakle house of mud and sticks

jefe: the boss man

mañana: tomorrow or the sometime later

mestizo(s); person of mixed Spanish and Indian (m)

mestiza(s): person of mixed Spanish and Indian (f)

mierda: same as shit (a curse word)

mi hijito; hijo; mijo; hijita; hija; mija: my son; daughter

muchacho(s); muchacha(s): like saying 'the guys' (m;f)

nada: no or nothing

Nana; Tata: nickname for grandmother; grandfather

padre: head friar, monk, minister, priest

pantalones: pants

paseo: the road, boulevard; place to stroll or ride

patrón; patróna: formal for a boss; a mistress (m;f)

pendejo(s); pendeja(s): slang for asshole (a curse)

pene(s): slang for a penis

peón(s): a peasant

peso(s): Mexican money

picaro: a womanizer

pinche: fucking (a curse word)

plata: silver

primo(s); prima(s): cousin (m;f)

pulque; pulqueria: a poor man's drink in Mexico

puta(s): a whore (a slang or curse word)

que?: what or why

querido; querida: affectionate meaning my dear (m;f)

rayo: thunderbolt

sarape: cape, loose coat or blanket

señor(es); señora(s): like saying Mr. or Mrs.

señorita(s): like saying Miss (young woman or girl)

sí: yes

tío; tía: uncle; aunt (m;f)

traje(s): ornate Spanish aristocrat's style of suit

vaquero(s): livestock herder or cowboy

vámonos or vamos: let's go, get out of here